BUZZ KILL

ALSO BY J. ROBERT LENNON

Hard Girls
Subdivision
Let Me Think: Stories
Broken River
See You in Paradise: Stories
Familiar
Castle
Pieces for the Left Hand: 100 Anecdotes
Happyland
Mailman
On the Night Plain
The Funnies
The Light of Falling Stars

BUZZ KILL

A Jane and Lila Pool Thriller

J. ROBERT LENNON

MULHOLLAND BOOKS
LITTLE, BROWN AND COMPANY
NEW YORK   BOSTON   LONDON

The characters and events in this book are fictitious. Any similarity to real persons, living or dead, is coincidental and not intended by the author.

Copyright © 2025 by J. Robert Lennon

Hachette Book Group supports the right to free expression and the value of copyright. The purpose of copyright is to encourage writers and artists to produce the creative works that enrich our culture.

The scanning, uploading, and distribution of this book without permission is a theft of the author's intellectual property. If you would like permission to use material from the book (other than for review purposes), please contact permissions@hbgusa.com. Thank you for your support of the author's rights.

Mulholland Books / Little, Brown and Company
Hachette Book Group
1290 Avenue of the Americas, New York, NY 10104
mulhollandbooks.com

First Edition: March 2025

Mulholland Books is an imprint of Little, Brown and Company, a division of Hachette Book Group, Inc. The Mulholland Books name and logo are trademarks of Hachette Book Group, Inc.

The publisher is not responsible for websites (or their content) that are not owned by the publisher.

The Hachette Speakers Bureau provides a wide range of authors for speaking events. To find out more, go to hachettespeakersbureau.com or email hachettespeakers@hbgusa.com.

Little, Brown and Company books may be purchased in bulk for business, educational, or promotional use. For information, please contact your local bookseller or the Hachette Book Group Special Markets Department at special.markets@hbgusa.com.

ISBN 9780316551403
LCCN 2024941724

Printing 1, 2024

LSC-C

Printed in the United States of America

BUZZ KILL

Prologue

They applauded when she stepped into the dayroom, and though she'd vowed to play it cool, Shelly burst into tears. They were all there: Shonda who shared her crime and romance novels, Katelynn who sang beside her when they put on *The Wiz,* Kendra the rapper, Jada the seamstress, Tam who tried to beat her up and failed and became her friend. They even let Starr trade shifts in the laundry so that she could be here. A sea of smiling women in gray, standing to greet her, surrounding her, taking her into their arms, hugging her tight, saying goodbye. Shelly even caught sight of a guard drying her eyes with a sleeve.

How could it be otherwise? She'd never had a family closer than these women and probably never would. Nearly two decades inside, and for next to nothing: a ride-along during a drug deal that went wrong, her idiot boyfriend the principal offender, dead on the scene. Shelly arrested, dragged out of the car, where they found weed, fentanyl, cocaine cut with Yes, two Glocks with the serial numbers filed off. A massacre in the house, Shelly too high to even know what was going on.

Inside, she got clean, let go of her anger. Stopped blaming other people for her misfortune. She was a big woman, and in prison she became a strong one, too, in body and mind. Took new inmates under her wing, protected them from each other. She was only twenty-six when she came here but the younger girls called her Mom, first sarcastically and later in earnest. She taught herself to cook and then taught other people. Her brother, Luke, the only person on the outside who'd stayed loyal to her, sent her the Indonesian ramen she loved, and she made savory noodles with onions and garlic and fried eggs whenever the prison had the ingredients and let her use them. That's what she was doing this morning—she'd made the women breakfast, ate with them as the gray upstate light filled the caged windows.

By the end of this day, Shelly would get to stroll out into that light anytime she pleased. Conversation over breakfast was all about what she would do with her freedom—eat a steak, dance in a nightclub, get some D, jump in a lake—but the truth they all understood and didn't voice was that Shelly was as fearful as she was eager. The idea of freedom was terrifying. She had a couple of job prospects thanks to Luke, who had gotten online and started searching for her: the Walmart, the Subway. There was a charitable organization in Nestor that tried to place ex-cons in jobs, including some in state and local government, and Luke had set up an interview for her.

Shelly was lucky to have Luke, lucky to have a home to return to. But the best thing of all was something she found in the back pages of a literary magazine that had been donated to the library: a summer writers' workshop for women that offered one slot, completely free, to a formerly incarcerated writer. She'd applied for it, and she won it, and in a couple of weeks she'd be attending it to work on a memoir of her life inside and outside of prison. She wanted to talk about injustice, sexism, life and death. She wanted to correct some misconceptions about crimes and why people commit them. She had three notebooks full of memories, and she was ready to work. She couldn't wait.

And yet, she dreaded the end of this day. She would miss these women so much. She would write, she would visit, but it would never be the same. She hoped she'd see them on the outside, but they'd likely be wrapped up in their own lives—and some of them, inevitably, in their own bad habits. Shelly had no illusions about her own chances without the structure of prison life; even well-intentioned people could end up back in. That's why the memoir was so important to her. It was something to work on every day, as the notebooks had been. It was a way of making sense of her chaotic, foolish, tragic, and, yes, she truly believed it, beautiful life.

It was nearly ten, time for the women to go. Shelly followed her friends out the dayroom door and into the complex, and as they peeled off to return to their cells, Shelly hugged them, told them she loved them. Outside her own cell, she said goodbye to the last few, gave to them the things she didn't need to keep: some paperbacks, her soap, her CD boombox. When they were gone, she gathered up her notebooks and the clothes her brother had sent her and followed a guard to Medical to pick up her pills. Another guard met her at the gate, drove her to Receiving and Departure in a golf cart. She got fingerprinted and sat down for her exit interrogation: basic questions about her age, date and place of birth, her parents. She understood this was to make sure she was who she claimed—stories of prisoners impersonating other prisoners and escaping were legion, some of them maybe even true. She answered correctly, automatically, but was she that woman anymore, really? No, the Shelly who was leaving Boynton Ridge today was born on the inside.

There were papers to sign. They took her ID card and added a sticker that read RELEASED, then handed it back to her along with a prepaid credit card worth three hundred bucks plus whatever was left on her commissary account. They gave her a cheap backpack to put her stuff in and the handful of garbage that had been in her pockets when they arrested her, including her old wallet and half a roll of breath mints. She changed into her new clothes—jeans, sneakers, fresh white socks, a V-neck tee, a Buffalo Bills ball cap—and handed over her uniform. Finally it was time. They led her across the front lot to the gate, which she hadn't seen in five years, since her furlough for her parents' funeral. The gate rolled open and she stepped through, and there was Luke, leaning against his car. He pushed himself off and walked effortfully, with a cane and a limp—the COVID that killed their parents had fucked up his joints somehow, and nobody had been able to fix them—across the parking lot and into her arms. His hairline had receded and his beard had some gray, but he seemed possessed by a new, intense energy that he was struggling to keep in check. Emotion, she guessed, not something he was good at expressing. He was shaking. He said, "Hey, sis."

"How's my little bro." Tears in their eyes.

"Aw, you know. Missed you."

"Missed you too."

"Right, so..."

"Yeah. Can we go home?"

"You bet, Shel," Luke said. "Let's go home."

She knew it wouldn't be easy moving in with her brother, but within a few days it became clear to Shelly that Luke wasn't well. He'd been suffering from what they called long COVID, though he refused to admit it. She overheard him telling a friend that their parents had died from "complications of pneumonia" and hung his head when Shelly butted in and corrected him. She was adamant about this. COVID had ravaged the prison and killed several of her friends—she wasn't going to let Luke pretend it didn't exist.

She might never have learned what killed their parents if she hadn't gotten out for the funeral and a friend of their mother's hadn't pulled her aside and told her the truth. Shelly wasted hours of her brief time on the outside looking for the death certificates in the messy house; she found them, and they confirmed what the woman had said. But when she confronted Luke, it became clear that he didn't believe in the disease at all. He thought it was a conspiracy theory, it was just the normal flu and only old people died of it, and they were trying to lock down America because they wanted to control the population. For what purpose, he couldn't explain. She was pretty sure he had brainwashed their parents too, or maybe it was the other way around. Wouldn't have put it past her dad. She spent the rest of her furlough trying to talk sense into Luke, but she ran out of time, and then it was back to Boynton for another nickel.

Shelly got COVID twice, once before the vax and once after. The first was worse, but both were bad. She weathered it and now felt good, but if she knew anything, it was that the damn disease was real. You had to be pretty brainwashed to watch it rip through a prison, leaving corpses in its wake, and deny that anything noteworthy was happening.

At the funeral, Luke had been short of breath; this and his inflamed joints meant he could barely walk around the block before he had to lie down for the rest of the day. He'd kept forgetting things and would kind of drift away mid-conversation, his mouth hanging open. And he was depressed, by more than just their parents' deaths, she thought. Now some of these things seemed to have improved. He was walking easier, and he seemed capable of being up and around more often. But something new had set in: his hands trembled, his eyes darted. His energy had returned, but it seemed to have no practical value; the house was a catastrophe. He'd clearly tried to clean up for her but had gotten either tired or distracted; the kitchen was tidy and swept, but the living room had bags of garbage piled everywhere and you could barely open the door to what used to be their parents' room. He'd been living off disability checks, remote IT work, and some savings their parents left.

It wasn't just Luke, though—everyone seemed different out in the world. Tempers were shorter, boundaries were more porous than she remembered. Customers in the supermarket muscled her aside or got into arguments with checkout clerks. Drivers ran red lights with impunity and followed her too close behind, engines roaring. When this happened, she began to panic and had taken to pulling over to let them pass. (She would not, could not, drive over the limit. She never wanted a cop at her window again.) Usually her tormentors raced around her, tires screeching; sometimes they honked or flipped her the middle finger. One guy in a black pickup, flags flying over the cargo bed, pulled over behind her and idled there for two interminable minutes, leaning on his horn and screaming. She'd tried not to look in the rearview, just locked her doors and waited it out. But she couldn't stop peeking. The man was mesmerizing, his mouth moving wildly, his eyes like televisions in a shop window, brightness dimed, tuned to no station. Prison could be dangerous, and there were a lot of angry people, but you could at least count on the order, the structure. Outside was freaking her out.

Shelly had learned to look on the sunny side of things, though, and regarded her situation as extraordinarily lucky, especially compared to what many of her incarcerated friends came home to—no home at all, often. Luke and Shelly owned their house outright. This gave them some latitude to get their shit together. It was a couple of lots off Route 7 in Onteo, right near a church, an auto-body shop, and a Dr. O's. (Somehow, during her time inside, *Donuts* had disappeared from the name, though the donuts themselves hadn't, thank god.) The neighbors looked askance; their house was the jankiest place on the block, and now it was home to an ex-con. She rented a dumpster and spent most of her three hundred bucks of gate money having all the junk hauled away. She bought a gallon of bleach, sponges, and gloves and disinfected the entire house. She also got a cheap phone, and she had Luke drive her down to Nestor to talk to the job-placement people. She wrote a little in her journals every morning, getting her thoughts in order for the writers' conference. When she felt the panic creeping in, she just returned to her room—her old bedroom, which their parents hadn't touched since she left home, and, luckily, Luke hadn't touched either—and shut the door. After a few days she managed to stop herself from reflexively getting up to open it and then again to close it. She longed for the protection and privacy of a lock, yet missed the reinforced plastic window of her old cell door. She vacillated between agoraphobia and claustrophobia. Her nightmares were of pandemic lockdowns.

One night she and Luke splurged on Outback Steakhouse. For most of the meal he seemed like his old self—he kept making puns and filled her in on the plots of superhero movies she'd missed. But then he grew irritated and paranoid, slumping at the table, peering furtively around the room, flinching whenever plates clanked or the song changed on the radio. By the time they left, he was shaking again, and she threw an arm around him on the way to the parking lot.

They came home to find the front door hanging open. "Oh, fuck," Shelly said, climbing out of the car.

"Don't go in!" Luke said, reaching for her.

"Why not?"

"Just don't. What if...what if they're still there?"

"Pfft," Shelly said, and shook his hand loose. She marched up the weedy front walk, shouted, "Hey!" and flipped on the lights.

It looked worse than it was. Tables and chairs were knocked over, a lamp was damaged, and a radio had been taken. (Briefly, Shelly wished she hadn't given her boombox away; now she'd have to clean in silence.) But not much else had been disturbed. They didn't keep cash around. The kitchen wasn't vandalized. She peered into Luke's bedroom, where he kept his computer equipment, and, incredibly, it was still there. Maybe because the clutter had made the space resemble a storeroom. "Luke!" she shouted. "It's all clear!" Maybe something had scared them off, and they ran so fast they didn't shut the door? Tweakers, probably. You could frighten those people whispering *Boo*.

Luke came in, head hanging, shoulders bent. Strange that Luke would feel so traumatized, Shelly so chill, but she was in her element now, taking charge, giving comfort, putting things in order. They closed and bolted the door, and Shelly was glad Luke had forgotten to lock it when they left; the thieves would probably have busted a window. They righted the furniture. Luke found a new light bulb and managed to bend the lampshade back into shape.

Everything was more or less back to normal by the time Shelly went to bed, or seemed that way until she reached under the mattress for her current notebook. It wasn't there. Maybe she put it in the prison backpack with the others—but when she got on her knees and felt around under the bed, the backpack wasn't there either. She looked in the closet, the dresser, under the folding buffet table that served as a desk, on top of the bookcase.

The backpack was gone. The notebooks were gone.

Luke wasn't in his room. She found him in the kitchen, gripping the table with both hands, teeth chattering.

"Dude," Shelly said. "They stole my notebooks."

He looked up at her, red-eyed. For a moment, she again wondered if he was on something. But she'd searched the house when she cleaned it, even tossed his room when he was briefly out, using the key she knew he hid, poorly, behind a loose part of the doorframe. She'd found nothing. It wasn't a surprise, really—Luke had never been a user or even a drinker, and Shelly wouldn't allow booze in the house, let alone drugs—but she half wished she'd turned up some kind of explanation for his behavior.

Luke said, "Your what?"

"My notebooks, knucklehead. My prison journals. Did you move them?"

He shook his head.

"What the fuck," Shelly said. "Why would anyone steal a bunch of notebooks?"

"No cops," Luke said.

"What?"

"Don't call the cops."

"No shit!" Of course not—the cops would find a way to blame her for whatever misfortune befell her. But why on earth would Luke say that? "I don't wanna deal with cops, but why can't you?" she said.

"That's why," he said after a moment of what seemed to Shelly like frantic thought.

"*What's* why?"

"Because you don't want them."

"So why are you telling *me* not to call them?"

"I wasn't," Luke said, staring at the floor. "I was just saying it." A rhythmic thumping filled the silence: Luke's heel gently thudding against the linoleum.

"Okay, bro," Shelly said, thinking hard now. The break-in just didn't make sense. Luke's room was closer to the front door than hers; any sensible thief would have looked in there first and taken all his shit, despite the teetering piles of food wrappers and scrap cardboard. The radio they'd stolen was just a cheap old thing. And her notebooks were worth even less. Who would want them? A rival writer? Nobody even knew she was planning to write something. Even *she* hadn't known until a couple of months ago.

She went back down the hall and examined her room more carefully. Things *had* been disturbed, but gently—the drawers opened, the clothes pushed aside. Shoes askew in the closet. Someone had come in here, meticulously searched for the notebooks, and taken only them.

"Luke," she said, back in the kitchen. He'd shaken a bunch of salt onto the formica surface and was tracing patterns in it with a finger. "Did you mention to anybody that I was writing something?"

"No," he said.

"Are you sure? Like, even in passing?"

He shook his head.

Then, suddenly, she knew what to do. She went back to her room and rifled through the papers lying on a corner of the buffet table until she found her address book: a little stack of notebook pages held together with a paper clip. She'd compiled the pages over the past few years in preparation for her eventual release: phone numbers and addresses of useful contacts, job prospects, prison friends who'd served out their sentences. Thank god she'd torn the pages out. There was one friend she'd met early on, the one who'd had a kid in Boynton Ridge. One she'd stayed in touch with, who had resources, a place to crash, and a business that, in a recent letter, she had called "a general problem-solving agency," whatever that meant. A friend Shelly had protected, and who'd promised to lend her a hand anytime, for any reason.

She would call Jane.

1

Jane Pool was hunched over the computer keyboard in her home office, typing up notes on the most boring domestic-dispute surveillance case she'd yet drawn in her grim year of boring domestic-dispute surveillance cases. She'd been hired by a woman—the only kind of domestic case she would agree to take—to spy on her husband, whom she suspected of infidelity. "I know he's cheating," the client had told Jane, "he *has* to be." But over the course of three weeks, it had become clear that it was the client, not the husband, who was doing the cheating, and the woman's accusations were the product of wishful thinking, a desire to find a justification for her own behavior. The husband, a mild-mannered lawyer with a gentle smile and a graying tonsure, went to his office, met with clients, went to court, went to lunch, went to the office, met with clients, left the office, went to the supermarket, bought eggs (or bread, or orange juice, or salsa), went home. Innocently worked or read a book with his socked feet up on the coffee table while he waited for Jane's client, also a lawyer, to come home. He did these things every day. On the weekends, he went fishing or played racquetball or tennis (weather depending) or worked or read a book with his socked feet up on the coffee table while Jane's client had sex with a colleague at her office. The search was costing the client a lot of money, and she was becoming increasingly angry at the lack of results, and decreasingly tolerant of Jane's insistence that these *were* the results, just not the results she wanted.

During their weekly videoconference the other day, her sister, Lila, ostensible equal partner in the business who, in her office five states away, seemed always to end up with the more interesting, adventurous, and lucrative cases, told Jane that she had better arrange to get paid before exposing the client's infidelity to her husband.

"I am not planning to expose her to her husband, Lila."

"Why not?"

"He isn't our client! She is."

"There is a greater client than the client," Lila said, glancing at something off-screen, probably another screen displaying something more exciting than their meeting. "And that client is justice."

Oh, for fuck's sake. "I do not recall that being on the business card," Jane said.

"Of course not. Nobody would hire us."

Before she started the company with her sister, she'd been the accountant in the history department of the nearby college where her father, Harry, taught, and hadn't seen or spoken to Lila in a decade. She'd been unhappily married and felt like a disappointment to everyone around her, especially her daughter, Chloe, a precocious adolescent with a keen sixth sense for adult problems. Now she was divorced, working for herself, and on good terms with Chloe; Jane's father was retired and worked alongside her as researcher and emotional-support elder, and her estrangement from Lila had come to a dramatic end with this business partnership. The two were fraternal twins and dissimilar in outlook, appearance, and expertise. And though they were once again, for the most part, in each other's good graces, Jane could feel that old resentment creeping back—at Lila's bullheadedness, her self-absorption, her unwillingness to relinquish even the slightest degree of control. Since the dust hadn't yet settled on their uncomfortably illuminating reunion, and for the sake of the business, she had tried to tamp down her growing frustration with Lila, to keep the edge out of her voice when they talked.

But Jesus Christ was Jane bored. Notes complete, she leaned back in her desk chair and pressed her palms against her eyes. Words swam in her field of vision: *Subject ate two-thirds of burrito, requested to-go bag for the remaining third.* Lila's last case—that is, the last one she deigned to inform Jane about—had involved tracking a stolen prototype sniper rifle to a wealthy collector's mountaintop retreat and retrieving it for its owner in a daring heist, then stiffing the client, a hired killer, blackmailing him with his own collection of snuff pornography, and throwing the gun into the sea. Where did she find these cases? Jane once demanded. The cases tended to find her. How could she afford to alienate wealthy and dangerous men? The less Jane knew, the better.

Her thoughts were interrupted, mercifully, by the house-shaking entrance of her daughter, who flung the front door open with enough force to make Jane's ears pop. "I'm home!" Chloe shouted, as though the place were a thirty-room mansion instead of the drafty twelve-hundred-square-foot ranch it actually was. Jane and Lila had grown up here, raised by their father in a manner Jane had generously retconned as benign neglect. The house had also been neglected, and since her divorce and the establishment of the agency, Jane had moved back and was trying to fix things and make improvements, occasionally with the help of her ex-husband, Chloe's father, Chance, a stonemason and all-around handyman. Still, you could describe the house as rickety at the best of times, and Chloe's presence made it feel ricketier still.

"Hi!" Jane shouted, also pointlessly. "I'm in the office!"

"Mailbag," Chloe said, appearing in the doorway, holding a pile of envelopes and packages. She was thirteen, pale-skinned and fine-haired, with large piercing eyes and a charmingly lopsided face. She compensated for her congenital insecurity—an unfortunate inheritance from Harry, which Jane shared and wouldn't admit to out loud—with a bumptiously theatrical overconfidence. Divorce had damaged their relationship, but it had improved steadily ever since, as Chloe watched her parents learn how to get along and as calm descended over both their households. About the divorce, Jane felt guilt but no regret. Life was better now for everyone.

"What is this all about?" Chloe asked now, holding up a padded envelope addressed to Jane that had been ripped messily open at one end.

"Why are you opening my mail?"

"It's business mail, isn't it? And I'm part of the business? It says Perks Locksmith right there on the address. And on the return address too."

"It's from Lila?"

"Unless there's a third Perks we don't know about."

Lila's arm of the business, the original one, was tucked away in a small town in Missouri and offered a range of services, among them the tracking of people and money, corporate espionage, government intelligence contracting, and IT security, including protection against cyberattacks or, depending on the client, the execution of cyberattacks. Perks had grown from Lila's vocational training as an actual locksmith, hence the name. Jane had suggested that perhaps the East Coast satellite office should be called something different, to reflect what the business actually intended to do, but Lila had insisted on keeping the name, for reasons that remained mysterious.

Among the recent promises Lila had made was to help Jane find an office space and get it set up. Since their last conference call, Jane had been expecting a list of locations to check out and landlords to contact, presumably via email. But none had been forthcoming. This package bulged in the middle and bore the logo of an overnight shipping service.

"Give it here," Jane said.

To her surprise, the return address wasn't Lila's—her actual location was, anyway, a secret to all but a few trusted associates—but one here in Nestor. Perks Locksmith, via Ten County Retail LLC, 2301 Linwood Drive, Nestor, New York. Inside, Jane found a resealable plastic bag full of keys, each bearing a paper tag on a loop of string. One tag read SPACE #27, another MAIN DOORS, another STORAGE.

"What on earth is this," Jane said, her jaw tightening.

"That's what I'm asking."

She typed the address into her computer and up popped a map. "It's out near the mall."

"Is it our new office?" Chloe said, her voice excited.

"It had better not be. I want something downtown that I can walk to."

"Well? What are we waiting for?"

The two drove north on the highway climbing above Onteo Lake while AM radio played a talk show about farming. It was early afternoon, an unseasonably cool midsummer's day, and little clouds were moving briskly across a blue sky. A good day for sailing, it looked like; sailboats, flecks of white, moved on the lake's surface like germs in a petri dish. Nestor was the tiny college town at the southern end of the lake, the dot of its exclamation mark. Sometimes Jane marveled at her return here, the place she'd grown up. Most people come home in the wake of a failed career, to care for an ailing parent, or out of simple love for the place that made them. Jane came home to confess to a killing, and ultimately to receive a prison sentence for voluntary manslaughter. Chloe had spent the first few months of her life in the nursery at the nearby Boynton Ridge Correctional Facility for Women and emerged into a marriage already doomed to failure. And yet, look at her now, a poised, eccentric, independent-minded young woman. Jane herself didn't feel grown up—how could this child be hers?

Jane let her phone guide her to the College Heights exit, and then left, over the overpass and through the traffic light. The half-abandoned shopping mall came into view, and it was Chloe, squinting at her own phone, who realized: "That address isn't *near* the mall. It *is* the mall."

"It's gotta just be the address of the landlord. She wouldn't dare."

As they pulled into the sparsely populated parking lot, a notification arrived on Jane's phone: an encrypted text from Lila. *There should be a panel van waiting,* it read.

"Did she literally track us here?" Jane wondered out loud.

"Of course she did!" Chloe said, not bothering to conceal her delight. She was impressed with her aunt, and clearly regarded her as the more dynamic, fearless, and brilliant of the two sisters. But that was natural, wasn't it? One's mother could not be cool; it was a rule of adolescence. Jane had coasted awhile on having done time, a fact that she and Chance had once concealed from Chloe; for some months after learning the truth, Chloe would tell anyone she met that she had been born in prison. But the novelty had worn off and she had come to regard her aunt's adventures as more compelling, more daring, more impressive than her mother's. What Chloe didn't understand was that Lila was also more selfish, more impulsive, less reliable. More ruthless, more violent.

"There!" Chloe was pointing to a featureless white delivery truck, parked near the main entrance, above which the mall's tan lines spelled out the ghostly word SEARS. A skinny guy with a mustache was leaning against the driver's-side door, smoking a cigarette. As they pulled up, he threw it on the ground and crushed it underfoot.

"Perks?" he asked as they emerged from the car.

"That's us!" Chloe said.

"So where am I taking this stuff?"

"You're probably going to be taking it right back where you got it," Jane said.

"Happy to get paid all over again" was his reply.

They followed the guy through the double doors and into the dim confines of the mall's main corridor. In Jane's memory, this mall had never thrived; a few years ago it had almost shut down. Now it was showing weedy signs of life: Though every third storefront was empty behind its metal grate, the remaining spaces had spawned strange new businesses scattered among the few familiar retailers. Beside Claire's, a mini–flea market. Nestled between Spencer's and Talbots, a place called Only Canoes. (Inside, the inventory lived up to the promise of the sign, a vinyl banner dangling over the disused logo of the Gap.) The food court was half empty, too, but a couple of the chains had been supplanted by offshoots from local restaurants: Vegan Delights, Tofu Tom, Chickentown Deli.

"I guess we're looking for number twenty-seven?" Jane said to no one in particular.

"Map's over there," the delivery guy said.

The glowing map kiosk was woefully outdated, but its colorful blocks were indeed identified by number, and 27 was up ahead, occupying a corner space. "There!" Chloe said, pointing.

They were greeted silently at the entrance by a woman who was applying the finishing touches to a vinyl logo on the glass front wall: a big gold key, anchoring the words

PERKS LOCKSMITH
"ALL OUR CUSTOMERS GET THE PERKS"

"You have got to be fucking kidding me," Jane said.

The delivery guy headed to the truck, and the sign woman stood back to admire her work. When Jane asked if she was expecting to get paid for this, she was told she already had been. Of course.

A moment later Jane and Chloe were alone in the empty space—an awkward, lopped-off triangle equipped with a couple of countertops, some desks, a few room dividers, and a cluster of rotating display towers shoved off in a corner. A few random tools had been left behind under the counters: a tape dispenser, a box cutter. Everything was scratched, dented, and nicked, and everything was beige. This was what Lila regarded as Jane's rightful place: a shitty storefront in a garbage mall. The sign on the door might as well have read FOREVER 36.

"Wait, what are the other keys for?" Chloe wanted to know.

"Don't know, don't care," Jane muttered, aware of how petulant she sounded, incapable of sounding any other way. A moment later Chloe was heading for a door in the back of the room, or really a hinged, flush section of carpeted wall. She opened it and stuck her head through.

"Oh my god," Chloe said. "Backstage at the mall!"

Reluctantly, Jane followed her into a cavernous industrial hallway with a concrete floor and exposed steel wall studs threaded with thick wires. They wandered around, occasionally encountering some retail employee busily moving merchandise in a rolling canvas cart. They eventually arrived at a storage mini-warehouse, where they found a bunch of empty shelves, high and deep, allotted to number 27.

Back in the corner space, they were met by the delivery guy dropping off his first round of boxes.

"Wait, wait!" Jane said, waving her arms. "I don't want this stuff!"

"Lady," the guy told her with a sigh, "I don't get paid until I send somebody a picture of all these boxes piled up in this space. I've got a shipping manifest and a rental contract that says it's legit. If you want to pay me again later to come pick it up and bring it someplace else, you can, but..."

He let the sentence trail off and left with his hand truck to get more boxes. Fine. If that imperious psycho wanted to waste her money dumping a pile of garbage into an empty office, Jane couldn't stop her. She wasn't going to give her sister the satisfaction of occupying this awful space; she wasn't even going to open the boxes.

From behind her, the stutter of packing tape, the guttural honk of tearing cardboard. "What the heck!" She turned to find Chloe with her hands deep in one of the boxes.

"Chloe!"

"What is this stuff?" The girl pulled out a couple of brass objects—key cores for door locks, Jane knew from her half-assed maintenance of her father's house. As Chloe tore open the other boxes, Jane peered inside. They contained the typical inventory of a real locksmith shop. In addition to the cores, a laser key-cutting machine, blank keys. A utility box with picks, a tension wrench, a stethoscope like a doctor would have, and various other tools Jane couldn't even identify. While Chloe marveled over these, the delivery man returned with another load, this time things Jane recalled seeing in Lila's office in Missouri: an unbranded tower computer and an enormous monitor, a soldering station, a metal punch, a printer and laminator.

"She cannot be serious," Jane said to no one in particular. "I'm not running a locksmith shop out of a shopping mall."

"It's fun," Chloe said, holding up a rotating display stand for key blanks. "Like a puzzle!"

"I admire your optimism, Chloe, but no. This isn't what we agreed to."

A few minutes later, Jane received another text. "'She'll be right there,'" she read aloud to Chloe. "*Who* will be right here?" Her thumbs were poised over the phone's keyboard, ready to issue a scathing rejoinder, but no. That's what Lila wanted. Jane wasn't going to give her the satisfaction.

Her question was answered a few minutes later in the form of a tall, lanky, broad-shouldered woman wearing aviator eyeglasses, her auburn hair pulled back in a low, tidy bun. For a moment, Jane just gawped in surprise; it was Chloe who took her head out of a box and said, "Oh my god, are you Loretta?"

"Ladies," the woman said.

Loretta was Lila's associate in the main office in Missouri. A former army staff sergeant who served in Afghanistan, she now maintained the front for Lila's business, a sleepy antiques shop, and handled Lila's travel arrangements, meetings, and schedule. Jane hugged her and introduced Chloe.

"So who's minding the store back home?" Jane said.

"It's peak bass season," Loretta told her. "The sign on the door says 'Gone Fishing.' I think we'll survive the lost income."

"Well, sorry you wasted your time. We are not going along with this bullshit."

Loretta was nodding. "I told her that's what you'd say."

"Like, what am I supposed to do here? I assume this locksmith stuff is supposed to be a front, like your shop?"

The woman shrugged. "I think mostly? With Lila, sometimes it's easier to just go with the flow."

"I am the damn flow! It's a partnership!"

"You're preaching to the choir," Loretta told her, holding up her hands.

"And I guess you're here to set all of this up?"

"And give you a few pointers."

"Great. What, locksmith lessons?"

"I think you're kidding," she said. "But...you really could learn. Most people take a course, then apprentice. You already have all the stuff right here. You could teach yourself."

"Come on, man!"

"Loretta!" Chloe said, behind her, excited. "What is this thing!"

Jane gazed around the room in despair as Chloe and Loretta chatted, wondering if she'd ever be permitted to feel like her sister's equal, if the whole thing had been a mistake. At least in the history department, she'd had a clearly defined task that only she was authorized to perform. And she preferred, in most ways, her small, reliable salary to the largesse of Lila's mysteriously deep pockets, likely the spoils of undocumented activity if not outright crime.

"I don't get why it has to be an actual locksmith," Jane said, approaching the two as they unpacked.

Chloe said, "Because it's cool, obviously."

Loretta laughed. Somehow this was what sent Jane over the edge. She kicked one of the boxes, and whatever heavy object was in there immediately sent a bolt of pain all the way up to her shoulders. "Fuck!"

They looked up at her, startled.

"Is this all some kind of joke to you two? I do not want to run a locksmith shop at a mall!"

Loretta stood, brushing off her hands. "I get it. I do. But...to your sister, this really is a good-faith gesture to get you up to speed with stuff she already knows. I know a...normal person would have discussed it with you first. But..." She gestured around the room. "Some of these tools you're going to actually need. And it could be a good summer job for Chloe."

"Seriously?" Chloe said.

"I mean...that's up to your mom."

Chloe pulled out her phone. "I already bookmarked a couple of videos. Like, the basics—duplicating keys, replacing...cores?"

"Right," Loretta said.

Jane could feel herself weakening, getting pulled off balance, falling in slow motion into Lila's now-familiar black hole of single-mindedness. It was like a drug, this blithe confidence. When they were young, the only kind of real ambition they could have outside of schoolwork was social—

drawing people into their sphere. The two were never popular, but Jane knew how to cajole and persuade and, later, to flirt. Between the two of them, she was the leader. She was an actor and a charmer, and she liked attracting boys and men. The girls joined the theater club together, went to parties, made friends.

All of that culminated in the night their theater director roofied Jane and tried to rape her. He ended up dead, and the girls went on the run. They were sixteen. Eventually, Jane turned herself in and served her sentence at Boynton Ridge, but until then they learned to survive, to manipulate people, to take what they needed. And Lila emerged as the leader in this new, unfamiliar life. She didn't need to be loved, and she didn't have a conscience, or not much of one. Her risks tended to pay off, and she didn't mind hurting people on the way to getting what she wanted. Jane never did figure out how to achieve balance with Lila; it seemed that one of them always had to be on top.

They'd reunited to figure out where their mother had disappeared to, and once that question was answered, they decided to go into business together. And Lila, it was clear, was still on top. And yet...Jane had to admit this location wasn't without charm. Lila could probably have talked her into it if she'd tried. Plenty of parking, old folks speed-walking by, quiet music warbling in from the hall, all the hot pretzels your heart desired.

As if reading her mind, Chloe interrupted to ask for money—she wanted to go find something to eat. Jane handed it over and, checking her phone, noticed that somebody had called.

"So...should I get to work on all this?" Loretta asked her, pointing a thumb at the computer equipment in the back of the room. "Or are we pumping the brakes?"

Jane could only sigh. The fight was draining out of her. "Sometimes I want to kill her, Loretta."

"I hear you," Loretta said. "The first half hour of the drive out here was a one-sided screaming fight. If only she'd been in the car to hear it."

"You *drove*? From Missouri?"

"That's how we roll."

"Fine," Jane said. "If Chloe's into it, I guess I'll go along, for now."

Loretta nodded, then headed to the computers, swiping a box cutter off the counter on the way.

Jane sat down on a folding chair and opened up the phone app. Some old-school stranger had left a voicemail, which the phone had attempted to transcribe. *Jane hi its Shelly bees lean from _____ ridge I got out a couple weeks ago Annie dear help...*

Surprised, she hit play and raised the phone to her ear. "Jane," came a voice she hadn't heard in years. "Hi, it's Shelly Beasley from Boynton Ridge. I got out a couple weeks ago and I need your help with something. It's kind of urgent. You said I should call you anytime so I hope it's not an imposition or anything. Uh, that's all, I guess...Call me back? It's weird and complicated out here, man! Say what you will about Boynton, you always knew what was gonna happen next. Well, usually. Okay, bye."

While her mother made a phone call, Chloe set out to explore the new digs. If you'd told her just a couple of hours earlier that she'd be spending her summer at the stupid mall, she would have laughed in your face. But the reality of the place had surprised her. She hadn't been here since the frozen yogurt stand closed three years ago, and things had changed. It was weird now! Somebody must have taken it over as a rehab project and lowered the rents. Almost all the national chains that made a mall a mall were gone, and in their places were random people selling random things: drug paraphernalia, used sneakers. Clothes that made you look like an animal, which she suspected was a sex thing but didn't want to ask anyone or look up. The "Snake Shop"?

The most shocking thing about the mall, though, was the abundance of hidden areas most people didn't get to see. The illuminated maps were lies! There were whole rooms and corridors in between and behind the ones the maps let you see. Grandpa Harry had taught her the difference between misinformation—information that was simply incorrect or mistaken—and *dis*information, false information given with the intent to deceive. The public mall maps were the latter.

Chloe explored as far as their set of keys allowed; she had access to about a quarter, she believed, of the mall's secret corridors and chambers. Occasionally a passing retail employee or custodian would smile at her, but most people narrowed their eyes, and she had to hold up and shake the keys to prove her legitimacy. She was at the age—too old to be cute, too young to have responsibilities—when people unfairly suspected her of all manner of mischief. On the other hand, this was also the perfect age: she was young enough to have free time, old enough to be smarter than people suspected. What she would accomplish with these covert advantages was something she needed to figure out.

She slipped out the workmen's door leading to an empty storefront and popped out into the mall proper from behind a giant GREAT DEALS COMING SOON! sign. Another piece of disinformation: she happened to know there was bupkes being readied behind that wall. In the food court, she got in line at the pretzel stand behind some high school freaks with a rat on a leash. Or maybe it was a ferret. Except for rabbits, rodents as pets seemed like a real statement to Chloe; it put you in a special social category where only other rodent folk resided. No, thanks.

Pretzel in hand, she headed for the seating area of the food court to kick back and stare at her phone. But she was distracted by a pack of loud girls blithely strolling by: Addison Kunstler and her smarmy pals. Addison was two things to Chloe: a rich girl with important parents, and her rival for president of the eighth-grade class. They both went to Tarbox Beals, the private school about an hour from Nestor that Chloe was required to attend for at least one more year and that her father's mother, Grandma Susan, was paying for. (Her parents had been mum about who paid for what, she supposed to keep things chill in the wake of the divorce, but Grandma Susan was the kind of lady who always let you know when you owed her one.) Most of the kids who went there were from Rochester, but Addison was one of a handful of Nestorians who made the long commute. Her mother's suggestion that they carpool was among the most appalling she had ever proposed, and Chloe's straight-up tantrum had resulted in a rare reprieve. Chloe figured that was because her mother (1) sort of enjoyed the drive and didn't want someone else's child in her car anyway, and (2) disliked Addison's mother. She did some money-related thing at Nestor College, and Addison's father was a computer scientist who had developed some kind of valuable software. Addison made it sound like they were royalty or some such, though Grandpa Harry hadn't heard of them. Of course, he was old and had just retired.

The funny thing about Addison was that they'd started out as friends when she arrived at the school last year. Chloe had been appointed by the principal to be her mentor for her first few weeks. This was a Tarbox Beals tradition: every new student got assigned a pal who was supposed to show them the ropes. Usually the kids were besties for a couple of weeks until the new ones found their rightful place in the social scene, but it wasn't like that with Addison and Chloe. They really liked each other! It was a rare treat when a new Nestorian showed up at Beals; Addison used to come downtown and spend the day just walking around with Chloe. You couldn't really do that in her neighborhood, Addison said; there was nothing to do, same as with her old town. She was talkative and funny, and they mostly complained to each other about boys from school.

And then something happened, Chloe still didn't know what. Addison stopped texting her back and rolled her eyes at the lunch table whenever Chloe spoke. It wasn't long before the other girls in that friend group began to follow her lead, and pretty soon Chloe was entirely on the outs with everyone she used to like, with literally no explanation. She resisted the urge to tell her mom, preferring to lick her wounds in private. But it was a hard time, and still a mystery.

Now Chloe followed the girls as they went into the rude gift shop, where the clerks flirted with them, and the jewelry store, where the clerks chased them away. They got coffee from Hot Beanz 2 and tried to shake free gumballs out of the gumball machine.

The school election was part of a yearlong civics unit. They chose the candidates in the spring, when the United States had its primaries, and elected a president in the fall, when the US had its elections. You had to make up a party to be in, with values and everything; Addison had run on the Security Party ticket, which was dedicated to improving the school's computer system. If elected, she said, her dad would help. Chloe had created the Cooperative Party, which promised to get more kids involved with more stuff and get the parents to cough up money to create new clubs. Chloe knew the class president wouldn't have much power, but it sometimes surprised her how many good things could happen if somebody just said out loud that those things were worth doing.

Anyway, Chloe and Addison had gotten the most votes in the primary and were supposed to spend the summer planning their fall campaigns. Maybe she should take some spy pictures of Addison knocking over a display of barrettes in Claire's and not picking it up or Addison harassing the security guard about why she didn't carry a gun. But no—she would beat Addison on the issues, not with some frivolous gimmick.

Pretzel finished, Chloe wiped the Parmesan cheese off her hands and headed back toward Perks. She hadn't been walking for more than a minute before she felt someone touch her shoulder and turned to find Addison's crew staring her down with their hands on their hips. All except one of them, a girl named Kay, who wouldn't meet her gaze.

"Just so you know," Addison said, "we saw you following us. In case you thought your *obsession* was a secret."

"Oh, hey, guys," Chloe said. "I didn't realize it was you. I thought it was just a bunch of ten-year-olds."

"That's going in my oppo. You're a stalker."

"Dude, your whole campaign is that you want to do surveillance. That's why it's called the Stalker Party."

That touched a nerve. "It's not surveillance! It's *security*!"

"Whatever, Zuck."

She rolled her eyes. "That's a compliment. My dad met Mark Zuckerberg once."

"What a cool pal to have. Maybe he can give you some debate tips."

"Actually," Addison said, "my dad's going to help me with that. He's a professor. He teaches in big lecture halls. Also, I'm not afraid of public speaking."

"Well, neither am I." Chloe didn't mention that her grandfather had also been a professor; she got the impression from her mother that he'd spent most of his career hiding in his office. "May the best woman win."

They were at a stalemate. Addison turned her back and the girls moved away. Kay's hands were shoved deep into her hoodie pockets, and her head hung; of the group, she alone peered back over her shoulder at Chloe, who waved. The girl quickly turned away.

Interesting.

2

Not long after reuniting with her sister and inviting her to join the business, Lila Pool set up a custom server dedicated entirely to detecting web searches for her various public and private identities, and all of Jane's, and the names and aliases of her extended family members, business associates, rivals, and intelligence contacts. Her custom code directed the searches to a dummy website, to which analytics were applied, with certain combinations of people, places, and events leading to an alert. If, for instance, somebody looking for information about Lila's connection to Central Intelligence—tenuous and antagonistic, but real—also seemed aware that she had a niece named Chloe, she wanted to know right away. If someone appeared to have discovered that Anabel Bortnik, former Iran-Contra-era spy and Panamanian drug capo with delusions of freedom-fighting grandeur, was in fact her mother, then Lila wanted to have a talk with that someone, possibly in their bedroom at three a.m., possibly with a knife at their throat. In Lila's line of work, it was impossible to be too careful or too prepared.

And because she was so careful and so prepared, those alerts rarely sounded. The server was hooked up to some cheap computer speakers that lived on a shelf on the rack in the back of her office, so old and decrepit that every now and then she plugged them into her CD walkman to make sure they still worked. They always did, and probably always would.

Lila's office occupied the top floor of a small warehouse in downtown Timber Fell, a quaint village in the Lake of the Ozarks region of Missouri whose economy was largely based on fishing and hunting. The ground floor was an antiques shop, which she had bought along with the building; she ended up retaining its manager, Loretta, as her assistant and keeping the shop intact. Once the top floor had been cleared of old junk, she brought in work tables, office chairs, and equipment for creating and modifying electronics. Her computers were hand-built PC towers running a customized version of Kali Linux. She used a large-format printer to create fake ID badges and big maps that she could bring on the road. She didn't like to use anything that could be tracked, including conventional phones and other GPS-equipped devices. In truth, she didn't really need the maps; she had road atlases for all fifty states, many of them enhanced with handwritten notes, and she possessed a natural sense of direction.

This room was high-ceilinged and bright, its many windows equipped with sheer light-filtering roller shades, for privacy; a small open bedroom area occupied one corner, an enclosed bathroom another. A storeroom of shelf-stable food and water could be found at the back, in case she ever needed to lie low for a few days or weeks or just wanted to, recreationally. The warehouse was her workplace and her home, and she saw no reason to separate the two.

Though Lila was not without emotions—she had been married briefly, and her relationship with Loretta was complicated—she generally preferred not to feel them, and the best way to accomplish this was to be alone. Sometimes she sent Loretta into the field to do things she could have done herself just to achieve the solitude.

Loretta's current assignment in Nestor was serving that purpose. Lately she kept ending up in Lila's bed, then wondering aloud if she was supposed to stay there or what. Lila hadn't managed to give her the courtesy of a definitive answer. She knew she was being mercurial and hurtful, but she also felt like she couldn't help it. So she'd banished Loretta for a couple of weeks and vowed to get it together.

And she had woken up on this first day alone full of simmering energy and excitement. It was a sunny morning in July. Her plan for these weeks was to upgrade the server software, review a few potential clients, look into getting a new GPS and RF sniffer, work on her bike, and play some Dwarf Fortress. She might actually take the Volvo, a heavily modified 960 Wagon from 1997, down to the lake to fish. A recent investment had been a secluded patch of lakefront about twenty miles north of here, where she had spent a couple of weeks upgrading an old cabin with a new roof, solar panels, and a woodstove—the perfect place for getting away from already being away from it all.

She got out of bed, took a shower, and pulled on a tee shirt and jeans. She fried a couple of eggs and ate them with an energy bar and a cup of black coffee. Then she refilled the coffee cup, sat down at her desk, and opened up her text editor.

Two hours later, something metal fell over in a corner of the room. She jumped out of her chair and fell into a crouch, her heart racing. Then the sound repeated itself and she realized it was a bell—the bell sound she had designated as the alert for her web scraper and that was coming through her dusty old speakers. Jesus Christ!

She reached behind her monitor and flipped the HDMI switch box over to the server. Its spare desktop flickered to life, and she opened her analytics application. A red line of text had appeared at the bottom of a long column of white, and it read

> SEARCH TERMS "LILA POOL" + "JANE" + "RUTH BORTNIK" DETECTED
> 45.52.226.143 NEBRASKA

Which told her that somebody in Nebraska had searched for both her and her sister, along with, surprisingly, their aunt.

Aunt Ruth had been an attorney and law professor based in Chicago. Their mother's sister, the woman could be described as cold, remote, and austere, but she had sheltered them for a week when they'd gone on the run twenty years before. Lila remained grateful but had never visited again and still felt some vestigial guilt over it; Ruth had ended her own life in 2011. There had been no funeral, and her husband, a mild-mannered older man named Lloyd, had sold the house in Evanston and disappeared somewhere, presumably to live out his remaining years in grief. They had no children.

Searches for Aunt Ruth were common, as she had authored or coauthored several important papers and had prosecuted a few landmark cases in intellectual property and energy rights, her overlapping specialties. But Lila had never seen a search connecting her to her twin nieces.

She dug a little deeper. The IP address had been assigned by a service provider in Omaha, a local one, luckily, which was more likely to have exploitable security flaws. Indeed, Lila quickly discovered it used BGPv4, a weak legacy routing protocol, and was soon able to spoof her way into the routing tables and identify the user's private IP and her name: Padma Nagarajan.

It didn't ring a bell. A simple search produced the information that Nagarajan was also a lawyer, a senior associate at Giscombe, Koch, and Hathaway, a large firm in Omaha. Their website provided a formal headshot of a smooth-faced, middle-aged woman, probably Indian or Pakistani, with a placid, confident smile. The picture *did* ring a bell, and after a few minutes Lila had it: this woman was a professional contact of Aunt Ruth's. When, back in 2006, Lila and Jane had arrived at the only address they had for their aunt, this lady was living there. She had a different name then—Diaz, maybe, or Cruz. She'd phoned Ruth, gotten her new—and final—address, and passed it along to the girls. Then they said goodbye to her, presumably forever.

But here she was, trying to find Lila and Jane. From a locked storage case, Lila removed a fresh burner phone from its plastic clamshell, activated it, took note of the number, and called the law firm. She was routed to an assistant, who said that Ms. Nagarajan was on a call. "Please interrupt. Tell her it's Lila Pool. I'll hold."

"This is an incredible coincidence," Padma said when she came on the line, and her voice brought Lila back to those exhilarating days, independent and free, their shattered lives on the cusp of rebirth. "I was literally just searching for you on my lunch hour."

"Not a coincidence. I noticed you doing it."

A silence. "Right. Of course. Do you remember me?"

"Yes," Lila said. "I'm grateful for the help you gave us back then."

"Well, I'm glad to have helped. Ruth kept me updated, a little, until she died. It sounds like things were hard for you, for a while."

"For my sister. But she got past it. She has a daughter. We're in business together."

"Yes," Padma said. "I found that. I was going to call her."

There was a long pause, as though she didn't know how to proceed. Lila let the silence stretch out.

"I feel a bit foolish about this. It seems far-fetched."

"Try me," Lila said.

"It's about your aunt. You know she passed away, correct?"

"I do."

Her voice fell to a near-whisper. "It was...they ruled it...self-inflicted. With a gun. Not many women use a gun, but I believed at the time that Ruth would. It was her own gun, for which she had a license and the proper training. I got the sense that your mother was...is...they were fierce women, is what I'm saying."

"That's right."

"However," Padma said. "However, I have reason to believe that this death may have been...that it was...it was not self-inflicted."

"Okay..."

"I'm sorry, I'm limited in what I can say right now. Hold on." Lila heard her get up, shuffle some papers, open a door. She asked somebody to run something to another office, presumably the assistant who'd answered the phone. The door shut and she returned. "Sorry. The information I have comes from a client. A very important and powerful one, represented by one of the senior partners. Most of those records are visible only on a need-to-know basis, but they farmed out some research to me, and I found—"

"Padma," Lila said, "let me stop you there." She was already mentally rearranging the next few days, and brought up her map-viewer app. "What are you doing in...six hours or so?"

"Uh...eating dinner? With my husband?"

"Why don't you plan to have it with me instead. Someplace public where you've never eaten before."

"Are you serious?"

"Yes. No more about this on the phone, especially not while you're at work."

"Oh! All right, good. Thank you."

"When you have the location, text it to me at this number. With the address, please."

"I will."

Lila hung up, put her workstation to sleep. She packed a bag, locked and alarmed the door, and headed to the garage where she kept the Volvo and her two vintage motorcycles, a fully restored BMW R90S and a new acquisition, a late R69S from 1968 that she was still sourcing parts for.

She threw her bag into the back of the Volvo, glanced dolefully at the fishing gear it sat beside, and opened up the reinforced military case where she kept her road atlases. She found the Omaha page in the Nebraska one, then climbed in behind the wheel and pulled out of the garage. The heavy door clanked shut behind her. She made her way north out of town, on the lettered highways along the reservoir, to Route 7, which would take her toward Kansas City.

Lila liked to drive, and she liked to do it in silence. She did not get bored or lonely. Sometimes she wished she could achieve, at home, the level and flavor of concentration that driving afforded her; the mechanics of travel freed her mind in a way that no other activity did. Greenfields, junkyards, forests drifted by outside; she crossed the reservoir, low to the water on both sides, and the rankness of fish and mud reached her through the open window. She hadn't driven this way since her journey with Jane to find their mother, which had brought them all the way to the Pacific Northwest, and then to Central America. They found her, all right, and Lila burned her house down. She'd be happy to never see her again.

She understood that Jane was upset with her. It was true that she'd presented their journey last year as one of renewal and discovery, and she could see why Jane would feel betrayed that they ended up narrowly escaping with their lives. But to Lila, that *was* discovery, that *was* renewal. The two had bonded in their teens over what Lila now knew to be the defining event of their lives: the justifiable homicide of their high school theater director, George Framingham. Framingham was a lecher, a creep, and their mother's lover; he'd roofied Jane at a party and Lila clocked him with a concrete candleholder. She hadn't intended to kill him; she only wanted him to stop raping her sister. They dumped his body into the lake and left town.

For Lila, this series of events had been miraculously liberating. An introvert who didn't see the point of social customs, she'd discovered a strength deep within herself while murdering a pervert, and a new, exhilarating source of pleasure and satisfaction. It felt good to put things right, and to devise a plan to bury the evidence forever. The latter was a failure—eventually the body had been discovered, and her trail of false evidence unraveled—but it wasn't a bad attempt for a girl of sixteen, and the next time she killed somebody, she didn't make the same mistakes.

As for Jane, she couldn't deal with the guilt, even though none of it had been her fault. It had all been George Framingham's fault. His actions amounted to a formal request for a candleholder to the forehead. But Jane seemed to feel worse and worse the longer they wandered together, and she started drinking and doing drugs when they settled down out west, and pretty soon wouldn't leave their apartment. Lila eventually moved out—or, rather, she took longer and longer trips with dumber and dumber people, learning how to gain their trust, take advantage of them. On impulse, she decided to learn a trade and became certified as a locksmith in California, where they were living at the time. This taught her a lot about people's houses, particularly how easy it was to enter them undetected. A sideline in electronic locks got her interested in hacking and encryption. Already adept at computers, she learned programming in earnest, did some corporate espionage, eventually hung out an IT security shingle. She discovered just how sloppy other people were. Initially, she hadn't thought of her particular skill set as unique or even unusual; she'd assumed most people were cautious, well informed, heavily defended. It turned out that the opposite was true. People were a vulnerable mess, and it was rare for Lila to encounter one who presented much resistance at all.

She had not understood Jane's misery and couldn't figure out how to help. Jane accused her of not wanting to—called her cold and unfeeling—but once Lila realized there was nothing she could do, why would she have pretended otherwise? Was she supposed to sit all day on the bed, holding her greasy hand? Telling her everything would be all right when it clearly wouldn't? Lila didn't like to drink or smoke or take drugs, didn't understand the mentality. If Jane was going to survive, she would have to figure it out herself.

At that point, they were both well into their twenties, and Framingham's death was nearly a decade behind them. Lila did not regard it as a loose end; it was done. Overworked local cops three thousand miles away did not worry her. Everyone knew Framingham was a monster, no one cared that he was gone. The case would remain cold. So it was a genuine surprise to Lila when Jane turned herself in.

If that's what Jane needed to do to assuage her guilt and kick her addictions, it was hardly Lila's place to complain. But it seemed to her a pointless gesture. Anyway, she wasn't given the opportunity to weigh in; Jane had left a note and headed east without consulting her. She supposed Jane had expected to be acquitted, but Lila could have told her that was never going to happen. The teen seductress, girl of loose morals, had to go to jail—that's how America worked. Lila read the Nestor news, kept tabs on her sister, was aware she was married and had had a child in prison. She'd always meant to get in touch, but every time she came close to doing it, she hesitated. Her life was stable and efficient. Personal entanglements would just get in the way. She found Timber Fell and Loretta and didn't look back—until she learned that their mother was alive and about to set foot on American soil for the first time in twenty years. That's when she finally got in touch with her sister—and when she realized she had missed her, just a little.

The business arrangement they'd arrived at in the wake of their adventure had served Lila well; Jane's satellite office had taken some of the drudgery off her shoulders and given Jane and their father something useful to do. In an emotional outburst around the time they made their deal, Jane had demanded an equal share of the agency's more dangerous and complicated cases, but she couldn't have known what this entailed and anyway didn't really mean it. She'd just needed to assert herself, and Lila was glad she had. Their weekly calls had convinced her that Jane was doing a fine job, and now that Lila had provided her with a real office, she expected the work to be even better.

She was making good time and decided to bypass Kansas City and head west to Topeka and pick up Route 75 north. Lila didn't like cities. Los Angeles had provided an object lesson in human nature, but now that she'd found her middle-of-nowhere, there was no going back. She didn't like interstate highways and she didn't like traffic. She liked towns past their prime, low buildings, and blank skies, space to think. North of Topeka, 75 was gloriously flat and straight, a gallery of grain silos, peeling paint, false brick fronts with blank windows, gas stations and warehouses. It didn't make her proud to be an American, but it made her glad to be in America.

She drove fast, and at a quarter to six, she neared the outskirts of Omaha and checked the screen of her burner. The place Padma had suggested was called Woodsmoke Bistro and it was in a strip mall on Pacific Street at Eighty-Seventh. She came into town via Fourteenth—passing housing developments half hidden behind concrete barriers, light-industrial campuses, a shopping mall, a car dealership—and, after a quick look at her printed map, turned right onto Pacific. She would arrive early, with enough time to check out the location and determine if it would suit their needs.

In fact it was perfect. The strip mall was laid out in a C-shape and housed several cafés and restaurants, a liquor store, and a drive-through bank. The smell of woodsmoke, as promised, filled the air. The restaurant had south-facing outdoor tables, which, in the heat and glare, were unoccupied save for an old man and a companion who could have been his daughter or his nurse. She took a table as far from them as possible and left her driving sunglasses on.

From a teenage waitress she ordered a black coffee. The girl told her they didn't have regular coffee but offered an Americano, which Lila accepted. She sipped it and watched cars pull in and out of the lot. It was a Friday evening. The bank was closed. Most people here were stopping at the liquor store on their way home from work. As she waited, traffic to the cafés increased; business-casual was the predominant mode of dress. There were office parks nearby; these customers were most likely doctors, lawyers, real estate agents.

A sixth sense told her that the bright red Prius pulling into the lot was Padma's, and she was right. The woman climbed out of the car and squinted in the sunlight, held her palm up to her brow, and scanned the strip mall's facade. Lila raised a hand and Padma approached the table.

Padma Nagarajan was about sixty and had a round, inquisitive face. She said, "Maybe we can go inside—we're right in the sun," but before Lila could object she added, "No, you're right, let's stay here." She sat down and ordered a salad and a glass of white wine, and Lila ordered the same salad and a glass of ice water, disappointing the waitress.

"It's nice to see you," Padma said. "You haven't changed."

"Neither have you." They were lying. This was one of those conventions Lila didn't like or understand but could force herself to abide by when necessary. She said, "Why don't you tell me what you discovered about Ruth's death."

Padma appeared flustered, evidently expecting more small talk. But she adjusted quickly and cleared her throat. "The client this information comes from is Travis Nutt. It's a distinctive name, and as soon as I heard it, I remembered that he'd been one of Ruth's clients too. He's based in Arizona—somewhere in Arizona—and he's a cattle rancher."

"Why doesn't he have a lawyer closer to home?"

"He probably does, for basic legal representation. But our firm is the best in the country in land-and-water-rights law, which is his primary need for this case and others we've handled. Also, Brian—Brian Hathaway, one of the partners—is friends with him. I'm not sure if they're friends because we represent him or the other way around."

"Why aren't you a partner?" Lila asked.

The question seemed to startle her. "I...various reasons. I came to the firm recently because I relocated with my husband. He's in food science and works for Conagra. I guess I'm in line for junior partner. I did give that up at my old job. And I started late in this field. Is that relevant?"

"I don't know yet. Go on."

She gathered herself, then said, "So, I get the sense that the current case is very lucrative, and Brian asked me to do some research on the statutes and regulations and relevant case law. I don't usually do this kind of thing—I have my own clients and cases—but this is one of those clients the whole firm works for, when we have to. The materials he gave me are heavily redacted. It's clear that Nutt is planning to sue the State of Arizona for access to irrigation from particular waterways or an increased share of the water he's already using. But the redactions make it impossible for me to know where in the state he's based."

"Is this kind of secrecy common?"

"No," Padma said. She paused as the waitress brought their salads and drinks, then asked them if they needed anything further. She was clearly annoyed that they didn't, but this meant she'd be unlikely to return soon, exactly what Lila wanted. When she was gone, Padma said, "When a partner asks for this kind of help, they always give us all the information on the case. So the redactions are definitely weird. Although, if you know Nutt, they're not that surprising."

"You know him, then?"

"Not *know* him. I've met him several times. Or seen him. He's got an air of self-importance and power about him—he barely speaks but when he does, it's very quiet, so the room has to fall absolutely silent to hear. He's small, pale, wears a Stetson. I mean...he sounds like a joke, the way I'm describing him, but it's very intimidating in practice.

"Anyway," Padma went on after a bite of her meal. "Among the research materials I was given were records of the case Ruth handled back in 2010. Before that, Nutt had been a university chemistry professor and researcher at Northwestern, where Ruth worked. He was a founder of something called the Agriculture and Food Production Symposium, a think tank devoted to innovation in the ag sector. He'd developed a livestock drug, a synthetic opioid that was supposed to revolutionize pain management on factory farms, and he ended up in a dispute with the university about manufacturing and marketing variations on it. They rightly thought they owned the compounds they funded, but he wanted to branch out and build on that research in the private sector. Ruth represented him on the case, and it looked like she was going to lose."

"I assume she didn't usually lose cases like this," Lila said.

"No, she did not. On the merits alone, she probably would have turned it down. But Nutt had been friends with her husband, Lloyd. It was sort of a favor for him. Nutt was a very unreasonable client who often acted against counsel's advice and seemed resistant to compromise. He kept…"

"Stepping on his own dick?"

"Uh, I was going to say 'getting in his own way,' but sure. Hold on, let me eat, I'm ridiculously hungry. Somebody stole my sack lunch from the work fridge." Lila picked at her own salad while Padma pushed forkfuls of hers into her mouth. It was perfectly good, but Lila was too distracted. She was trying to puzzle out where the danger was going to come from in this story. Padma flagged down the waitress and asked for some bread, and when it came she buttered a piece and ate that too. "Jesus, okay. Are you going to eat?"

"Eventually," Lila said. "Did the guy go rogue? With the drug?"

"How did you know that?" Padma said. When Lila didn't reply, she went on. "But first, what happened was, in the chem building where Nutt worked, a custodian heard a woman screaming and went into the lab to find two grad students there, naked and clearly high. They'd been using cocaine laced with this stuff, the veterinary drug. The woman would later say that she was being raped, but the man's response was that it was nonconsensual for *him* too. That the drug had driven them both wild with lust and they couldn't stop, that was his defense."

Lila's body was flooding with adrenaline. She said, "Bullshit."

"No doubt," Padma said coolly. "Anyway, there was no trial. He was a foreign national, so the university arranged to have him deported. The woman sued them, and Nutt dropped his doomed case and disappeared. Then the drug started turning up everywhere. He used the student's defense as a marketing tool and got investment money from some high-level reps of a drug cartel with a wing operating inside the United States."

Lila had a sick feeling about what was coming. "The drug is Yes, isn't it."

"That's the street name, yeah. It's a fentanyl derivative."

Lila knew this but didn't bother to tell Padma. Yes was a cocaine adulterant that had the reputation of being an aphrodisiac, though she'd seen a study that had debunked the idea. Nevertheless it was beloved by finance bros and wannabe crypto high rollers for its reputation as a premium product. It wasn't surprising to learn that this was the result of a calculated marketing push, but that wasn't the part that made her feel sick.

"And you know this how?"

Padma shrugged. "Some of it, news reports, though the further the events recede into the past, the less anyone seems to care. Nutt dropped out of the news entirely after a couple of years. So when I was in Chicago visiting family, I went to the Northwestern library and—"

"Her papers."

"Exactly. Lloyd must have sold them to the university. I wanted to talk to him but I couldn't find him. Lots of scholars have their archives preserved by libraries; you can go and page through them. I found her files for the Nutt case in the law library—you'd think this would be a liability for the university, but maybe nobody noticed."

"People are sloppy," Lila said.

"Anyway, that's where I got the stuff about the cartel funding. Which brings me to why I was looking for you now." She reached into her bag and pulled out her phone. She tapped and swiped for a moment. "First of all, I know where Nutt is going to be next week. Brian is meeting him there—the National Stockyards in Oklahoma City. He's showing off some new cattle or something, and Brian's an investor." She handed the phone to Lila. "And I found this."

The screen displayed a photograph of a yellow legal pad covered in Aunt Ruth's notes. Her handwriting was spiky, with a pronounced rightward slant; Lila identified her as a lefty who'd been taught to overwrite. She zoomed in. The top half of the page identified Nutt as the inventor of

Yes and noted some of its proven effects and dangers. Then there was a blank space, and beneath it, several more notes, messier than the others, as though written in haste:

snowmen/holy ghost
$$$ > cow/ashes/purify and rebuild
az, elections?
am I in danger

Lila's heart clenched. Padma said, "I don't know what she's getting at with the ashes, but like I said, Nutt's a cattleman, I guess he put his drug profits into that. He's based in Arizona, so maybe he wants to influence the elections there. As far as I can tell, the Snowmen are the drug cartel that funded him. They're based in Seattle."

"Right."

"But I don't think you write 'Am I in danger' to yourself because you're depressed and want to die. You write it because you're worried somebody might kill you."

"Yeah."

"Oh, and I haven't been able to figure out what 'holy ghost' is."

"Who it is."

"What?"

"Who, not what," Lila said, handing the phone back. "The Holy Ghost is a person."

"How do you know that?"

Lila said nothing in response, except, a few seconds later, "Thanks for telling me all this. I've got to go."

Later, Lila pulled over at a rest stop, parked in a patch of shade, and opened up her laptop. It found a satellite signal, and she searched the internet for videos of Nutt through her VPN. There weren't many. In one from a decade ago, he was being interviewed outside a courthouse, his face indistinct in the shadow of his wide-brimmed hat. His voice was nasal yet powerful, like a fire alarm, as he denounced the university that had taken him to court. There was a news report with a clip from some kind of zoning or environmental variance meeting in Phoenix where Nutt spoke about the need for rural businesses to operate independently of state regulations. It sounded like a bunch of self-serving bullshit to Lila, but people in the room seemed to appreciate it. And there was one other video, from seven years ago, an advertisement for a business called Maynard Sands Truck and Trailer, a dealer and customizer of big rigs in Nevada. It was one of a series of testimonials from the business's prominent clients. Nutt was dressed in a western shirt and suit coat, and the morning sun sneaked under his hat and made him squint. He was trying to smile. It looked like he wasn't enjoying the process.

After that, nothing. His name came up in a few publicly available documents on the Arizona State Library's website, mostly relating to trademarks and patents. Lila wasn't sure how relevant these were to her aims, but she downloaded them and perused a few. A mechanical system for streamlining the delivery of medication to livestock. A paper about repurposing known vectors for cattle disease. A bunch of names for medicines she supposed he was reserving for future use. She filed these away, planning to give them a more careful read later. An index on the site also referred to documents about land ownership and variance, but these had either been redacted or had never been publicly available.

She put the computer away, got a couple more road atlases out of the military case in the trunk, and plotted tomorrow's route to Oklahoma City. She was going to need to see this guy firsthand and figure out where he lived. She would determine what had frightened her aunt about him, and what his relationship was to her mother—the drug capo and self-styled freedom fighter known as the Holy Ghost.

3

The news had arrived via email in the form of a link to something called the *Ghorum Gossip,* and Harry Pool clicked it with the sinking feeling that he was succumbing to a scam. He was in the age group scammers targeted the most, and someone was always threatening to take his Social Security away, warning him his computer had a virus and was going to be wiped, informing him of fake COVID-19 programs he'd forgotten to take advantage of and sweepstakes he'd won. He was an educated man—a professor emeritus of history, no less—yet he felt vulnerable every time one of these emails arrived, as though upon retirement, he'd crossed some Rubicon and lost the power to resist.

Also, now that Perks Locksmith had been given its own office, and his home office would again be his alone, he had realized that solitude—his profoundest lifelong need, as vital to his survival as food, water, and air—no longer held the appeal to him that it once had. He loved having Jane living here again, loved helping her rehabilitate the house, and loved spending time with Chloe, whom he was presently assisting in her campaign for class president. Harry had studied an election or two in his day, though he hoped Chloe's school would run theirs better than the regimes he'd spent his career investigating.

But right now, with the girls at the mall and his academic career behind him, Harry felt lonely and defenseless, and winced as a website sprang to life on his laptop screen.

It wasn't what he'd expected. No pop-up ads, no malware warnings. Instead, a quaint electronic newsletter from a small town with sidebar listings for classified ads, sporting events, and gardening lectures. The headline before him read "Husband, Father, Nestor College Administrator Dead at 84," and he suddenly remembered where Ghorum was and who had lived there. Oh, no.

> Franklin P. Hastings of Ghorum, NY, died peacefully at his home on July 10. He was 84. He was predeceased by his loving wife, Georgina, who passed away in 1978, and son, Hubert, who perished of a childhood illness.
>
> Franklin was proud to have served in the US Army from 1962 to 1964 and to have accepted government contracting work in the years that followed. He worked for many years as assistant director of the Nestor College financial aid office before his retirement in 2014. He is survived by a nephew, Vincent. A memorial service will take place on Saturday, July 19, 11 a.m., at the Ghorum Public Library. Donations in his memory may be sent to the Ghorum Public Library, 14 Main Street, Ghorum.

Harry returned to the email and noticed that it had been sent by vthastings78@gmail.com and that the link was accompanied by the single line *Please come I have something for you.*

He remembered Vincent Hastings very well. They'd met when Harry visited Franklin for the last time, at his home deep in the woods, situated at the end of a long gravel drive, on a burbling creek. Vincent was the goombah who smacked him on the side of the head and took his pistol from him. Yes, it was true that Harry had intended to murder Franklin Hastings and so deserved the roughing up, but he'd known deep down he wasn't really going to do it, and so did Franklin. They had a history. Harry had thought of him as the Factor; he'd been Harry's CIA handler, or so Harry believed at the time. He sort of really was at some point, but after a while it turned out that they were both pretenders, pantomiming the gestures of spycraft to occupy their sad old lonely time. The real agent, Harry's wife, Anabel, was long gone by then, and he'd come out to Ghorum to settle the score. But life had already punished Franklin Hastings enough, and he wasn't really Harry's worst enemy. Harry himself was.

Anyhow, that was all water under the bridge. Franklin was actually dead now, and with any luck Vincent's mysterious gift was something other than a knuckle sandwich.

Saturday began in a mad rush. Jane was off to look into a break-in at her friend's house, and then would be leaving town to attend some conference with the woman. This was somehow supposed to be a case she was on, but Perks wasn't getting paid for it, and it sounded to Harry more like a vacation. At seven thirty in the morning he found his granddaughter frying eggs at the stove and Jane bent over the kitchen table jotting things down in a pocket notebook she'd swiped from Harry's office.

"Good morning," Harry said.

"Dad!" Jane said, patting his shoulder. "I'm glad you're up. Do you think you can bring Chloe to Chance's?" The girl typically spent one week a month with her father, and this was supposed to be one of them.

"Ah, did you forget? I have a memorial service to attend."

"What! You didn't tell me!"

Hm. Maybe he hadn't. "I'm sorry. It's my old friend the Factor. He's the one who—"

"I remember who he is, Dad."

"Also, Mom?" Chloe said. "Dad's out of town, remember? He's getting Grandma Susan and Grandpa Chip moved out of their condo in Palm Beach for the season. I'm supposed to be with you all week." Before Jane could react to this—it was clear to Harry that she had completely forgotten and was too abashed for a moment to speak—Chloe asked Harry, "Is the Factor the CIA guy? The one who recruited my grandmother?" She set the plate of eggs before Jane, who was too busy gazing imploringly at Harry to notice. *Could you babysit this week?* her eyes pleaded.

"That's the one," Harry told Chloe.

"Will there be spooks there? Unmarked black cars?"

"I don't think so. Maybe?"

"I'll come with you," Chloe told him.

"Oh god," Jane said, her mouth now stuffed with egg. "Dad? You wouldn't mind?"

"It's a two-hour drive to a coffin and back," Harry warned Chloe. "But I'd love to have you along."

Jane gathered her notes and car keys, then stood up and kissed Chloe on the head. To Harry, she said, "You're really all right to babysit this week? You'll hardly have to do anything. She can take care of herself. You'd just have to be on call."

"Also," Chloe said, "not a baby."

"It's a figure of speech," her mother said, groaning.

"It's fine, Jane," Harry said. This kind of thing had happened before. Chloe was a good companion, and he didn't mind. He tried to cling to some scraps of anger out of principle, but it was futile; when push came to shove, he felt bad for having been an inattentive father—when Jane was Chloe's age, he was a gloomy drunk locked in his office, writing letters to his absent wife and never sending them. He valued the opportunity to make up for it now.

An hour later Harry and Chloe were on the road in Harry's Subaru, listening to country radio, which the girl had chosen. Rather than singing along, she was leaning over, concentrating on the lyrics. "The women are all warning each other about the men," she said. "But the men are all just proud of how American they are."

"They do seem rather extra-American," Harry said. He'd chosen a tan linen suit and dreaded stepping out of the air-conditioning and into the summer heat. Chloe wore a black dress, her only black dress, which she'd gotten for a dance. It wasn't very funereal, but she was a child, no one would mind. After a while she turned the radio off and Harry thought she'd fallen asleep, but she was just gazing out the window.

"I need to think of a campaign slogan," she said.

"What's your party affiliation, again?"

"The Cooperative Party! I'm supposed to get kids to help with stuff. Suddenly it seems dumb, though. Who wants to vote for the girl who likes chores?"

"That's what a slogan is for," Harry said. "To make that not seem dumb."

"So what were some good ones?"

After a moment, Harry said, "I can only think of the bad ones. In the thirties, there was a guy named Alf Landon, and his slogan was 'Let's Make It a Landon-Slide.'"

"Let me guess, he won?"

"Ha. And an anti-prohibition candidate in the twenties named Al Smith went with 'Make Your Wet Dreams Come True.'"

"Grandpa, come on!"

Buzz Kill

"He meant alcohol! That's what was being prohibited!"

Chloe rolled her eyes but he could tell she was amused. "Right. Alcohol."

Woods and hills sped by. They passed over a creek and then the same creek, doubling back on itself. At some point a black pickup raced up behind him, gunning its engine; Harry stole glances in the rearview and saw two men, yellow ball caps pulled down low, sunglasses on. Gun rack behind them, flags flying. The wheels jacked up so high he could see daylight underneath the grille. They would fall back a little, then speed up again, nearly touching his back bumper. There was plenty of room to pass; the men were just enjoying themselves at his expense. At some point in recent memory Harry had thought such people would recede into the background, that this strain of Americanness would be diluted and die out. Now he knew there would be black pickups bearing down on him until his death. Which he hoped wouldn't be today.

He drove onto the shoulder and slowed down, and the truck roared past, horn blaring, threadbare flags madly flapping. One was the Gadsden Flag, the one with the rattlesnake and the legend DONT TREAD ON ME. Did these libertarian gun nuts realize it was first flown on the *Alfred*, flagship of the Continental navy, in 1775? It was supposed to be a symbol of colonial unity, not anti-American domestic terrorism! He pulled back onto the road without stopping.

"What's up with those guys?" Chloe said.

"I wish I knew," Harry replied. "Or, on second thought, maybe I don't."

I won't let those men ruin my day, he thought. It was good that he was going to pay his last respects to the Factor. It was good that Chloe was along for the ride. He felt like he was being a good grandfather and a good friend. A good posthumous friend, anyway. *Steady as she goes, old man.*

"As for you," he said to Chloe, trying to keep the tremor out of his voice, "cooperating isn't a bad platform. Roosevelt ran on everyone pitching in and helping, and he gave people jobs to do. It feels good to help."

"Yeah, I guess," Chloe said. And then, after a minute, "'It Feels Good to Help.'"

"'It Feels Good to Help.'"

"'It Feels Good to Help.' Yeah, maybe."

Ghorum was a village located in a corner of its namesake township, a quaint assemblage of offices, bars, and bungalows sitting shoulder to shoulder among a handful of quiet intersections. There was one traffic light, and the church and the library faced each other across it. Nothing was bustling, exactly, but the small library parking lot was half full—not of mysterious black cars, to Chloe's disappointment. Harry recognized an old red Mercedes sedan, sitting a little low on its shocks, the paint faded and blistered in patches.

Inside, old people in suits or dresses were milling around, picking up hardcover books and idly reading the flap copy, drinking orange juice out of plastic cups. Harry noticed his old dean, Julius, and a couple of other people he seemed to remember passing on the Arts Quad every now and then but whose names he didn't know. Chloe impressed him by immediately learning their names, introducing herself, explaining that she was Harry's granddaughter ("He was acquainted with the deceased"), and offering her condolences. Most of them seemed charmed and amused, and no one seemed terribly sad. Harry was sad, not about the loss of the Factor, which had little effect on him other than to remind him of his own mortality, but rather in contemplation of the Factor's past: a single son who died in childhood, a devoted wife who died weeks after he retired, and a lifetime of probable closeted sexual frustration. He would have thrived in another age, in another place; if he'd been born a decade earlier, he could have participated more fully in the era of campus CIA recruitment. Instead, he was a leftover, a glorified intelligence hobbyist who had used Harry to feel better about himself, to give himself a sense of purpose. Somehow this had rendered the Factor a friend rather than an enemy.

Harry was shaken from his thoughts by the room-dominating figure of Vincent, moving toward him through the crowd. Well—not a crowd, exactly, but any room with Vincent in it seemed crowded. "Hey," he said.

"Hello, Vincent. Did I miss the...ceremony?"

He shook his head. "This is it. Nobody really knew him but me. I'm no good at speeches. You can say something if you want."

"No."

"You wanna come out to the car?"

Harry left Chloe to her mingling and headed back into the heat under the protection of Vincent's shadow. "You don't look much like your uncle," Harry said.

"His wife was my mom's sister," Vincent replied. "Mom was big."

"Right."

They arrived at the Mercedes and Vincent threw open the trunk. He lifted out a milk crate full of binders. A taped-on piece of paper was markered with Harry's name in a shaky hand. "I looked through them a little," Vincent said. "It's his notes. Everybody he met, every little piece of information he learned. You write history books, right?"

"In theory," Harry said with a sigh.

Vincent handed over the crate and waited while Harry put it in the back of his car. They backtracked across the parking lot together.

"Looks like you inherited the car."

"Yeah," said Vincent. "It's too small. My Jeep fell in a ravine."

"Sorry to hear it?"

"I appreciate you coming out," Vincent said as they passed back into the cool of the library. "I really liked the old guy. He was funny."

Harry tried to hobnob a little longer. He talked with his old dean about retirement. "You should be glad you're gone," Julius said. "The campus is being transformed overnight by all this tech money. New buildings, new faculty. Forget hiring in the humanities for a couple of years, they won't even let me deal with attrition. I look out my window at what used to be a wooded hillside, and now it's the Kunstler Center for the Ethical Advancement of Artificial Intelligence. Ugly as sin, Harry, blinding panels of glass, you can't even look straight at it."

"Even the acronym is ugly," Harry pointed out.

"The computer scientists have no taste! And suddenly we've had to hire more security. Angry people protesting things like art exhibits and plays, shouting things I don't even understand. There's a theater professor who's transgender, and they barged into her lecture on Byzantine pantomime and started calling her woke."

"Oh, dear."

"And when the donors got wind of this, they asked me why I hired the professor in the first place. Honestly, Harry, your timing was impeccable. Pretty soon all your department will be allowed to teach is how wonderful the Greeks were."

He extricated himself from the conversation to find that a respectable amount of time had passed, enough to justify leaving. Harry cast his gaze around for Chloe and found her at the circulation desk with a pile of books. "I got a library card!" she said.

"But when will we ever come back here?"

"We're part of the Finger Lakes Library Alliance," explained the circulation clerk, a fiftyish woman with a lively air about her. "She can return them at the NPL."

"This is Margaret," Chloe said, "she's into spies and made sure the library acquired all these books." Harry saw novels and historical monographs, including a prizewinning brick about Central Intelligence that he had read with interest when it came out. He did not mention that Chloe's grandmother was cited in it, but, knowing his granddaughter, she probably turned straight to the index to check.

Harry shook the woman's hand. She was attractive. No ring. Perhaps older than he initially thought—nearly age-appropriate, in fact. He immediately became sweaty and flustered and pulled his hand back with awkward alacrity. "Chloe says you're a historian," the woman said with a smile.

"Um, yes, well. I was."

"Grandpa, they have your Cold War book."

"Ah!" Harry said. "Well. Thank you."

"My pleasure."

Her pleasure!

They said their goodbyes and left. In the car, Chloe read while Harry went over his brief conversation with the circulation-desk woman again and again. He marveled at his capacity to be turned to jelly by a pretty lady, even at seventy-five. What was the evolutionary advantage? Coupling at his age meant only that the lions hunting you would have twice as much to eat.

At home, he hauled the crate into his office—again, how lonely!—and began to peruse the binders. For the first time in months, he wanted a drink. Before the girls had joined forces, he'd been in a bad state, peering down from a precipice and contemplating tumbling off it; this period had ended with him waking up on the floor soaked in his own urine and nearly accidentally killing the cleaning lady. He'd gone cold turkey and, a year and a few lapses later, at last was able to spend entire hours on end not longing for oblivion. The binders, however, brought him back. It was the Factor who turned him on to gin and who initiated the period of his life about which he felt the most shame.

But the man had stories, many of them untold. And here were some of them—or clues to them, anyway. The Factor, it seemed, had had an interest in coup attempts, particularly Agency involvement in them. A voluble and charming man, he had gotten a lot of people to talk to him over the years, and seemed to have jotted down everything that they said. The binder's pages had clearly been torn from a series of three-hole-punched wide-ruled legal pads and were covered in his hurried, maximalist handwriting. It was hard to read at first, but Harry soon got used to it, the way he'd gotten used to the man himself. The Factor had met someone—back in the seventies, no doubt, when his association with intelligence began—who'd been involved in the Dominican occupation of the 1920s; he'd met a woman whose father was part of the failed expeditionary force that invaded Siberia in 1918 in support of the White Russians against the Bolsheviks. He'd met some of the Allied architects of Philippine postwar independence, and a guy who claimed to have been the Agency's negotiator with the anti-Communist "Holy Bond" of Greek military officers in the late forties. It was all hearsay, probably liars and exaggerators speaking through the words of a liar and exaggerator, but it was fascinating reading. Harry loved disorganized information because it gave him something to organize. It made him happy, and it made him want to drink.

At some point, as though reading his mind, Chloe brought him a coffee and a peanut butter and jelly sandwich. He looked up in surprise. "I forgot about lunch!" he said.

She laughed. "I figured."

"Do you need—can I—"

"You're good, Grandpa. I'm working on something. Can I get you anything else?"

"No, dear. Not now."

Harry ate his meal, then read for a few more hours. Only when he was beginning to tire did he discover something truly surprising—a reference to a minor coup that he hadn't thought of in years. It had been orchestrated by the CIA in the contested microstate of Plácidia, a small archipelago off the coast of French Guiana, in the mid-sixties, a sideshow to the Agency's "successful" efforts to destabilize the Communist government of Brazil. Harry looked it up online to refresh his memory: the tiny country's leader, Alain Rampersaud, who had inherited the job from his father, Christophe, had been assassinated by unknown parties sympathetic to the Brazilian military, and control of the country was ceded to them. Plácidia eventually regained its independence in a negotiation around Brazil's 1988 constitution, and was now a popular tourist destination.

But according to the Factor's notes, the Plácidian coup was not what it seemed. *AR alive, secretly living in the US, I just met him!!* The man had introduced himself to the Factor (at what gathering or where had not been recorded), and while drunk revealed just enough to convince the Factor he was legitimately Alain Rampersaud. It was true that Rampersaud's body was never found; local lore held that he had been thrown from cliffs overlooking the sea and washed away. Maybe he really was alive. The only breadcrumbs the Factor had left were that he loved to fish, lived near a lake, and enjoyed the snow—something he had presumably never experienced in his youth. And there was one cryptic note: *Ask PTJ!*

So where was the man? Harry wondered. And who the hell was PTJ?

He was shaken out of his reverie by a scream. "Jane?" he shouted, leaping to his feet. Then he remembered that Jane was grown up and out of town and that Chloe was the one who was here. He made for the doorway only to see Chloe materialize in it, clutching her phone.

"Are you all right?"

"No!" the girl said. "Look!" And she thrust the phone into his hands.

Harry wasn't sure what he was looking at. A video, yes, displayed inside some kind of social media application and played in a loop. It appeared to take place in a school cafeteria; a group of girls, Chloe among them, were seated around a lunch table.

It was, he realized, the Tarbox Beals School, where Chloe was running for class president. Chloe was the subject of the video. She was visible at the top of the screen; it looked as if the person making the video was pretending to check texts while actually recording. Over and over, Harry watched and heard Chloe tell the other girls, "I think Addison's gay. She tried to kiss me in gym." This was followed by the noise of the cafeteria filling the stunned, offended silence from her friends.

"Oh, dear," Harry said. "Did that really happen?"

"Grandpa, *no*. That didn't happen, and I didn't even *say* it happened."

"I don't understand."

She snatched the phone back. "It's *fake*! I wouldn't care if Addison was gay! But also, she didn't do that and I didn't tell those people she did! And if she did do it, I wouldn't talk about it that way!"

"Fake?"

The girl looked almost as exasperated by him as she was by the video. She pocketed the phone so she could clench her hands into claws. "*Yes,* Grandpa, a deepfake video? Have you heard of this?"

"Oh!" he said. "The Russians making Zelensky appear to surrender."

"Yes! Yes, exactly!"

"But...I don't think Russians would make something like this, Chloe."

Chloe growled. "It's not, like, fancy technology, Grandpa, *anyone* can do it."

"Really? Can you do it?"

"Okay, not *anybody,* but, you know, anybody who knows how."

"But who would do this?"

"Addison would! Like how you told me about Hitler and that building they burned down and blamed it on the good guys?"

"A false flag?"

"Yes!"

"Except don't compare her to Hitler, that doesn't usually go well for politicians."

"Grandpa, I'm not giving a speech, I am talking to you. What do I do? If I get online and start denying it, I'm going to look ridiculous. Maybe I'll call Mom."

"You could," Harry said. "But you might be better off..."

"Aunt Lila?"

"Aunt Lila."

4

While her daughter and father drove northeast to attend the Factor's memorial, Jane headed southeast to Onteo, where Shelly Beasley lived with her brother. Half a dozen years had passed since she had seen her friend and protector in the flesh; she'd gone to visit exactly once before deciding that she would never return to Boynton Ridge again. She wouldn't claim to suffer PTSD, but the panic attack she experienced passing through that gate again, the nausea and shortness of breath that gripped her in the visiting room, were enough to keep her away forever. She had written, dutifully, to Shelly every six months since then and gotten the idea that this was more than most people from Shelly's past had done. But she still felt guilty.

Shelly had saved her life, or at least Chloe's. There had been a couple of women in Boynton Ridge who took an instant dislike to Jane—sensed, she supposed, that she came from a different world from them, understood she was afraid, took any opportunity they could to harass her, hurt her, steal from her. Soon after Jane realized she was pregnant, she would clutch her belly as she passed these women, instinctively trying to protect the baby whose life she was already threatening with her incarceration. She was racked with guilt and fear, lost her appetite, refused to talk about what was happening in group therapy. Shelly, benign but imposing in manner, approached her in the yard, took her under her wing, guessed what she was harboring beneath her perpetually crossed arms. Until a medical exam proved what she'd suspected and her lawyer managed to secure her a spot in the nursery wing, Shelly protected her and the baby, helped her open up about her experiences on the run, made the prison feel almost like home.

If it weren't for Chloe and Shelly, Jane might have ended her own life at Boynton Ridge. She would never tell Chloe this. Shelly knew it without having to be told. Prison was a bottleneck she would not have been able to wriggle through on her own. And so when Shelly called, she dropped everything to help.

"Maybe you could come take a look at our place," Shelly had said on the phone. "Because I can't figure out why these jackasses broke in. All they took were my notebooks and a radio."

"Of course," Jane had told her. "I mean, I'm not, like, a detective-detective. I can't dust for prints."

"Oh, yeah, I get it. But...there's something else. I'm attending this conference—it's like a memoir-writing retreat. It starts on Sunday. Women only. I'm gonna write my story, Jane. The way I figure, everything I went through, maybe knowing about it would make it easier for some other girl, or maybe keep her from ending up in jail in the first place."

"That's a great idea."

"Well, what I'm asking is, maybe you'd want to come. There's a couple of slots still open. You could help me remember the stuff that was in the notebooks they took. And also...you've had an interesting life, too. Maybe you should write about it."

Shelly was the only person, aside from her ex-husband, Chance, who knew the truth about the crime that landed Jane in Boynton Ridge—namely, that she hadn't really committed it. She could never tell the real story. Could she?

"And you know I can take care of myself, but, maybe this break-in has something to do with the conference, you know? It sounds crazy, but..."

"It's not crazy."

"Okay, thank you. So, you could come along and...you know, keep an eye out. For what, I don't know."

Jane didn't know either, and couldn't imagine. But she'd said yes. For Shelly, and for herself. Maybe writing it all down would help. Nobody ever had to read it—she would do it to remember, to satisfy herself that it was all real. And maybe she could get to the bottom of whatever had happened to Shelly. She'd called the conference—the Douglas Creek Writers' Conference—and booked herself a week of classes, cafeteria meals, and a cabin in the woods. She didn't bother to tell Lila she was taking the week off. If Lila wanted to be in charge, let her figure it out.

Onteo was a small city of about ten thousand just off Interstate 88, a couple of hours' drive from Nestor. Jane's phone took her off the highway west of town and shunted her into a suburban neighborhood bordering a half-abandoned commercial strip. Shelly and her brother lived just off the strip, in a tidy bungalow with a fenced yard and gravel drive. When Jane pulled up, it was eleven in the morning, and the brother was standing in the back, peering over the chain-link fence with his hands in his pockets toward the parking lot of the church that dominated the block behind. Balding, pale-skinned, he had bad posture and looked up only briefly when Jane's tires crunched on the drive. He was wearing a yellow tee shirt, baggy on his thick frame, and a pair of jeans. A wooden cane leaned against the fence beside him.

Shelly filled the narrow front doorway like a mismatched bit of masonry, broad-shouldered, thick-waisted, radiating strength and vitality despite her hair gone gray. Her smile was wide and she bounded down the steps and took Jane into her arms like a tree swallowing a fence post. In spite of herself, Jane burst into tears.

"There, there, kiddo," Shelly said. "I'm the one that got robbed."

"I missed you, Shel."

"Missed you too, little Jane. How's that girl of yours?"

"Not quite as grown up as she thinks."

Shelly laughed. "Well, that'll never get her into trouble. Let me show you around."

The house was spare and organized and smelled clean, though everything in it was old and broken: the sprung sofa and chairs, nicked and warped dining table, threadbare carpets with tracks worn into them. Shelly had said they'd inherited the place from their parents, and it appeared unchanged since the seventies.

"So, that table got knocked over," Shelly said, "and they took the radio off of the counter there. The couch cushions were all scattered." Jane followed her into her bedroom.

"Yeah."

"My notebook, the latest one I was writing in, was under the mattress, and the rest were in my backpack under the bed, and they were all gone."

"How much of the stuff in there do you remember?" Jane asked.

"Actually," Shelly said brightly, "a lot of it, it turns out. When I was inside I used to read over what I'd written all the time. I was already thinking about how to write a book with it all. So over the past few days I've been taking notes on the notes. I think I have it. The one thing I'll really miss is the quotes. Do you remember Starr?"

"All the things her potty-mouthed grandma used to say!"

"The one about warts on a donkey's dick! And remember Ace? Rest in peace."

"International person of mystery," Jane said. "They could always break up an argument with some baffling non sequitur."

"It was like a magic spell—everybody left scratching their heads."

The two of them stood there, nodding and grinning at each other. "Don't say it!" Shelly said.

"Say what?"

"That you think I miss it! I don't miss it!"

"I wasn't going to say that," Jane said. "But it's okay if you miss it a little."

"Well, thanks. I am just trying to get my shit together out here and this is not helping. I say this as somebody who has broken into houses to steal money for drugs many times...this seems weird, right?"

"Yeah," Jane said. "You're right, it really seems like they wanted the notebooks."

"They didn't go any farther inside. I mean, all the valuable stuff is Luke's."

"Can I see his room?"

They went outside to ask him if Jane could take a look. He seemed startled to meet her, as if he hadn't just watched her climb out of her car ten minutes before. She could see now that his yellow shirt bore a cartoon bee with Xs for eyes hovering over the words PROUD DRONE. He was trembling a little and kept looking over her shoulder.

"They didn't go in there," he said.

"Are you sure?"

"They would have had to break the lock."

"Luke's an IT freelancer," Shelly said with a bit of pride in her voice. Jane figured this explained the shirt. "He's seriously keeping us afloat until I get situated."

Luke shrugged, managing a very small smile. "I'm just glad you're home."

Back inside, over glasses of ice water at the kitchen table, Jane said, "So what do you think this is about? Why would anyone want the notebooks?"

"No idea. I mean, there's stories about lots of people in there." She laughed. "And they're all criminals! But it's not like I'm gonna expose any secrets. Everybody was already inside for the stuff they did."

"Do you remember anyone over the years who particularly resented you or felt you'd wounded them?"

"Well, I definitely wounded a few people. But I get your meaning. No, not that I can think of."

"I don't suppose Luke installed any security stuff, like a doorbell camera?"

"Nah. I bet he will now, though."

Since the subject of Luke had been broached, Jane said, as gently as she could, "So…what's up with him? He seemed kind of wound up."

Shelly nodded. "Yeah, no, he is."

"Do you know what's wrong?"

"Long COVID, maybe? Which he doesn't acknowledge, he thinks it was all a scam. Like, he thinks it's from getting too close to people who got vaccinated. He made me promise not to get any boosters, so I lied and said sure. Early on, he had the fatigue and the brain fog, but those things got better. The joint stuff is the main thing left."

"Okay," Jane said. "But there's nothing else? He's all furtive and shaky. Like, if he's on something, you know—"

"Yeah, I know. Believe me, I've been watching him like a hawk. I search his room regularly. I search the car. We've both been there, Jane, so you know I would know if he was using."

"I believe you."

Outside, Jane walked around the yard, trying to picture the crime. There were cars parked on both Shelly's street and the commercial strip; it wouldn't have seemed unusual for someone to pull up here in the evening. She should ask around. Out in the street, she peered up toward the main road. Just opposite Shelly's place was a shared parking lot for a donut shop and an auto-parts store. The buildings' high corners were clearly visible, and as she moved closer, she could see that a security camera was perched on each.

Of the four neighbors near enough to have noticed a car pulling up that night, one didn't answer the door, two had seen and heard nothing, and one, across the street and two houses down, noticed a car at around the right time but didn't note the make or model. The neighbor in question, a seemingly solitary man wearing a cardigan sweater in his heavily air-conditioned house, had been having a problem with his Wi-Fi router and wanted to ask Luke for help. "I heard a car stop and a door slam, but when I looked out the window, it wasn't their minivan." He didn't see anyone get into or out of the car, and could only say it hadn't been an SUV or van. "A sedan or station wagon or something," he said. "I just saw the taillights. Sorry."

Jane sat on the hood of her car and considered her next move. She knew what she ought to do: ask Lila to get the security camera footage. But the last thing she wanted to do was ask her sister for a favor.

In the end, she had no other option; she was here to help Shelly. She called the 800 number for Perks, then put in the code that would ring whatever phone Lila happened to be using. Her sister swore by low-tech burners; Jane had watched her, at seemingly random moments, pull her phone from her pocket, crush it under her boot heel, and throw the pieces into a creek or a lake or a dumpster.

Lila took the call without speaking, as was her habit. In the background: the hum of tires against pavement. "It's me," Jane said. "Where are you?"

"On my way to Oklahoma City," said Lila.

"Okay...why?"

"Livestock auction."

"No kidding."

"Largest in America, in fact. Do you remember Padma, the woman we met in Chicago who helped us find Aunt Ruth?"

"Jesus," Jane said. "Sort of? We were literally children."

"Well, she's a lawyer in Omaha now, and she tracked us down to give us some interesting information. She thinks somebody murdered Aunt Ruth."

"What!"

Lila filled her in on the meeting with Padma and gave her some vaguely worded background information about the man she was investigating. Jane grew increasingly irritated and finally broke in with "When were you going to tell me this?"

"Tomorrow, during our usual call."

"You find out our aunt was murdered and you decide to wait until the end of the week to tell me?"

"*Might* have been murdered. Anyway, I figured you and Loretta had your hands full in the shop."

"Well, maybe Loretta does, but I don't," Jane said. Trying to keep the indignation out of her voice, she told Lila what she was working on, and that a couple of security cameras might produce a useful clue. "I remember that trick you pulled with the cameras at the airport in Seattle. Can you, like, hack into these and see the footage for a certain day?"

"Depends on what their system is," Lila said. "Most likely it's old, and the footage is just saved on a computer in the shop or maybe even on tapes. If it's more recent, they probably have a service, and it might be something I can crack. Are they chain businesses?"

"Dr. O's and Quick-N-Done Auto Parts."

"Not sure offhand but Quick-N-Done might be a win. I think I've used their cameras before. I'll get back to you."

"I'm going to be at a thing with Shelly for a week, starting tomorrow," she said as casually as she could manage. "But I can probably get away if you need me."

She expected, at the very least, to be asked what thing with Shelly, but Lila barely seemed to hear her. "Sure, sure," she said.

"Because if we're going to be bringing our aunt's murderer to justice, I'd like to participate, if that isn't too much to ask."

Lila emitted a little grunt, like a dog trying to get through a cat door. "If you want to make yourself useful..." she said.

"Wow, yeah, that would be great."

"You can find Lloyd. He's missing. Or hiding. No idea what his role was in all this."

"Hm. Would he even be alive?"

"Maybe not. But if he's dead, he didn't die as Lloyd Davies. Not publicly, anyway. I checked."

"Do we even know what he did for work? I just remember him as a quiet old guy with a newspaper."

"Same. It seems he was on a lot of boards. Of profitable enterprises."

"Okay, great," Jane said. "Got anything else?"

On the main drag, cars whizzed past in the sun. Somewhere, a child shouted, a crow cawed.

"Lila?"
But she'd hung up. Of course.

Jane told Shelly she'd meet her the next day at the conference and headed back to Nestor. The cassette deck in her car had been broken for ages; it had swallowed up a tape and would still default to playing it when she switched the radio on. The tape was a self-help lecture she'd bought back before her incarceration to keep her off booze and drugs. It hadn't worked then, but she'd been clean now for nearly fifteen years, and she didn't mind hearing the guy's soothing voice reminding her that she could choose her destiny every day of her life. "Yesterday doesn't matter," he told her now. "Tomorrow isn't real. There's only today, the day you tell the demons no, and the angels yes."

It was late afternoon when she arrived at the mall. Loretta had the shop mostly set up. Jane had to admit that it looked good—professional and inviting—although she wondered if that might be the opposite of what they wanted. "I'm setting up a little training area for Chloe," Loretta said, gesturing to a space on the back desk. "We're going to go over the different kinds of keyways and interchangeable cores. I'll have her practice swapping a few."

"Great, I guess?" Jane said. "Did we get any customers?"

"Somebody wanted me to show him how to change the text size on his phone. Then he asked me if I was a man or a woman."

"Oh god."

Lila had rented Loretta a hotel room but she accepted Jane's offer to come over for dinner. She followed Jane in her car. At home, Chloe was pacing circles around the house; Harry hadn't changed out of his suit and was sitting in his office with a three-inch looseleaf binder open on his lap. Jane ordered takeout and watched a video on Chloe's phone with Loretta that Chloe insisted had been faked. In it, Chloe was saying something about another girl being gay. It seemed to Jane a stretch to claim it was fake—kids said dumb things they regretted all the time. Couldn't Chloe have said what she said and forgotten?

But—"There's definitely something going on there," Loretta said, pointing. "Your mouth is weird. Look," she said, poking at the screen. It was true, Chloe's mouth moved strangely, as if the skin were loose. "Your best bet is to talk to whoever took the video and try to get the original. That way you can prove it's not real."

"But I don't know who took it!"

Jane watched as her daughter scrutinized the phone, scrubbing the video back and forth, trying to pick out the details. It was jarring how much Chloe resembled Lila at moments like these and how hurt Jane felt imagining that the girl's DNA had somehow opted out of her own influence. Now she felt bad for assuming the worst about Chloe—of course she hadn't shamed her friend at the lunch table. At rest, she resembled her father, Chance, whose preternatural ability to relax, to accept whatever situation he found himself in, was both the largest part of his appeal and the reason they'd been a poor match. And under stress, Chloe turned into her aunt, quick to anger, laser-focused on her next move. It wasn't that Jane wanted Chloe to beg her to stay home this week—the girl was nearly fourteen, and her parents were the last thing on her mind—but faced with a crisis, Chloe could have at least called her own mother for advice first.

In the morning, she packed a duffel with her notepad, laptop, and a week's worth of essentials. She considered rousing Chloe to say goodbye and listened outside her door for a moment in the hope that she was already stirring. But in the end she crept back down the hall, climbed into the car, and set off for Douglas Creek.

5

The drive to Oklahoma City had taken Lila most of Saturday. She skirted Topeka and Wichita and followed Route 35 south in blinding sun. The road cleared her mind of clutter and helped her put off the call she had to make.

The call would be to an Agency man she knew as Knight. He'd been a part of her life, for better or worse, for more than a decade, but they'd met in person only once, several years ago, in a truck-stop diner outside Pine Bluff, Arkansas, when Lila was on a case she was certain no one knew about or could possibly know about. Yet Knight had walked in the door, slid into the booth across from her, and greeted her by name. He was the man who'd inherited her mother when her old handler retired, and it was his intention, he'd made clear when he first contacted her, to keep her—and Lila along with her—in the fold.

Anabel Bortnik hadn't been around much when Lila and Jane were girls, and eventually they figured out why. She'd been recruited by the CIA when she was an undergraduate and worked throughout Central America monitoring Russian involvement in the manipulation of various national governments. The daughter of diplomats, one Russian and one Spanish, an angry narcissist who both adored and despised men, she was perfect for the role. Indeed, she was so good at it that she effortlessly betrayed her handlers, retreated to the mountains of northern Panama, and began attempting to wrest control of the international cocaine market from the capos of Colombia and Bolivia. Knight had wanted Lila's help to disrupt her mother's efforts, and in exchange, he said, the Agency would refrain from blowing her cover and crushing her business.

Up until that meeting in Arkansas, Knight hadn't asked much of Lila and often fed her helpful bits of information, coincidentally right at the moments she needed them. She thought he'd been establishing a useful symbiosis based on mutual respect, but what he said to her at that truck stop suggested that he'd just been warming her up for this big ask. "Give me a fucking break" was Lila's reply to the spook, who responded with a condescending smile. The man was tall and cadaverous, with hollow cheeks and bright green eyes, and he nodded, idly smoothing his black western shirt against his sunken chest. He might have been thirty or he might have been sixty, and Lila could have sworn his preternaturally smooth skin was the result of carefully applied makeup—not for fashion, but as though he were starring in a noir TV series about spies, filmed via hidden cameras, and had just spent two hours in his trailer being prepped for this scene.

Lila hadn't wanted to do Knight's bidding, and considered refusing outright. Instead, she capitulated, then roped her long-estranged twin sister into the cross-continental hunt. Lila wasn't one to interrogate her own motivations much, and at the time convinced herself and Jane both that she could use the help. But in a truth arrived at only after the fact, she had missed Jane and was looking for an excuse to reunite. She supposed she also wanted to spread the blame around if things went bad.

In spite of herself, Lila actually got interested in the task and was reluctantly impressed by their mother's extraordinary ambition and skill. Her interest in horticulture, the hobby she'd employed to ease the burdens of motherhood, had sparked innovation in the development of the coca plant, and her new variety was hardy and potent enough that its production could be decentralized and placed in the hands of small, independent farmers. Cocaine, for their mother, had become a political project. The obnoxious alias—Espiritu Santo, the Holy Ghost—derived from the name of the white blossom that was the national flower of Panama and had originally been meant as a joke among the citizens of Nacimiento, the city she'd settled near. Nobody joked about it anymore. Lila wondered if her mother had devised the name and then engineered its adoption, the way she'd engineered so many things about her productive and disreputable life.

In the end, Lila and Jane found Anabel Bortnik and hurt her, and Lila had hoped that the bill was paid and that her relationship with the Agency was over. But those hopes seemed foolish now that their mother seemed to be connected to her own sister's death. Surely this wasn't a coincidence, Ruth Bortnik representing the man who had made a fortune collaborating with her sister. But who knew what, and when? Did Ruth take on the client knowing Anabel was involved and wanting to either contact her or punish her? Or did Nutt see an advantage in retaining Ruth—maybe thinking it would give him some leverage in the event that his dangerous collaborator turned against him? Or was Anabel the one who had recommended Ruth to Nutt, seeking some inscrutable advantage of her own? And how did Lloyd fit in? Someone had made the connection and begun moving pieces into place to serve their needs. But who? And what needs?

Lila had to gather more information. She'd find some in Oklahoma City, but that wouldn't get her everything she wanted. She was going to have to contact Knight.

Before she could, her burner chimed with a call from her service, and she recognized the number as her sister's. Reluctantly, she took the call—but better Jane than Knight. Jane needed help with some trivial matter involving a break-in, and Lila filed away the information for when she had a moment to look into it. Dutifully, she filled Jane in on what was going on with their aunt's death, and predictably, Jane found a way to get angry about it. Lila had been planning to tell her about their mother's connection to everything, but in the end she didn't bother, partly because she wanted to have all the facts first, and partly out of spite.

Lila ended the call. She'd call Knight another time—right now she was too annoyed. Besides, she would doubtless have to deal with other people later and needed to conserve her limited reserves of social energy. Fucking vampires.

She'd made a reservation at a hotel in Bricktown, the commercial district nearest the stockyards, using a prepaid credit card bought with cash and registered under a fake name and address for which she had a convincing driver's license. She got off the highway early and tooled down Northeast Fourth Street, a flat and lonesome two-lane that brought her past disused farmland, a couple of business parks, a few churches, and, eventually, a low, brown, fenced suburban area before spilling her out into downtown Oklahoma City.

The hotel was decorated in the kind of gratuitously luxe bad taste that wealthy cattlemen might like—marble floors, a fake cactus garden, golden wall sconces in the shape of steer horns—and as she checked in, she saw a few of them passing through the lobby in their baggy boot-cut jeans and big dusty hats. Her room was also as expected: full of worthless pieces of technology equipped with intensely bright LEDs. The staff had tried to conceal the electrical outlets behind heavy pieces of furniture, but Lila muscled these out of the way and unplugged everything. The windows opened, but only a couple of inches, so she got out a screwdriver and removed the anti-suicide flanges fixed to the bottom channel. Finally she could breathe.

The hotel was an unconscionable four miles from the stockyards. A bus ran every half an hour from the botanical garden near the hotel, but Lila suspected most people drove. She put on her sunglasses and a ball cap and walked. Reno Avenue's sidewalks extended far out into the commercial wasteland that made up most of the route, and she passed a vet clinic, a storage warehouse, an abandoned motel, and a towing service before reaching the stockyards' immediate neighborhood half an hour later. Commerce thickened up, the various single-story buildings crowding closer and closer together and increasingly relevant to the needs of visiting livestock buyers and sellers: a bail bondsman, a bar, a truck mechanic. WELCOME TO HISTORIC STOCKYARDS CITY read a sign, and she entered a fairly lively shopping and entertainment district. After passing the giant lot where the rest of the hotel's guests probably parked, she went through a large entry arch announcing the stockyards themselves. Big rigs towing ventilated trailers rumbled past, and the sound of mooing reached her from a seemingly endless holding area off to her right. The trucks turned into a loading zone, and men shouted to each other over the noise, directing traffic, throwing open pen doors, and leading animals down narrow chutes of bent and rusted steel pipe. Lila leaned against a wooden fence, taking stock of the whole spread, which just now seemed to be waking up for Monday's auction, a day and a half away. The animals stood on what seemed like packed dirt, but after a moment's observation she could see that it was brick—the whole massive agglomeration of pens was paved with broad bricks, worn smooth at the edges. She supposed that was where the neighborhood got its name.

She found an entrance gate and soon was wandering among the pens along a series of narrow paths not dissimilar to the ones she saw the cattle being forced down. Surely the animals understood these were the channels that led, eventually, to death? She'd read online that only "feeders" were bought and sold here—young cattle that would be raised someplace else. This was probably the young animals' first exposure to the complicated system that would eventually slaughter them. Some cows were heading toward her, led by a couple of cowboys, and she hopped up on a length of wooden fence and straddled it to let them pass. The animals' hot, soft flanks brushed against her jeans.

The pens were labeled with stenciled black numbers on a white-painted background. A few large signs were visible sticking up above the pens: B&B COMMISSION CO., P. F. LAKE COMMISSION CO., STOCKMAN'S PRIDE, CENTRAL LIVESTOCK. A heavyset middle-aged man was working under one of them, preparing one of the pens for the impending arrival of some livestock.

"Hey," she said, pointing, "are these the names of the ranchers?"

"The sellers, you mean?" the man said, wiping some sweat off his brow. His ball cap was so stained with sweat and salt that its logo had been completely obscured. "Naw, these are the commission companies."

"I'm new here," she said, leaning against the fence. "What do they do?"

"Oh. We bring the animals to the pens, feed 'em, look after 'em. It would be a nuthouse here if every seller had to find their stall. You're not supposed to be here, really." But he looked her up and down as though he didn't mind.

"So where am I supposed to be?"

He grinned and gestured above his head to a catwalk that ran over and around the pens. "I could show you around if you wanted."

"Maybe later," she said, trying to match the man's bored sexual energy. "You know a guy named Nutt? Travis Nutt?"

"Seller? Can't say I've heard of him," the man said. "Not one of ours, anyway."

"Thanks. What's your name."

"I'm Okie. That's a nickname."

Lila forced a laugh. "You don't say."

"I grew up outside of Norman, so when I lived in Texas for a while, people called me Okie. It stuck, even after I came back."

"Right. I'm Heidi." That was the name on the fake ID she was using. "Maybe I'll see you around, Okie."

"I like to say I grew up outside of Norman, but I grew up inside of Irene!"

"Haha."

"That's my mom."

"I figured."

"You know where to find me!"

She continued to wander, seeking out each of the commission companies' signs. Nobody was around at the first couple of them she found; two more were staffed but didn't have Nutt for a client. But near the sign for a company called Land Trust, she encountered the first woman she'd seen on the premises. She was around fifty, muscular and stocky, with her hair bundled up beneath a trucker cap. She was sitting on the fence rail holding open a gate for half a dozen head of black cattle that were being led into one of the pens. When the animals had gone through, the woman hopped down and pulled the gate shut. Lila greeted her with a wave.

"No time to chat," the woman said.

"Understood," Lila replied. There was clearly not much going on here yet, but she herself had put off plenty of people this way. The woman had an air of self-containment and efficiency that Lila recognized and respected. "I'm just looking for Nutt."

"Ain't here yet," the woman said. "They'll roll in late, I'm sure."

There it was. "Sounds like Nutt."

The woman shook her head. "A text would be nice so I'll know when I can go take a shit."

It was getting to be around dinnertime, but Lila wasn't hungry. She decided to explore a little and found her way to the wooden catwalk Okie had pointed out to her. It gave her a good view of the whole yard, which was even larger than she'd thought. In a registration office, a distracted girl scrolling on her phone directed her across the catwalk to the little red barn where the auctions took place. Lila picked up a pamphlet on the way out and read it while crossing over the pens—fifty acres of them, the pamphlet told her. There used to be more, a whole complex of slaughterhouses and packing plants, back when the railroads were more active, and also other animals—sheep, horses, hogs. But it was only cattle now. Lila got the idea the place was culturally important but superfluous to the larger industry, which the pamphlet told her was content with feedlot auctions or sales conducted remotely via video.

She found the auction floor, which was located in an old hay barn. A hundred tiered seats were arranged in an arc facing a central semicircular pen that itself held a raised auctioneer's platform. Above the platform was a widescreen monitor, now blank. A couple of kids sat in the back row horsing around. A woman walked in from a door behind the platform, dropped off a clipboard, and said, "Just looking around?"

"I'm surprised it's so small," Lila said.

"Everyone's gotta see what they're bidding on. We sell half a million head a year in this room."

"Wow."

"Happens real fast. Come back Monday."

Outside, the sun was low in the sky, and the air had begun to cool. The commercial area around the stockyards was showing signs of life now; people walked in and out of bars and restaurants clutching shopping bags.

Lila ate a hamburger and drank a beer at the bar in a steak house and listened to cowboys bantering. They didn't talk about work, they talked about rodeo and auto racing and women. Nobody mentioned Travis Nutt, but she didn't expect they would. She headed back toward the hotel as the sun set. A few men leaned out of pickup windows and yelled at her.

In her room, she opened her laptop and found a message from her niece asking if she could examine a video. Chloe said that the video wasn't real and was being used to sway the voters in a school election. Lila gave her instructions to upload it to her secure FTP, and ten minutes later, she was scrubbing slowly through it in her video editor.

The girl was right, this video had been faked. The resolution in the mouth area was slightly different from the surrounding part of the image; it appeared stretched or nudged. The sound had been edited as well, even more poorly than the video; it was possible to hear a background voice cutting off mid-sentence and a different voice cutting in, but more quietly, as though farther away: *...going to wear the jeans with the flower p...ver if my mother lets me go.* The voice that uttered the words "I think Addison's gay. She tried to kiss me in gym" did sound like Chloe's, but it wouldn't have taken a genius to fake that. The forger would have needed a clear sample of Chloe's speech. Lila opened up her browser and visited the Tarbox Beals website. A menu led her to the school's YouTube channel, where she quickly discovered a video of a recent debate competition. Chloe was on the debate club and gave a persuasive speech about the benefits of universal basic income. The audio had been taken not from the camera but from the podium mic and was clear and consistent, without background noise or echo. A perfect sample.

Lila downloaded the video, stripped out the audio, and compiled a deep-learning application from GitHub. After finding three typos in the README and noting them as comments on the programmer's pull request, she generated an automated transcript of Chloe's speech, edited out the handful of transcription errors, and fed the audio and text into the app. It took her twenty minutes or so to get a decent approximation of Chloe's faked slur and another ten to improve on it significantly in an audio editor by tweaking the inflection and the duration of each word.

It wasn't impossible that a child had created this video alone, but it was highly improbable. The mouth could have been animated in Blender or some other commercially available 3D graphics package, but the audio required programming knowledge that someone Chloe's age was unlikely to possess. Lila strongly suspected that a parent or older sibling had been involved. She did a search for Addison Kunstler, Chloe's opponent, and learned that her father, Tibor Kunstler, was a programmer turned CEO. He headed up an AI think tank at Nestor College and had donated money for a new building. He also had involved himself, more recently, in election politics, publicly offering to examine the software of voting machines in an apparent effort to gather evidence that fraud had taken place in the last presidential election. A couple of state legislatures, it seemed, had taken him up on it.

Lila stared at Kunstler's portrait on her screen. This was the grown man who had created a deepfake video of her niece, this bespectacled, smooth-skinned loser with a monobrow and enough money to buy and sell the entire school. What a prick.

It was getting late but she called Chloe and told her what she'd discovered. The girl was elated. "Right on! Let's take her down!"

"Well," said Lila, "let's consider. Is that really what you want?"

"Uh...yes?"

"Think. Getting help from her powerful family is exactly what Addison did. You might want to see if you can arrive at the same answer on your own, without any input from me. There are a bunch of girls around that lunch table in the video, right? You know them?"

"Sure. They're my friends. Or I thought they were."

"There you go," Lila said. "They probably know you didn't say what it looks like you said. But they're afraid of Addison and her popularity and her rich dad."

"Kids are cowards," Chloe said.

"So are adults," Lila told her. "Anyway, start with them. Peel them away. Figure out who took the video in the first place."

"Actually," Chloe said after a moment, "I think I know."

"So that's your first mark. Get to work. When you bring down this house of cards, I'll be there to back you up."

In the morning, Lila went downstairs for coffee and a banana to fuel her work on Jane's surveillance cameras. As she was passing through the lobby, she noticed a couple of men checking in, one gray-haired, the other younger. The older man was dressed in a black ankle-length coat and black pants despite the heat. He had a thick gray beard and long curled sidelocks. The younger man filled out a dark blue tailored business suit. Both men wore skullcaps. Lila wouldn't have expected Oklahoma City to be a destination for observant Jews. She chastised herself for the mistaken assumption and continued back upstairs.

It was fortuitous that the auto-parts place at the end of Jane's friend's street was a Quick-N-Done. The company was presently in dire straits; it had declared bankruptcy several years ago and closed more than half its locations. IT security upgrades were not likely to be high on its list of priorities. QND employed a surveillance company called Nimbus that had recently suffered a devastating hack that exposed its entire user database, including every client's password, to the world. Doubtless the company had sent out a warning to all its customers to reset their passwords, but not many managers bothered to do this, or even to read the email in the first place.

As a result, once she'd logged in to her satellite internet, Lila was able to access the live feeds from all the cameras at the Onteo QND. At the moment, its parking lot and retail space were empty of customers, and its clerk had his hand in his pants underneath the front counter as he watched pornography on his phone. Some enterprising script kiddie was probably posting this feed on 4chan right now.

But what Lila wanted—and swiftly got—was access to the cloud storage for QND's Nimbus account, which was hosted behind a web interface that appeared to have been designed around 2008. She found the folder that contained the video archive for the day of the break-in and scrubbed through it until she could see the crime in progress.

The camera wasn't great, the resolution was low, and streetlight offered scant illumination. A car pulled up in front of Jane's friend's house and discharged one person from the passenger side. This person disappeared from the frame, then returned a few minutes later, walking briskly. It appeared to be a man, fairly athletic, with a slight build. He wore a black hoodie. The headlights obscured the make and model of the car, but then the thieves did something surprising: they drove to the end of the street, turned left, apparently realized they'd made a mistake, and pulled through the QND parking lot to correct it. As a result, Lila could tell that the car was a white 2016 Honda Accord. The car's trim and a quick web search told her it was the LX variant. New York plates, but motion blur rendered the number illegible. The driver was a white woman, probably in her late twenties, with straight light brown hair, bangs, and a long, thin nose.

When Lila called her sister, she heard loud talking, music—the sounds of a party. "I thought you were with writers," she said.

"I am. I'm at an orientation event. Hold on."

When Jane had made her way to someplace quiet, Lila filled her in on what she'd discovered. "Does any of this sound familiar?"

"Not to me, but I'll ask Shelly. A white woman driving a Honda Accord isn't exactly a zinger."

"Just telling you what I found."

"Hey, also, did you tell Chloe to do something? About the fake video? I just talked to her and Dad. He said she's taking notes for some kind of grand plan."

"Perfect," Lila said. "Yeah, it turns out the kid, Addison, her dad made the video for her. But I told Chloe to try to get to that answer her own way."

"Jesus, okay. She didn't tell me that."

"So," Lila said, "can I consider this our Sunday call? Since we're both working?"

Lila told her what she'd done over the past twenty-four hours. "Presumably Nutt is here now. I've got the lay of the land. I'll find him and Padma's boss and see what develops. Hey," she said, "by the way, what's your cover?"

"What?"

"You're at a writers' conference, what, just hanging around?"

"I'm here as a writer."

"What are you telling people you write?"

"No, I mean I paid for a slot," Jane said. "I'm taking a class. I'm literally writing a book. Or I'm going to. Every day from eleven until five is writing time, and I'm going to the library with my computer in…ten minutes."

"What, a romance novel?" Lila said.

"Haha. It's a memoir class."

Lila could feel herself tensing up. She'd been lying on the hotel bed, her head propped on the pillows; now she sat up, dropped her legs to the floor. "You're not going to spend the week spilling our secrets to a bunch of strangers, Jane."

"We all had to sign an agreement not to poach each other's material. It'll be fine."

"I don't care about some dumb bitch stealing your ideas. I care about the security of our firm."

"Jesus, okay," Jane said. "It's not like I plan to name names."

"Or places, or events? I don't want any of it out there."

"Well, then, I don't know what to tell you."

A tense silence extended between them for several seconds. Lila employed a trick she'd taught herself to put sources of anxiety out of her mind. She imagined a high-backed wooden chair standing in the foreground of a featureless black expanse. Now Jane materialized in the chair, thick ropes binding her at the ankles and wrists, a gag filling her mouth. After a moment, the chair began to move away, slowly at first, then gaining speed, propelling her sister deeper and deeper into the void until she was nothing but an undetectable speck in the distance.

"Hello? Are you still there?" Jane said now, but to Lila, the voice was small and insignificant.

"I need to get back to work. Good luck." She ended the call.

Today there was more action at the stockyards; the air was thick with diesel fumes, the anxious lowing of the animals, men's shouts. Lila peered down from the catwalk, searching the area occupied by Land Trust's customers for somebody who matched Nutt's description. But it was hopeless; the yard was too large, the scene too chaotic. She would have to get down there and mingle. On a whim, she walked over to the shopping district and, at a western outfitter's, bought a pair of embroidered work boots and a wide-brimmed straw hat with a leather band. She was already wearing a chambray pearl-snap shirt; now she could conceivably pass as a native.

On the way back to the yard she ducked into a desolate little grassy lot behind a bar and scuffed up her purchases in a patch of ground that had been worn to dirt, probably by a dog. A guy wearing an apron watched her from the picnic table where he was perched beside the propped-open rear door. She sat next to him, removed her tennis shoes, and pulled the boots on. "Mind if I leave these here?" she said, setting the tennis shoes on the ground. "I'll come back for them."

"So long as you come back, I'm happy," the guy said.

Lila put her hair in a single braid, the style she'd seen a few women wearing in the shopping district, and fastened it with an elastic band. The guy watched her do it. She put on the hat, said thanks, and returned to the yard. In the parking lot she saw a truck she hadn't noticed before, a Peterbilt with an extra-long cab, black metal flake paint, green and silver accents, vintage-style round headlights. Arizona plates. She didn't know much about big rigs, but it looked expensive, a custom job. She remembered Nutt's testimonial video for the truck dealer. Her money was on it being his.

She walked onto the bricks like she knew what she was doing. After a minute she found the woman from before. She was dragging a hose over to a trough to fill it. "Nutt?" she said to Lila.

"Right."

"They got in a little after ten. I think his guy's over there." She pointed with her chin. "C twenty-seven. You got your hat on backward."

"Do I?" Lila said, not touching it.

The woman grinned. "Nah."

Lila made her way over to the right stall, dodging little herds of stock as she went. A few men nodded as she passed them. Nobody told her she didn't belong. Finally she found a medium-sized pen with half a dozen young cattle milling around in it, and a couple more sitting on the ground. They were distinctive, even to her, someone who'd never given cattle much thought: from nose to tail, their coats were shiny, unblemished, and a deep, roasted-chestnut red. In the blue shade of the barn's morning shadow, they glowed like campfire embers. They struck Lila as some of the most beautiful animals she had ever seen, and they stood out here like celebrities on a busy city sidewalk.

A man sat on the fence laughing at something on his phone. He was lanky and chiseled, a day of stubble. His jeans were dirty but his shirt and hat were immaculate. Late twenties, early thirties. Lila got the impression he had a high opinion of himself. She spied a wedding ring.

There were a few ways to proceed. She could pretend to need to see Nutt for some business reason and straight-up ask what his schedule was. But that could lead to actually having to talk to the man. She didn't know enough about his work, the legitimate kind, to fake it. Better to feign ignorance, appear bored and a little dumb, and draw this guy out.

"Hey," Lila said. "Cute cows."

"These are heifers."

"What's that?"

"A heifer's a girl who's never been kissed," he told her, laughing.

"Well, no wonder I didn't recognize 'em," she said.

The man let his gaze linger on her. He put away his phone.

Lila had lived through this moment hundreds of times—the moment when a guy decided that, however ignorable you'd seemed a second ago, on balance, he wouldn't turn down an opportunity to fuck you. Half the time the guy didn't even realize he'd made the call. It was instinct, a weakness of the species that most men had to train out of themselves, though in her experience few bothered. They tended to like being this way. She made a few subtle adjustments to her stance—shifted some weight to one leg, moved her hands to her hips, drew breath so that her chest rose just a little. Lila had five years to a decade on this guy, but she took care of herself and this was a work trip. It wouldn't be hard, if it came to that.

"I'm Remy," the guy said.

"Heidi."

"What's your story, Heidi? Most people hanging around down here know what a heifer is."

"That's my brother-in-law's business," she said with a dismissive wave. "I'm just along for the ride with him and my sister. She thought it'd be good for me. I'm a dental hygienist in Little Rock."

"Well, teeth are important in this line of work."

"Oh, yeah? How do mine look?" She gave him what she hoped was a big old country grin.

"I'd bid on you," he said, grinning back.

"So where are you from?" she said.

A look crossed his face, so quick you might've missed it, of extreme seriousness and caution, as though she'd just asked him for the code to his cash card. Then it was gone and he was back to his corn-syrup flirting. "A little place called Bumblefuck, Arizona," he said. "Good for you how?"

"Huh?"

"Your sister thought it'd be good for you."

"Oh. You know," Lila said. "Got a divorce. Stuck in a rut. Watching too much reality TV." She hoped, belatedly, that that was still something people watched.

"Aw, sorry to hear that," he lied.

"So, these are your...heifers, then?" she said, edging closer along the fenceline. "I thought you guys hired people to look after them."

"Oh," he said. "Right. Well, yeah, we do, but my partner here—well, let's be honest, my boss—is a little particular. And these girls are real special. We've got some potential buyers coming by the pen for a sneak peek at, uh, they were supposed to be here half an hour ago? So I'm just sitting here waiting for them to show up."

"People here seem pretty busy. I wondered why you were sitting still."

"Yeah, it's kind of a whirlwind usually." He glanced over her shoulder, slid down from the fence, and slipped his phone into his pocket. "Sorry, Heidi, here they come. Hey, what are you doing later?"

"What's the opposite of working in a dental office?"

He laughed. "I think I got something in mind. Meet me at the Rolling K on Agnew. How's eight?"

"Perfect."

She left him with a wink and turned in time to see three men coming toward her along the path. One she recognized immediately from Padma's law firm's website: Brian Hathaway, the senior partner. He was a tall, olive-skinned white man with long fleshy ears and a heavily moisturized face that looked like it had been crumpled up and smoothed out too many times. He was wearing a suit without a tie and looked ill at ease. Only his well-worn boots spoke of some history with the region. He didn't seem to notice Lila at all.

Her eye was next drawn to the man who was surely Travis Nutt. Padma was right; he radiated power and confidence despite his small stature and comically wide-brimmed hat. His pearl-snap shirt was elaborately embroidered, his jeans were brand-new, and his square-toed work boots were black and polished. Under the hat, Nutt's skin was as pale and smooth as a cue ball despite his age, which was around sixty. His hands were small and fine and unblemished—very strange for a man who'd spent his life in the laboratory and on a ranch. It was like he was made of some space-age wax that couldn't be penetrated and didn't melt in the sun. She could see, dangling from a gold chain around his neck, a small, tarnished cross. It looked cheap, out of place with the rest of his self-presentation. She suspected it had some sentimental or nostalgic significance. Nutt's eyes took her in and dismissed her.

The third man, to Lila's surprise, was the older Jewish man from the hotel. He was sweating profusely in the heat but appeared familiar with this kind of discomfort and unfazed by it. His shoes were off-brand black sneakers, thick soles, wide at the toe. He had a lively step and a skeptical expression on his face. He alone met Lila's gaze and nodded in friendly recognition, whether because he remembered her or simply for their shared humanity, she couldn't tell.

None of the men seemed particularly fond of the others or enthusiastic about whatever they were doing. They passed Lila in a cloud of aftershave—Hathaway's, she assumed.

She didn't want to be seen to care about their business, so she continued on her way, then turned left and headed back to the main office and catwalk. Now that she knew where Nutt's stall was, she could make them out in the distance, gathered around the cluster of red coats like cowboys around a campfire. It was impossible, of course, to know what they were saying, but Nutt seemed to be holding forth, his hand on one of the heifers' backs, while Remy looked on, arms crossed. The third man nodded. Every now and then, Hathaway would interject something. After a while, the men left and parted at the exit from the bricks.

Lila went back to the spot behind the bar where she'd left her tennis shoes, put them on, then carried her new boots back to the hotel to rest up and shower before her date with Remy. She was thinking about the scribbled note from Aunt Ruth's legal pad: *cow/ashes/purify and rebuild*. Her goals tonight were to find out what that meant and to discover exactly which Arizona Bumblefuck Nutt and Remy hailed from. She had a feeling she would end up there before long.

6

Her grandfather thought she should go with him on his research trip on Sunday, and it took Chloe a good half hour to prove to him that she was capable of being left alone for the day. In the end, she succeeded by making him breakfast, brewing the coffee, and serving it to him the way he liked it, with cream and two cubes of sugar. She sat down across from him, placidly sipping her own cup, black.

"You see? I won't starve," she said, gesturing toward his eggs and toast.

"You're not going to eat?"

"Grandpa, I ate an hour ago. I get up early."

"I'm not sure that coffee is good for someone your age," he said.

"It isn't good for anyone!"

"Oh, dear," he said, pushing his own mug away.

She pushed it back. "Grandpa. Seriously. Drink your coffee."

With faux reluctance, he complied. "Tell me," he said, "your plans. I'll be more comfortable with this arrangement if I know exactly where you are."

"First, I have a few things to work on here. Then I'll take the bus to the mall."

"You've done this before?"

"Many times. The sixty-seven stops at the apartments behind the high school at ten fifty-one. It will drop me off at the mall at eleven oh three."

"All right, all right."

"Loretta is setting up the computer system today. She promised to show me how to use it. Then, around lunchtime, I have a meeting in the food court."

Grandpa Harry winced. "With a boy?"

"No, Grandpa. It's just politics."

That seemed to perk him up. "Oh! I see. 'It Feels Good to Help'!"

"Exactly! Anyway, after the meeting, I'll maybe practice my locks, then take the bus home and sit on the porch and read. And you'll be back for dinner, right?"

"Yes, yes. What do you want to eat?"

"Anything's fine."

"I usually make myself a grilled cheese sandwich on a Sunday evening."

"Perfect."

A schedule, Chloe knew, always made her grandfather feel better, and before long he had shrugged on his stained blue blazer, slipped into his loafers and sunglasses, and gathered up his satchel. The shoulder strap had broken a long time ago—before she was born, he had told her—and the handle had broken last year, so he'd just been carrying the thing around in his arms. "Does this look odd?" he'd asked her a few months ago, and it certainly did the way he was holding it, like a parachute he'd grabbed at the last second before jumping out of an airplane. She told him to treat it like a clutch bag. Once she explained what that was, he seemed to get it, and now, climbing into his Subaru, he looked like a princess entering a limousine. Or slightly more like one, anyway.

When he was gone, Chloe picked up her phone and began composing a text message to Kay, the girl she believed could be the key to undermining Addison. She was the one who had peered mournfully over her shoulder at Chloe at the mall before the video dropped. And, in Chloe's memory, she was the one sitting at the lunch table about where the camera was positioned. Chloe believed Kay was the camerawoman, chosen by Addison for her ability to blend in and her reluctance to challenge authority.

The video had blown up online and Chloe had had to silence her notifications or she wouldn't have gotten a moment of sleep. Last night she had taken her pillow into the closet, sat down on the floor, pressed it to her face, and cried. She'd resisted the impulse to talk to her mother, who had her own problems to worry about, and tried to take a page from

Aunt Lila's playbook: be cool, keep your mouth shut, and do the work. She was initially disappointed that Aunt Lila wouldn't help her expose Addison's dad, but when she woke up this morning, she could see the value in doing it herself. She would repair her own reputation and show her opponent's weakness.

Another thing she realized: Addison had made a mistake attempting to ruin her so long before school started. Nobody cared about the election right now. She'd given people time to forget and Chloe time to plot against her.

She'd gone over a hundred possibilities for this text to Kay while lying awake last night but had settled on the simplest, least revealing, and most likely to appeal to Kay's guilty conscience: *I need your help. Pizza at the mall?*

I have to practice the flute came the reply.

All day?

No

So, 1 pm? On me

It took a while, but by the time Chloe reached the bus stop, she got the reply she wanted. *Ok.*

Chloe was only a couple of years and change away from her learner's permit, and it was an article of faith among her friends that they couldn't wait for the freedom that cars would bring. But, though she kept this to herself, Chloe didn't mind the wait. She liked riding the bus. Not school buses, which, thank god, she didn't have to ride on except for field trips, but city buses, with their charming mix of old people and college students and local weirdos, most of whom had not yet leered at or harassed her. The 67 took her up the lake's edge into the hills, and she could peer down at all the sailboats and weekend fishermen down there enjoying the wind and sun. A lo-fi beats playlist filled her ears, and her heart lifted.

The mall was more lively than she'd expected; a branch of the local animal shelter had opened up where Old Navy used to be, and children and their parents had flocked here for Kitten Day. Behind the glass facade of Perks Locksmith, however, everything was quiet and calm. Some strange and soothing music was playing, a distant and watery piano with notes spilling out in an order that wasn't random but didn't seem fully human either. As she approached the back desk, the piano was joined by a cello.

"What's this?" she asked Loretta.

"It's generative music," Loretta said. She was dressed in a mixture of sixties and nineties styles, a short-sleeved white linen blouse with a big black bow, a tartan skirt, combat boots. Actual army-issue ones, too, in which, Chloe supposed, Loretta had experienced actual combat.

"Like AI?"

"Uh, no. More like Brian Eno." Chloe nodded as though she knew who that was and made a mental note to look it up. "Just a little program I wrote. I've been tweaking the parameters all morning. I don't know what I think. It's been throwing a tuba in every ten minutes or so without asking permission."

"Whoa."

"Hey, do you mind if we save the computer work for another time? We got an actual emergency call from some lady down on the lake."

"I thought we were closed today?"

Loretta shrugged. "I answered the phone—my bad, I guess. Anyway, this will be a useful lesson for you."

"As long as I'm back by one? I have a meeting."

"Piece of cake," Loretta said, and they packed a tool bag and headed out in her rental car.

The house was a recently constructed lakeside mansion with giant windows facing the water, a dock with a boathouse, and a three-car garage with a Land Rover parked outside. Its owner was a lady in her thirties wearing ripped jeans, a flannel shirt, and pearls, and she stared bewildered at Loretta and Chloe with her arms crossed. It was in the high seventies outside, but she was shivering in her air-conditioning, which billowed out of the house like a mudslide. She appeared to have been crying. It was pretty clear she'd been expecting some dude in coveralls.

"Thank you for coming on a Sunday. I kicked my husband out."

"Sorry to hear it, ma'am," Loretta said.

"You shouldn't be, he fucked his graduate student." The woman appeared startled at her own outburst and apologized to Chloe.

"My assistant has heard it all," Loretta said.

The woman handed them the door key and disappeared into the recesses of the house, and Loretta pulled some equipment out of the bag. "This lock is pretty easy to rekey," she said. The lock had a traditional keyhole beneath a new-looking numeric touchpad. "And you can use your phone to open it." It took her only a few minutes to disassemble the mechanism and replace the core, and once it was finished, she gently pulled the door closed. "Locked, see?"

"Yep," said Chloe.

"Come here." Loretta led her ten feet down the front walk to a wrought-iron bench surrounded by shrubs in a modest front garden. Chloe had the feeling they were the first people ever to sit on it.

From the tool bag, Loretta pulled out a little hacked-together device that consisted of a miniature touchscreen computer, an antenna, a folding keyboard, and a USB dongle with an exposed circuit board the size of a stick of gum. Loretta powered up the machine, and some code flowed down the screen. She handed Chloe a piece of paper with eight digits on it. "Here's the factory passcode for the new lock," she said. "Go punch that in."

Chloe went to the door and entered the code. The lock clicked as expected. She returned to the bench.

"Now watch," Loretta said. She typed a few commands into the little computer and the code flowed again. A second later, Chloe heard the sound of the lock opening, ten feet away.

"I just used what's called a Bluetooth sniffer. All this equipment costs about two hundred bucks. Our customer will change that password, or she should, but it doesn't matter. Anyone could hide in the bushes when she comes home and use this to read whatever she types in. Then they'd have her passcode and could enter the house anytime, completely undetected."

"Whoa."

"Other brands of lock have other vulnerabilities. Some, you can issue broken commands that will send the lock to an error state. Some, you can spoof the key fob. Also, the password for pretty much any electronic lock can be brute-forced. Set up this rig in a secluded spot, like the boathouse. If you don't mind getting a little wet, you can get in there easy and hide it. Let it quietly try all combinations until one works." She demonstrated, typing in a command and letting the little computer begin a rapid run through all the possible codes. The screen bloomed with text. "Then come back and just stroll in the front door."

"People *do* that?"

"Usually, no," Loretta said. "Regardless, every house is unsafe. Most break-ins are for fast cash. People will just smash a window, grab a laptop, and run away, and unless you have bars on your windows or a big angry dog, you're not gonna prevent that. But I wanted to illustrate that these new technologies aren't any more secure than a traditional dead bolt and key. And sometimes, in our business, you need to get in and out undetected."

"You don't mean the locksmith business," Chloe said.

"No," Loretta agreed, putting her tools away. "Not the locksmith business."

They returned to the mall with time to spare, and Chloe got a hot pretzel and watched lock-picking videos at a table in the food court while she waited for Kay to show up. It had been a long time since she'd believed that adults had their shit together and that the world was relatively safe, but these past couple of days had been a real eye-opener for her. It was becoming clear that when things didn't break, when people didn't get hurt, it was mostly because nobody had thought to do the breaking or hurting. So much of the world depended on everyone's good intentions, and in her limited experience, there weren't enough of these to go around.

A sixth sense made her look up. Kay was standing about thirty feet away, half concealed by what, a few months ago, had been the mall Santa's throne but that now supported a toddler sliding board. The whole Santa enclosure had been transformed into "Keep It Cool Playland," where small children played with blocks and dolls amid the winter decor. Kay stared blankly at them as if longing for simpler times. Then she raised her head, saw that she'd been clocked.

"Hi," she said, having approached just close enough to be heard but not close enough to be tackled or grabbed. Not that Chloe was going to. Kay was a slight, diminutive girl with poor posture. She was pretty but it was hard to make out her face; her lank black hair was always dangling over it. At school, she somehow managed to make the bright Tarbox Beals uniform look like an old washcloth. Now she was dressed in the same black jeans and hoodie from the other day, her hands buried deep in the pockets.

"Do you want to sit down?"

"I guess," Kay said, not moving.

"Well...please sit down?"

There were four swivel chairs attached to the table. Kay took the opposite from Chloe and began, nervously, to swivel.

"I'm not mad at you or anything," Chloe said.

"Why would you be?"

"You took the video."

"Did I?"

Chloe nodded. "It took me a little while to remember. It was last October. You can tell from the Seneca Nation mural on the wall behind me that we made for Indigenous Peoples' Day. We were talking about Halloween and I was bragging about my thunderstorm costume from two years ago."

The girl shrugged.

"Why were you taking the video in the first place?"

"I just was."

"Well, why did you give it to Addison?"

Kay stopped swiveling and faced Chloe for the first time. The one eye Chloe could see behind the hair was narrowed. "I *didn't*. I left my phone unlocked when I went to pee, and she texted it to herself. I didn't even know until later."

"Okay. I believe you."

"Good," Kay said fiercely. "I don't like what she did. We even had a fight about it."

"So she admits she made the fake?"

"Her dad's the computer guy. It's probably him."

Chloe shook her head. "I can't believe an adult would do that. Like, why would he even care? It's just a stupid school election."

Kay looked at her for a few seconds as if making a calculation. Chloe held her gaze. Finally Kay looked away, saying, "Addison's all right, but that family is fucked up, that's all I can say." Almost as an afterthought, she added, "They're on vacation this month to *both* Disneys, how sicko is that." It seemed to Chloe that Kay could say even more, maybe that she wanted to, but at least for now that wasn't going to happen.

Chloe stood up. "Well, thanks for meeting me. I know you're Addison's friend, but if you want to help with my campaign, I could use you."

The girl sat there, mouth hanging open, looking offended.

"What?" Chloe said.

"Pizza?" She held up her phone. "On you?"

After a second, Chloe laughed. "Right," she said. "Pizza on me. Come on."

7

The drive to the Douglas Creek Retreat took her along a series of winding country two-lanes through woods and farms. Jane dangled her arm out the window and tapped the door in rhythm with a song on the radio. She'd signed up for the conference under the name she'd adopted after she got out of prison and assumed the role of suburban wife and mother: Martina Kelleher. It was legally and habitually her real name, the name she went by at school functions, the name on the checks. But she'd never truly inhabited it. To her family, to Shelly, and in her own mind, she was the permanently searchable Jane Pool, voluntary manslaughterer.

She crested a hill and Douglas Creek came into view, spread out in the valley below like a model train diorama: the meandering brook, the church spire, the little houses dotting the flats and climbing quaintly up the hills. Off in the distance, behind the school sports fields, woods surrounded a small lake. Even from here, Jane could make out the retreat, a series of log cabins created for corporate and academic gatherings clustered around a broad dock and a meeting hall. This was her destination.

The first right before town proper began led her past homemade posters that had been laminated and taped to various street signs and light poles. WRITER'S CONFERENCE, they read, and someone had used a red marker to copyedit the apostrophe to its rightful place at the end of the first word. She didn't know whether to regard this as a good or bad omen.

Jane pulled into a broad gravel lot enclosed by split-rail fence and punctuated with yellow-painted concrete parking stops. She stepped out, stretched, grabbed her duffel and laptop bag, and followed a shady footpath to the cluster of buildings in the distance. The place had been built to resemble a Catskills resort circa 1950, each cabin crisply painted and surrounded by an apron of shrubbery and flowering perennials, each intersection of paths marked by arrow-shaped wooden signs: CAFETERIA, CONFERENCE CENTER, OWL CABINS, DUCK CABINS, DEER CABINS. It was made to appeal to the nostalgia of people in their fifties and older, professors and local corporate leaders, government officials. But Jane liked it immediately. It was clean and organized and easy to escape from if necessary.

WELCOME WRITERS! REPORT TO CONFERENCE CENTER! read another laminated sign, and Jane trailed a group of women to a three-story glass-and-log structure with a sharply angled roof overlooking the lake. A few people piloted rowboats on the water, and beyond the lake the rooftops of Douglas Creek were visible among the trees.

The mood inside was buoyant. There were about three dozen women here: a few teenagers, a few grandmas, all manner of people in between, all talking and laughing in the high-ceilinged, echoing lobby. Jane's heart skipped a beat; for a moment it felt like the Boynton Ridge common room, or some idealized version of it from a dream. She spied Shelly and approached.

"Hey!" Shelly called out. "This is Hannah and Kim, they're in our class. Guys, this is——" She raised an eyebrow at Jane. "Martina?"

"Hi!" she said to the two, a girl of around twenty and a woman in her sixties. "Friends call me Jane. My middle name." The younger woman seemed shy behind her smudged eyeglasses; the older one was tall and thin with close-cut gray hair. A bit of conversation revealed that Hannah was writing about sexual assault—"My professor at school told me not to workshop it there"—and Kim about her cancer treatment. Kim asked Jane what she was writing about, and she stammered for a moment before Shelly stepped in and said, "I told 'em we did time."

"Oh."

"Sorry, I figured they'd find out soon enough!"

The women directed her to a little rustic building with a sign that read, incongruously, CONCIERGE SERVICES. It resembled a roadside farm stand. A teenage girl was stationed between a wooden counter and a wall that bore a honeycomb of mail cubbies beside a hook board covered with dangling keys. The girl checked Jane's name off on a clipboard, then gave her a key and a map. She made her way to Owl Cabins. Cabin C was a one-room cottage with a twin bed, a gas fireplace, a sofa, and a kitchenette. It would do fine. She returned to the conference center and joined the other writers in an auditorium, where the conference director, a sternly enthusiastic woman named Beth, introduced herself and the week's schedule.

"After lunch," she said, gesturing toward a projected copy of the paper they were all holding in their hands, "you'll break into your class groups and have an icebreaker session. Then you'll have writing time in your cabins—or wherever you feel those creative juices flowing!—then dinner in the cafeteria and the evening reading event. Feel free to explore, ladies, and be sure to wear a life vest for any water-related activities! We are not liable for your water-involved actions!"

Jane sat down to lunch with Shelly and their classmates. A fifth woman, Tilly, had joined them. A cheerful person around Jane's age, Tilly wore her hair in curls and published a book blog called *Curly Quotes*. She used her phone to show them the blog, which featured a winking, stylized illustration of her face and hair and a recommendation feature called "Curl Up With…"

"I'm on social as Curly Quotes, that's where you probably recognize me from."

"I didn't recognize you," Kim said, scowling.

"It's mostly for younger readers," Tilly said. Kim's scowl intensified.

The food was pretty good for a conference buffet, though people complained about it. "I think that's the memoir teacher, Heather Wooster Steyer," Hannah said with a gasp, gazing starstruck at a woman drifting by in flowy, flaxen earth tones, holding a tray. She went to sit at what Jane took to be the extemporaneously created faculty table. "Her collection *Drunk Notes* is one of my favorite books pretty much ever."

"Aren't there supposed to be six of us?" Kim asked.

"According to Beth," Tilly said with a little shake of her hair, "one's coming late. Her name's Marin. Like the county."

Jane took a moment to field a call from Lila in which she learned that the robbers' getaway car was a white Accord, driven by a white woman. Then Lila scolded her for attending the conference. They argued about it briefly and, as usual, pointlessly, until Lila hung up. The others had already made their way to the location indicated in their packet, a small conference room off the main hall with windows facing the woods, and Jane joined her classmates there. After a moment Heather Wooster Steyer arrived and said, "You may call me Heather," before telling them a bit about herself: thrice-divorced alcoholic and two-time National Book Award longlistee whose father had been an atomic scientist and whose mother was a "tragic ballet prodigy." Her prematurely silver hair was long and seemed to move of its own volition, cascading like water over her narrow shoulders.

Each participant offered a few facts about herself. Kim's illness had ruined her marriage, and she intended to write about that. Hannah had once been pulled onstage to accompany Alanis Morissette on the drums for one song. "I'm a drummer," she clarified. "Among other things."

"What song?" Shelly wanted to know.

"'Hand in My Pocket,'" Hannah coolly replied.

Shelly talked about her incarceration and her brother, and Tilly shared some instances of anti-curly discrimination while Kim glared.

"Martina?" Heather asked, glancing up from her notebook.

"Call me Jane. I, uh," she said, then surprised herself by continuing, "confessed to a crime my sister committed and served a year in state prison for it."

Appreciative noises went up around the room. Heather sat up a little straighter. "I, for one, would like to know why. Will your memoir tell us?"

"I...sure," Jane said. The women nodded, eager to know the story.

"I'm told that..." Heather glanced down again at her notebook. "I'm told that Marin will be arriving this evening and is willing to present her work on Tuesday. Would any of you like to volunteer for tomorrow?"

"I volunteer Jane!" Tilly said.

"I'll go," Kim said. "I've already got copies."

"Excellent," Heather said as Kim began to pass around stapled sheaves of paper. "We should all be prepared to offer our thoughts to Kim tomorrow. And your first reading should already be in your packets: a lyric essay on the concept of the zoo, written by me. Good luck with your work this afternoon, and I will see you all tomorrow."

"That was quick," Kim said when she was gone. They stood up and gathered their things in the wake of Heather's swift and silent glide to the exit. Shelly and Tilly each said they were going to find somewhere peaceful to write; Kim and Hannah announced their intention to chat by the lake and went off together, heads close in conversation.

Jane returned to Cabin C. She'd known, of course, that she would have to actually write something, but the reality of the situation had sneaked up on her. She hadn't done any sustained writing since group therapy at Boynton, where they'd written letters to dead relatives and to their childhood selves for purposes that were never really clear to her. Now she actually had to be...profound? Or entertaining, at least. She had no idea where to begin.

Her short-term solution was to not. Instead she plugged in the satellite router Lila had given her, opened her work laptop, and signed onto their network. She began to search for their missing uncle, dimly aware that Lila could likely track everything she did and had probably already tried everything it would occur to Jane to do.

In the months since they'd started the new expanded Perks, Jane had followed Lila's advice and taken a few online courses, read some books, watched some tutorials. Via their anonymized subscriptions and backdoor hacks into various information databases, and using a custom interface of Lila's that consolidated them, she could comb through government, criminal, genealogical, and academic records for references to Lloyd Davies and any aliases he had.

Lila might have been the computer expert, but Jane knew more about Uncle Lloyd than her sister did. When the girls were teen runaways, he and Aunt Ruth had offered their home as a safe haven for one week a year along with an annual allowance. Only Jane had taken them up on it. Lloyd was a man of few words, but Jane had noticed a few things about him, like his penchant for horse racing and Arizona Diamondbacks baseball. He often took calls from a woman with a husky voice—Gina, maybe?—who Jane believed was an assistant or financial adviser who handled his business affairs. Jane understood these to involve real estate. Lloyd often emerged from his study smelling of pipe smoke; Jane got the idea Aunt Ruth didn't allow him to smoke it elsewhere in the house. He preferred a particular tobacco that had been discontinued years before, and he had sourced, he told Jane, "a lifetime supply."

"It's important in life," he told her once, "to figure out what you like, and to stick with it." He never explained why.

Jane quickly found the correct Lloyd Davies by cross-referencing his name with his old address; she made a note of his birth date and Social Security number. Real estate records had him buying the house she remembered, on Orrington Avenue in Evanston, with Aunt Ruth in 1998. He appeared to have lived there until her death in 2011, at which point he became the sole owner. Then, in 2012, the house was sold, and Lloyd's address changed to one on the ten-thousand block of West Belmont Avenue in Chicago. This seemed strange to Jane; with street view, she discovered that the property was a warehouse or depot of some kind. Another search identified it as a mail-forwarding service. Around this same time, Lloyd's name ceased regular use and dropped out of banking records and credit reports, and his Illinois driver's license expired and wasn't renewed.

Jane had no doubt that Lila had learned all this. She probably hadn't done a search for Lloyd's special tobacco, though: Blackmoor Extra Distinguished Long-Burning Plug Slice. Jane remembered it because she used to ponder whether the name meant that Blackmoor Extra was distinguished or that Blackmoor was extra-distinguished, and when she asked Lloyd, he thought she was mocking him and refused to reply. (He was right.) She could picture the tin it was packed in: white with black printing, a slab typeface over various ribbons and filigrees, like a dollar bill. A search confirmed her memory; it was made in Britain, had been in production between 1901 and 1992, and was described as "pure burley with a mild liquorice topping and slight oatmeal sweetness," whatever that meant.

If Lloyd had bought a lifetime supply of the stuff, he had to keep it stored someplace. She looked up how to do this. Best practices ranged from just putting it on a shelf in a closet to having a special temperature-and-humidity-controlled room for it. Lloyd seemed to her like the kind of guy who would favor the latter. Remembering a trick of her sister's, she did a web search for the tobacco, narrowed it to 2011 and 2012, and checked results from various messageboards and Reddit.

As it happened, not many people had talked online about Blackmoor Extra Distinguished Long-Burning Plug Slice (sometimes styled, amusingly, as BEDLBPS) during those years. There were a number of pipe-enthusiast communities out there, but Blackmoor had the most hits on one called Pipeman's Lounge, and most of these were posted by a smoker named DiamondD1951. One of the threads this person started was titled "Moving Collection?"

> Pipemen—I will soon be moving cross-country and will need to relocate my extensive collection of out-of-production tobaccos and rare and antique pipes. I live in a cold, damp part of the US and am going someplace hot and arid. I want to avoid drying and cracking on the journey and also in the new climate. Any tips would be welcome.

People had very strong opinions on the matter and weighed the various packing options as well as the question of next-day shipping versus moving with the furniture. *Not bringing much furniture,* DiamondD1951 wrote. In the end, consensus emerged around just driving the supplies to the new location in his car. *Don't leave it in the sun too long!* somebody advised.

Was this man Lloyd? The screen name was certainly plausible. She read back through his posts and found him making some restaurant recommendations to someone visiting Chicago in the early 2000s. There weren't many posts after 2012, though; he'd ignored requests for an update on his "Moving Collection?" thread and offered only one-word replies to a few other requests for recommendations. By early 2013, he'd disappeared from the board entirely.

Next, she clicked on the tab in Lila's application marked FACE RECOGNITION. She'd already uploaded some photos of Lloyd to their server—besuited, posed photos from various corporate boards he'd served on—and done a rudimentary search, but it had mostly turned up generic-looking middle-aged white men posed similarly. After a moment's thought, she went online and found a novelty website that would age a person in a photo for you. She plugged in Lloyd's portrait and tried the face search again, this time narrowing it geographically to the Southwest. Thousands of hits came up, again without many plausible results.

But there were two that might have been him. One was a figure in the periphery of a newspaper photo printed in the *Arizona Republic* in 2017 of a man standing in the bleachers of a baseball game triumphantly holding up a baseball while his wife and children clapped with joy. A Diamondbacks pitcher, the caption explained, having thrown a no-hitter, had tossed the ball he'd used to do it into the stands along the first-base line, and this man had caught it. The man who resembled Lloyd was standing next to him, leaning slightly away, as though in a strong wind. He wore a cap and clutched a pair of sunglasses in his hand, revealing a face that instantly brought back Jane's memories of Chicago—but the more she stared at it, the less sure she was. The shot was clear but high contrast; shadows obscured, slightly, his features.

It was the second photo, however, that convinced her both were Lloyd, a promotional snapshot for the newly unveiled smokers' patio at a "dog-friendly gastropub" in Prescott. It was taken in 2022 and showed diners enjoying cigarettes along with their steaks underneath a white-painted latticed pergola that hadn't had the chance to grow in yet. One man dined alone, a golden retriever at his feet, reading a print newspaper and smoking a pipe. It was undeniably Lloyd.

Jane tried a couple of other regions of the country to assure herself the world wasn't crawling with plausible false Lloyds, then sent the two photos to Lila via their encrypted chat. *Prescott, AZ, a few years ago?* she wrote, then checked the time and realized she was ten minutes late for dinner. She hadn't worked on her memoir at all.

Dinner was much like lunch except that her group had begun to separate into factions. Hannah and Kim were fast friends, and Tilly, sensing that she'd somehow alienated the others, concentrated on her phone, occasionally holding it up and posing for a selfie. Jane wondered why she kept at this for so long, then realized she was attempting to compose a shot with appealing-looking passersby in the background. At one point their esteemed teacher drifted past and Tilly let out a triumphant cackle. "Got ya!" she said.

Shelly was talking about the progress she'd made. "I'm starting with the day I got out. It'll be, like, I go through the whole process, the fingerprinting, the exit interview, getting my old clothes back, and feeling free and being, like, afraid of my freedom and afraid of missing all the girls and the routine. That's the prologue."

"I like that," Jane said.

Shelly forked a meatball into her mouth and said thanks, through meat.

They talked more about various people they both knew. "Did you overlap with Zora?" Shelly asked.

"The girl with the dice? It was after I moved to the nursery wing. But I heard about her."

"She fleeced one of the guards for a couple hundred bucks. A legend."

"And who was it that drew mazes and made those absurdly hard crosswords," Jane said.

"That was Ace. I kept a couple of them in the notebooks."

"Do you know what happened to Ace?"

"Leukemia," Shelly said, shaking her head. "They got diagnosed at Boynton. Warden gave them medical parole so they could die on the outside. I don't know where they went or who with, though. Their family was the devil incarnate."

Jane barely had time to register this sad fact before Beth, the conference organizer, approached their table with a young woman at her side. The newcomer was white, nondescript, and extremely nervous. Rapidly blinking, heavily made-up eyes peered out from beneath a mousy cap of hair, and she seemed to have a tic of wiping her long, narrow, and apparently dry nose with the back of her hand. A white oxford shirt, buttoned to the neck, was tucked into high-waisted jeans. The jeans had been pseudo-randomly smeared with several different colors of paint as though by a careful brush, and her black trucker-style cap bore the image of a skeletal hand curled into devil horns.

"Ladies," Beth said, "this is Marin. She just arrived from New Jersey. She'll be part of your workshop."

They all said hello. "Where in New Jersey are you from?" Hannah asked. "I grew up in Morristown."

The woman froze. "I live in Trenton momentarily," she said.

Beth led her away to the buffet while the women exchanged puzzled glances. "Well, she should be interesting," Kim drawled.

"I approve of the hat," Hannah said.

Marin returned with modest servings of chicken breast and roasted potatoes pushed to opposite sides of an otherwise empty plate. Next to the plate she set down a tall glass of what looked like skim milk. She pulled her cap lower and slouched into her seat.

"Marin, what are you working on?" Shelly asked.

"Chicken and potatoes," Marin said.

"No, I mean for the conference. Your writing."

"Oh." Her shoulders hitched and something like a chuckle escaped her tightly compressed lips. "Uh, it's a thing about the environment." After a moment, she added, "How it's important, and companies and whatever are trying to ruin it for, uh, profits."

"Are you an activist?" Tilly asked brightly.

She seemed to consider before answering. "I identify as an artist. Also, my pronouns are her and hers."

"Good to know," Kim said.

Conversation moved on, but Marin kept her head down, pecking diligently away at the food, and occasionally popping her head up to take in her classmates, like a crow observing passing traffic from its meal of roadkill. Of course Jane was immediately suspicious. Marin was ill at ease and matched the description Lila had given her of the woman in the car. Her eyes darted, and she would sometimes get a faraway look, as though transfixed by something in a parallel dimension. She snapped back to attention, however, when Shelly resumed talking about her prison memoir.

After dinner, they all went to an event in the main auditorium. The author was an award-winning poet whose reading featured numbered sections and extremely long pauses. Jane bought her book. It was quite thick for a volume of poetry but sparsely populated with text, four or five words per page at most, and the signature she added for Jane resembled Morse code. When they all emerged from the conference center, they discovered that a fire had been built on the beach, and people were milling around, sipping wine from plastic cups. Jane found the bar, a repositionable structure made of thick twigs, and got herself some seltzer. The poet stood at the water's edge, gazing out into the distance as admirers approached.

Marin soon peeled off into the darkness, and Jane followed from a respectable distance all the way to her cabin, which proved to be Owl E. Back at the beach, Jane found Shelly and said, "Come with me."

"So—Marin," Shelly said as they walked down the path toward the arrow signs. "Weird, right?"

"That's what I wanted to talk to you about. I had my sister look into the surveillance footage from the auto-parts shop at the end of your street. She got a glimpse of the people who might have broken into your house."

"Wait, she can do that?" Shelly said.

"Sometimes. Anyway, the driver was a woman. It was blurry, but the description matches Marin." They reached the intersection and Jane led them down the path marked PARKING. "And she got the make and model of the car."

"Seriously?" Shelly said. "They followed me here? For real?"

"Maybe?" A minute later they'd arrived at the parking lot. Arc lamps cast a cold light over the gravel and scattered cars. "We're looking for a white Honda."

"There!" Shelly said. It was parked far from the other cars, in the shade of a large tree, a white Accord with New York plates.

"Do you have your phone?" Jane said. She had Shelly look up images of a 2016 Honda Accord LX. This car was definitely the right model. It was badly cared for, with cracked trim and a mismatched replacement door. There had been stickers on the rear bumper that were recently scraped or peeled off, a few incompletely. Jane knelt in the gravel and ran her fingers over the residue. The glue was still sticky. One had been a bright yellow circle with some kind of cartoon on it—there wasn't enough left to identify it.

And a couple of new stickers had been affixed. One read PROUD LIBERAL LEFT-WING COMMIE SOCIALIST ON BOARD! The other simply said WHALES.

Shelly crouched beside her. Her jaw was tight. "So it's her? This is the asshole who stole my notebooks?"

"Her passenger was the one who broke in, a guy in a hoodie. But Lila didn't get a good look at him."

"Fuck a duck," Shelly said. "I don't get it!"

"Me neither."

They were about to return to the cabins when they heard the crunch of gravel at the north end of the lot. Marin was standing, deerlike, in the pool of light beneath a streetlamp. As they watched, she snapped her fingers as if suddenly remembering something, pulled her hat down over her face, and hurried off toward the trails.

8

The Rolling K bar was located in a one-story brick building on the busiest street in Stockyards City. Inside, it was loud and dim, decorated with wagon wheels, acoustic guitars, and black-and-white photos of Conestoga wagons and men riding horses. The place teemed with cattle ranchers and their families; a few tourists looked happy and out of place in their sweatshirts and sneakers. Their shouted conversation mostly drowned out a classic-country playlist blasting in the background. Lila had worn her jeans, new boots, and a clean pearl-snap. She'd undone an extra snap at the neck and rolled the sleeves up above the elbow, revealing a gold charm bracelet that Loretta had modified for her. People were lined up two deep at the bar or crowded around little round dining tables made of old-growth pine slabs sanded and varnished to a dull shine.

Remy sat at one of them, alone, with a pint glass of beer he'd barely touched. He'd set his hat upturned on the table in front of an unoccupied chair, saving her place. When he saw her, he hung the hat over his knee and gestured with a chivalrous sweep of his hand for her to sit down. She did so, tucking her own hat underneath her chair.

"Charming spot," she said, almost meaning it.

"It's been here for eighty-nine years," he replied, leaning close so that he wouldn't have to yell. He smelled pretty good: dusty, leathery, and clean.

"I've been here eight seconds," she said, "and there still isn't a beer in front of me." It sounded, she thought, like something a person who liked beer might say.

He laughed, waved a waitress over, indicated another for the lady. "You hungry? It's bar food, but it ain't bad."

"Sure."

They ordered burgers. Remy asked her about life in Little Rock and she invented some stuff, trying to make life in the imaginary dental office sound a little bit sexy. Their food came, and while they ate, Remy glanced over his shoulder every couple of minutes. He seemed to be focused on a door in the back of the bar marked PRIVATE.

"You want to switch places?" Lila said. "That way you can look at me and that door at the same time."

He laughed, but she could tell he was a little disconcerted. "Sorry. Look, I'll be honest with you, I'm kinda on the clock right now. The boss is back there taking a meeting."

"Who with?"

"Some guy he wants to work with, put it that way. Once they clear out of there, we can do whatever."

"I like whatever," she said.

"I bet you do" was the response, delivered with a wink. It was becoming clear she was going to have to have sex with this guy, which she thought she could manage to enjoy. He hadn't bothered to take off the wedding ring. She respected him for that, anyway; there wasn't any confusion about what they were doing and it would have been pointless to complicate it with a white lie. She drank some of the beer and forced a satisfied smile.

At some point during their meal he checked his phone, presumably for a message from Nutt. He used its facial-recognition feature to log in. His lock screen, she noticed, featured a photo of his wife and child—a girl of around five—standing in a pasture with a mountain in the background.

"Sorry," he said, putting the phone away, but at that moment the PRIVATE door opened and the Orthodox Jewish man from earlier emerged, clearly in a state of agitation, his younger companion in tow. They elbowed their way through the crowd to the exit and disappeared. A minute later, the office door opened again and Hathaway and Nutt came out, the former looking embarrassed, the latter cool. To Lila's surprise, several people got up from their seats—a few lone men and a couple, a man and a woman, who abandoned their two children at their table—and mobbed Nutt at the bar. They all looked excited. Nutt placidly spoke to them while Brian Hathaway backed awkwardly out of the way. "Excuse me," Remy said to Lila and met the group at the bar.

Remy laid a hand on the shoulder of one of the men and seemed to be asking him to move along. A tense exchange resulted, which culminated with Nutt shaking hands with everyone and signing autographs for a few of them. The couple were wearing yellow ball caps, and one of the other men had a black tee shirt printed with a fierce yellow cartoon bee. Once Nutt's fans had returned to their seats, Remy, Hathaway, and Nutt had a curt, intense discussion. They were joined briefly by another man who emerged from behind the bar—the owner, no doubt. Hathaway paid the tab, hands were shaken, and the meeting broke up. Hathaway and Nutt left.

Remy returned, looking a little deflated.

"Who were those guys in there with them?" Lila said.

He sat down, scooping his hat up from the chair where he'd left it. "Ah, just business. Boss was hoping to work with that rabbi fella but it seems like it's a no-go."

"What is it," Lila asked, "some kinda religious thing? Your boss is a Christian, right?"

He gave her a wary look. "I don't think I mentioned that."

She touched her neck, letting her fingers linger there a moment before letting them slide down over her chest. His eyes followed. "Around his neck," she said. "The cross."

"Oh, yeah. Yeah. He's pretty churchy. Doesn't like to work on Sundays, actually, so we usually wouldn't be here until later tonight. But the rabbi doesn't work on Saturdays, so..."

"Got it. What's a rabbi want with cattle, anyway?"

His eyebrows went up. "Everybody likes beef, Heidi, and for some people it's gotta be kosher. They got their own way of doing it."

"Sure, sure. Well, your cows looked good to me—what didn't he like about them?"

"Heifers. Beats me. That's above my pay grade." His sour expression suggested that he knew more than he was saying and would prefer to be talking about something else.

"And those superfans with the yellow hats. What was that all about?"

"Oh, boy," Remy said with a nervous laugh.

"I don't mean to pry! Just, what's the deal with you guys, exactly? I know there's money in the cattle industry, but your boss seems like quite the high roller. Was that his custom Peterbilt in the lot?"

He'd appeared unnerved by this line of questioning, but he clearly couldn't resist the opportunity to talk about the truck. "Yeah, it is!" he said. "The flattop? Black and green?"

"That's the one," she said.

"Seventy-two-inch sleeper with a three-hundred-inch wheelbase. That's a 2023 three eighty-nine. He used to have a 2010 but when he heard they were discontinuing the model, he went for broke."

"He let you drive it?"

A belly laugh. "Oh, hell no! Honestly, we don't need to come here at all, I think it's mostly an excuse for him to drive the damn truck."

"Can't blame him."

"Naw, it's a beauty. Anyway…" He paused, took a long draft of his beer. "The boss's deal is, he was doing work on genetically engineered livestock pretty much before anybody, back when you couldn't put 'em on the market. He was one of the guys who got the FDA to change the rules."

"Seriously?"

"Well," Remy said, waving a hand in the air, "him and some other guys lobbied our senator who's on the committee that got the FDA to change the rules. Or something like that. He literally drove the truck—the old truck—to DC with a big banner on the side."

"That's dedication."

"That's business," he said. "By the time the rules changed, he was ready with a bunch of new strains of cattle, some disease-resistant ones, some with short hair that don't mind the heat. He's also working on ones that miscarry less. And polled dairy breeds."

"Polled?"

"Sorry. No horns. When your bulls have horns, cows get gored, people get gored. It's easier to breed 'em out with beef cattle but tougher with the dairy stock. So if you could snap your fingers and get rid of the horns on dairy cattle, that's worth a lot of money."

"Wow."

"Except every time you make a genetic change, you gotta get the FDA to approve it, and they'll only approve it once they know it's safe, yada yada. So a lot of his money's going into politics. Getting people elected, so they can get people appointed, so they can do the right thing for the industry."

"Is that what the rabbi wanted? Polled cattle?"

He grew uncomfortable again. "Uh, yeah, probably something like that. Like I said, above my pay grade."

"How'd he get into genetics in the first place?"

"He's a chemical engineer," Remy said with something like pride. "Used to be a professor, he did all kinds of lab research. I was his student back in the day. So he came at the industry from a science angle." A waitress walked by and he made a signature motion in the air with an invisible pen. "Hey, you wanna get out of here?" he said. "Hotel bar's a little quieter."

"Sounds good."

He used his phone to order a ride. Outside, the air had cooled and rain had begun to fall. She wasn't uncomfortable but nestled up to him, feigning the need for warmth. He asked her about her upbringing, and when she said, "You first" (meaning "Me never"), he told her about his rural Arizona childhood, lake fishing and desert camping, shooting rattlesnakes and turkey vultures with the 7mm-08 Remington he got for his tenth birthday. "In the army, I won competitions with that rifle," he said, and she sensed he was trying to impress himself, gassing himself up for seduction, as much as he was trying to impress her. He drew her close, sliding his hand down her arm, letting his fingertips make contact with her breast. In the car, she put her hand on his knee and slowly moved it up toward his thigh. He let out a snicker at his obvious arousal.

"Maybe let's skip the bar," he said as they dashed for the automatic doors of the hotel.

"Fine by me."

They made out in the elevator. He kissed her neck and separated her legs with his knee. Bold. She let out a moan that she almost meant. In his room, they got undressed on the way to the bed. He ducked into the bathroom. She watched through the open door as he set down his phone by the sink and tore a condom off a strip stashed in his Dopp kit.

Lila liked sex well enough, though it had been a while since she'd done it with a man. Remy was a perfectly fine partner, if a little too eager. She had to push him away to set the proper pace, bringing herself closer to the edge before climbing on and fucking him. Some guys didn't like to see a woman touch herself, but he did. She didn't understand the transformation that desire brought to some people, men and women both; people would tie their lives in knots for sex, leave themselves vulnerable to all manner of devastation: emotional, financial, familial. She could probably ruin Remy's marriage in minutes if she wanted.

She didn't want that, though. She wanted to find out more about this failed business deal and discover where Nutt's ranch was. If she could catch the rabbi before he left town, maybe she could figure out the former, but the answer to the latter was probably here in this hotel suite.

She quietly finished and waited for him to do the same. Then she rolled off him and let him encircle her with his arm.

"That was nice," he said.

"Yeah."

"I hope you don't think I do this every time I'm out of town," he said, disappointing her. "To be honest, I'm a workaholic. My wife and I have an understanding but I don't take advantage of it very often."

She doubted that, but also she didn't give a shit. "You don't seem like that kind of guy," she made herself say.

"I'm not. And you seem like a nice kind of girl."

"I'm not," she said, and they laughed. "I'm the kind of girl who has to piss. Be right back."

In the bathroom, she ran the faucet and examined his phone. She'd hoped to see the smudges of his fingers on the keypad, but the display was clean. She tapped it with a knuckle, making sure not to move it, and brought up the lock screen. His wife was conventionally pretty, a buxom cowgirl, the kid like any other child. Lila raised her wrist and searched through the charms on her bracelet—a heart, a sun, a fish—until she reached the log cabin. Where its front door should have been, a little camera lens lurked. Its chimney snapped the photo. Loretta had installed the electronics, a tiny sensor and logic board usually found in medical instruments or virtual-reality headsets, so Lila wouldn't have to carry a phone into sensitive places. It wasn't exactly a vital piece of tech and had been given more as a sweet and clever gift from a friend than as a crucial tool. But Lila liked it. She snapped a few photos of the lock screen, positioning it slightly differently each time to make sure she got a good shot of the mountain in the background. Then she used the toilet, turned off the water, and went back out.

She'd hoped Remy would have fallen asleep, but he was sitting up in bed. That ruled out searching his wallet, but if he was as smart as she assumed he was, it wouldn't contain any evidence of the ranch's location. He seemed like a pretty basic guy but no fool. "Welcome back," he said. "I don't mean to be rude..."

"But you have to work tomorrow," Lila said, bending down for her underwear.

"I gotta get up at four."

"Ouch."

"So, yeah. Thanks for a fun night. Hope we see each other again sometime."

"Count on it, cowboy." He didn't mean what he'd said, but she did. She'd be in Arizona before long, at the base of that mountain, figuring out why her aunt was dead. The thing he truly ought to hope for was that he didn't get in her way.

Dressed, her hair tied back, she blew him a kiss and walked out the door.

Back in her room, Lila showered, then connected the bracelet to her laptop with a miniature cable and downloaded the photos she'd taken of Remy's phone. Resolution was low but it would be enough. She logged into the satellite internet and VPN, then dragged the photos into her image-recognition application. The mountain—a glorified hill, really—was in Skeleton Flats, an unincorporated town in Yavapai County, Arizona. It had a population of 714 people, an elementary school, and a post office. In her maps app, Lila zoomed to check out the view from the road. With a bit of clicking, she was able to determine the exact spot where the photo had been taken: just off Route 10, beside the log-gate entrance to a ranch. The map didn't identify the ranch the way it did most other ranches; there was just a pale blocky area in the otherwise featureless expanse. The road that led to the area was called Affirmation. She switched to the satellite view and was rewarded, to her surprise, with a large brown blur.

Affirmation? That is...Yes? Could Nutt really be that vain and stupid?

He could, of course. It had to be the spot.

She searched for the cartoon bee that Nutt's fan had displayed on his shirt. Eventually she found examples of it in crowd scenes, some at theme parks and concerts, others at parks and on city streets. There didn't seem to be much in common among the people wearing the tees other than a handful she found attending political demonstrations. She filed away a few of these for future reference. For now, sleep.

Lila woke at six, took the stairs down to the lobby, and helped herself to a cup of weak coffee and a morning newspaper from the meager continental breakfast spread. A couple of tables were positioned at the threshold of the café, and she took one and pulled her chair around to face the bank of elevators.

A lot of her work featured some degree of waiting. One mark of a professional, in her estimation, was imperviousness to boredom, but the smartphone had robbed humanity of this ability. Most people couldn't stand in line at the supermarket without pulling theirs out. In addition, the modern phone had an unreasonable degree of security risk, and that, along with Lila's extreme distaste for interruption and for other people in general, gave her an excellent excuse for not carrying one. Patience, once table stakes in her line of work, now seemed like a superpower.

Memorable stakeouts included a chilly all-nighter in a burned-out air traffic control tower in Belarus, a stifling day hiding out under a reeking canvas tarp in a rowboat on a Texas reservoir, and five hours in a tree in a rainstorm in Bang Suan, Thailand, peering in the window of a farmhouse and wishing she'd chosen a better spot. Today's task, sitting quietly in a temperature-controlled hotel lobby waiting for the most easily identifiable man in Oklahoma City, was not likely to present much of a challenge in comparison.

Nevertheless, she almost missed him while she was refilling her coffee. The rabbi and his companion were clearly in a hurry; she saw them sailing past the check-in desk with their wheeled suitcases just as she turned from the urn. She put the cup down and went after them, calmly but briskly, and caught them just outside the automatic doors loading their luggage into the trunk of an Uber.

"Excuse me, sirs?"

They seemed to jump, as if she'd delivered an electric shock with her eyes. The rabbi stared at her blankly, but the younger man recognized her. Not a great sign.

"What is it?" the younger man said.

"Sorry to bother you. I see that you're in a hurry."

"That's right," the man said. The rabbi looked on, clearly curious.

"If you don't mind talking to me before you go, I'll pay for your ride. I'm a reporter," Lila said. "Doing a story on biotech in the cattle industry. I heard you were working on something with Travis Nutt, who's something of a pioneer in the field."

"A *reporter*," the young man said.

"Yes, for a trade journal. I have to admit, it's been something of a bust, I could really use some quotes. Maybe I can take you both out for coffee or—"

"No, you're not," the man said, his eyes narrowed.

"No, I'm not what?"

He raised an angry finger to her face. "Not a reporter. Not doing a story. And you're not going to talk to my father and me. You are a liar and we are leaving this place."

"Avner," said the rabbi, touching his shoulder.

"No, Dad, we are not talking to her," he said, brushing the hand away. He turned back to Lila. "I saw you last night with his man. Flirting with him. You are working with them. You don't deserve an explanation from us."

"Avner, wait," the rabbi said. And, to Lila: "Is this true? You are with them?"

"It's not true."

The three stood for a moment, taking stock. Then the rabbi said, "Whoever you are, my son is right, you can't be trusted. But I will tell you this for your story or whatever it is you're doing. He is not a scientist, he is a madman. We thought he understood our aims and wanted to help!"

"What aims, Rabbi?" Lila said.

"Dad," said the son, but the rabbi silenced him with a hand.

"We are trying to nourish the souls of the Jewish people, to deliver unparalleled peace and harmony to all of humanity. We wish to be spiritually ready for climactic times, not to bring them on. Your Nutt has sadly misunderstood our mission. We want to build the Temple for peace! He wants only to destroy. He can keep his heifers, we wish failure upon all his endeavors."

"I'm not sure I understand," Lila said.

"Yes, you do," the son spat. He slammed the trunk shut and tenderly pushed his father toward the car door. "My father has nothing more to say to you." Nevertheless, the older man couldn't resist handing Lila a business card.

Seconds later, they were gone.

Back in the hotel room, Lila packed up her clothes. She was finished here. It looked like she was headed to Arizona. If she left immediately, she could beat Remy and Nutt to their ranch, break in, learn what she needed to know, and make a plan. She could be there this time tomorrow, sooner if she budgeted less time for sleep. Afterward, based on the information that Jane had sent her, she could go find Lloyd and determine what he had to do with any of this and how much mercy he should or shouldn't be shown. The fire was in her now, and she was eager to start crossing items, and possibly people, off her list.

She could even skip all that, figure out what room Nutt was in, and go murder him in his sleep. Her fingers were twitching just thinking about it.

But no, she had to be sure. And she wanted to know exactly why and how Aunt Ruth lost her life and how her mother was involved. She wanted to know what Ruth's cryptic notes meant and what Nutt had said to the rabbi to make him and his son so angry. *He wants only to destroy,* the man had said. Destroy what? And why?

And, if she was being completely honest with herself, she thought that Jane was just a little bit right about the business—Lila *had* been sidelining her. It wasn't anything personal; she just liked working alone. It was easier to just do something than to teach somebody else to do it. But she was actually impressed by the work Jane had done on Lloyd. Those pictures were definitely of him, and she still didn't know how her sister had pulled it off.

Lila put on her sunglasses and hat, shouldered her bags, and made her way to the parking garage. The Volvo was already gassed and ready to go. She navigated through Bricktown traffic to OC Boulevard and followed the signs to I-40. Her instinct wanted to send her beneath the overpass and left onto the on-ramp west. But in the end she signaled right, got into the exit lane. Maybe her sister wouldn't mind a visit. They could plan the trip to Arizona together.

Also, Lila could make sure the memoir situation wasn't getting out of hand.

The light turned green, and she headed east.

9

Harry had spent a couple of days searching for something—anything—placing Alain Rampersaud in central New York, even a single breadcrumb. So far he'd come up short. He'd mostly spent his time in the humanities library at Nestor College, sitting in his carrel reading or on one of the public computers, searching online archives.

In 1964, with the clandestine help of the Agency, the Brazilian military overthrew the government of president João Goulart. Plácidia, under the elder Rampersaud, Christophe, managed to reach an uneasy détente with the new regime, perhaps hoping that the island's small size and strategic unimportance would cause these increasingly hard-line leaders to forget it existed. But as things deteriorated on the mainland throughout the sixties—the suspension of civil rights, the abolition of political parties, and the disappearance or exile of countless artists and activists—Christophe grew restless and began to speak out. In response, the military junta threatened to seize the southern half of Plácidia—historically a place of lush forests and paradisial shores and home to the Rampersaud clan's retreat—for air and sea bases and a munitions factory.

Christophe had thought Plácidians were on his side. He was mistaken. His ill-gained riches had caused immense resentment among the miners and fishermen who made up most of the population, and they turned against him. Somehow—and the research wasn't clear on the details—Christophe was deposed, most likely murdered by these local sympathizers, and the expectation was that the Brazilian generals would choose a successor from the mainland to replace him.

But that's not what happened. Instead, an election was held in Brazil, and the presidency won by Emílio Garrastazu Médici, the junta-backed (and only) candidate for the job. And somehow, Alain Rampersaud ended up as president of Plácidia and remained in office for a year and a half, seeming to placate both the locals and Médici, despite the latter's penchant for repression, censorship, torture, and murder. Plans for the military base were put on hold, and Rampersaud the younger, whether out of generosity or simple self-preservation, converted his family's land into a national park, with the former vacation house serving as a natural history museum. Harry couldn't determine if this was a popular decision at the time—the family's enemies might very well have wanted the land for themselves—but it had legs; the Parque Nacional do Plácidia survived through the remainder of Brazil's military dictatorship and its attendant economic woes. (Harry surmised that its survival was more the result of that economic slump than any fondness for nature among the mainland's leaders.) Today it was home to unique species of birds, frogs, and insects and a major destination for ecotourists and naturalists.

But what had happened to Alain Rampersaud? Anecdotally, his détente with Médici wore thin, and agents were sent to toss him off the cliffs and onto the jagged wave-washed rocks below. Different versions of the story had him defenestrated from the presidential mansion, impaled on a flagpole, executed by rifle fire on a cliff's edge, or—more charitably, Harry supposed—simply thrown off the deck of a ship and left to drown. In all variations on the story that Harry could find and in the meager government records he could access, the man was quite dead.

At home late Monday afternoon, Harry found a note from Chloe: *Going to friend's for dinner, don't wait up!* He was disappointed, having looked forward to reporting his findings to his granddaughter, but also relieved, as he could now dine alone on toast with broiled cheddar cheese and yellow mustard, a childhood comfort food that he craved and was too embarrassed to eat in front of her. He reviewed his notes and the Factor's while he ate, again came across the mysterious *Ask PTJ!*, and impulsively decided to track this person down. He picked up his phone and called Vincent.

"Professor Pool," the big man answered with surprising jollity. Harry could hear the burble of a creek and the caw of a crow in the background.

"Hello, Vincent, thank you for picking up. How are you doing today?"

"Sad. Tired."

"You're at your uncle's?"

"Taking a break from cleaning," he said with a grunt. Harry pictured him standing, walking to the edge of the Factor's deck, peering out over the creek and into the woods. "He had a lot of blankets."

"Is that so?"

"I guess my aunt made them. Knitted. Crocheted? Don't know the difference. She made a lot of goddamn blankets, Professor, and he kept them all. How you doing with those binders?"

"Quite well. That's why I'm calling, Vincent. Your uncle left a note to himself, probably jotted not so long ago, to query someone with the initials PTJ. It's about a historical thing—a coup in South America in the seventies. Do you know who this might be?"

"No, Professor, sorry," he said. "Uncle Franklin didn't have many friends, I don't think. He sent emails. Maybe he was writing to a PTJ."

"Can you find out for me? When you have the chance, I mean."

"Got nothing but time. Can I call you back?"

"Of course."

Harry finished eating while staring out his office window at the street. A couple of bicyclists zipped by, followed by the top-hatted street magician and failed mayoral candidate known as Rick the Trick, pushing his grocery cart full of gear home to his apartment behind the high school. Harry had just decided to launder the curtains for the first time in thirty years when the phone rang.

"Professor, I can't find anybody. I'm sorry."

"No worries, Vincent. It could be some kind of code. Your uncle was a mysterious man."

"I tried to think of who mighta come to see him but it was hardly no one. And all he ever did was go to church and the library."

"It's fine."

"Oh, wait."

"Yes?"

"The library. Isn't that lady there called Peggy?"

Harry's toes began to tingle. He cracked them, sat up straight, and said, "Peggy."

"Yeah, hold on." Harry heard typing. "Here's the website. Margaret J., it says. Margarets are Peggys, right? He sometimes talked about his friend Peggy at the library."

It had to be her—he wished it fervently. His own computer confirmed it. The Ghorum Public Library staffers were listed only by first name and last initial, but there it was, beneath a fetching headshot: one Margaret J., Reference Librarian. Her head was tilted forward just slightly, a half smile on her lips, as if she were about to impart an amusing secret.

"Want me to call and find out for ya, Professor?"

"No, Vincent, you've done enough...I'll call myself. Or, better yet, stop by. I've got a book or two to return, anyway." Of course he didn't— Chloe had taken the books out just the other day, and it was unlikely she'd finished any. But he could always just take them out again for her. He ended the call with Vincent, craved a glass of wine, and popped open a can of diet soda instead. He had to admit that he was rather beside himself. Somehow he'd get himself to sleep tonight, and in the morning he'd drop in on Margaret J., reference librarian.

Alone in the house that morning, Chloe had been beside herself as well. Against her better judgment, and without any adults around to prevent it, she'd been digging hard into the social media furor surrounding the deepfake video, watching her classmates attack her, defend her, persuade one another to switch sides. Her biggest mistake so far was recording a response video, just a couple of seconds of herself sitting up in bed, her hair a mess, saying, "It's *fake*." She superimposed the word FAKE in all caps, idiotically checked *Allow comments,* and posted it.

The resulting deluge had occupied the past hour of her life. She was still in bed, trembling from the three cups of coffee she'd drunk, realizing she should delete the video but unwilling to back down. Both videos had now spread far beyond the Tarbox Beals community; random strangers were weighing in on the veracity of *both* videos and also on Chloe's morality (low), bitchiness (high), and level of attractiveness (mixed, though all responses made her feel like shit about herself). *I'm thirteen!* she shouted in her own head. *Leave me alone!* But she had asked for it, hadn't she, by rekindling a flame that would doubtless have died by the day's end. What an idiot!

She made the extreme decision to delete the video, knowing that it would be a black mark on her integrity, mostly because if she didn't, her mom would eventually see it and be mad at her and feel bad for not being home to prevent her from posting it in the first place. And then she made the even extremer decision to power down her phone, stick it in a drawer, and take the bus to the mall without it.

Loretta was there, routing cables and installing software. Chloe busied herself creating attractive arrangements of retail products and learning how to use the key cutter. She got a slice of pizza, ate it while walking listlessly around like some kind of degenerate, and petted some puppies at the animal shelter, who were extra-excited because of the pizza smell. Then Loretta went out on a job—it was looking more and more like they were an actual locksmith rather than merely a front?—and Chloe checked in on her socials via a browser tab on the store's computer. There really was no getting away, was there. Addison was posting from Florida: she was at Disney Star Wars, or whatever it was called, making her own lightsaber. Chloe smirked—they were too old for that kind of crap!—but deep down she knew that if somebody took *her* to Disney Star Wars, she would absolutely make her own lightsaber, and probably bring it home and hang it on her wall like a spoil of war.

Exhausted, discouraged, she sat down hard on the stool behind the counter and lowered her face into her hands. And when she looked up again, she was confronted by a lidless cardboard box tucked onto a low shelf out of which peeked a familiar little black plastic nubbin. She pulled the box out, and there lay Loretta's kludged-together Bluetooth sniffer: the microcomputer, the keyboard, and the antenna that had been sticking out, all of it lashed to a rechargeable lithium-ion battery pack. Above her, on the computer screen, Addison, safely hundreds of miles away, lunged and dodged and swung her stupid toy, and an idea began to coalesce in Chloe's mind.

She opened up her backpack, emptied it of its contents—water bottle, extra tee shirt and underwear, pads—and replaced them with the sniffer. Then she shoved the box back into place and stood up. She glanced at her watch. Loretta should be back soon, and Chloe could leave. Then what? The bus home, and make a plan.

In a browser tab, she tried to find Addison's address by searching for her parents, but all she got were their offices at the college. After a moment's thought, she went to the Tarbox Beals website and clicked LOG IN. She knew that the office manager, Mrs. Feeney, had access to everyone's address. The school's emails all had the same format: first initial, last name, at tbschoolny.com. She racked her brain for Mrs. Feeney's first name, then remembered it by picturing her cluttered desk with its plastic nameplate: Darlene! So, dfeeney@tbschoolny.com. Now the password. Mrs. Feeney had a cat, everyone knew it was called Paws, the desk had a picture frame with the name on it. Chloe tried *paws, pawscat, pawspurr, catpaws*. There were grandchildren too, right? Aiden and something? She talked about them every time you needed to borrow a stapler or whatever. It was something weird and annoying, like Rebel or Raven.

Revel! Aiden and Revel. She tried both, and *aidenrevel*, and *revelaiden*, and nothing worked. She tried *password, pa$$word*, and *1234567890*. Nope.

This whole time, Chloe's fingers and toes were twitching, and she was pitting out like crazy. A lady came in and she panicked but it turned out she was just looking for the nail salon that used to be here when the mall was still normal. Eventually Loretta returned and praised the meager work Chloe had done as Chloe hastily closed her browser. "You've mastered the cutter?"

"Uhhhh, I guess? You have to rotate the clamp for the different car keys, right? That's the part I'm not sure about."

"Yeah," Loretta said, coming around the counter to demonstrate. She gripped the clamp handle on the machine and adjusted it. "If there's a centerline on the key, you put it here, and if it's off-center, here, okay? Honda and Mazda are the ones where you have to move it to A. You'll get it with experience."

"Okay, thanks." The backpack at her feet radiated deception; she half expected it to start shrieking an alarm.

"By the time I leave next week, you'll be able to take over this part of the business, and you can continue with the online course."

"It's a lot to remember." Glancing down, Chloe saw the tie-dyed sleeve of her NERDSTOR, NEW DORK tee shirt poking out of the cardboard box.

"You'll get it! And I'll always be just a phone call away."

"Unless you're busy, like, slamming some redneck's arm in a car door."

"I can multitask." Loretta smiled, so Chloe smiled, then worried she wasn't smiling hard enough and smiled much harder. Loretta asked if she was okay and Chloe said absolutely. "I think I'll head out, if that's all right."

"Thanks for minding the shop!"

"Okay, then!"

"Okay!"

Chloe bent down to pick up the backpack and casually bumped the box with her elbow, pushing it farther back on the shelf. She shouldered the pack and edged around Loretta, who had turned to the computer. Oh god. She hadn't cleared the browser cache. Too late now.

At home, her grandfather was still out, thank god. She raced for her bedroom and reunited with her phone. She wanted to kiss it. She immediately texted Kay.

Where does Addison live

What for? came the reply a minute later.

I want to send her a letter to clear the air

OK. I dunno. It's a coldasack in a rich people neighborhood. I could ask my mom, she drives me there

This gave Chloe pause. She didn't want adults involved. It was already risky involving Kay, whose loyalty she hadn't yet fully earned. She was going to have to manage that relationship to keep her plans secret. But she didn't see what other options she had at this point. She texted, *Would you?* and a few minutes later Kay came back with *6 Cherry Tree Lane.*

Thank youuuuuu. Do you want to hang out soon

When

Tomorrow?

A very long pause before Kay typed *OK*. Chloe waited, but there was nothing more. It was clear that Kay wasn't going to help her out with this friendship. She texted back, *Awesome I will text you tomorrow maybe we can hang out downtown where do you live*

Downtown

Perfect later

She typed the address into the maps app and her heart sank—it was way out behind the college, in the hills, and of course the buses didn't go there. But she had a bike she hadn't used in a hundred years that she assumed was out in the crumbling shed where her mother and aunt used to smoke weed and talk about boys, or so they claimed. She could bus to Nestor College and bike out to Addison's place, then coast all the way home.

She needed darkness to fall. But she also needed to get out of here soon, before her grandfather came home, so she wouldn't have to explain where she was going. She ate a PB&J, shrugged on her backpack, and left a Post-it saying she was having dinner at a friend's and he shouldn't wait up. Then she put on her sunglasses and ball cap and headed for the shed

The bike was a pink Schwinn with a white plastic basket that her Grandma Susan had bought her when she was eight. She remembered now why she'd left it in the shed—it was immensely silly. If she had undertaken this mission a year ago, she probably would have been too embarrassed to even get it out of the shed, but now it was like a little piece of performative nostalgia. Both tires were flat, so she wheeled it to the gas station on Route 13 and shoved a handful of quarters into the pump. The bike rattled and squeaked, but it rolled. She felt almost proud latching it onto the front rack of a city bus, then removing it ten minutes later at the Kunstler Center for the Ethical Advancement of Artificial Intelligence, the building Addison's father had funded and now worked in, creating the sentient computers that would someday rule over humanity. It was blindingly ugly in the setting summer sun, like an upturned laundry basket to which somebody had glued shards of broken glass. These were supposedly some new type of solar panel that subtly moved with the sun. She would have thought the building was kind of cool if it hadn't been the lair of her tormentor. After checking to make sure nobody was looking at her, she gave the building the finger, then let her phone lead her through campus and toward the woodsy hills where all the deans, economists, and science geniuses lived.

The neighborhood was called University Heights, even though Nestor wasn't a university but a lowly college. Not that Chloe knew the difference, and she suspected nobody else did either. It had a small commercial district with a couple of restaurants (filling up now that the sun was going down), some clothing shops, a community center, and a firehouse. Across from it was a wedge-shaped park with one rounded end, like an ice cream cone. All the streets here, she realized, went willy-nilly, at weird angles and in unexpected curves, probably to make people who didn't live here feel like they didn't belong.

It was working on her. As she leaned her bike against a park bench and pulled her backpack onto her lap, she felt like she was being watched, and probably was, by surveillance cameras. Loretta had a device that could check, she bet.

She pulled out the backpack's contents and switched the device on. The little screen showed a boot message and then a colorful line of text; the antenna unit blinked its LEDs, then settled into a steady green. Chloe realized she didn't know what she was doing. She unfolded the portable keyboard and tried to remember what Loretta had typed into it. After a few minutes' research on her phone, though, she figured out she wasn't close enough to any houses to sniff their locks. She bundled the tech, still powered up, into her bike basket and crossed the street to the sidewalk; now she could monitor people going in and out. Sure enough, the screen lit up with text whenever someone used their garage door opener or electronic door lock. A lady walking a dog passed her with a tight smile before veering off into her house; Chloe watched in amazement as the screen displayed the code the lady punched in. It was a shame it wasn't her house Chloe wanted to break into.

Of course, she wouldn't be able to break into the Kunstlers' house this way unless she was there when somebody entered. Maybe they'd hired somebody to bring in the mail or water the plants, but she'd have to be very patient or very lucky to intercept them.

She continued to wander around the neighborhood, taking to the street edge when the sidewalk ran out, the little display lighting up whenever somebody used a wireless or computer anything. What an amazing device! It was like a sixth sense. What would it be like, she wondered, to feel this invisible world with her actual body? The whole spectrum of phone calls, internet, Bluetooth, the plain old radio: signals that hadn't even existed for countless millennia and now filled the air as abundantly as, like, ocean waves crashing and the wind whistling through trees. Maybe animals were right this minute evolving new organs for detecting it. Or maybe this wasn't how evolution worked. A girl could dream!

The sun had set, and Chloe's phone informed her that the Kunstlers' place was just around the corner. This dead end was silent, wooded, and creepy. She could still turn back—it was all downhill from here, all the way to Mom's!—but no, she was committed. Whatever the consequences, Aunt Lila would back her up.

Addison's actual house was a mild surprise. It appeared at first to be almost quaint, a sort of chalet set back from the road and gently embraced by trees. Only when you got close did you realize how huge it was, getting larger the farther back it went, with all kinds of balconies and turrets and sunporches, and roofs going in all directions. Like a pile of wood and glass that had been dropped here and accidentally formed a house. Behind it lay a gigantic aboveground pool with a cover over it; the delicious smell of chlorine filled the air, and from inside a cedar shed—its own miniature chalet, Swiss as hell, with a cute eave and a bunch of little windows—came the thrumming sound of a water filter.

The shed! She was reminded of what Loretta told her—if you wanted to brute-force a lock, all you had to do was leave the device somewhere unobtrusive and let it work. Addison's family would be out of town for a while, right?

After a quick glance around, she entered the woods at the edge of the Kunstlers' yard, leaned the bike against a tree, and scurried up behind the pool shed. It had a simple wooden door with a loose-looking hasp and padlock. Hm. It was full-on dark now, so she crept out of the shelter of the trees to start trying the windows and was immediately terrified by the sudden illumination of the entire pool area by an automatic spotlight. She let out a small scream and held her breath, waiting to see what would happen next.

The answer was nothing. No alarm. It was a simple motion-detection light, probably more for convenience than security. It probably went on and off a dozen times a night, whenever a raccoon or fox ambled by. Luckily the shed was largely in shadow, and no neighbor was close enough to see it, so she checked each window, hoping one was unlocked.

As it turned out, none was unlocked or locked, because they didn't open. But she did find, to her delight, a key to the padlock sitting on the top of the frame, and a few seconds later she was inside.

It was warm and moist and close here. The filter resembled a big gray Minion and it burbled happily away. She placed the device on a shelf near the back window with its little solar panel directly beneath it and typed in the command she recalled Loretta executing back at the sad rich lady's place. The screen lit up with digits, a new series of them every couple of seconds. It was really doing it!

The lights outside the shed switched off, and Chloe was alone in the darkness. She laid her hand on the Minion and wished she could live here. She could just lie down in the corner on a pile of inflatable pool toys and forage for food at night. If it worked for the raccoons, right?

Instead, she pocketed the key, opened the door, and sneaked back into the woods as the motion lights flooded the yard. A minute later she was cruising back into town on her bike along the untrafficked suburban streets, feeling as marvelously, verifiably alive as she ever had. The wind in her face, the stars above, the hum of the bike tires beneath her—it was all so real, even realer than a movie. It was perfect.

10

Before class, the women milled around outside the conference center as they waited for Marin and Heather Wooster Steyer to show up. Shelly smoked a cigarette while Tilly responded to comments on her social media accounts. They got to talking about friends and relatives they'd grown apart from, mostly because of politics and conspiracy theories.

"I don't talk to my sister anymore," Kim said. "She told me my cancer came from 5G towers. The entire time I was going through treatment, I would get these printed-out articles in the mail, paranoid nonsense that made me feel worse. She signed my email up for newsletters about Fauci controlling world governments and Michelle Obama being secretly transgender. My spam folder is full of this garbage, I can't unsubscribe."

"My brother-in-law went off the deep end," Hannah said, accepting a puff from Shelly. "He wouldn't vax and got obsessed with the dead skin my sister and nephews were shedding. At first, she liked that he was finally cleaning the house for a change. But it got out of hand. He shaved the kids' heads and buried their hair in the woods."

"What!" Jane said.

"No," Tilly said, looking up from her phone, "I am not one bit surprised about that. I had a stalker who was into that stuff. First it was just dick pics, then I posted about getting vaxxed—this was right when it came out, when everybody was so excited and happy—and that set him off. He begged me to purge myself or something? Like, with bleach? And then he came to my town and tried to prevent me from voting."

"Jesus lizard!" Shelly said.

"The poll workers called the cops on him, but I actually talked to him for a minute, and he was just this kid, jumping out of his skin, telling me the voting machines had the same nano-whatevers as the vaccines, and the president was reprogramming people who came to vote. He was like, 'They don't have to change your vote anymore, they can change your mind!' I almost felt bad for him."

"I wouldn't," said Kim in a rare moment of sympathy.

Tilly shrugged. "I'm not saying he didn't scare the shit out of me. Just, after the cops took him away, I was like, sucks to be him. I got to go home afterward and have a Dove bar. He went to jail." She looked up at Shelly and Jane. "No offense."

"None taken," Shelly said.

Eventually Heather Wooster Steyer appeared, drifting toward them with Marin close at her heels. The group got settled in the classroom as the clouds parted, drenching the lake outside in sunshine.

"Who," asked Heather Wooster Steyer in an unflappably professional tone gently laced with barely detectable irony, "would like to offer Marin *one* item of praise and *one* item of constructive criticism?"

The tiny seminar room was silent save for the gentle rustling of notebook pages and the hiss of the air conditioner laboring against the relentless efforts of the sun through the floor-to-ceiling east-facing windows. It was Tuesday morning. Yesterday, the group had given notes on Kim's cancer memoir, which Jane had found engaging and—surprisingly—uplifting. The excerpt they'd read was an extended riff on the husband who abandoned her in her time of need, and she'd managed to imbue him with genuine pathos, processing his family trauma, his mother's death, and his father's absence in a way that the man himself had clearly been incapable of. Shelly said, "He doesn't deserve this," Tilly said it wasn't her kind of thing but it sure was well done, Hannah quietly wept, and Marin silently sulked. That night, Marin disappeared, but the rest of them gathered on the beach, drank their wine or seltzer, and laughed. Jane bonded with Kim over their divorces, Hannah with Shelly over their love of the New York Yankees. The whole day had been a pleasure from start to finish and, they'd thought, prepared them well for anything the morning might bring.

Then, of course, they'd all woken up and read Marin's memoir. Now they had to find something to say about it.

"Anyone?" Heather Wooster Steyer said. "Hannah? An item of praise?"

The young woman appeared startled. She brought her hand to her face and literally bit her knuckle. She said, "Uh...I appreciate the...uh...energy you bring to the page, Marin. It's, yeah, it's a lot. Um, and as for the criticism..."

"*Constructive* criticism," Heather Wooster Steyer reiterated.

"Yeah." Hannah flipped her notebook page forward and back as if hoping to discover a gentle tweak she'd forgotten about. "Uh...I think things could be more...modulated? It's all in one, I guess you could say, register. It's sort of on blast, if you get what I mean. Maybe your reader would like...a break now and then." She let out breath, clearly relieved to be finished.

Marin sat with her arms crossed over her chest and glared at Hannah. "Well, maybe some people aren't snowflakes who hate conflict, and you don't know what you're talking about."

"Marin," said Heather Wooster Steyer, "please remember, you're supposed to remain silent during this stage of the conversation. You'll be able to speak shortly."

"I don't find silence conductive to my needs as an artist," Marin replied. She was dressed today, despite the heat outside, in a big, baggy tie-dyed sweatshirt bearing the Coexist logo, a tiny pair of bike shorts, and thick-soled rave boots featuring five buckles, each a different color of the rainbow.

"Okay. Shelly?"

Shelly cleared her throat. "Yeah, well, this guy, the ex-boyfriend character? I guess I'm kinda interested in him, he's got some potential. But, like...I'm sure there's more to it than this, but you broke up with him because of...recycling?"

"He didn't respect the earth," Marin said. Across the table, Heather Wooster Steyer's mouth opened with a quiet pop, then closed.

Kim jumped in without prompting. "My praise is that this manuscript is absolutely deranged," she said. "I was never bored, I'll give you that. My criticism is that you made up the entire thing?"

Heather Wooster Steyer groaned. Marin said, "Oh, yeah? Maybe you did too?"

"Pardon me?" Kim said, genuinely shocked.

"You're just making stuff up to be a victim so everybody will suck up to you!"

Everyone started speaking at once except for Heather Wooster Steyer, who pushed her wheeled chair back from the table until it bumped into the wall. She remained there, waiting for the furor to die down.

The fact was, Kim was right—Marin had obviously made everything up. It was clear by now that she'd come here under false pretenses and was posing as an aspiring memoirist to get something out of Shelly, something that the notebooks—presumably in her possession, or perhaps already disposed of—hadn't managed to provide.

But what? After their encounter in the parking lot the other night, Jane and Shelly had tried to talk through the possibilities. Marin didn't seem like an emissary from some criminal enterprise, despite the break-in. She obviously wasn't any good at crime. Everything about her was fake. And so far she'd paid only cursory attention to Shelly with the exception of some long, puzzled glances. Last night, Jane had ventured out to spy on her after everyone had retired to their cabins. She saw a haggard-looking man a dozen or so years Marin's senior in the cabin with her, but the window was closed, so Jane wasn't able to make out their words. Marin was sitting on the bed, shaking her head, her palms out in a gesture of exasperation. She looked like she'd been crying. The man paced the room. He resembled the man in the surveillance video, thin and a little stooped. A pack of cigarettes was rolled up in the sleeve of his tee shirt. After a moment, he sat down and put his arm around Marin. Jane abandoned her hiding spot in the trees when they started groping each other.

In addition to being annoyed that Marin had sneaked a man into the conference, Shelly admitted that his presence just deepened her confusion. Jane agreed. They decided to wait and see what happened Wednesday, when Shelly's work went up on the chopping block, and if they were still confused, they'd just confront Marin.

But now it seemed like they weren't the only ones who'd been looking forward to confronting Marin. Tilly, who'd been uncharacteristically silent for most of the session so far, briefly tried to defend her, urging everyone to give her the benefit of the doubt, but somehow this led to Marin telling Tilly that her voice and hair were obnoxious and that she didn't need her pity.

After a few more minutes of this, Heather Wooster Steyer interrupted and said, "It isn't appropriate to question the veracity of the work. But it is appropriate to point out, Marin, that it doesn't *ring* true. Strange things do happen, sometimes so strange that you would never put them in fiction. But you have to present them to us using the kind of details that make them persuasive."

Everyone fell silent. Marin sulked.

"Also, I think Hannah's right," Heather Wooster Steyer went on. "The work is too eager to tell us how to interpret events. Just show them to us, let us decide for ourselves."

The conversation continued with the nominal participation of Marin, but she remained silent for the rest of the session, her jaw tight. When it was over, Shelly passed out copies of what she'd written for the session the next day, and the group broke up.

As they filed out, Jane and Shelly watched Marin speed-walk to the conference center's exit, flipping the pages of Shelly's manuscript. Wordlessly, they agreed to follow. Marin raced through the woods to her cabin, and the two women listened at the door. It sounded like she was on the phone. Her voice was largely muffled, but occasionally a phrase came through, amplified by despair.

Walking toward Shelly's cabin, the two of them compared notes. "Did she say something about a code?" Jane said.

"Also," Shelly said, "I could swear she said 'Ace.' I think it was, 'Not much about Ace.'"

"Ace as in *Ace*?" Jane said. "From Boynton?"

"Why the fuck would somebody be looking for information about Ace? They've been dead for years—leave them to rest, for shit's sake."

Jane tried to remember everything she could about Ace, whom she had known only briefly. They had been a beloved figure in that era of Boynton; with their shaved head and cryptic neck tattoos, their slight build and retiring character, they used to slouch through the inmates' daily routine like a friendly wraith. Ace looked like they would flinch if you touched them, hide if you called out their name—but in fact, they came to life when you sat down beside them. Their tired eyes sparkled, their voice cracked as though long disused, but Ace would tell great stories about their life as a runaway. They were young—in their mid-twenties then, Jane guessed—but seemed to have encountered a lifetime's worth of weirdos, grifters, and freaks, or at least had the gift of being able to describe them, to turn their random lives into coherent narratives full of hilarious twists and turns

Ace had also been good with technology and design. They described themself as an artist—a claim that, issuing from somebody else, might have resulted in an eyeroll at best or bullying at worst. But Ace was the real thing and the women respected it. Ace had their own notebooks, in fact, full of drawings of other inmates, any of which they would rip out and hand to its subject if asked. In those days, almost everyone's cell had an Ace portrait hanging in it. They had a way of bringing out, somehow, your most ideal self. In Ace's eyes, all the women were thoughtful and strong and beautiful. The mazes they drew and word puzzles they devised were distributed in a prison newsletter they'd started and that they managed to make look fantastic despite limited access to the computer, which was old and ran primitive desktop-publishing software, in the library.

Given a different kind of life, Ace could have been famous—a bestselling novelist or beloved illustrator. Instead, kicked out of their parents' house, a mansion (as they described it) in suburban Albany, for being queer, they drifted around the East Coast, living on the streets in various cities, becoming a junkie. Ace's mother, Ainsley Winter, was a Republican congresswoman, once a pro-business, anti-crime moderate, later radicalized by election conspiracies, and now mostly known for complaining about widespread voter fraud, election-machine hacking, secret fake balloting, and other debunked theories. Her voice tended to dominate hearings on these subjects, which were frequent and fruitless, and could often be heard blasting out of TVs in car dealerships, truck stops, roadhouses, and muffler shops across America. The story of Representative Winter's relationship with her child would probably have tanked the career of some public figures, but her voter base admired her for it, and she'd won her last election by a landslide.

As for Ace, they provided heroin to a friend who overdosed, and they were charged with manslaughter and sentenced to seventeen years, thanks to changes in state drug-prosecution laws that their mother had championed. When asked whether she regretted this legislation in the wake of Ace's conviction, the congresswoman said that, on the contrary, her daughter Katie deserved the sentence she was given, and she hoped that it would "cure" her. The misgendering and deadnaming were pointed and deliberate, and her constituents noticed.

But Ace, as Jane recalled, also thought they deserved the sentence.

The friend's death really was their fault, Ace would tell anyone who asked. And Boynton's state-mandated substance-abuse treatment had indeed gotten them off heroin, though Jane assumed that it was the queerness, not the drug addiction, that Ainsley Winter had believed needed to be cured. In any event, the Ace Jane knew was contrite and unembittered, and didn't complain about their mother. If they had lived long enough to earn a conventional release, Jane thought they would have thrived on the outside.

Jane and Shelly strolled in silence for a moment, then Jane said, "Do you think it's about their mother? Is somebody looking for dirt on the congresswoman?"

"Maybe? Although Winter cut them off, right? What could they have known that would do any damage?"

"Yeah," Jane agreed. "And it would be secondhand and several years old."

"I assume that bitch got Ace's papers and what have you when they died."

"Or whoever they were staying with did?"

"Well," Shelly said, "it wasn't me, so I don't know why I'm so fucking important."

"There's got to be something in Marin's cabin that identifies her. We should break in." To Shelly's brooding silence, she added, "Sorry. *I* should. Forget I mentioned it."

"Thanks," Shelly said with a grunt. "I'm not going back to prison for another drive-along."

"Right."

Shelly gave her a look. "Do you do this kind of thing all the time, or..."

"Over the past year, I've mostly been doing desk work."

"And your sister?"

"Yeah," Jane said, "she's in the field."

"You sound pissed about it."

"I am," Jane said. "It was supposed to be an equal partnership. And I guess it is, on paper. But when the rubber hits the road..."

"Lila's driving."

"Right. I'm sick of being sidelined."

After a moment, Shelly said, "Sidelined isn't so bad, is it? You've got your kid. Do you really want to risk your freedom so you can be a part of the action?"

"I hardly think Marin's going to call the cops on me," Jane said, bristling. They'd arrived at Deer D, Shelly's cabin. "And I'm not going to get caught."

Shelly laughed. "Listen to yourself! You sound like everybody in group therapy at Boynton!" Jane must have looked angry or offended at this, because she added, "Sorry, man, I'm not trying to be judgmental or anything. And I'm grateful you're here with me. Just…don't do anything stupid on my account. You know I can protect myself against these jackasses. I mostly just want your moral support."

"No, it's all right. You're right."

Shelly clapped a big hand on Jane's shoulder, and it let loose a flood of some unidentifiable emotion: nostalgia tinged with regret, a longing for some simpler time that probably never existed. In a flash, she missed her last days at Boynton Ridge, out of the main population, when she'd just held and nursed Chloe all day, waiting for her sentence to end. She missed being a child herself. She missed the feeling of having a mother.

Back in Owl C, Jane opened up her manuscript and ticked listlessly away at it. After fifteen minutes, she thought she might fall asleep, so she called Chloe. The call went to voicemail. She glanced at the time, lay on the bed for ten minutes. Tried to write some more, then opened a browser and started researching Ainsley Winter. If she knew more about the woman, maybe she'd learn who was pulling the strings.

Winter had graduated from NYTech in 1989 with a degree in industrial and labor relations, started her political career as an intern for an agricultural lobbyist, and eventually worked in her congressional predecessor's office as a staff assistant. She proved good at talking to the press and, as a conventionally attractive, articulate woman who seemed unfazed by reporters' aggressive questions, became a familiar figure in upstate politics. She ran for, and won, a seat in the statehouse, then ran for, and won, a special US congressional election after her boss died suddenly in office. She was the fourth-youngest woman ever elected to the US House of Representatives.

Jane's interest was piqued by a piece in the *Times Union* about Winter's recent divorce. Most congressional marriages went largely unnoticed by the general public, even when they ended; this article was buried deep on the newspaper's website. It had happened a year and a half ago. Winter's ex-husband was a real estate developer with lots of property on and near Lake Ontario and had never been a big part of the congresswoman's public life. He did seem to be the source of her wealth, though; Winter had grown up middle class in Ogdensburg, where her parents owned a hardware store. The two had met in college, it seemed. There had been no scandalous rumors or accusations before the split, and it was announced via a simple press release half a year after Ace died. The congresswoman was popular, and who would make a big deal out of somebody's divorce such a short time after the demise of her estranged child?

Jane wondered if there was something there. The congresswoman no longer lived in the house Ace grew up in; it had been sold in the wake of the divorce. An article from a year or so ago, this one about voting-machine crackpots, mentioned a conspiracy theorist who had accused Winter of "working for the other side" because her apartment in Albany was located next to a Chinese restaurant that had been closed as part of an organized-crime crackdown. The charges the restaurant owners faced were unrelated to elections or politics, but the (racist and, as far as Jane could tell, nonsensical) theory was so prevalent for several months that Winter had to publicly smack it down at a press conference about something else.

But what was the well-heeled Winter doing living in an apartment next to a restaurant in Albany? Jane had pictured a housing complex on a golf course or something, but no, a little more research turned up the apartment in question, actually a poorly maintained half a double on Jefferson Street, just a few blocks from the state capitol building. It was hard not to come to the conclusion that, however polished her public image, Winter had fallen on hard times since her divorce. Could this be connected to someone's search, via these obscure and mysterious means, for information about Ace?

Jane knew what it was like to have your life fall apart, how fast it could happen, how hard it could be to come back from. Before she turned herself in, Jane hadn't expected to live to her current age, let alone have a daughter, a reliable car, a job, an ex-husband. Even for a rich lady like Ainsley Winter, life could turn on a dime. Like mother, like child, she supposed.

And in an instant, she was actually interested in the memoir she was supposed to be writing. She'd describe those years, the ones that led up to her false confession. Let Shelly have prison life—Jane wasn't inside long enough to own the subject, anyway. Like mother, like daughter—she'd write about her estrangement from her own mother, and her fears of estrangement from her daughter, the one she was ignoring right this minute!

Rain began to fall and raked the cabin; it was extraordinarily noisy against the metal roof, and gradually came to blot out the entire world. For an hour and a half, Jane wrote about her mother's affair with George Framingham, then leader of the sisters' theater camp. About the complexity of her own feelings for him years later when he came to teach theater at her own high school. About the fateful party where he sexually assaulted her—and her rescue by Lila.

She had years and pages to go before she'd turned herself in for what Lila did, but that was enough for now. The rain was slowing. Hunger was gnawing at her belly. She snapped the laptop closed, slipped on a poncho, threw open the door, and gasped at the sight of a man standing just outside it. She'd nearly knocked him over, in fact. He was wearing a black hoodie and holding what she recognized, thanks to Lila and Loretta, as lockpick tools. He was haggard and pale with a scarred hatchet face, and she recognized the look of somebody who'd come back from addiction, probably meth, probably while in prison.

"What the fuck?" she said.

For a moment, he looked like he was going to run, and he did, but first he lunged forward and slammed his hands into her shoulders. As she hit the floor, Jane scolded herself for being caught off guard and for letting out a squeal of surprise. Shit, Lila was right, she'd gone soft! Gasping for breath, she got to her feet and peered out the door. There he went, racing down the path toward the parking lot, his sneakered feet flying like a child's. Jane went out, slammed the door behind her, and took off after him, passing a few startled women on the way. She followed him toward the parking lot, gaining on him steadily. His running style was highly inefficient, and he was slow, and as the parking lot came into view beneath the trees, she grabbed his flopping hood and jerked him back. He lost his footing, and the two of them tumbled to the ground.

Back when she and Lila were runaways, they'd learned self-defense from books, then YouTube, and later from a guy named Rayburn, an amiable Christian who ran a dojo in Flagstaff. They worked for him for a while, helping to bring girls to the business, most of whom were eventually driven away by Rayburn's friendly but off-putting proselytizing. The proselytizing was part of his three-point philosophy: fend off your attacker by using words first (that's where Jesus came in, in his case), the attacker's own momentum second, and violent force only as a last resort. Once, Jane had watched Rayburn flatten a drunk outside a Chili's after muttering, "May the Lord forgive me for what I'm about to do."

Jane didn't say that before, using muscle memory, she flipped her attacker over, planted a knee firmly in his crotch, and put a hand around his throat, more as a genial warning than an actual effort to inflict suffering. "What the fuck do you want, man?" she said through her teeth.

But she should have gone for the hands. She heard the knife before she saw it, scraping along the gravel on its way to her throat, and she rolled off him. He could have stabbed her then—she was supine and disoriented for a couple of seconds—but instead he flipped the knife closed, got up, turned around, and ran. Jane watched him climb into Marin's car—or maybe it was his—and peel off, gravel and mud spraying out behind him.

Panting, infuriated, she stalked back toward the conference center, muttering under her breath. The creep! She was going to wake up tomorrow aching and bruised. At least the rain had stopped; she was only a little wet from the scuffle. Outside the main building, still panting, she found Shelly walking with Hannah and Kim. "Are you all right?" Kim wanted to know.

"Fine, fine, just back from a run." She turned to Shelly. "Can I talk to you for a sec?"

They stood on a drainage grate under an awning that had been claimed as a smokers' porch. A couple of women stood six feet away, placidly puffing and looking at their phones. Jane filled Shelly in.

"What the fuck?"

"That's literally what I said."

Shelly sighed. "Well, I guess she's gonna fly the coop, then? I mean, good riddance, but I wanted to crack this case."

"No, listen," Jane said. "She doesn't know we know he's connected to her, right? Let's just pretend we're afraid because some man showed up and tried to get into my cabin."

"Okay, you tell Beth, I'll back you up."

"Also, about Ace. I did some research. Did you know their parents divorced, and their mom is living in a cheap apartment in Albany when Congress isn't in session? I'm beginning to wonder if the lady got into financial trouble or something and if Marin and this guy are connected to her."

"So what the hell do they want from me? Ace died. They were poor."

Jane had to admit she didn't have a clue. "But lemme do some more research tonight."

They went inside and told Beth what had happened. Jane left out the assault, which would just complicate the issue. And she didn't want to bear the burden of anyone's sympathy. Beth reacted with incredulity at first; it was clear she didn't want the problem to exist. But once it sank in, she found some resolve. Clutching her clipboard, she climbed up onto a chair by the windows and shouted for attention.

The room fell silent. People turned from the chow line and looked up from their plates. "It has come to my attention," Beth said, "that a strange man was seen attempting to enter one of the cabins. He was quickly chased off the premises. I don't think there's any danger. But should any of you see a thin man in a black hoodie, please notify me immediately. Meanwhile I will contact security and have them patrol the grounds, and please be sure to secure any possessions you have left unattended. I'll give you an update via email later this evening."

A hubbub ensued. A few women left their tables or their places in line and hurried off, presumably to check the locks on their cabins. Jane saw Marin, standing with a plate in her hand near the front of the line, and watched her carefully for signs of disturbance. To her credit, she didn't panic, but if she really wanted to convincingly fake it, she should have freaked out just a little bit.

Jane was mildly surprised when Marin joined them at their class's usual table. Kim arched an eyebrow at her, Hannah smiled uncomfortably, and Tilly said, "Wow, hi."

"Hi," Marin said.

Everyone ate, making small talk about the work they were doing. Jane told them she'd had a breakthrough and would be ready with work to pass out tomorrow. A murmur of congratulations went up. After a while, Marin said, "So, Shelly. I read your story for tomorrow. It's so good."

"Thanks, Marin," Shelly said warily.

"That person Ace sure seems interesting."

Shelly didn't glance at Jane. She said, "Yeah, Ace was something else."

"Was?" Marin said. "Oh no, did she die?"

"They died of leukemia a few years ago."

"That's so sad," Marin said, spearing a roasted potato with her fork. "It would be so interesting to hear more about her. They."

"Well," Shelly said, "I loved Ace, but they're just a small part of my whole project. What do you want to know?"

"I liked the part about the puzzles and what have you," Marin said. "I bet she—they—had a lot of puzzles and codes and stuff that they shared."

Shelly paused as though racking her brain to recover some dusty old memory. "You know," she said, "now that you mention it, there was one thing Ace always used to say, and I never knew what it meant. I always wondered if it was some kind of mystery they wanted us to solve."

Voice trembling, Marin said, "Oh, yeah? What was that?" She popped the potato into her mouth and chewed fast, rabbit-like.

"Something about a horse. Or a...shadow. Do you know what I'm talking about, Jane?" As Marin's head swiveled to Jane, Shelly shot her a pleading look.

"Uh, you mean that thing about the...horseman's shadow? And it was touching something, right?"

"That was it. The horseman's shadow."

"Touching the compass rose!"

"There you go."

"Whenever things were uncertain, or somebody was worried," Jane said, "Ace would just wink and say, 'The answer lies...'"

"'Where the horseman's shadow touches the compass rose,'" Shelly said.

"Which, what on earth does that mean?"

"It has to mean something, knowing Ace."

The other women listened with interest, not seeming to know whether they were kidding or not. Marin, however, was all in. She wolfed the rest of her meal and scurried off with a muttered goodbye. They watched her speed-walk out the double doors and down the path toward the cabins.

Back in her cabin later that evening, Jane opened her laptop and worked more on her memoir. Darkness fell. She was getting tired, her shoulders were killing her, and she wanted to shower and go to bed. She saved the file, and then, as a quick and dirty backup, sent it as an attachment to her Perks email account.

Curiosity kept her from getting ready for sleep, though, and she dived further into Ainsley Winter's career. She learned that the congresswoman enjoyed tennis and horseback riding (a fortuitous coincidence, given the impromptu false clues they'd just fed Marin), that she was a devout Christian, and that she was for free speech and against woke corporations. No surprises there. Jane searched her campaign website and her official congressional web page for a directory of staff members, but it didn't seem to exist. She did, however, turn up a list of salary disclosures, arranged by year, going back decades in the congresswoman's career. These were alphabetical listings of everyone in Winter's employ, what they did, and how much they were paid. So Jane opened up Lila's custom search application and began looking for information on each staffer and former staffer.

It took about fifteen minutes to hit pay dirt. Four years ago, around the time the congresswoman's marriage was collapsing, around the time she went all in on election conspiracy and culture-war grievance, she employed a woman named Imogen Freele as "assistant regional liaison" in her Albany office. Freele earned a paltry $17,500 in this position, and seemed to have been in it for about a year and a half.

Imogen Freele didn't seem to have any social media presence but was identified in a few of Winter's publicity photos from the time, including one celebrating a rural broadband initiative, and another the reversal of military personnel cuts at Fort Drum. At the broadband event, Freele was one of several people wearing matching black tee shirts with a yellow logo too grainy to make out and giving a thumbs-up. The Fort Drum photo was clearer; in it, she was standing off at one end of a line of functionaries, wearing a white cardigan and a lanyard over a black dress and looking ill at ease. She also looked an awful lot like Marin.

Then a knock came at the door.

11

The previous night, Lila had been lying under the stars on a low hill somewhere east of Gratis, Ohio, at a campground whose eccentric signs she'd followed off of Route 40 and into a grid of cornfields and pastures. It was unclear how the hill had ended up here, in this region of comically reliable flatness; maybe this was where the glaciers gave up the ghost ten thousand years ago. The signs depicted a couple of cartoon women wearing big glasses. WOMEN OWNED! the signs claimed. FAMILY ORIENTED! They led her down a lonesome two-lane that kinked around a small cluster of lakes, one of which the campground, Lazy Acres, overlooked.

Only one of the women was on duty this afternoon, an elderly lesbian with a pronounced limp and a trucker hat embroidered with a cartoon pig holding a knife and fork. She wore the glasses from the signs and said, "I could give you Eagle's Perch, that's up top of the hill. Or Bear's Den, in the woods."

"Is there something down on the lake?"

The woman nodded. "Here's a map," she said. "Why don't you take Salamander's Grove. Got a little woods, a little grass, a little lake. It's close enough so you can steal my Wi-Fi, password's *lazygals*."

"I appreciate that," Lila said. She pointed to a metal rack of snacks. "I'll take cheesy pretzels. And a ginger ale from the cooler, if you have one."

"A 7Up?"

"Sure."

Buzz Kill

"And how about a little firewood?"

A gravel access road led her to a hand-painted arrow marking her campground. The woman was right, it was a collection of Ohio biomes in miniature: frogs croaked, insects chirped, and the *saw-whet* of an owl sounded from across the placid water. Lila unpacked her folding stool and one-woman tent but after setting the tent up decided she didn't need it. The day was still bright but the sun and temperature were falling. She built a fire inside a ring of stones, ate her pretzels and drank her soda, then took out her laptop, connected to the satellite, and did a little research into the man who had handed her his card at the hotel, Rabbi Ephraim Luntschitz, and his son Avner.

She should have looked them up sooner. Luntschitz was the founder of the Holy Temple Center, an organization dedicated to ushering in "a great new epoch" in Judaism by building, on Jerusalem's Mount Moriah, the Third Temple. The first, Solomon's Temple, was known only through stories in the Hebrew Bible and was believed to have existed for several hundred years, until it was destroyed by Nebuchadnezzar and the Babylonians in the early sixth century BCE. Eventually the Babylonians were driven out by the Persians, and the Second Temple, later known as Herod's Temple, was built.

The Romans destroyed that one, and since then, two thousand years had gone by without a third being built. Constructing this theoretical Third Temple—"a house of prayer for all nations," the Torah said—was seen as a sacred ambition by some Orthodox Jews; it would bring about the restoration of certain ancient traditions along with a new flowering of the Jewish faith that would unite the world in peace.

That was Rabbi Luntschitz's goal, anyway. His website was a charming mishmash of outdated CSS and cornily Photoshopped images of the Temple Mount glowing with God's light, and his message of relentless optimism and good cheer was laced with frequent exclamation marks. Lila was confident that the entire site had been written by the man she'd briefly met in Oklahoma City.

Lila clicked a menu item marked RED HEIFER. This was clearly where Travis Nutt had come in. According to the Bible, in order for the Third Temple to be built, a perfect red heifer had to be sacrificed. The requirements for this animal were stringent, having been derived from rabbinical interpretations of biblical verses. According to Luntschitz's site, the heifer had to be at least three years old and "of perfect redness. Two or more hairs of any color other than red will disqualify the animal!" Even the hooves had to be red, and the heifer was required to be "absent any physical deformity or imperfection whatsoever, *external* or *internal*!" The heifer could never in her short lifetime have been used for labor. "This would seem very simple!" the rabbi wrote. "But in fact the heifer must experience *very special treatment* to avoid even the remotest hint of exertion in the service of work. She must never be yoked or ridden, and so, it is best never to so much as touch the animal except to protect her from herself. One cannot so much as reach over her or lean against her."

The result of all this was that the heifer was nearly impossible to produce. Her care would require special facilities and techniques that lay outside the purview of most cattle breeders, and bringing an adequate candidate into existence would require nearly unachievable precision. And how would one determine whether a cow was internally perfect? What, in fact, would that even mean? Nutt, as a pioneer in genetically engineered livestock, must have been a very appealing partner for Luntschitz; in theory, he could use science to guarantee the total redness of a prospective heifer and probably had the kind of equipment that would enable a team of biblical scholars to determine whether her guts passed muster. There were several breeders mentioned on the site who routinely shipped candidates to Jerusalem for examination, but so far, none of these rouge ladies of leisure had been approved for slaughter.

The rabbi's site didn't mention what became of the rejects, but Lila supposed they were slaughtered anyway, outside the holy trappings reserved for the One True Cow, and eaten. Maybe there were some nice red handbags out there, who knew.

Luntschitz had denounced Nutt as a madman, someone who wanted to destroy. Lila did a quick search for Christian takes on the red heifer, which were unsurprisingly absent from the rabbi's site, and learned that some Christians believed the building of the Temple would result in the Second Coming of Jesus and that this would cause the Jews to accept him as their savior. Some people who believed this thought this would be a good and peaceful outcome, and others thought it would bring about the rise of the Antichrist and the end of the world.

From the rabbi's words, he seemed to have the idea that Nutt was in the latter camp.

Darkness was falling. Lila had been dimly aware of an increase in noise from up on the hill—apelike hoots and recreational squeals, little snatches of music coming from a phone. Somebody had shown up and camped out on Eagle's Perch, she guessed. Women were issuing jokey groans, the kind they used to protest male behavior that they truly objected to but weren't willing to risk seeming uncool to stop. Lila was good at tuning this kind of thing out, but it was about to become unavoidable: here they came, crashing through the shrubs that separated the various campsites, the men entirely nude, hands cupping their dicks, the women reluctantly shrugging off their bras. There were five of them, all in their twenties, probably drunk and stoned. One of the women streaked determinedly after the men, but the other two paused by Lila's fire. "Hey," one said, panting and pointing at the ground. "You mind?"

Lila snapped her laptop shut and gestured toward the grass. The two lowered themselves and, as if compelled by some internal synchronization, sat cross-legged and folded their arms over their chests. They were similar in appearance, narrow-hipped, straight brown hair. The shorter one seemed nervous; her cheeks were flushed and she bit her lip. She was cute and kept looking over her shoulder at her friends, who were now screaming with horrified delight in the intensely cold water. The taller girl had large, expressive eyes and idly clenched the toes of one foot, smacking her flip-flop against her heel. She peered into the fire, sighing.

"Water's a little cold for skinny-dipping," Lila said.

"Tell me about it," said the nervous girl.

The tall one said, "Come on, Gaby, this is your chance."

"At what?"

"Caleb."

The girl sputtered. "I don't want Caleb!"

"You've always wanted Caleb. Even when he was with me." Tall laughed at her friend's reaction, which was an expression of obviously feigned shock. "It's okay, he wanted you too. I mean, we did break up."

Gaby turned to Lila, leaned in. "Caleb's married."

"Not to me," said Tall. "Some lady in Cincinnati. Separated." Warmed by the fire, they let their arms fall, stretched out their legs. She turned back to Lila and added, "*Recently* separated."

"You guys are what," Lila said, "college friends?"

"High school," Tall said. "All back in the area coincidentally. Caleb's camped out in his folks' basement, licking his wounds. Becca's sister got married in Bellbrook over the weekend. Gaby's mom broke her ankle and she's helping out. Kev still lives here."

"Well, in Dayton," Gaby said. "Kev owns a party-rental store with his brother. He had the tents."

"Sorry about your mom," Lila said. And, to Tall, "How about you?"

Tall just shrugged. "I'm Brooke, by the way."

"Brooke mysteriously appears and disappears, that's her job," Gaby said. From the lake came demands for the girls to come and swim. Lila could make them out, pale streaks in the dark. A meteor shot across the sky above them, but only Lila seemed to notice it.

"I work for a logistics company," she told Lila, leveling a direct and lingering look.

"Gaby!" came a voice from the lake. One of the boys was waving his arms. The other had the third girl on his shoulders; with a yelp, they fell backward into the water.

"All right," Gaby said, standing and stretching. "I'm going in. Wish me luck."

"He's the one who needs the luck," Brooke told her.

"Haha. I meant luck at not getting a fucking heart attack." She gathered breath, let out a scream, sprinted down the grass to the shore, and dived in, barely making a ripple. A moment later she popped out in front of Caleb, sputtering and swearing. Lila and Brooke watched the others playing, watched the stars.

"Got something for you," Brooke said, eyes on the lake.

"I'm probably not into it," Lila said, "but thanks."

She turned, scratched a bare ankle with her toe. "Oh, I see. No, not drugs."

What, then? For a moment, Lila wondered if she meant sex. A little jolt of desire ran through her, and she felt annoyed with herself for feeling it and with the younger woman for making her feel it. Brooke shifted her legs now, turned a little, offering Lila a better view.

"I mean a package."

Now Lila locked onto the woman's eyes. "What?"

"You're Lila, right?"

Every muscle in her body tensed.

"Easy," Brooke said. "I'm not a threat."

"What the fuck is this?"

"Just trying to combine business and pleasure. Relax."

"Don't tell me to fucking relax."

The girl sighed. "I don't work for a logistics company. I'm a courier. I got a call."

They stared each other down. Lila pointed at the lake, said, "And all of them?"

"High school friends. For real. We were out for beers and I was brought a package and told to come here. As it happens," Brooke said, scratching the leg with her fingers this time, "we used to come every weekend the summer before college. Once more, for old times, I said. A nostalgic brainstorm."

"This is sloppy. You shouldn't have brought them."

"It's good cover, though, don't you think? Better than just telling them I had to leave," she said with a shrug. From the lake, splashing and screaming. "Anyway, it's a document." She smiled, looked down at herself. She seemed amused by her nakedness, the play of firelight on her body. "I don't have it on me."

"Go get it."

"Happy to. I'm gonna take a dip right now, though. Maybe you'd like to join us. Join me," she amended, expressionlessly meeting Lila's gaze.

"How old are you?" Lila said.

"Twenty-six." When Lila didn't react, she went on. "My dad was air force, he's retired now. We traveled a lot when I was a kid, but when I started high school he was working at Wright-Patterson." She gestured east with a nod of the head. "After college I said I wanted to work in government so he recommended me for a job at the National Archives. That led me to the GSA under Homeland Security, and eventually somebody tapped me for interagency work. I like it. I'm technically employed by Central Intelligence, but I pollinate a lot of flowers." She winked, slipped an elastic band off her wrist, tied her hair back. "In case you're interested in my *story*. So. How old are *you*, Lila? I'm guessing…seventy-five."

"You shouldn't have brought your friends."

"Let's go swimming."

"Let's go get my document."

The two gazed at each other for another few seconds. Then Brooke stood up, kicked away her flip-flops, pushed her panties off, and walked calmly into the frigid water. Lila noted a shudder moving up her back and across her shoulders. Then Brooke vanished beneath the surface.

"For fuck's sake," Lila said. She went to the Volvo, secured her laptop in the footlocker, locked the car, and stashed the keys under a rock. She returned to the fire, threw on a couple of extra logs, and took off her clothes.

The water was fucking excruciating. She was angry at Brooke for talking her into this and angry at herself for doing it. She swam out to where Brooke stood in chest-deep water waiting for her. The others seemed to have disappeared. The two of them were alone.

"Cold?" Brooke asked. Under the water, she took Lila's hand, pulled her closer. Lila let her. Brooke had a couple of inches on her. Her head was garlanded in stars.

"Do you seduce everybody you deliver documents to?"

"Sure don't. You're shivering."

"I miss the fire."

"No doubt that's where we'll end up."

In the morning, Lila watched Brooke crawl out of the sleeping bag, put her underwear on, and trudge up the hill through the shrubs. It was nearly six a.m. While she was gone, Lila pulled on pants and shirt and threw the last of the logs on the embers. She poked them with a twig until the fire was crackling again. Brooke came back dressed, carrying a Halliburton case, two tin mugs, and a dented percolator. She unlocked the case and took out a pen, a form for Lila to sign, and a manila envelope.

"I'm not going to open this while you're here."

Brooke scowled. "I'm not an amateur."

"Sorry." Lila signed, handed back the form, and went to lock up the envelope. Then she returned to the fireside.

"Time for a coffee?" Brooke wanted to know.

"Gotta get on the road soon," Lila said, but of course she didn't. "It'd be a shame to waste the fire, though."

Brooke nestled the percolator in the embers, then sat beside Lila on a log. A minute later she inched closer. The water boiled and the coffee brewed. When it started to smell good, Brooke used her hoodie sleeve as a potholder and poured the coffee into the mugs. They drank it.

"Maybe I'll see you again sometime," Brooke said. It was uncool. Lila liked it.

"Doubtful."

"Well."

"Well."

They undressed and climbed back into the bag. The sun rose and the fire died. "Wait here," Lila said as they got dressed again. She dug up her keys, went to the car, and took a rubber-banded stack of business cards out of the glovebox. She brought one back to Brooke. It read

PERKS LOCKSMITH SERVICES
"ALL OUR CUSTOMERS GET THE PERKS"

NORTH MAIN ST., RIVERSIDE
LOOK FOR THE BIG GOLD KEY

Beneath the text was a phone number.

"Riverside where?"

"Just Riverside."

"So whenever I happen across a Riverside, there you'll be?"

Lila shrugged. "I can be a lot of places."

Brooke kissed her. "Thanks for the perks. I'll call this one of these days. Here." She dug through her things, retrieved the pen. Took Lila's hand in hers and wrote a number on her palm. Lila stared at it, memorized it. Closed her fingers over it.

It seemed like they might say something more, but they didn't. Brooke turned and made her way through the hedge and didn't look back. Lila doused the embers, packed away her bedding, steered the Volvo out of the campground, and turned left onto the two-lane that led to the highway. She bought gas with cash and found a wide place in the road, far from any surveillance cameras, to pull over and examine the package Brooke had given her. She broke the seal on the envelope and pulled out three pages, fastened with a paper clip. The top one, a cover sheet, was bordered in red and bore the familiar SECRET label. Underneath that was a letter from Knight. It consisted of a single sentence.

Why haven't you called me?

Lila swore under her breath and turned to the sheet below it. It was a heavily redacted nth-generation copy of a document from a few months before. Knight had used a red pen to circle a passage in the middle of the page.

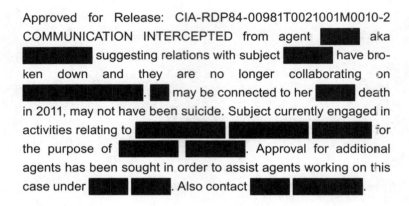

Lila sighed. The wind picked up; dark clouds were massing to the north. It would rain soon. She leaned into the car, got her Zippo from the glovebox, and set fire to the document and its envelope. Then she returned to the footlocker, pulled out a fresh burner, liberated it from its blister pack, and plugged it into the car's cigarette lighter. While she was trying to activate it, a passing SUV slowed and she looked up, ready to bolt or fight. But it was Brooke driving, with Gaby in the passenger seat. For a second it seemed she might stop. But she just raised a hand, honked the horn, and accelerated over the rise.

Lila snorted in self-disgust as she pushed a small measure of emotion away and punched in a phone number and then a code. A comically long series of clicks and buzzes ensued, as if the Agency's directory were staffed by rogue apes, randomly pulling and patching switchboard cables.

"Hold please for Knight," said a woman's voice.

"What, are you in a hotel room with him? Is he hiding in the bathroom?"

"I'm in Langley, ma'am. He is in the field and I'm trying to reach him."

She sighed. "Sorry. That was mean."

"I've heard it all, ma'am."

A couple of minutes passed. The ashes of Knight's secret communiqué skittered across the road in the wind. Finally he came on the line. "I assume you were already aware that something involving your mother is on our radar."

"I assumed," Lila said. A pickup rattled by, towing a couple of ATVs chained to a trailer. Country music issued from the windows.

"What hicksville are you in, anyway?"

"The same one you sent the courier to. I'm still here."

"Nice to know you're sleeping in these days."

"That's me," Lila said, "kicking back and watching the world go by."

"Maybe you'd like to meet, since you have so much free time."

"You know where I'm at."

"As it happens," Knight said, "I can get there lickety-split, thanks to the bottomless resources of the United States of America."

"Wow."

"There's a charming little spot east of Lewisburg called Dull Woods Diner."

"Jesus, Knight, where do you find these places?"

"Again, the bottomless resources of the United States of America. This is what you're missing, staying out in the cold."

"Access to spook Yelp? Kicking myself."

"Would you like coordinates or can you make your way there with your primitive civilian technology? I'll be there in an hour."

"I'll ask a farmer for directions," she said, and hung up.

It was shaping up to be a beautiful summer morning. On a long, straight, flat road north that separated two counties, she drove with the windows down, tried not to think about Brooke, gave up, thought about Brooke. Farms and horse barns. A suburb. Churches.

It wasn't clear to Lila why Knight was so preoccupied with her mother. Was it some kind of professional vendetta, an unquenchable fury about the agent who got away? Or just mommy issues? Either way, Lila was perpetually annoyed by the man's desire to return her to the fold, as though turning the daughter would send some kind of message to the mother. Lila had news for Knight: her mother wouldn't give a shit.

And yet Lila had to admit, she enjoyed the Agency's pining; everybody wanted to be wanted, right? Knight had been useful to her from time to time, and she had been useful to him. She hadn't liked it when he made her go to Panama and burn her mother's house down, but once the deed was done, she was glad she'd had the opportunity to do it. She hadn't felt so alive since clocking George Framingham in his tiki rape cellar.

Besides...she didn't like to imagine what it would be like to try and cut the man off entirely. Whether or not she could do it depended on how badly he wanted to keep her in his sights, and she feared she knew the answer: badly enough to make her life miserable by demonstrating the limits of her power and independence. She wasn't eager to learn what those were.

Knight had been quiet since Panama, and she'd taken it as a signal that she'd done well and had earned the right to be left alone. Now, just maybe, Knight was planning to offer her help. Or maybe he was planning to extort her again. Or both.

The diner, at the intersection of two country roads, was just somebody's modest ranch house—or what used to be somebody's modest ranch house. A new house, larger and uglier, had been built at the rear of the lot, a gable-encrusted McMansion nestled up against a cornfield, and this seemed to be where the owners actually lived. That's where their trucks were, anyway. Children played outside, and chickens browsed in a fenced area anchored by a henhouse.

She found Knight sitting by a window at a rickety table draped in a gingham tablecloth. The only other customer was an old man drinking coffee in the next room, out of earshot. Knight wore black pants and a windbreaker, despite the growing heat, and a collared shirt with no tie. He'd let his graying hair grow longer and it was combed over both ears, suspended there with some kind of gel. He looked no different from the last time she'd seen him, years ago, strengthening the impression of creepy agelessness. She said, "What a great place to meet. You blend right in."

"You must have me confused with someone else. I'm just taking a break from threshing."

"Har har." Lila lowered herself into the creaky cane chair that faced him and ordered black coffee from a skeptical-looking middle-aged waitress, doubtless the owner. She said, "It's hard to imagine this couldn't have been done over the phone. Or via the supersecret spy package you sent me."

"I'm old-fashioned. I like a little face time."

"Well, here you go."

"You're looking well," he said. "None the worse for wear, anyway, after your grand adventure."

"You mean stopping by Mom's? There have been adventures since then, Knight."

"Oh, we know. But it seems as though you're pretty eager to get back into the Mom business."

The waitress returned with two coffees and, for Knight, a thick slice of banana cream pie. For just a second, his sardonic leer dissolved and he gazed at the pie with genuine affection. "Aren't you going to eat?"

"Eventually," she said, sipping her coffee. "Please, tuck in. And no, I don't particularly want to be in the Mom business, but her holiness keeps popping up. I assume we're here to help each other out, so maybe you'd like to tell me what you do and don't know?"

"Your understanding of our relationship is charmingly whimsical," he said through a mouthful of pie.

"Come on, man."

Knight dabbed his lips with a paper napkin. Outside the window, a tiny child rumbled by on a tiny motorized SUV, a determined expression on her face. "All right, all right. I gather you've had contact with our mysterious cattleman, yes?"

"Glancing," she said.

"We've known about his connection with your mother for a while. There's some alchemy going on between the product that made his fortune and her product. Or at least there's widespread perception that there is, which is all that matters in this business."

"You haven't tested it personally, I assume?"

"Yes? No," he said. "I mean no, I haven't tested Yes. But we have. It's been tested, I mean. It doesn't have the aphrodisiac effect it advertises, or not any more than any other combination of that sort, but it sure does have some effect. Whatever you happen to want to do, you'll probably be more interested in doing it on this stuff. The main problem with it is, sometimes, instead of the little death, you get the big one." He seemed pleased with this joke as he forked up another hunk of pie.

"I guess your interest in it is to protect the American people from this deadly scourge?"

"Uh, no, not really."

"I was kidding, Knight."

Mouth full, he nodded his understanding. Once he'd cleansed his palate with coffee, he said, "I'm more concerned about the uses to which the drug's profits are being put. And I'm trying to figure out how involved your mother is."

"Are you talking about the cows?"

Knight gestured out the window. "I'm not sure how much of a kook your little cowboy is. Is this just a fun hobby, trying to bring about the end of the world? Or is he orchestrating something else with the heifers as a pretense? There are groups we suspect him of being in cahoots with, but it's proving hard to, you know, prove." He gestured to Lila with his fork, then speared the last pie hunk. "He reminds me of you, actually."

"Sorry, was that a compliment?"

"Sure was," he said, and ate.

"All I really care about," Lila said, "is what happened to my aunt. Once I have that information, I'll act on it, and I'll be finished. You can take the rest." She gestured at his empty plate. "Of the pie, if you will."

"I just did," he said, raising his mug. "And the surgical precision of your intent is admirable. If only my august institution possessed a shred of your restraint. Unfortunately, you are not going to be able to choose your favorite parts of this complicated business and leave the mess to us."

"Oh, no?"

He shook his head. "In finding out what you wish to know, you are inevitably going to find out things I want to know. And, forgive me, if you fuck it up, you could prevent me from ever knowing what I want to know. Or, worse, hasten the catastrophic outcome I fear our target desires."

"Not my problem."

For the first time, Knight betrayed a measure of genuine annoyance. "I don't believe you actually feel that way. Innocent people's lives could be at stake. You're not a psychopath."

She sighed. "Tell me what you want, please."

He removed a bankroll from his pocket, dropped a twenty-dollar bill on the table. "Don't make me have to spy on you. Don't make me have to stop you. Keep the lines of communication open. Work with me."

He seemed to be speaking in earnest. She said, "Do you know what happened to my aunt?"

"Not suicide, is my best guess. But no, nothing beyond that. I don't mean to be callous, it just isn't a priority."

"Understood."

"Is the husband alive? Have you found him?"

"We think so," Lila said.

Knight nodded, stood up, waved thanks to the waitress, who was on the way to collect his plate and mug. "Start there, then," he said. "And be a dear and tell me what you find out?"

"I'd expect the same from you."

"Deal," he said as though he were about to stick his hand out for a shake. But he didn't. "Drink your coffee. You don't want to fall asleep at the wheel." And with a wink, he was gone.

Back in the car, Lila looked at her watch, then her map. It was still early. She could get to her sister in a day or so if she took the interstate. They could compare notes, make plans. And maybe Lila could sneak a look at whatever Jane was writing. Maybe make a few edits. Maybe one big edit.

She pulled onto the county line road pointed north, and drove.

12

The day after planting the Bluetooth sniffer, Chloe met Kay at the playground on Nestor Square, the weedy pedestrian mall that interrupted traffic in the middle of downtown. The Square had seen better days, apparently, but Chloe hadn't been alive for them; now it was as scruffy and commerce-unfriendly as she'd ever known it to be. She had fond memories of this playground, of a wooden structure, smoothed by decades of hands, shaped like a castle. She used to sit on the benches beside it, eating black-and-white cookies from the old bakery with her mother.

Kay was waiting on one of those benches, buried in her black hoodie despite the heat. She raised her head at Chloe's approach and threw off the hood. Kay seemed both more wilted and more pretty today, like something growing in secret in the shade of a tree in some jungle, and Chloe felt kind of cool trying to become her friend. She said, "Hey."

"Hey."

"What do you want to do?"

Kay shrugged. "Walk around?"

They headed east, away from Nestor Square, past the tattoo parlors and porn shop that somehow still existed, the free clinic and the auto mechanics. Every minute or so they'd bump into each other and one of them would apologize. In the empty lot next to the abandoned firehouse, a little cluster of boys were milling around, their hats at weird angles, bouncing a gigantic pink ball. They shouted gross things and Kay gave them the finger. She said, "Pizza?"

"Yeah."

Outside Sicilian Experience, they sat in the alley. Chloe could smell a dryer venting someplace nearby; the sound of a video game came out of an apartment window. Kay said, "Yeah, so, my dad's cool and nice and everything is fine at my house, in case you were wondering."

"I wasn't?"

Kay glared.

"Seriously," Chloe said. "I don't even know what you're talking about. I'm glad you like your dad." When Kay averted her eyes, she added, "That sounds wrong. I totally mean it."

"It's like," Kay said, "my dad grew up poor, my mom grew up rich. My grandma put me in Tarbox Beals, and then my mom died, and my grandma doesn't like my dad, and it's this whole thing. I assume everyone at school knows this."

"Oh my god," Chloe said. "My grandma's rich and put me in Tarbox Beals too." Then she gasped. "I'm sorry! I'm sorry about your mom, I should have said that first. I didn't know any of this."

"It was a while ago, it's fine. I mean," Kay said, "it's not *fine,* but you know what I mean."

"My parents are divorced and my grandma hates my mom, but it's mostly just funny now. I was very mad when all that happened."

"Well," Kay said, "I was sad about my mom, but yeah."

"I didn't mean—"

Kay waved a hand in the air. "It's whatever, it's cool, I know what you meant."

They were silent for a long while. They ate their slices. Chloe tried not to watch Kay too carefully but stole glances at her while pretending to gaze down the alley at the back of the dry cleaner's. She'd always seen Kay as just a depressed stoner or something—one of those lifeless kids who don't care about anything, or pretend not to. But Kay seemed different to her now. Where before she'd seen laziness, now she saw... restraint. Where before she'd seen a follower, now she saw somebody who just did her own thing. Chloe had gnawed her slice down to the crust, so she set it down on her paper plate and said, "So, why are you friends with Addison? Not that you shouldn't be, just..."

"I know, it's weird."

"Not *weird,* just—"

"When she started talking to me, I was like, what do *you* want, bitch? Her whole deal is, like, straight out of *Euphoria* or something. But she turns out to be kind of secretly interesting. She's into noise music and survival horror and writes for hours in her notebooks, like, stream-of-consciousness made-up shit."

"Okay."

"I know why you're trying to be friends with me," Kay said.

"Why am I trying to be friends with you?"

A suspicious look. "You think I'm the weak link."

Chloe didn't say anything.

"But Addison's cool, and you're cool, and I think you should just be friends. Or, friends again, I guess. That's all." She sat up a little straighter. "Also, I lied to you about something. I didn't leave my phone unlocked. That's not how she got the video."

A little chill ran up Chloe's spine. "So how?"

"She asked for it. I showed it to her on my phone and she wanted it, so I sent it. I'm really pissed at her for the deepfake thing. It wasn't cool, it makes all of this seem like it's my fault."

"Wait," Chloe said, "why did you take it in the first place? Why did she want it?"

Kay shrugged and, to Chloe's surprise, allowed a little smile to cross her face. "You were being funny, that's all. It was"—and now she legit grinned—"a *precious moment* I was trying to capture."

After a silence, they both broke into hysterics. Chloe pretended she hadn't noticed that Kay ignored the second question.

They walked to the inlet and watched college crew teams racing boats. Clouds rolled in over the lake and the temperature dropped by ten degrees. Chloe thought it would rain, but it didn't. Her phone buzzed with a notification and she glanced down at a text from Loretta: *Have you seen the Bluetooth sniffer?* Chloe replied with a shrug emoji. She tried to suppress the waves of anxiety rising in her by observing the waves of water the wind was making. There was a path that ran northeast along the lake and they followed it to the farmers' market, where they bought strawberry lemonades and talked to some toddlers who wanted to engage in speculation about the new dog their dad was bringing home. Her grandfather texted, said something about going out to dinner with a research subject and he'd be home late, was that all right? She told him sure, she was going to bed early. There. That left her some cover unless he was in the habit of peeking in on her at night, which she doubted.

She and Kay took the path past the sewage-treatment plant and hospital annex to the city park and then over the footbridge toward town. A couple of black pickup trucks rumbled by, equipped with roll bars and jacked up on big knobby wheels, flags flying. One driver, a redneck in sunglasses and a yellow ball cap, leered out the window at them, shouted, "Hey, girls!" The guy laughed at Kay's middle finger and gave her a thumbs-up. At some point Chloe would have to eat again, and she was plotting some way to do this with Kay—maybe she could invite her over for pancakes or egg salad or something? Would that be weird?—when another text came in from Loretta. It read *Call me ASAP* and was accompanied by a screenshot of Loretta's phone displaying what appeared to be random numbers, but that Chloe soon realized was a notification from the Bluetooth sniffer telling her that the Kunstlers' door code was 830672.

"Oh, shit," Chloe said, coming to a dead stop.

"What's up?"

"I have...uh, I have to go."

"Okay?"

"I mean, we're already going, I guess. So let's keep going. But then I have to go home and, uh, do something."

"What's up?" Kay asked again. She didn't seem offended or anything, but she was clearly very curious.

"It's about...I have to help my grandpa."

Kay laughed. "No, you don't! I mean, you don't have to tell me if it's private, but don't lie."

For a moment, Chloe considered telling her. But...Kay would try to stop her. Which probably meant that she should stop? Which was not something she wanted to think about? The entire situation was very upsetting. She said, "Uh, sorry, yeah, no, it's not my grandpa, but I can't talk about it. Yet."

"That's cool," Kay said and kept walking.

Chloe trotted to catch up. Kay seemed to be walking faster than before. "I really want to tell you, I just can't."

"No, I get it."

They walked briskly and in silence. Not a terrible silence, but not the same easy one as before. Chloe considered just bailing on the sleuthing, confessing to Loretta, and telling Kay everything over egg salad sandwiches, but then Kay said, "This is my turn," and Chloe said, "Oh, okay, cool," and Kay said, "So, yeah, see ya," and Chloe said, "Text me?" and Kay said, "Sure," and she was gone.

Well, damn. Chloe went home, considered cooking for herself, then made a PB&J again and ate it with a glass of water. The house was silent. Loretta kept calling—Chloe let it go to voicemail—and texting: *Chloe, what are you doing? Please call back. Don't do anything foolish.* She realized that eventually Loretta would just drive her rental car down here and that, if Chloe was going to execute the plan, she should leave immediately.

She powered down her phone and left it on her bed. She threw a water bottle into her backpack, got on her bike, and rode to the bus station, where she hoisted the bike onto the rack and rode up to campus the way she had yesterday. This time, when she got off, Addison's father's building, the one named after him, appeared menacing, reflecting the low orange sun through racing clouds, and she turned away from it.

She tooled aimlessly around until sunset and returned to the woods she'd entered the night before. There, she sat at the base of a tree and pondered the correct approach. Maybe she shouldn't have gone into the woods at all—it would be better to be caught pretending to belong than to be caught sneaking. She could have just ridden her bike up the driveway, dumped it on the ground, and walked in like a house-sitter. She wished she'd thought of this sooner.

In the end, she decided the best thing to do was retrieve the sniffer, stash it with her bike, and go in the back way. The floodlights would turn on, but if she punched the code in quick enough, she'd be inside before it occurred to anyone to see what was going on.

But did the back door have a digital combination lock? She moved through the trees trying to get a look, but something was always in the way—the shed, the deck rail, the pool, a bush. If she wanted to go in the back, she was going to have to just run up there, assess the situation, and either punch in the code or return to her hiding place as quickly as possible.

Okay. It was time. She crept up to the pool shed without triggering the lights, retrieved the key, unlocked the door. The sniffer was undisturbed there. She switched it off, stashed it in her bag, and returned to the trees to hang the bag from the handlebars of her bike. Then, before she had a chance to chicken out, she strode out of the woods, up the steps, and across the deck to the door. The floodlights came on and she had to shield her eyes from the glare. But there it was, another keypad. She punched in the code the sniffer had produced and the lock disengaged with a click and a hum. She stepped inside and shut the door behind her.

The house was quiet and smelled like nothing. She was in the kitchen, which was dominated by a huge marble island and a skylight above it. The floodlights outside switched off, and suddenly Chloe could see the stars and moon, and the wisps of clouds zooming beneath them. "Okay," she said out loud to herself and began to move through the house, exploring.

For rich people, the Kunstlers didn't seem to have much stuff. There were some abstract paintings on the walls and a couple of sculptures in alcoves; they had the same big TV everybody but her grandfather had, in a spacious but somehow cold living room dominated by a fireplace with no wood or ashes in it. (*Give them some credit, Chloe,* she told herself; *it's summer, maybe they just keep it clean.*) The wood floors were unscratched and, she realized after a moment, weren't wood but some kind of woodlike synthetic substance. Oriental rugs were everywhere.

She peered into the parents' bedroom, which was neat and unremarkable, and Addison's, which was the same. At some point in her past, Addison seemed to have stopped updating her room. The bed had stuffed animals, doubtless from her childhood, and the walls had posters of, like, *How to Train Your Dragon* and *The Lego Movie* and *The Force Awakens*. In the closet she found a box of Hatchimals and LOL Surprise dolls, a BB-8 robot, and the box for a Nintendo Switch that she doubtless had taken with her on the trip. There was no computer here—presumably that had gone along too.

There was a home office between the two bedrooms, and Chloe assumed it was the dad's. An iMac sat on a desk, and there was a bookcase and a leather couch. The desk drawers were full of junk—old USB cables, a portable hard drive, sticky notes. Only now did it occur to her that computers had passwords—how was she supposed to get in? She sat at the desk and touched the computer's keyboard, and the screen offered several users—Mom, Dad, and Addison—each represented by a little cartoon version of each person. Dad's and Addison's accounts each asked for a password, but to Chloe's surprise, Mom's did not. She clicked it, and it let her right in.

Mom's desktop screen was a mess—icons everywhere, overlapping each other, not even locked to the grid. Most of them seemed to be business stuff—invoices, spreadsheets, that kind of thing. She opened up the photos app and found the family's entire past, going all the way back to Addison's birth and before. Addison was cute right from the start, with big expressive eyes and a big lock of hair. Also, her mom was pretty. There were photos of her nursing the baby, her breast exposed, and Chloe quickly scrolled back to the present, embarrassed.

She was briefly alarmed when new photos suddenly appeared of the family at Disney World. Addison was posing in a full Rey costume wielding a lightsaber, and it was so corny it was cool. Her dad wore exactly what he probably did at work, an oxford button-down tucked into blue slacks, and her mom wore a black ball cap and a black tee shirt with a cartoon bee on it. She was giving a double thumbs-up, except with the thumbs bent at the knuckle, for some reason. They were in line at the Tron coaster. Chloe supposed they had their phones synced with this computer, and the pictures were appearing automatically. They were obviously having fun together, and Chloe felt bad both for spying on them and because she'd never really had this kind of fun with her parents. Not that she'd longed for it before, but she did now. She closed the app.

She sort of wanted to just leave. Instead, she decided to do her due diligence and opened the applications folder. Alongside the apps the computer came with and some business stuff, she found Blender, the graphic design app, and when she opened it, it loaded the last project the user had worked on, which was a picture of her.

Of *her,* Chloe!

The picture was a frame from the cafeteria video. She clicked on the collections tab in the menu on the right, and inside it were Kay's original video, a video of her giving a debate speech, and a bunch of photographs of her that she supposed Addison had taken. When she clicked playback, the active project ran, and the video proved to be the fake that had started this whole drama.

It wasn't Addison's father who had made the video. It was her mom.

She closed the app and put the computer to sleep, then sat there in the dark trying to process this information. Why had it made sense when she thought it was the dad but didn't now that it was the mom? Chloe didn't know anything about the lady other than that she worked at Nestor College. Was she one of those power moms who would stop at nothing to advance her daughter's career?

What would it be like to have one of those?

Chloe became aware of a change in the ambient light through the windows—a blue and red pulsing. Now she heard car doors slamming. She looked over her shoulder and out an alcove window across the hall, and there, at the curb, were two police cars. Four cops were coming toward the house, and as she watched, two peeled off to cover the back.

The house must have had an alarm. She was going to get arrested. Without thinking, she threw open the desk drawer, grabbed the portable hard drive, and shoved it into the back pocket of her jeans.

Everything after that was automatic. She sprinted down the long upstairs hall toward the woods-facing side of the house. She tried to remember the confusing pattern of gables and rooflines she'd sneered at yesterday when she'd cased the joint, but couldn't bring them to mind. *Note to self: case better.* At the end of the hall there was a double-paned window behind a little wooden table bearing a vase of plastic flowers. With shaking hands, she disengaged the lock and threw up the sash, knocking the vase over. She could hear the cops banging on the door; doubtless they had the combination and would be inside in seconds.

A window screen was blocking her exit to the roof, and she couldn't figure out the mechanism for getting it open, so she pushed the little table aside and kicked it. Its white plastic frame bowed and snapped, and the screen clattered onto the roof. Below her, the cops said, "Stay where you are, we're police officers!" A moment later, another door opened—the other two had come in via the deck.

Chloe stepped carefully through the window and onto the roof. The night air was cool and she heard the cry of some bird. The sky had cleared and the wispy clouds stilled, and the moon traced everything in sharp relief. She crept down to the rain gutter and peered over.

There was a second roof below her, angling off to the left, and that one sloped right. Its edge was maybe a dozen feet off the ground. The trees were a bare few feet away, though—she could jump out, grab a branch, and break her fall. She didn't give herself time to be frightened—she hopped down, followed the roofline to its lowest point, and, after drawing a breath, jumped.

It almost worked. There was a big bushy fir down there, like a Christmas tree that had gotten out of hand. She got fingers around a bough and for a moment thought she'd just slide down the tree like she was exiting a burning plane. But the needles folded up and slipped out of her hand, and her momentum carried her off to the side, deeper into the trees, and dumped her onto the ground, hard, before she could put her hands out to cushion the fall. Her arm got trapped underneath her, and her breaking wrist was as loud in her ears, and in her nerves, as the thump of a bass drum. Her whole body screamed, but not her mouth.

She leapt to her feet. The cops were probably at the top of the stairs by now. Her bike was just a few yards into the cover of the trees—she could see it from here. In seconds, she'd made her way to it across the soft humus-y ground, gripped one handlebar with her uninjured hand, and pushed out the other side of the little woods. She was standing behind somebody's privacy fence on the block in back of Addison's house. There was no time to think about what to do next—she turned right, ran to the end of the fence, the bike clattering, then turned left.

It was dark. She was in a grassy declivity between two houses. She didn't want to look down at her arm, which she was clutching to her side, but she had to get the backpack on. It felt like the wrist was growing...like it was the size of a beachball and would shortly balloon to envelop her entirely. It was sort of numb now, but she could feel the pain lurking underneath the numbness, like the hump of a whale about to surface from the ocean. She started to cry, looked down.

It was bad. It was bent! The bone wasn't sticking out, that was a blessing, but it was just...not the right shape. She felt like she might pass out, so she took a deep breath and looked up at the moon. Imagined herself standing up there, looking back at the Earth. *See? It's just a blue-and-green ball, it's so far away, and nothing matters.* In school they told her that when people saw the first pictures of Earth from space, they thought it would end cruelty and strife, because everyone would suddenly realize that we're all in it together. Chloe thought more people had the opposite reaction: if it's all just a colorful dot, we might as well invade Ukraine.

Gingerly, she slipped the backpack strap under the wounded arm and up onto her shoulder. In a moment, she had the pack on and was wobbling out to the edge of the grass. She turned right and wended her way through the dark and quiet streets, trying to go generally downward and toward the lake, where the hospital stood perched on a cliff edge just off the county highway. Blood pounded in her arm and pain was coming in waves. A glance down showed her that swelling had commenced; she'd soon look like Popeye the sailor man. Police lights flashed at the edge of her vision, but she was in fate's hands now; if the cops found her, they found her.

But they didn't. She coasted, switching back and forth as she descended, over creeks and through woods, past the big stone houses where deans lived. She realized her wrist felt better if she whimpered, so she whimpered a little louder with every breath.

In the end, she discovered that she had miscalculated only slightly. She popped out on the highway a hundred yards south of and slightly downhill from the hospital. She had to pedal up the smooth incline as the headlights of oncoming cars blinded her. The pain was intensifying, radiating out to her shoulder and chest, and her heartbeat was a bully pushing her up against the lockers. An approaching sound from behind alarmed her—a chorus of roaring, sputtering engines, like a swarm of gigantic broken hornets—and she watched as a slow convoy of pickups, like the ones she'd seen earlier, rolled past her toward town. Most were jacked up, and all were flying flags: the American flag, but also the snake one, the Confederate one, a black one with a yellow cartoon bee. *Where did I just see that bee?* she asked herself. There were guys—and a few women—standing up in the beds of the trucks, and though it was dark, and though she was delirious with pain from her arm, Chloe thought some of them were holding guns, assault-rifle-type guns, across their chests, like military guards or something.

And then, at last, she was there. Through the parking lot to the emergency room entrance. Her breaths were quick and shallow now and she wanted to scream. She got herself off the bike and let it fall to the pavement and stumbled through the automatic doors and met the eye of a nurse before something in her just seized up and she fell on the ground.

Her last thought before passing out was that she was impressed with herself for having the presence of mind to twist her body to protect the wrist. *Great job, Chloe. Good night!*

A bunch of stuff happened: voices, movements, bright lights, loud beeps, and jabs in the arm. People asked her questions and she tried to mumble answers. Eventually everything calmed down and they left her to sleep. When she came to, there was a man in blue standing beside her and she tried to say, "I'm just a kid, please don't put me in jail," but she couldn't form the words. Also, the man turned out not to be a cop but a nurse. He was young and potbellied and when he heard her slurred voice, he said, "Oop!" and hurried out of the room.

It was still night, judging from the window beside her. There were other beds here, empty. Her head was elevated and she gazed down on her poor hideous arm, black and blue, the wrist as plump as a leg of lamb and immobilized by something she supposed must be a splint: a long piece of beige plastic secured by Velcro straps. Beneath it, the arm throbbed numbly.

She fell asleep again, maybe for thirty seconds, maybe for three days. Now there was a doctor, a tiny woman with a suspicious air. She said hello.

"Hi."

"We aren't sure who you are. The police say no children are missing. You are a minor, correct?"

"I'm almost fourteen," Chloe said. Her mouth was so dry. "Can I have some water?" The nurse from earlier, loitering in the background, ducked out.

"You said your name was Chloe. Chloe what?"

"Kelleher."

The doctor asked Chloe if she knew where she was and how she had gotten here. Asked her if she had any allergies, if she was on any medications. The answers seemed to satisfy her. Then: "Chloe, do your parents know you're not at home?"

"No. My mom's away for the week. I live with her and my grandfather. He probably thinks I'm in my room."

"Is your father in the picture?"

"Yes, ma'am." She was thinking more clearly now. The nurse returned and handed her a Styrofoam cup with a straw. In it was the coldest, most delicious ice water she had ever tasted. "I stay with him some weeks. He's on vacation with my grandma."

"Chloe, are you safe? Did someone cause this injury?"

"No, no. Just me being dumb. My parents aren't like that."

"Your grandfather?"

Ugh. "You'll meet him soon, I guess. He would never hurt me."

"Does your mother have a boyfriend or girlfriend?"

"Nobody is abusing me, ma'am."

The doctor stared at her and Chloe stared back. The doctor pointed at Chloe's backpack, sitting on a chair. She said, "We brought your backpack and bicycle in. There was no phone and no ID. Do you usually go out without those things?"

"Uh, yeah, I like to switch off sometimes. I left my phone at home."

"All that was in there was a digital device." She paused a moment to let that sink in. "A computer with an antenna?"

"I'm in the computer club at school. That's my project."

"Can you tell me exactly how this happened to you?" She pointed her chin at the splinted arm.

"I fell off a roof." Idiot! Surely she could have come up with something better than the truth?

"Okay. What roof?"

"My roof. At home." She thought about her father's house, an hour from here—her other grandfather, an idle, rich land developer, was wasting away there and had made Dad install this elaborate weather station on the roof so he could monitor the wind speed or something, for fun. "I was trying to install a weather station up there," she lied. "I was going to collect the data on my computer. And I slipped and fell."

"Where do you live, Chloe?"

She rattled off the address. "It's downtown, next to the creek."

The doctor was nodding. "So you were alone at home, where your phone is? And you fell off the roof, and, instead of calling someone, you got on your bike, with a broken arm, and rode it here."

Oh god. "I know it sounds stupid. I didn't want to worry my grandfather."

"You say he's probably at home now? We need to talk to him."

"Okay, sure."

"We need his phone number, Chloe."

"Oh! Sorry. Uh, I don't know it."

The doctor just looked at her.

"Well, come on," Chloe asked her, "do you know anyone's number?"

A raised eyebrow. "We could ask the police to go over there and tell him where you are."

"Oh god. No." The doctor stared, awaiting an explanation. "It's just," Chloe went on, "he's an old guy, I don't want to give him a heart attack."

"They could lead with reassurances."

They stared at each other.

"Please, no police," she said quietly.

The doctor sighed. "Why don't you tell me his name, and we'll try to get in touch. The police are all too busy to bother with you, anyway. There was some kind of demonstration and people are getting into fistfights on the Square."

"Wait," Chloe said. "The guys in the pickup trucks? With the flags and the guns? That was real?"

The doctor said, "I didn't see them, but that sounds like the ones. They paraded around trying to frighten people, and some downtown kids jumped onto the trucks at a traffic light and attacked them." She pointed with her thumb over her shoulder. "We've got both sides in the ED. Lucky for you, it's a big night."

"Lucky for me," Chloe said.

Around the time Chloe was headed out to meet Kay, Harry was an hour into his journey to the village of Ghorum, one of Chloe's library books—a rather lurid monograph about the Russia of the 1990s by a former rival he would rather not have the girl become a fan of—on the seat beside him as a prop, with the relevant sheet from the Factor's binders folded and tucked between the pages. He was thinking a little about how Alain Rampersaud might have escaped death, but mostly he was thinking about what he would say when he saw Peggy J., how he would frame his question to make it clear he also wanted to talk with her in general, not just about the history of a tiny island off the Brazilian coast.

Was this what people called a crush? He had been in the woman's presence for only a few minutes, but he was blushing, right now, alone in a car, thinking about her! He spent the rest of the ride muttering to himself or to the her in his head, preparing speeches, practicing his casual jokes. He got himself so worked up that when he arrived at the public library, he had to sit in the car for a spell with one leg sticking out the door. Two young women emerged from a nearby park, a rope extended between them, and half a dozen small children clutched the rope, like a tiny chain gang. They passed his car on the way to the library and the children peered in the open door to get a glimpse of the weird old man. Yes, yes, hello, hello. When the children had passed, Harry gathered his book and his courage and headed into the shady cool of the library.

Peggy wasn't there, though. Instead, behind the MARGARET T. JANSSON, REFERENCE LIBRARIAN nameplate (Jansson! He should have remembered) sat…some guy. Forties, little beard, little glasses, apathetic look. Just a guy. "Yes?" said the guy.

"Ah," Harry said, faced with possibly the only conversational scenario he had failed to prepare for on the ride here, "yes, um, I wanted to, that is…this book. To return it."

"Circulation," the guy said, pointing.

"Well, also," Harry added, "Mrs. Jansson, that is, Margaret, that is, Peggy recommended it. And I was going to thank her for the…ah… fascinating—"

"She's off today," said the guy.

"Oh. Ah. All right, then."

Dejected, he exited, dumping the book in the circulation slot on the way out. He felt excessively moist and floppy and wished he'd just put on a tee shirt like the drunk he used to be instead of a neat button-down oxford. He unbuttoned a button and rolled up the sleeves. Alas. Might as well eat alone the lunch he'd hoped to eat with Peggy Jansson.

And then he walked to the nearest, probably the only, restaurant—a little café called the Cake and Kettle, on the ground floor of an old hotel—and there she was. Alone! Eating a salad by a window and reading a book from the library he'd just left. She looked up and saw him at the hostess station and smiled. She recognized him!

"Hello, Professor," she said as he approached her table.

"Mrs. Jansson! You remember me."

She held up the book she was reading. It was his one and only. "After meeting you and your granddaughter, I decided to read it. It's very good!"

"Well," he said, "you're only halfway through."

"I've already finished. Just taking another look at the photos. Would you like to join me?"

How could this be so easy? He sat down and they talked about his book for ten minutes while he sipped a mug of coffee and waited for the sandwich he ordered. When it arrived, he experienced a moment of regret—no one can eat a sandwich tidily; what was he thinking?—then just...let it go. It didn't matter. This nice woman had watched a man eat a sandwich before. It would be fine.

Eventually he admitted that he'd come to town to see her. Her look of pleasure faded only slightly when he specified that he'd wanted her to answer questions about Plácidia and Alain Rampersaud. "There's a note in the Factor's journals about this coup—"

"I'm sorry," Peggy said, wiping her hands with a napkin, "the Factor?"

"Oh." He felt himself blush again. At least now there was someone here to be embarrassed in front of. "Franklin. Franklin Hastings. That's my...ah...private nickname for him."

"I'd love to know the story of how you came to have a private nickname for Franklin!"

"Haha, well, all in good time, I guess! Anyway, his notes say that he met this man, the onetime benevolent dictator, in person, despite rumors of his demise in, I believe, 1971. He had jotted this down with great excitement, it seemed to me—" He patted his pockets, searching for the note, but realized he had left it in the book he'd just dropped off at the library. "Oh no. Oh, dear." He explained to Peggy what he'd done, and she laughed—not in a mocking way!—and suggested they go recover the page.

In the library, she disappeared behind the circulation counter and emerged holding his folded page. "Come on over to my place," she said, handing it to him. "We can sit in the garden and puzzle over this." She led him through the shady streets to a charming bungalow with a fenced yard and a swing-bearing sugar maple. "For my granddaughter," she explained about the swing, "though I wonder if she'll have outgrown it by the time she comes again." Harry did some rapid math in his head.

"I'm sixty-three," she said, reading his mind. "Hailey is twelve and lives in Wisconsin. My daughter's a doctor there. They spent a lot of time here in the summers the few years after Paul, my husband, died, but this year they might skip it."

"I'm sorry."

"About which?" she said, leading him in the back door to a neat, old-fashioned kitchen decorated in shades of yellow and white. "My daughter being too busy to visit or my husband dying?"

"Both, I guess?"

"Thanks, Harry. It's been a while. Also, we were in the middle of a divorce. It wasn't pleasant, but I didn't wish the man dead."

"He died young," Harry said, wincing inwardly. "Pardon me."

She laughed at him. "Not so young. Your age, actually," she said, smacking him on the chest. A chill ran through him.

They sat out back, under the tree, drinking iced tea and eating cookies. Somehow the conversation got off track before it even began, or maybe this was the track it was always headed for. She asked him about his marriage and he talked for an hour. He realized he'd never done this before—actually shared the strange story of his marriage to Anabel—and at last recognized it for the astounding tale of international intrigue it was. "You're telling me that your ex-wife is literally an international criminal mastermind," she said.

"I...I guess I am?"

"I can't compete with that! Paul just got addicted to online conspiracy and wouldn't go on trips with me anymore. The whole point of retirement was supposed to be getting to enjoy your time! I went to Cairo by myself in 2019, then called a lawyer. It turned out Paul cashed in our retirement accounts—he was in aerospace engineering—and gave it away to congressional ghouls and weirdos. So, once he'd passed, I got my old job back. I actually like it much more now that I need it."

"You do seem to like it very much."

"I get to recommend books to strangers every day—that's something I'd happily do for free."

One thing led to another. They never did get to the topic that had ostensibly brought him here. Harry picked up his phone at one point to call Chloe but decided to just text her—he was going to have dinner with a research subject, he told her, did she mind? *Nope,* she texted back, *I'm going to turn in early.* Perfect.

Peggy grilled a couple of steaks and some corn on the cob, and then she drank a glass of wine, he had more tea, and she took him to bed. He hadn't forgotten how—that is, he was able to! And she was beautiful, young and kind and generous. Afterward, although it was barely past eight, the sun was still out, they fell asleep. Harry dreamed that he was standing on a cliff's edge, gazing down at the sea. He understood that this was Plácidia, and the coup was underway. Soldiers were waiting behind him, and he could hear the rustle of their uniforms, the gentle clanking of the buckles and straps on their utility belts, the quiet click of a full magazine being fitted into an assault rifle. They were waiting for him to jump to his death. But instead of fear, instead of dread, he felt the yawning, infinite freedom that death would bring, and he was filled with joy. It wasn't necessary to get a running start, he could just jump. And he did, and the wind seized him and buoyed him, and he flew over the sea like a great bird, the crashing waves anointing his face with droplets of spray. On the shore behind him, the Plácidians were celebrating his flight on their steel drums, playing a careful, minimalistic, repeating pattern, and with each repetition of the pattern, the wind gathered underneath his arms and he was lifted again above the surface of the sea. When he woke, his face was wet—wet from the dream?—but no, wet from crying. He'd been crying! It was dark, he was in an unfamiliar bed, and the steel drums played on.

"Harry?"

"Hm."

"Harry, your phone?"

Who was that? Oh, yes, Peggy! He remembered their day together, laughed.

"Harry, are you all right? Your face."

"I had a dream. A joyful dream!"

"Do you want to get your phone?"

"Yes, yes," he said. "I have so much to talk to you about."

She laughed. "But make the ringing stop first, Harry."

The phone told him it was 3:14 a.m. The number was unfamiliar. He said hello and a voice asked, "Is this Harry Pool?"

"Yes?"

"I'm Dr. Juniper Lin, calling from Onteo County Hospital. I'm sorry to wake you. It's about your granddaughter, Chloe. She is fine."

"Oh, no."

"She showed up here on a bicycle with a broken wrist. She claims that you're looking after her this week, is that true?"

"Oh, no. Yes, that's true. Oh, dear."

"She says she fell off the roof of your home. Are you there now, sir?"

"Yes. Oh. Oh, no. No, I'm not. I should be. I'm so sorry." The doctor asked a few questions about Chloe's medical history, which he answered. "I'll come right away," he said. "It may take me a short while."

He hung up, got out of bed, was startled to find himself naked. He wiped the tears from his face, barely remembering why he'd shed them. Something about the sea? "I have to go. I've been a terrible father. Grandfather. Oh, poor Chloe." He answered Peggy's startled look with "I shouldn't have fallen asleep! She broke her wrist somehow. Why didn't she call me? I have to go."

"I'll come with you," she said, pulling on her jeans.

"No, no."

"I insist, Harry. It's as much my fault as yours."

He searched the floor for his clothes, gathered them up. "I should call her mother. I should call her father." Should he, though? What had Chloe been doing on the roof? That couldn't be right.

He didn't realize he was standing frozen beside the bed, clutching his wadded-up clothes, until Peggy, fully dressed, quietly spoke his name. "Harry," she said. "Harry, do you want to call Chloe's parents?"

He blinked, glanced down at his watch. "No," he said. "Not yet."

Five minutes later, they were on the road.

13

Jane glanced at her watch. It was nearly eleven—way past bedtime for anyone in this studious crew to be knocking on her cabin door. She looked around for something heavy enough to hurt a person and seized on the only substantive thing within reach—the poet's mostly blank hardcover volume of inscrutable word salad Jane had repurposed as a notebook. Weapon in hand, she crept across the room, raised her arm, and threw open the door.

On the threshold, Lila laughed. "You look like a TV preacher!"

Jane threw the book onto the bed. "What the hell are you doing here?"

"That's how you greet the sister you haven't seen in months?"

"Nearly a year."

"Time flies, I guess." Lila flopped down on the bed. She looked different. Less guarded, less composed. Her V-neck tee shirt, sweaty, was tucked into jeans with some kind of black smears on them. She wore tennis shoes with no socks, and her hair was half escaping the nylon band it was perpetually gathered into. She smelled like...woodsmoke?

"You didn't answer my question."

"What was it again?" She lay back on the pillow, hands behind her head. Her eyes took in the room, lingering briefly on Jane's open laptop, which displayed the memoir in progress. Jane snapped it closed.

"What are you doing here?" she asked again.

"Ah! I was thinking about what you said. You know, about our collaboration being imbalanced. This thing with Aunt Ruth, I think we should be together on it from here on in, don't you? You should come to Arizona with me."

"How many hours did you have to drive to say this to me in person?"

"Twenty, give or take. Not too many."

Jane sat down at the foot of the bed. Automatically, she gripped Lila's ankle, then pulled her hand away, embarrassed. Goddamn it. She'd missed her sister, missed being alone with her. She said, "Look. You're right, I'm sick of being sidelined. And I want to figure out what happened to Ruth. Probably more than you do."

"It's not a contest."

"All right, all right. But I have to see this through for Shelly. And I finally made some progress with my writing. Plus I've left Chloe alone with Dad for a week, I need to spend some time with her before I go off on some goose chase with you."

"So you're saying you're not *really* committed to doing this together."

Jane had drawn a breath to scream and her hands had balled into fists before she noticed the grin on her sister's face. "You asshole."

"Fill me in," Lila said, "on the tweakers who stole your friend's stuff. And I'll fill you in on Aunt Ruth."

Over the course of a few minutes, Jane described her research into Marin, the congresswoman she'd worked for, and Ace. She told Lila about the ridiculous lie they'd told Marin and about the guy who tried to break into her cabin earlier that night.

"I didn't see the car in the lot," Lila said. "Do you think Marin took off with him? The thing about the horseman's shadow is kind of brilliant—I wouldn't be surprised if they brought that back to Ainsley Winter and her red-yarn board. You might be free of them for now."

"So you think I'm right about this? They're working for Winter?"

"Probably," Lila said. "And it involves money, I'm sure."

"Yeah, but how? Ace was poor. They died poor."

"I agree it doesn't make sense. But it will eventually." Lila sat up. "Do you want to hear where I'm at with the Arizona stuff?"

"Sure."

There wasn't much, to Jane's surprise. She'd boned a guy and figured out where Nutt's compound was. And had a conversation with an angry rabbi who refused to work with him. Nutt seemed to be some apocalyptic goober with a weird hobby, and it wasn't clear how any of it was connected to Aunt Ruth. Lila hadn't even pursued the leads to Uncle Lloyd that Jane had produced. For a moment, Jane allowed herself a feeling of triumph—she wasn't being upstaged by her twin for a change—but then it became clear that Lila was leaving something out. Jane asked, "What about Mom? How is she involved?"

"Not clear. My contacts haven't been helpful with that."

"But you've been in contact with contacts."

"Some."

"Agency contacts?"

Lila said, piqued, "Just people I know."

Hm. She'd leave it for now. "So look," she said, "stick around with me for the rest of the week, relax here, do some research. Let me finish my class. Then we'll go home and regroup with Chloe and Dad and make a plan. Deal?"

"Deal," Lila said. They shook.

Shoulders sore, adrenaline pumping from the chase, Jane was wide awake. Lila was still wired from the highway. They agreed to take a walk through the moonlit woods and down to the lake. A few minutes later they were gazing out across the water, watching little white rectangles bobbing in the distance: people on a dock, looking at their phones. "It's weird to me," Lila said, "that people come all the way out here to be off the grid, then broadcast their exact coordinates to the world."

"Maybe they're not trying to get off the grid," Jane said. "Maybe they just want to look at their phones next to water."

Lila was scowling. "I don't get it. They take a lake selfie, put it on social media, pretty soon they're getting ads for sunscreen and dock shoes. How can they be so stupid? These corporations are reading their minds."

"It's not stupid," Jane said. "It's lonely being a person. Sometimes it's a comfort to know somebody's paying attention."

"Seriously?" Lila said, truly annoyed now. "You're telling me it's a comfort to you when publicly traded entities know you're on the rag?"

Jane sighed. "Sometimes."

They went back to the cabin in silence. While Jane was in the bathroom, she could hear Lila moving around, trying to get comfortable in the space. She came out to find her sister already asleep, or pretending to be, face to the wall, her own balled-up jeans for a pillow.

Jane climbed in next to Lila and threw an arm over her, sought her hand. Lila stirred, entwined her fingers with Jane's.

"You're different," Lila muttered.

"*You're* different."

They snickered, then were silent for a little while. "We're not different at all, actually," Jane said, but Lila was asleep again, or faking it again.

Marin didn't show up for breakfast, or for class. Heather Wooster Steyer seemed relieved. She regarded Lila's arrival with apparent equanimity but Jane's fellow students were burning with curiosity. When she wasn't around her sister, Jane tended to forget her weird energy, a kind of star power. Guys in truck stops had asked them more than once if they were famous. "Weren't you in that cop show?" This didn't happen when Jane was alone. Lila pushed her chair back to the edge of the room as the women discussed Shelly's memoir; instead of fading into the background, the gesture somehow elicited greater attention. Legs crossed, chin in hand, she had the air of a casting director coolly regarding a performance from deep in shadow, a void that devoured everything. Even Heather Wooster Steyer, ordinarily aloof, seemed flustered. Jane tried not to appear exasperated. Only Shelly seemed unaffected, and indifferent to everyone else's agitation.

The excerpt went over well. Jane liked it immensely, could imagine it being published. Everyone praised Shelly's descriptions of character and longed for more encounters with the colorful women of Boynton Ridge. Everyone was filing out of the room to head for the cafeteria when Jane felt her phone buzz. The sensation instantly filled her with guilt—it was probably Chloe, who she should have called last night—but when she answered, it was her father's voice that said, "Hi, honey, please don't panic."

"Oh no." She held up a finger to Lila, scuttled out the door. Low dark clouds raced, promising rain wherever they were headed, but not here. "What happened."

"Well, she's all right."

"It's Chloe? Where are you?"

"Well, we're at the hospital—"

"Oh my god."

"—but, as I said, it's fine, just a broken wrist."

"How did it happen?"

"I guess she was up on the roof?"

"Dad! Why did you let her go on the roof!"

"W-well," her father stammered, "you see...the thing is...it wasn't that I was exactly there to—"

"Is she there now, Dad? Just put her on."

"I'm sorry, Mom," Chloe said, coming onto the line after a few seconds of fumbling and scraping.

"Honey, are you in pain?"

"No. I mean, I guess I would be if they didn't give me drugs."

"What happened?"

Chloe told her some story about working on a summer project for school involving the weather and getting up on the roof to scout out locations for a weather station. She slipped and fell, broke the wrist, and rode her bike to the hospital. Even if the details hadn't sounded like nonsense—the only bike Chloe could have ridden had been left to rot in the basement or the shed years before, and they didn't even own a ladder—Jane would have recognized the lying from Chloe's tone.

"Hm. Well, I'm sorry I wasn't there for you. I'm on my way. Also, your aunt is here."

"No way!" Chloe said. "Will I get to see her?"

"I suppose so?"

"And you'll get to meet Peggy."

"Who's Peggy?"

Chloe explained that her grandfather had shown up with the lady from the library in Ghorum, and that's why he hadn't been home when she fell off the roof, and the lady was nice.

"Why do you know a librarian in Ghorum?"

"The memorial we went to over the weekend?"

Jane had already forgotten about that. Fortunately, Chloe's lies were taking the edge off the guilt. The apple, she supposed, hadn't fallen far from the tree; Chloe was bound to have her own private life she didn't tell her mother about. Maybe that was a good thing. Or maybe Jane was excusing herself from having to care about the lies.

She ended the call, then turned to go back to the conference center. Lila was standing just outside the door, pocketing a burner phone. "I'm sorry, change of plans. Chloe broke her wrist falling off the roof. I guess she was working on a school project?"

"No, she wasn't," Lila said. "I just got off the phone with Loretta. It seems like Chloe borrowed a Bluetooth sniffer from the office without permission. Loretta thinks she was trying to break into somebody's house."

"What!"

"I'll follow you home. We'll sort it all out there."

There was something about Lila's tone she didn't like—the implicit assumption that she, not Jane, was more qualified to deal with a family matter, despite her complete detachment from everyone and everything. But Lila always talked with plausible deniability in mind; if Jane called her out, Lila would say she was crazy, and Jane would be left humiliated and seething. She decided to just seethe instead.

They said their goodbyes to the writing group, with apologies to Shelly. "I think your thieves are gone for now," Jane said. "Can we pick up the trail again when the conference is over?"

"Sure," Shelly said. "But you were going to workshop tomorrow! Can you send us your piece?"

"Yeah," Hannah said. "I was looking forward to that."

"Same here," said Kim. Tilly was off by the trees taking a selfie with the racing clouds in the background.

"Sure. And, Hannah, I'll comment on your piece, too, just send it along."

The women exchanged hugs and phone numbers while Lila stood off to the side, arms crossed. When they parted, and the sisters had returned to the cabin, Jane took a moment to open her laptop and send the women her memoir. But the document wasn't where she had left it on the desktop. She opened the word processor and peered at the recently opened files, and it wasn't there either.

"What the hell?"

Behind her, she heard Lila shoving things into her bag and zipping it up. "I'm ready to go," she said.

The implacable expression on her sister's face told the story: this was Lila's fault. Jane remembered hearing her moving around the cabin last night while she was in the bathroom. She'd obviously broken into Jane's laptop—having configured it for her, Lila probably included an admin backdoor—and deleted the file. It seemed almost unbelievable, even for Lila. "You didn't," Jane said.

"I couldn't let you risk the security of our business."

"There was nothing in it about our fucking business!"

"You wrote about your false confession to George Framingham's murder. That would expose me in ways that would affect my standing in the spaces that are important to me." In response to Jane's stunned silence, she continued: "You confessed for selfish reasons, and now you're writing this for selfish reasons."

"You absolute bitch!" was the only rejoinder Jane could come up with.

"Anyway," Lila went on, "you said you were here on a case. The writing was accessory to that. The case is on hold for now, so there's no reason to pretend the writing is important."

"It *was* important!"

But even as she used the past tense to refer to it, Jane remembered that the memoir *wasn't* gone. She'd emailed herself a backup. Unless Lila had thought to search the work inbox—but the idea was laughable. Lila was allergic to drudgery. Email was Jane's job—that was by design, part of the unbalanced and manipulative partnership Lila had conceived for them. When they got home, Jane would check—but she bet it was there.

"Not," Lila was saying, "more important than my privacy and reputation."

Something occurred to Jane. "Is this the real reason you drove all the way here? To delete my memoir?"

"It's one of the reasons I came. The other, the primary one, is the one I gave you. I think you're right that we should work together on more projects, especially one involving our family."

There was no reason to betray any further emotion. It always backfired with Lila. Jane wanted to scream at her, slap her, push her out the door, but there was no point. She had one up on her sister right now—best to keep it this way.

"Fine," Jane said through clenched teeth.

"Do you still want me to come home with you?"

"Yes. I'll need time to deal with Chloe, and then we can make a plan."

"We can have our first business meeting with the full staff," Lila said, suddenly cheerful. "If Dad can be dragged out of his research. Who's Peggy, by the way?"

"What?" Jane said.

"You asked Chloe who Peggy was."

"Chloe says Dad showed up at the hospital with a woman."

Lila raised an eyebrow. "Interesting."

They stared at each other. Jane understood that, according to the rules of their family dynamic, she was supposed to make nice now. Well, fuck that. "Give me five minutes. Then you can follow me home."

For a few seconds, waking up in the back of a car with a dull ache in her arm and the sound of a hard rain battering the window, Chloe thought, or maybe dreamed, that she was back in fourth grade, her last before Tarbox Beals, sent home after falling off the monkey bars. She remembered being put to bed once it had been determined she didn't have a concussion or a broken bone and half sleeping as she half listened to her parents and Grandma Susan arguing about which of them was worst, Mom or Dad. Now, coming to, she derived a grim satisfaction from knowing the question had been answered at last: it was Chloe herself who sucked.

Grandpa Harry and Peggy led her inside, all of them carefully hurrying through the downpour. "Cover your cast!" Grandpa Harry shouted, though she was already doing so with an old towel she'd found in the car; they'd sent her to ortho earlier this afternoon to get it put on, then home with painkillers. Inside, Peggy praised the house—charming, she called it, which seemed very diplomatic to Chloe—and set to brewing coffee. Grandpa apologized once, then again. Fully awake now, Chloe said she wanted to be alone and headed to the home office to look up Laurel Anne Kunstler, her new nemesis.

The office was half disassembled; most of the important stuff had already been moved up to the mall office, and the rest was in the process of being re-Grandpa'd: books, papers, multiple mugs of undrunk tea, half evaporated. There was a desktop computer here, which she supposed had been rendered obsolete by the fancy new Linux machines Loretta had set up at Perks. Maybe Chloe could have it for her room.

She lowered herself into her mother's swivel chair gingerly, avoiding contact with the armrest. She was beginning to feel some pain in the arm again, and considered taking a pill, but she wanted to see how bad it could get first. With her healthy arm she woke the machine and punched in, awkwardly, the passcode she'd cribbed last year by glancing over her mother's shoulder: the street address of the house, plus Chloe's name and birth year. Not very secure, Mom. The monitor flickered on, displaying a messy desktop with a background image of herself and her mother standing in Times Square in, like, 2019, striking stupid poses. They had gone to see *Wicked* and her mother, like an insane person, asked a stranger to take the shot. They were wearing *Wicked* shirts.

Laurel Anne Kunstler wasn't a professor like Addison's dad, it looked like. And while Chloe had somehow gotten the idea that she was some kind of money person—an accountant or whatever—she was actually a graphic designer in the marketing department of Nestor College. Chloe found a headshot and bio in the staff listings saying where she'd gone to school and that she specialized in making promotional videos for various departments and programs. Which, yeah, that made a lot of sense. Chloe went back to the search page and clicked around, hoping for more information about the lady, but none was forthcoming. Stuff from her college alumni magazine, her getting some dumb entrepreneurship award for a company she started that seemed to have died soon after. A picture of her standing with other moms at a fundraiser for Tarbox Beals. Automatically, Chloe searched the background for her mother, but of course Jane Pool aka Martina Kelleher would not be caught dead at such a thing. Glancing through the other photos on the school website, she *did* find her Grandma Susan lurking around. Of course.

Chloe closed the browser. Grandpa Harry and Peggy were speaking in low voices in the kitchen, about her, no doubt. Her mom and aunt and probably Loretta would be here soon, and there would be a grand inquiry into her dumb behavior. The truth would emerge, if not from the available evidence, then from her own mouth, because Chloe knew herself to be a pushover and a terrible liar.

There was an unread badge on the Perks email, and she idly clicked it. She was a Perks employee, right? In the inbox, accompanying several pieces of spam from imaginary lawyers in developing nations, was an email from her mother, addressed to herself, with the subject line TUES 5 PM DRAFT. Chloe opened it.

There was no text, just a file labeled *Retreat piece,* and when she clicked on the file, the word processor popped open.

The piece began with a bracketed bit of text reading *insert early childhood here? crib memory/dream?,* then got underway with a reminiscence about the greenhouse—the one just across the hall from where Chloe was sitting that was full of houseplants, and dust, and mice. It had apparently been where her mom spent time with Chloe's grandmother, the one who became a drug lord in Central America and maybe was alive and maybe was dead but who Chloe had never met. Sometimes she'd considered bragging about this grandmother at school, but it felt dangerous. Her mother had warned her against bringing it up and there'd been something convincing in her tone. She'd stayed mum. Nobody at school knew.

And, it turned out, Chloe didn't really know either. According to this...memoir, she guessed it was, Grandma Anabel had been a spy, and so had Grandpa Harry, sort of? She'd had affairs, disappeared for weeks at a time, and seduced her mother's theater camp director?

As she read, her excitement turned to dread, then to horror. The guy her mom had killed, the one who was trying to rape Aunt Lila, was the guy from camp. He had ended up teaching at their high school! Her grandmother had literally been...was having sex with...with her aunt's rapist? And then...

And then Chloe read a couple of pages past the murder before she got confused and had to go back. Then she read it again and went back again. And read it again.

It couldn't be right. Aunt Lila was the one who had killed George Framingham, not Mom? Mom was the drunk one? It was Mom who'd been flirting with George to get revenge on their mother or something, who got roofied and ended up on the futon in the sex dungeon. And Aunt Lila was the one who burst in and saved her. Clocked George on the head with a candlestick. Told Mom what to do next. Got the idea to haul the body into the boat and dump it in the lake.

Chloe had known all these details—she'd looked it up last year, after her mother told her only the sketchiest outline. At the time, she hadn't understood why Mom didn't want her to know the full story, because once she found out, she was deeply impressed. Mom had been a hero! And all of Aunt Lila's bravado had seemed to Chloe like compensation for her helplessness back in the day. Mom was the one who had done the right thing, had paid for it with her freedom.

But now it turned out that the roles were reversed. Aunt Lila was the hero.

So why did Mom go to prison?

She read on. After the killing, the two girls stole George Framingham's laptop and wallet, fled Nestor in his car. They took shelter with their aunt in Chicago, then traveled west. They lived in a squat, robbed a creepy kid in a church, stole another car, learned martial arts from some Christian guy. Eventually they made it to LA and lost track of each other. Then Mom became an addict, and after that it got so gross she couldn't go on.

No explanation for why Mom turned herself in. Why she'd lied to the judge, the jury, to everybody.

Chloe knew she ought to be mad but couldn't settle on who to be mad at. Her mom for lying? Aunt Lila for letting her? What about Grandpa Harry, did he know the truth? What about her dad, Grandma Susan? Were they all in on the lie?

Her arm throbbed. Actually, her whole body was throbbing. She was crying and the tears were falling onto her cast. Down the hall, doors were opening, people were arriving. She got up, effortlessly, from her mother's chair, leaving the memoir on the computer screen as a message. Limped to her bedroom, went inside, and locked the door behind her. Then she called her dad.

The line connected in a little flurry of bumping and scraping, like the phone had fallen out of his hand. "...my daughter," she thought she heard him say.

"Hi, Dad."

"Hey, bud, what's up?"

He sounded awkward and out of breath. "Not much," she lied. "Where are you? Who are you talking to?"

"Oh, yeah, I'm at the condo, that was Grandma."

Hm. He was lying too. "They all packed up?"

"Yeah, we're just, you know, enjoying the pool, taking in the air before we come home. You having a good week with Mom?"

"Yeah," she lied again. Not a good week. Not with Mom. Suddenly she wasn't sure why she'd called. She didn't want to rat out her mother; she didn't even want this new information to be real.

She heard more commotion on the line, and somebody saying they'd be right back, they were going to do something unintelligible. Her father mumbled some response. "Was that Grandma?" she said, knowing the answer.

"Oh, yeah." He sighed. "I mean...okay, bud, I'll be honest with you, no. Your grandparents flew home yesterday. I'm here with...I've been meaning to tell you..."

Oh god.

"Um, yeah, that's my friend, uh, Florabell. We've been kind of, yeah, seeing each other?"

"You have a girlfriend? In Florida?"

"No, she's...we're friends from home. I'm staying at the condo a few days as, like, a vacation. To see if we really like each other. And, yeah, we do. So..."

"So you're on vacation with the girlfriend you didn't tell me about."

"I mean, I'm telling you about her now. I didn't want to until I knew for sure."

"So...what? Are you getting married?" Chloe said, and the meekness of her voice embarrassed her, so she added, "Third time's the charm?"

A pause, during which she could hear children shouting and splashing, salsa music playing. Why wasn't she there? Why couldn't she just, like, have a cheesy vacation next to a pool while being annoyed with her father? But she would have said no if she'd been invited. And her father knew that. So he didn't invite her.

"Bud, that is out of line."

"Sorry."

"Sorry ain't gonna cut it," he said. But then there was a silence while they both pondered what actually could cut it. He sighed. "Fine. I guess I should have told you before this. I didn't know how you'd feel."

"You have your answer. I don't care."

"Okay, well, good, I guess."

"Good."

"Well, all right. I'll see you in a few days, then."

"Fine."

"Okay, bye. Love you."

"Bye," she said, and ended the call.

In the hallway, footsteps, voices. They were looking for her. She heard her mother entering the office, heard her pause as though brought up short. By the document open on her computer screen. Good.

Painfully, like an old lady, Chloe hauled herself up from the bed and went out the door to face the music.

14

Lila marveled at them all, gathered in the cramped, low, grimy kitchen around the bowed and broken table, sitting on the mismatched chairs and stools, gently simmering. Their father embarrassed that he'd let Chloe fall off a roof—if that was what really happened—and embarrassed to be accompanied by a strange woman. Chloe humiliated and in pain, but also angry, but also confused. Jane still pissed at Lila for deleting the file, angry at Chloe, angry at Harry—but, for some reason Lila couldn't determine, subdued. Perhaps the ride here had cooled her emotions. Loretta ashamed of having taught Chloe to use the Bluetooth sniffer, ashamed of failing to stop her from using it. And the woman, Peggy—actually, Peggy was surprisingly composed given her incongruousness here. Her presence was keeping them all quiet, perhaps out of politeness, more likely out of bafflement.

Lila was standing. Harry had offered her his chair but she'd shaken her head no. She didn't like to sit down in a strange place. Not that this place should feel strange—she had lived here for sixteen years—but it felt more peculiar, more alienating, to her than any random truck-stop diner or roadhouse might. It was the place she'd fled, intending never to look back.

If you'd asked her twenty years ago, or even ten, she would have predicted that today, her father would be dead and this house razed, replaced with a shitty apartment building for college students. Instead, both Harry and the house had remained, not only intact but unaltered. The same sagging roof, the same stained ceilings, the same tile floor dotted with bits of mouse shit. Their father looked his age, but he'd looked this age at fifty, too, and it gave the impression that nothing would ever change.

It freaked her out. She liked that things changed. She liked that she was good at putting them behind her. She leaned against the stove, arms crossed, watching and listening. Loretta introduced herself to Peggy. Chloe and Jane glowered at each other. Harry kept reaching out to Peggy as if to touch her, then jerking his arm back.

Chloe said, "Isn't anyone going to *say* something!"

"Peggy," said Lila, "it's nice to meet you."

"Likewise."

"How long have you two been together?"

The woman shook in closed-mouth laughter, and her eyes passed the question to Harry. "We're not," Harry said. "That is...we're here together. We're just not..."

"We just met," Peggy said. "I'm helping your father with a research project."

"Got it," Lila said. Peggy smiled at her, and Lila, uncharacteristically, felt her face contorting into a polite smile of its own. The woman's confidence was infectious. Why hadn't their father found somebody like this before? She turned and said, "Chloe."

"What," the girl replied with a resigned sigh.

"What really happened to you last night?"

Chloe hung her head as though contemplating resistance, then drew a breath and began to speak. She told them that, after talking to Lila on the phone a few days before, she decided that she needed to establish real evidence that her school rival's father had created the faked video of her that was still, as far as she knew, making the rounds on social media. "Not that I would know," she said, not without some pride. "I stopped looking at my phone." Loretta had taught her how to use the Bluetooth sniffer—across the table, Loretta pressed her lips together and squirmed in her chair—so she stole it from the Perks office and hid it in the pool shed behind the rival's house. She waited until the device had cracked their door code, broke in, and found the source of the video. Then, having tripped the house alarm, she broke her arm fleeing the cops and coasted down the hill to the hospital on her bike. Jane and Harry gaped at her, appalled.

"But get this," she told Lila triumphantly. "You were wrong. Her dad didn't make the video. Her mom did!"

"Very impressive," Lila told her.

Jane brought her palm down on the table. "Lila!"

"Admit it, it was risky and not very well executed, but not a bad plan overall."

"It was a terrible plan! Also, who appointed you head of this meeting?"

"Just filling the power vacuum," Lila informed her. "Loretta. How's progress on Perks East?"

"Ready to go."

"Excellent. Dad, maybe you can man the office for us, be on call to do some digging if necessary. Save the locksmith work for Jane and Chloe—"

"I didn't sign up to be a fucking locksmith," Jane said.

"And you and Peggy," Lila went on, ignoring her, "can pursue your research project on the side."

Harry stammered, "I-I-I don't know how to—"

"Great, thanks. Jane," she said, turning to her sister, whose anger was being undercut by some other emotion Lila couldn't identify. She seemed uncertain, fearful, above and beyond her daughter's accident, which had obviously not done the girl real harm, shooting Chloe sideways glances, hoping to catch her eye with some unspoken command. Lila made a mental note to pry the truth from her at some point. "We'll go to Arizona in the morning, work on finding Lloyd and scouting out Nutt's compound."

"Lila. You can't be serious. My daughter just got out of the hospital. I'm not going to Arizona with you."

Chloe rolled her eyes.

"She's coming," Lila said. "And Loretta. Two cars. Two teams."

"Wait," Chloe said. "You want to *drive* to Arizona?"

Lila shrugged. "It's a couple of days. We'll take turns sleeping. All interstates, straight shot."

"No," Jane said.

"Or I can get us a charter flight to north Texas. I know a guy there with cars."

"Like, a private plane?" Chloe said, excited.

"Yeah."

"I'm in," Chloe said. Her expression was fierce, defiant—not what Lila would have expected of her, given what had just happened.

"You don't get to just say you're in, Chloe," Jane said. She was slumped in her chair, hands out of sight beneath the table. Lila imagined them clutching and twisting.

Chloe turned to her and repeated, "I'm in."

A silence settled over the table. Then Jane stood up, leveled a look at Lila, and said, "I need to talk to you."

Lila followed her into their father's office. It was in disarray, but a new kind of disarray: disarray in progress. Books and papers were everywhere, but the windows were clean, the carpet was vacuumed, the empty tumblers bearing the tide marks of booze had been replaced by abandoned tea mugs. It no longer looked like a place where somebody was slowly dying.

Jane spun on her, arms crossed. "I don't appreciate your encouragement of Chloe's behavior. I'm going to have to discipline her, and you want to take her on an exciting trip! You're not her mother."

"Admit you're impressed with her, though."

"I am not impressed!" Jane spat.

Lila said, "Well, I am. Also, I don't think that's why you're mad. Something's going on between you two."

"What's going on is that my daughter invaded somebody's house and broke her arm fleeing the police!"

"Besides that," Lila said. "She's angry with *you*. And *you* think you deserve it. Why?"

Before her sister's face hardened, Lila caught a moment of vulnerability, a microscopic wince, a tilt of the head to hide it. Then, in an instant, Jane had reapplied her mask of inviolability. Lila knew a performance when she saw it. She snorted. "All right, fine, I don't know what I'm talking about."

"You sure don't," Jane said.

"But, Jane. You feel bad because you left her on her own, and she got hurt. And you're mad at me because I don't include you in our work. This could be the perfect way to set things right. We work together. You stick with Chloe and smooth things over. Anything dangerous, Loretta and I can handle. Or, if you want in, Loretta can babysit."

Jane turned her head to the window. "I don't want her to work with us, Lila. I want her to have a normal life."

Lila almost laughed, then realized it wasn't a joke. Her sister really did seem to think this was possible. "Jane," she said. "Come on. She was born in prison. Her whole family are criminals and spies. You think she's going to care about stuff like being class president for long? She didn't break into that girl's house because she wants to be a leader at school. She broke in because it's exciting. Because she wanted to prove she was better than those smug idiots."

"She broke in because you told her to."

"All I told her to do was find her own evidence! And she did it." Jane appeared close to boiling over, so she added, "Look, I'd be mad, too, if she was my kid. I get it. But her plan worked. And when she was hurt and in trouble, she got to safety all by herself." She reached out and laid a hand on her sister's shoulder. "The kid's a badass. You should be proud of her."

Jane slapped the hand away. "Excuse me, Lila, I *am* proud of her, and *also* I'm upset with her. The two things are not incompatible. You don't understand what it's like to be a mother."

"Fine, fine."

"And she *will* need to be disciplined for this. She broke the law and could have broken her neck. However."

Lila waited.

"However, maybe this trip could be good for us."

"Of course it could."

"But, Lila," she said, leveling a finger, "don't interfere with Chloe. Don't contradict me when I lay down the law. She already thinks you're a cooler version of me, I don't want you undermining me."

"I am literally a cooler version of you, though."

"Oh, fuck off" was the earnest reply, but Lila could tell she was softening, just a little.

"Fucking off is my superpower."

When they returned to the kitchen, Loretta was regaling the others with a story about searching for a soldier who went missing during a coalition raid on a bomb factory in Kandahar Province and eventually finding him hiding in a terrified civilian's house in a nearby village, curled up in a ball. "We'd lost another guy to a booby trap during the raid, and he just straight bugged out. The people whose house he was in thought we were going to kill them." Lila had heard it before.

Now the four of them looked up with questions in their eyes. Lila said, "We can drive or we can fly. Votes for taking two cars all the way?"

Lila raised her own hand. No others went up.

"Hm. So I guess we're flying?"

"Where's the airport?" Jane wanted to know.

"Altamont."

"So, that's, what, three hours?"

"If you're a slowpoke. I'll try to suppress my disgust at the idea of going east to go west, and I'll call my guy there. I doubt there's anything today but I bet he can free something up for tomorrow. He owes me one."

"Again?" Jane said.

"Chloe," Lila said to her niece, "let this be a lesson to you: make sure you've got a lot of guys who owe you one."

The guy in question was a friend of Gramps, her contact for motorcycle parts (and, as an added bonus, guns) in central Montana. In her early days as Perks, before she had her headquarters and more work than she had time to do, she sourced a lot of jobs through Gramps, who had bonded with her over classic BMW bikes. She probably also reminded him of the estranged daughter that his dissipated girlfriend spilled to her about one night when Lila was crashing at their compound. Anyway, the plane guy was named Louie Donough, his son had gone missing, and Lila tracked him down. The kid had gotten himself into some bad shit, which she extracted him from at some risk to her own safety, and Louie felt he owed her above and beyond the fee he'd paid.

He didn't, but Lila didn't disabuse him of the notion. He'd gotten his start as a truck driver for a grocery chain; now he was a logistics mogul with a specialization in sensitive and hazardous materials, particularly those that required a "cold chain," end-to-end refrigeration without interruption. His ElBeeDee rigs were a familiar sight on American highways with their distinctive shivering-beagle logo, but he also did some offshore work in the Northeast US and eastern Canada and he owned a fleet of small aircraft for urgent deliveries of small parcels, many of which Lila assumed required concealment from government regulatory bodies and law enforcement. He was the major client of this airport and ran a bunch of planes out of there, one of which they could doubtless hitch a ride on without ending up on any passenger manifest. It was likely they'd be sitting ten feet from a crate full of industrial toxins or black-market donor organs, but there was no reason to share that information with her sister.

Lila slipped into the office and made the call. Louie wasn't available to speak, but his assistant knew her and told her they had a shipment going out early the next morning to Little Rock. After that, the pilot could hop them to Amarillo for a nominal fee. Lila agreed, and arranged for a couple of cars for the week. She would pay via crypto after their phone call.

"As it happens," the assistant said, "Mr. Donough is doing business in Albany today. I'll let him know you'll be in Altamont in the morning."

"I'd love to see him."

"I know he'd love to see you as well, if time allows."

Back in the kitchen, she told everyone the plan. They'd leave Nestor at three thirty a.m. Chloe and Jane groaned. "We should all turn in early," she said, and Chloe said, "Duh." While Lila hauled out her laptop and paid for the trip, their father got cold cuts out of the fridge, and they all sat around the table eating sandwiches in silence. Peggy occasionally reached out and touched Harry's arm, and Lila surprised herself by feeling a little jolt of something, she didn't know what.

Oh, yes, she did.

"God," Chloe said. "How am I going to *sleep* with this thing?"

"I'll help you get settled," Jane said, getting up.

"No, thanks," Chloe muttered, and slouched past her down the hall. Jane sighed, then stole a glance at Lila. A brief standoff ensued during which each of them tried to appear more expressionless than the other. Then Jane gave up and turned in for the night.

Lila and Loretta chatted with Peggy and Harry for a while. Harry regaled them with stories of his ongoing research project, a mystery about a deposed South American strongman who was supposed to have been thrown off a cliff or something but might be living nearby under an assumed name. She hadn't seen him so animated in ages, but then again, aside from her brief visit here last year, she hadn't seen him at all. She said, "Dad, why do you care about this so much?"

He appeared taken aback. "I'm a historian! I don't like it when there's something that might stay unknown forever. I'm the only one who cares, I need to see it through."

"Do you think this guy wants to be found?"

"I...I don't know. Perhaps not?"

"I'm just saying," Lila told him. "I've tracked down a lot of missing people. They're usually not happy to see me."

"Are you...are you telling me to stop?"

Lila said, "I'm not telling you anything. But if you find him, maybe take a breath before you introduce yourself. You might avoid, I dunno, a punch in the face."

"He's older than I am," Harry said incredulously.

"I've been punched in the face by guys older than you, Dad," she said, getting up. To Peggy, she added, "A pleasure meeting you."

She left the two of them to their bewilderment and followed Loretta out to her rental car. They drove in silence to her hotel. Loretta admitted Lila into a spacious, clean suite overlooking an airport, post office, and community swimming pool. The last was closed for the night, but Lila stood at the window while Loretta prepared for bed, watching a lone employee sit placidly at the end of the diving board, bouncing gently and smoking a cigarette. The smoke rose into the pool of light cast by a security floodlight and dissolved in the air.

They shared the king-sized bed, two feet of space separating them. Neither of them went to sleep. Loretta said, "I feel bad for leading your niece down the garden path."

"Not your fault."

Five minutes passed. Headlights swept the ceiling. Outside, car doors slammed and children's voices echoed in the parking lot. "I'm glad we're leaving," Loretta said. "I was running out of things to pretend to have to do."

"Well, I appreciate it."

"So, I guess you've had enough space? Are we good?"

Lila suppressed anger that she knew was irrational and unfair. She didn't like it when people laid their feelings on the table. She didn't like being blindsided by the emotional needs of others. Of course, she'd been told that she did this herself to her friends, her lovers, her family. But in Lila's view, those weren't feelings she showed them—they were facts.

Loretta had dumped her a month before. No, she hadn't. But that was what Lila had been saying to herself, quietly, for weeks, alone in the car or the shower, under her breath on long walks, out loud alone in the office facing a screenful of code. *You dumped me!* The truth was, their relationship had kindled and burned out years before. They'd worked together in harmony ever since, but occasionally the romance would flare up, like a persistent, chronic rash. Sometimes it felt like a return to all that was normal and right. Most of the time it felt like what it actually was: an impulsive reaction to temporary loneliness. Earlier this year they'd seemed to be trying it for real again; it went on for months and they'd felt like a couple for the first time since the first time. But then Loretta had disappeared for a couple of days, and when she came back, she broke it off, told Lila they couldn't do this anymore, that if they kept at it, she would have to quit. This had resulted in the Perks East assignment, which both of them knew was unnecessary. Jane was perfectly capable of renting a space and setting up her own office. But planning it had given Lila something to do and a place to send Loretta while she got her thoughts straight in her head.

The Lila of last week would have reached out and taken Loretta's hand. But things had changed. "We're good," she said now.

"Are you sure?"

"I met somebody," Lila said.

She felt Loretta propping herself up on one elbow. "What? How?"

"Just the other day. In Ohio."

"You have to be fucking kidding me." She sounded angry—she probably was angry—but when Lila turned, Loretta's face showed only incredulous delight. "You absolute slut."

Lila said, "I don't know what to tell you. A girl brought me a package from Knight, and..."

"And you fucked her."

"Yeah."

"And you're, what...you're in love with her? After one night?"

"That's not a thing," Lila said. The result was uproarious laughter. "I'm sorry, what's so funny?"

"That very much is a thing." Loretta flopped down again. Lila felt through the mattress the back-and-forth movement of her head shaking in amazement. "Good for you, I guess." There was jealousy in this dismissal, a little bit, anyway, but what Lila mostly heard was grim satisfaction, as though Loretta would enjoy watching Lila fuck it up.

A deep, penetrating embarrassment settled in her body; she could have sworn she felt the bed creak under its strain. Why had she told Loretta about Brooke? It had just been one night, and she would probably never see the woman again. And despite what Loretta said, you couldn't be in love with someone after a few hours together. There was not enough data! Lila was infatuated, it was true, but not in love. And she wasn't the one who'd brought up the word. The very idea of it was absurd.

She wanted to call Brooke. She wanted to get up, go out to the pool, bum a smoke from the guy on the diving board, and call her.

Fucking pathetic. She closed her eyes as hard as the muscles would allow, and when she got tired of doing that, she went to sleep.

15

At three thirty, Chloe and her mother were ready and waiting at the door, standing with their backs to each other. They wordlessly threw their bags into Lila's Volvo, followed Loretta to the airport to drop off her rental, then hit the highway for Altamont. Chloe wanted to stay awake, piss off her mother by bonding with her aunt, enjoy the euphoria of having gotten away with something. But the thrum of the car's tires and the medication-dulled throb of her arm sent her back to sleep within minutes. She awoke to the crackle of an intercom, Aunt Lila's voice, the clatter of metal. A section of fence was moving aside, and a few moments later the car slotted into a spot in front of a large building, the kind of corrugated-metal half-tube that Chloe knew had a real name but that she'd always thought of as a HoHo Hangar, after the snack food it resembled. She chastised herself for the childish affectation: time to learn what things were called! Aunt Lila told everyone to wake up, then led them to the office door.

"He's a hugger," she whispered to Chloe, hand on the knob. "You just have to let it happen."

"Uh..."

They passed through into a cavernous space occupied by several small aircraft and lots of equipment, illuminated by floodlights. A buzzer sounded until the door shut behind them, and from the center of the hangar floor came a bearlike man with broad shoulders, smooth skin, and gray curls upon which a pair of aviator sunglasses was perched, as if he couldn't wait for the sun to come up.

"Everybody, this is Louie."

"My friends," Louie said. "Look at you all. Bright and early." He wore suit pants and a pin-striped shirt without a tie, and he clasped each person's hand in both of his and repeated his name. He hugged only Aunt Lila, to Chloe's relief.

"Louie, how's your boy," Aunt Lila said.

"I've brought him into the business," Louie said proudly. "He's working out of Texas, customizing our software. And he's getting his pilot's license. All thanks to you."

"It took a good father to keep him on track."

"You are too kind. Too kind."

Their plane was a small jet. Chloe had imagined something with propellers Amelia-Earharting them over the continent, wind tossing them to and fro. They would fly directly to Little Rock, Aunt Lila explained, to drop off Louie's client's cargo, then immediately take off for Amarillo, where their cars waited. The whole journey would take about four hours.

They climbed up into a cramped but clean cabin with two columns of what proved to be very comfortable seats. A man sat in the back row wearing a navy-blue suit and sunglasses—the client, Chloe supposed. The aisle beside him was occupied by a large battery-powered cooler with a digital readout and a keypad-operated lock strapped to a wheeled cart. The man didn't acknowledge them as they entered.

They took seats in the front, Aunt Lila with Loretta, Chloe stuck with her mother. She leaned across the aisle and whispered, "What's with the guy?"

"Do not look directly at the guy," Aunt Lila said. "Do not acknowledge the guy in any way."

In spite of herself, Chloe shuddered a little. "Are you serious?"

"Kidding," Aunt Lila said. "Sort of."

They slept, then woke when the wheels touched down in Arkansas. The cooler guy brushed Chloe's cast-encased arm as he wheeled the cooler out of the plane, and she jerked it away. For a second, she had to suppress a desire to punch the guy in the kidney. (Maybe the cooler contained kidneys. Stolen ones!) They were back in the sky in minutes.

The airport was not in Amarillo, Aunt Lila said, but twenty miles west along Route 40, and was even smaller than the one they'd taken off from: just an airstrip, a smaller hangar (though not as small as an actual HoHo), a control tower, and a lonely little office where a woman sat gazing out over the dry and featureless landscape. Chloe was astounded to see a genuine tumbleweed blow by. She pointed at the horizon. "Are those, like, mesas?"

"Yep," Lila said.

"They look like they're in a cartoon."

Their cars were white SUVs, spacious and comfortable marshmallows. Twenty minutes later they were sitting in a diner on the outskirts of Vega called Aunt Irma's: SINCE 1997, RIGHT WHERE THE PAVEMENT ENDS. As advertised, it stood on a dirt track on a lot beside a ranch house that doubtless belonged to Aunt Irma. HAIR BY BEX, read a sign in the yard. They ate greasy eggs and greasy potatoes among women with poofy hair and men who kept their hats on. Chloe felt an inexplicable joy. "This is the best thing that has ever happened to me," she said, and everyone laughed, even her mother. She had the waitress sign her cast, and when they got outside, she saw that the woman had drawn a cartoon of her own cleavage beneath the name *Jiffany*.

They gathered around the rear of one of the cars. With her laptop, Aunt Lila had found a lodge-style motel on the southwestern outskirts of Prescott, roughly equidistant between Skeleton Flats and the gastropub where her uncle had been photographed. It consisted of a collection of small freestanding cabins and was called Trout Brook Cottages. "Jane," she said, "what ID do you have with you?"

"Mine?"

Lila scowled. "You still have the Sarah Matthews passport, right?"

"Somewhere," her mother said, clearly exasperated. "Sorry."

Lila rummaged in her bag, removed a zip-lock baggie, pulled out a passport and driver's license, and handed them over. "You're Karen Pugh," she said, then made reservations under that name and another one. Aliases! "We can be there by dinnertime if we're fast," Lila said.

"Wait," Chloe blurted. *"Dinnertime?"*

Loretta said, "We need to cross New Mexico and half of Arizona."

"Things are big out here," her mother explained.

"Whoa," Chloe said. "Okay." How embarrassing.

The weather was sunny and mild. Chloe insisted on riding with Aunt Lila, causing her mother to open her mouth, then snap it closed without speaking. Chloe had intended to drill her aunt for information on this leg, starting with the provenance of the counterfeit passports, but she ended up just sleeping again. They drove for hours, then ate pretty good Mexican outside Moriarty, New Mexico. Chloe and her mother switched places, exchanging a glare as they did so, and Chloe slept next to Loretta for a while.

They crossed into Arizona a little after five in the afternoon. Somewhere in New Mexico Aunt Lila had taken them off the interstate and onto a two-lane highway, which led them onto another two-lane highway, and then another, by far the loneliest roads Chloe had ever seen in her life. Nothing but dust and brush, the occasional ranch, and distant hills that never seemed to get any closer. This landscape filled Chloe with longing, and she had to really think it over to determine what she was longing for—she was longing for this, this very place and very moment that she was experiencing right now, as though it were already years behind her. This seemed like a very adult feeling and she couldn't decide whether this meant she should look forward to adulthood or dread it.

Loretta's phone rang. She listened for a moment, hung up, and pulled the car over. "Let's stretch." They got out. The air was hot and clean and dry and smelled of some herbal sweetness; Chloe breathed it in and felt energized. She wandered off into the brush as the women conferred, and was immediately startled by a snake that came whiptailing out from the shade of the rock directly past her. It was big! She let out a yelp but held her ground as the animal continued on its way, following a wandering track in the dirt it seemed to have carved on its own, and disappeared.

By the time she rejoined the group, she had learned, from her phone, the snake's name (Sonoran gopher snake), whether it was venomous (no), and what it liked to eat (rodents, duh). She intended to brag about the sighting but the mood of the group was weird. Everyone was agitated; it seemed that her mom and aunt had exchanged words. Chloe tried to get back into the car with Loretta, but she said, "Why don't you ride with your mother."

"Because I don't feel like it?"

The response was a single arched eyebrow.

"Fine, fine," Chloe said with a sigh. She wasn't going to be able to avoid it forever, might as well face the music.

She managed to avoid facing it for another half hour of lonesome road before her mother said, "Well? Are you going to start?"

"You're the one who has all the explaining to do."

Her mother took in breath, held it, let it out. "I don't think I do. You weren't there, you don't understand, and you don't seem to want to."

"You *lied*! In court!"

"That's right, I lied. And I paid the price. I had my reasons. God forbid you should ever have the same ones yourself."

They drove in silence for a few miles. The landscape didn't change. The sun sank, but not far enough. Now it was below the level of their visors. Her mother had brought sunglasses, which she had annoyingly called sunnies ever since a trip to Australia she and Dad had taken without her, which Chloe guessed was meant to "save their marriage." It didn't work. Chloe, an idiot, had forgotten to pack her own sunglasses. She felt that this put her at a disadvantage in the conversation.

"Why didn't Aunt Lila confess?" she asked, trying to sound as angry as she'd been a few minutes ago.

"Because she didn't care. I'm the one who cared."

"But *why*?"

Her mother's response sounded like a formal declaration: "Because, Chloe, what we did was wrong, and somebody had to put it right."

"But it was Aunt Lila's idea to cover it up, not yours."

"I couldn't live with the guilt."

"I don't get it! It wasn't your fault!"

She didn't respond. Chloe assumed she was angry and returned her gaze to the bright empty road. But when she hazarded a glance back a few minutes later, her mother was biting her lip, and her face was wet.

"Mom?"

"It was driving me crazy," she said quietly. "Not the guilt. The waiting."

Chloe gave her a minute to elaborate and, when she didn't, said, "For what?"

Her mother wiped her cheek. "For them to find us. Your aunt just… didn't worry about things like that. The more time passed, the less she thought about it. She never looked back. To her, it was stupid that I worried. She was so dismissive, and it made me so angry. But for me…the more time passed, the more scared I was. I would dream of them breaking the door down, and wake up screaming. That's when I started using…It got to be the only way to sleep."

"Mom—" Chloe began, but her mother held up a hand.

"Also, I didn't think I'd go to prison. I really didn't. I thought...I thought I would just tell my story, and everyone would defend me, everyone would sympathize, and they'd just let me go. And then I could get on with my life. Your father and I..." She shook her head. "We were just so reckless and foolish. When we got married, it was, like, a news story. You know, the teen killer gets hitched. At the courthouse, I held up my hand with the ring and the reporters shouted questions and took pictures, and I felt brave and proud. But I was just a fool. Hand me one of those?"

She was pointing to the packet of tissues on the center console. Chloe pulled one out and her mother blew her nose into it.

"We weren't careful about getting pregnant. I would never have let it happen if I really thought they would convict me. I was just vain and irresponsible. And your aunt was right—stupid."

"You're not stupid."

"Thank you. But I was then." She turned to Chloe and the sun lit her eyes behind the glasses, and she said, "But, honey, I don't regret any of it, because I got you. If I had to do it all again, I would do it all again, to get you."

"Mom," Chloe said, and now she was crying too.

"Every mistake I made that led to you is the best dumb thing I ever did. I really mean it."

"I'm sorry I got mad."

"No, no, you were right to be mad," she said, turning back to the road. "I should have told you sooner."

"When were you planning to do it?"

Her mother sighed. "I told myself I was writing that memoir to piss off your aunt. But I think, deep down, I knew it was for you. I was going to give it to you. Eventually."

A big bug hit the windshield and left a gross smear. They both gasped, then they both laughed. Chloe stopped first. Her mother ran the windshield washer, and after a few minutes, she said, "You can have my sunnies if you want."

"You're *driving*."

"Suit yourself."

"Were you scared?" Chloe asked a while later.

"When? Lots of times. Until I got out of prison."

"No, I mean when it happened. When he took you down there. To the basement."

"I wasn't scared," her mother said. "I wasn't anything. I was drunk. I mean, if I felt anything while it was happening, I don't remember it. The first thing I remember is Lila kneeling there with the bloody candle thing. That scared me."

"It sounds scary."

"Everything about your aunt was scary from that moment on. She still scares me, a little."

"She's cool," Chloe said, not intending to hurt, but as soon as she said it, she knew it would.

"Yeah," her mother said, resigned. "She's cool."

Signs of civilization had begun to appear: little clusters of houses in the hills set along winding empty streets, hoping to become suburbs. A veterinary clinic, an antiques shop. A strip mall failing to look like an old adobe Pueblo house. They met up with the interstate and got on it. Prescott looked chill. It surprised her to see grass and shrubs, and she thought about what her science teacher had said about water in the West—who got to have it, who dried up and blew away. They passed the city and continued south along a narrow road that wound into, yes, the mountains, which had finally, stealthily arrived behind the sun's glare. They could see for miles across brush-covered valleys from the tightly curving road; it looked like a car commercial. It left her feeling light, feeling forgiving.

"Um, majestic vista much?" she quipped.

"These dope peaks are giving me life," said her mother.

Chloe snorted. "Mom, my god."

Trout Brook Cottages wildly exceeded her expectations. The one Chloe would share with her mom—an experience that she had been dreading all day and was now dreading slightly less—had three bedrooms, two on the first floor and one up on a loft overlooking the enormous living room, which featured a huge fireplace, log-frame sofas and chairs, and a couple of vintage video game arcade machines you didn't even have to put quarters in to play. "I get the loft!" Chloe shouted, as though there were siblings to compete with. The bed was huge and she had to crawl, in an awkward, arm-preserving scuttle, to get off it.

They dropped off their bags and met up with Loretta and Aunt Lila in the main lodge, which was dominated by a restaurant. Fishing shows played on several giant TVs hanging on the walls alongside trophy fish and the heads of elk and mountain lions mounted on varnished plaques. Chloe didn't usually eat meat but she ate it now, a hamburger as thick as a *Webster's Unabridged*. She tried not to look at the mountain lions. The place was packed, and they had to raise their voices to hear one another across the table.

It was decided that, in the morning, Chloe would accompany Loretta into town to try and track down Uncle Lloyd while Mom and Aunt Lila would see what they could find in Skeleton Flats. The plan seemed to leave Aunt Lila distracted and agitated, and she poked idly at her salad. "You know what?" she said, looking up. "I'm going to go out there tonight. To Skeleton Flats."

"Don't you want to rest up?" Mom asked her.

As if in answer, Aunt Lila raised a finger to a passing waitress, asked for coffee.

Resolve curled the corners of her mother's mouth down. "Wait," she said to the waitress. "Make that two."

"You're coming?" Aunt Lila asked.

"We're in this together. And I'm the one who actually knew Aunt Ruth, remember?"

"Did you, though? Or did you just cash the checks?"

"Oh, fuck off." She turned to Loretta. "Could you look after Chloe tonight?"

"Excuse me," Chloe said. "I don't need looking after. I'll lock the cabin door and, I dunno, get good at Dig Dug."

"Fine," said her mother, standing up. She glowered at her sister and said, "Let's get ready. I'll meet you at your cabin in fifteen minutes."

Chloe stood at the doorway to the bedroom while her mother, charged with anger, changed into a long-sleeved black shirt and jeans. She pulled her hair into a ponytail and popped it through the opening at the back of a black ball cap. Purple script on the front panel read *Sass*.

"That lid is fire," Chloe offered.

Her mother's only response was a tight smile. "Are you and I good for now?" she wanted to know. The strong subtext was that if they weren't, well, whatever. Chloe assumed it was the exchange over dinner with Aunt Lila that had put Mom into a shit mood and not their earlier conversation in the car, but she felt that some advantage she'd gained had been lost.

"We're okay."

"I'm sorry I didn't tell you the truth. I wasn't ready. But I was planning to, I promise." She removed a folding knife from her duffel, flipped it open, examined the blade. Folded it up and pocketed it.

"I'm sorry I snooped on your computer."

Her mother shrugged. "It's all right. I've got no more secrets from you now, though. There's no point in snooping."

"Okay." Chloe suddenly felt a tug of affection for her mother and wished she weren't going out. Maybe she could talk her into staying. They could curl up on the bed and make fun of TV. But she didn't ask. She said, "Don't die?"

"Not in the plan."

"Okay."

Another tight smile. Her mother's mind was out on the flats now. "Good night," she said, and walked out without another word.

For a little while, Chloe really did try to get good at Dig Dug. You had to control a little dude digging tunnels through the ground; every now and then a dragon would appear to harass you, and you could either crush it with a rock or inflate it with an air pump until it exploded. When you killed all the baddies, you got another level: more of them, moving faster.

It wasn't too bad for an old game. But once she realized this was all there was—the dirt, the rocks, the dragons—she lost interest. The other game was a racing thing, not her jam at all, and she couldn't move her busted arm quick enough to steer. She fooled around on her laptop for a while, using the lousy cabin Wi-Fi, then dug in her backpack to see if she had any gum.

Her hand found a cool little brushed-aluminum rectangle: the USB hard drive she'd grabbed from Addison's mom's home office. She'd entirely forgotten she'd taken it; they must have pulled it out of her pocket at the hospital when she was passed out and stuck it in the backpack. She got a little chill, remembering her mother's memoir and feeling the feeling that a stranger had touched her body without her knowledge or permission. Benignly, in her case, but still. She didn't like it. She regretted, briefly, getting mad at Mom.

She plugged in the hard drive, hearing the voices of Loretta and Aunt Lila screaming at her not to. But nothing untoward seemed to occur. The icon appeared on her desktop and she double-clicked it.

It was a backup. A backup of the whole computer! An initial rush of excitement gave way to indifference, though—Chloe had already gotten what she wanted from Addison's house, evidence of who had made the video. What use was there in looking further?

Well, maybe she could figure out *why*. Because it didn't really make sense, did it. Why would an adult act this way? Chloe thought about what good friends she and Addison had been for a minute and wondered if she'd even been aware of what her mom was doing. Maybe Addison had been horrified; maybe she was waiting for it all to go away, just like Chloe was. Chloe hadn't actually seen Addison participating in the frenzy of likes and shares and reaction videos, and she'd assumed this was just a mic drop. But maybe it wasn't.

She looked at the photos again. It appeared that the backup had been made a few weeks ago, so none of the Star Wars ones were here. There were lots of pictures of shoes and purses and things—maybe Mrs. Kunstler bought and sold a lot of stuff online. This made her check the mbox files where email was locally stored. Yeah, it was true, the lady bought and sold a crap-ton of stuff, some of it worth thousands of dollars. Judging from the receipts, she kept a purse for, like, two weeks on average. A sicko!

She also found a lot of receipts for something called USA Dronewave, marked "Thank you for your contribution," and with no web address. The emails were anonymized, from a different random-character address each time, and they recorded donations in the thousands of dollars. Chloe opened a browser and did a search. USA Dronewave was some kind of right-wing thing, on lots of progressive groups' watch lists. It had to do with elections or something. But it had no website Chloe could find. References to it were weirdly sparse, but she found pictures from some conservative conference: white people in suits shaking hands, ladies with sculpted hair and big boobs making mean sneers.

A look through Mrs. Kunstler's browser cache didn't turn up much, but she did seem to spend a lot of time on a website called ctznfrdm, which Chloe couldn't access without an account and that didn't seem publicly searchable. The login screen was nearly blank, just username and password fields.

But Chloe had the whole backup! She found Mrs. Kunstler's password-manager archive and grabbed the username (gnmenotice81) and password (random junk) from it. She switched back to the browser and logged in.

It took her a minute to understand what she was looking at. It was a messageboard, kind of janky-looking, with stupid little custom animated emojis and outsize user avatars that featured eagles and skull masks and flames and camouflage and assault rifles and characters from memes. There was a forum about outing pedophiles, one about murders supposedly committed by liberal politicians, one about voting machines, one about COVID. The one called Puppet Masters was full of anti-Semitic conspiracy theories. But the most active one was called... Dronewave.

Chloe realized she was sweating and that her mouth was dry. Her arm was throbbing. She went to the bathroom, took her pain reliever, and drank a glass of water. Her face in the mirror was pale. She should go across the way and get Loretta before reading anything more. Or maybe she should just close the browser, delete her cache, and get rid of Mrs. Kunstler's hard drive.

Instead, she climbed back into bed and kept reading. Dronewave seemed to be some kind of national movement to root out and punish supposed election fraudsters and strengthen right-wing power in swing states, so they intended to stage a series of demonstrations later in the summer in which election officials would be "held to account." Each user had a title under their name. Most people were labeled Proud Drone, with a little badge of a smiling cartoon bee with Xs for eyes. A few were Dronemother or Dronefather and these users were thanked in a thread called Affirmations. Their badges were bees, too, scowling, fierce ones; the Dronemother bees wore little skirts and eye makeup, and the Dronefather ones had biker vests. People posted that they needed Affirmations and provided addresses, and the Dronemothers and Dronefathers donated money to have the Affirmations sent. Many posts read AFFIRMED! with lots of animated flexing-arm-muscle emojis and bent-thumbs-ups that trembled and then exploded.

Now Chloe remembered the bee shirt Mrs. Kunstler was wearing in the Disney photos. It had the same design as the badge. And this reminded her of something else: the bent-thumbs-up gesture she was making in the Tron line was like the emoji here. At the time it had just seemed like some dumb out-of-touch-parent thing, but seeing the custom emoji, Chloe understood: with the cocked thumb, the gesture looked like a hand grenade. Like, a secret revolutionary code. She felt like she'd seen it before somewhere too. She was scrolling down, trying to fill in the details about the rallies, when a knock came at the door. It was Loretta. "I'm not here to babysit," she said, raising her hands in surrender. "I'm just sick of Donkey Kong Junior."

"Maybe take a look at this instead," Chloe said. She led Loretta to the bed, and the two sat cross-legged, gazing down at the laptop. Chloe explained what she'd found. "And now that I'm telling you, I just remembered something. Some guys in pickups were harassing my friend and me the day I broke my arm. They gave us the thumbs-up but I just realized, the thumb was bent, like this. And they turned out to be part of this movement or whatever that had a whole demonstration in Nestor and people got into fights."

Loretta snapped to attention, said, "May I?" and, at Chloe's nod of approval, scooped the computer into her lap. She clicked and swiped and searched. "Yeah, that's what I thought. Check it out." She showed Chloe the results: photos from all over of convoys of jacked-up pickups full of people with guns. "It's, like, open carry writ large. They've been going around to college towns all summer, places where there are lots of liberals and not much law enforcement, and putting on a show." She shook her head. "It was a whole thing when I was in the army," she said. "People don't like to talk about it because most grunts on the political right are law-abiding and respect the Constitution. But there is definitely an element that's just waiting for the coup. In the early 2010s some guys killed another soldier because they thought he was going to expose their plan to assassinate Obama."

"Whoa."

"Later, there was the guy who handed classified troop movements to a satanic cult in the UK, and the guy who helped bomb that base in Syria. They coordinate with foreign militaries too—the Germans and Italians are also dealing with this shit. It used to be those guys would wash out and go form militias or whatever. The brass doesn't want a bunch of extremist lunatics in uniform. But when I left, these guys were getting smarter about it. Less explicitly crazy, more—"

"More what?"

But Loretta was frozen, her mouth hanging open. "Wait."

"What!"

Loretta turned the laptop to face her. She pointed at a post in a long thread about the pending political rallies, then clicked it to reveal the poster's profile. The avatar was a fierce-looking bobcat head smoking a pipe. "This screen name. DiamondD1951. It's in the case file your aunt has been building. Your mom found it. It's one of the things that led us here."

Chloe stared.

"It's the guy we're supposed to be looking for tomorrow," Loretta said. "It's your great-uncle."

16

In the fading daylight, Jane watched Lila smooth a thick state atlas on the hood of the car, then pin it down with a laptop. They had driven ten miles to Skeleton Flats—a dusty sign riddled with bullet holes had charmingly marked the municipal boundary—and pulled over in the lee of some low, anonymous hill. Nothing but the road, a few boulders, and some brush was visible as far as Jane could make out. "Check it out," Lila said, opening the laptop. The screen snapped on, displaying a satellite view of brown, undulating terrain. "You see it?"

Jane had decided that she would suppress her anger and project confidence and calm on this recon mission. Act the way an equal would act. But already Lila was annoying her. "Just tell me what you want me to know," she said.

"This," Lila said, her finger thumping the hood, "is a topo map of the quadrant where Nutt's ranch is, just behind this rise. And this"—she pointed at the screen—"is the latest pass-over data from Landsat Eight. We're right about...here. Nutt's compound is...here."

On the paper map, a very narrow track led from the buildings back into the hills and ended in a depression. Two blank rectangles seemed to indicate some moderate-sized agricultural facilities. But the screen showed the path, now widened and fenced in, leading to two massive gray blocks connected by several covered passages. A slightly darker gray area in front of them suggested a parking or loading zone. "He's vastly expanded in the past few years. I think he's doing something new, something that Mom knows about. This is what I want to check out."

"Something besides the red heifers?"

"I looked into this some more," she said. "That rabbi I met in Oklahoma City—his whole thing is building the Third Temple to bring peace to the world through faith, which, good luck with that, I guess. Meanwhile Nutt's whole thing is to start World War Three."

"World War Three might not need his help."

"No, it probably doesn't," Lila said. "But look—I think he's up to something else, too. When I was in Oklahoma City, I saw him getting mobbed at a bar by a bunch of randos like he was some kind of celebrity. At first, I figured they're cattle people, he's probably some beloved breeder. But he's not. The real cattlemen think he's a hobbyist. These people knew him from something else." She tabbed over to another window on the laptop that displayed a series of photos: people driving pickup trucks, people standing in the truck beds holding guns. A crowd, fists in the air, groups of people yelling at each other. "It's some kind of libertarian movement. Started by a bunch of January Sixth rioters, former Proud Boys and Oath Keepers. Their symbol is this bee with Xs for eyes—that's how I found all these, I just searched for the bee. It looks like they've been going around harassing liberal strongholds, starting in Portland last year and popping up in Madison, Iowa City, and so on. College towns in swing states, mostly."

"What's Nutt have to do with them?"

"I don't know. But these people in the bar, they had hats and shirts with the bee on them. What I want to do," Lila said, closing the laptop, "is get into the house and see what we can find about Aunt Ruth and whatever legal matters Brian Hathaway is handling for Nutt. But... maybe we should sneak into that new facility, too, and see what he's cooking up. Maybe it's connected."

They drove the car along lonely roads for another twenty minutes until they found a place to stash it, down a dirt track that led into a blind gully. There was a little concrete hut here with a locked steel door, doubtless some utility or highway-maintenance structure. A line of phone poles passed overhead, sending a tendril through its roof. "I don't think anyone will be wandering down here tonight," Lila said. "Let's follow these lines."

They jogged across the two-lane highway, eager to avoid the gaze of any motorists. But there weren't any. They scaled a brush-covered hill and peered into the valley depicted on the maps: a flat plain cupped by low hills, invisible from the road. The buildings the satellite had seen were there, half a mile away, broad and featureless. A couple of white panel trucks were visible from where they stood, as was a tall fence topped with razor wire that stood between them and the facilities.

"I guess we try this place first?" Jane said.

"Might as well. Here." Lila unslung her backpack and removed from it a nylon shoulder holster and pistol, both the color of the sand they were standing on. Jane recognized it as a SIG Sauer of some kind, slightly different from the cop gun she'd learned on.

"What the hell?"

Lila was shrugging on her own holster. "Last time we worked together, it became necessary to defend ourselves."

Yeah, Jane thought, *no shit.* "I haven't touched a gun since then."

"You should practice once a month." Lila stared at Jane, waiting for her to arm herself.

"Uh-huh," Jane said; she accepted the holster and pulled it over her head. Once it was snug, she accepted the gun from Lila. She turned away, racked the slide, peered into the chamber. Lila handed her a full magazine and she clicked it into place, thumbed down the safety, and tucked it under her arm without chambering a round. She felt a mixture of confidence, power, and fear. Last year, after what happened in Panama and after establishing the business with Lila, she'd applied for and received a certificate of good conduct and had her firearm rights restored. But she knew that if she was convicted of a violent crime again, she'd likely go to prison for a long time, without the promise of a comfortable incarceration like the one she enjoyed in the Boynton Ridge nursery. She'd miss out on what was left of Chloe's childhood, not to mention the prime years of her adult life.

Yet here she was.

Wordlessly, Lila press-checked her gun, inserted a magazine. She shot Jane a look: *Sure you're ready for this?*

Jane ignored it. "I trust these are registered? You didn't just get them from Gramps?"

"Sure," Lila said. "Let's move out."

It was nearly dark now, and they could go down into the depression without fear of being seen unless Nutt employed some kind of heat-sensing perimeter defense. This seemed unlikely to Jane, though there would certainly be motion detectors inside.

They crept along the fenceline, alert for the presence of cameras and guards. There were two guard towers, reminiscent of the ones outside Boynton Ridge. A distant one overlooked the access road between the new facilities and two buildings that appeared to be a barn and a residence. The other, nearer tower monitored some low buildings now in darkness and the near side of the industrial structures. A faint glow was visible through the windows of the towers, doubtless the light from surveillance feeds. There were also a couple of guys walking slowly around the new facilities. Even from here, a good fifty yards away, they could smell the smoke from one guy's cigarette and make out the red dot pulsing at its tip. Lila raised an imaginary sniper rifle to her eye, jerked her hands, and quietly imitated, with her mouth, the sound of a single kill shot. She rolled her eyes.

"Don't get any ideas," Jane whispered.

They made their way all the way around the fence, taking care not to get too close to the section near the road that was interrupted by wheeled gates and illuminated by bright halogen lamps on poles. At one point they needed to hop over a shallow creek that ran through the property. The fence was secure. The only weak spot they found was a drainage outflow pipe at the creek's edge, large enough for them to crawl through but protected by thick steel mesh sunk directly into the concrete flange. There would be no cutting through it.

It was impossible to tell what was going on in these new buildings, though the sight of evenly spaced industrial vents and the sound of fans pushing air through them suggested that at least the nearer one was indeed full of animals. The smell of manure confirmed it. So maybe there was nothing more at stake than the heifers after all? As they watched, a tall loading-bay door on the farther building clattered open and rose; a panel van backed up, and a couple of people, a man and a woman, began loading some white corrugated postal bins into the back.

Lila pulled a small, expensive-looking pair of compact binoculars from a zipper pocket of her backpack. She raised them to her eyes and said, "Priority Mail boxes. They don't look very heavy." After half a dozen boxes had entered the truck, the bay door shut and the truck exited the compound.

"Weird time for a post office run," Jane said.

They backed away from the fence and moved up over the ridge in darkness to observe the main compound. They lay prone on the ground, and Lila passed the binocs to Jane, who scanned the other buildings while Lila pulled out her laptop and began sniffing for security flaws. That large, vulgar log residence was surely Nutt's. Beside it, a broad, smoothly paved lot accommodated two big rigs and a fleet of white panel trucks like the ones in the industrial area. A couple more guards were here, pacing around the compound. Out on the flats behind it was an equestrian barn, backed by hills. She could make out several animals in the shadows, dozing in their stables; a well-worn track ran through an area enclosed by white split-rail fence, interrupted by brush fences and other obstacles designed for jumping.

Another house, a low, more conventional ranch, stood nearer to them, outside the fence but apparently part of the compound. A family seemed to live there. A minivan and pickup were parked in a long paved driveway, and a massive play structure, half the size of the house itself, dominated the packed-dirt backyard. Jane remembered seeing, on the way here, a wide place in the road marked as a school bus turnoff; doubtless it existed to gather up whatever children lived here.

Lila paused in her clicking and typing. "That's Remy's," she said, nodding toward the house Jane was looking at.

"Your cowboy boyfriend."

"Yeah, exactly," Lila said, obviously peeved. "We're going steady."

"You just need to get rid of his wife."

"Look," Lila said, pointing. "That's Nutt's Peterbilt rig, the one he was showing off in Oklahoma. He's back."

"So what do we do?"

Lila snapped the laptop shut and stood. "Now? Nothing. We've got some information. We go back to the cabins and sleep, and in the morning we make a plan."

"Did you find some security holes?"

"Maybe," she said, and didn't elaborate—pointedly, Jane thought.

"I have a question."

"Shoot," Lila said.

"If he's a cattleman, where's the pasture? Like, don't cows need to go outside and eat grass or whatever?"

Lila frowned, ostensibly in concentration, but Jane thought she detected some annoyance that she herself hadn't thought of this. "Maybe they're all at auction."

"Yeah, but, does anything out there look like cattle have been walking around in it? You've seen farms and ranches before. It's weird, right?"

"Yeah, it's weird."

"So could they be…indoor cows?" Jane said. "Is that a thing?"

"Like cats."

"Yeah, hydroponic cat farming."

"Okay, now that would be weird," Lila said.

They hurried down the ridge and trudged back through the scrub to the road. After a few seconds of crouching in the ditch as a big rig passed by, they ran to the other side and into the gully where the car was. Jane wriggled out of her holster and tried to give the gun back to Lila.

"That's yours," Lila said, waving it off. She got behind the wheel. "You're going to need it."

Jane climbed into the car, still proffering the weapon. "I don't want to carry a gun that isn't registered to me."

Lila shook her head, her mouth a tight line. She started the car, grabbed the holster and gun, and threw them in the back seat. "Whatever," she said.

"Look, you don't have to like it, but I don't want to take unnecessary risks. I have a lot to lose."

"Yeah, I know, having a kid has made you precious."

"Hey!"

"I mean," Lila went on, skidding onto the road, "not so precious that you get resentful when I don't invite you on a life-threatening mission to somebody's drug compound."

"That's different!"

"It isn't. It's just hypocrisy, plain and simple. Unless you're more afraid of feeling guilty in jail than you are of being dead."

Jane opened her mouth to argue, but a moment later snapped it shut. Her sister was once again, exasperatingly, correct. She would rather be out in the field than sitting at home feeling inferior to Lila, but she would also rather be dead than back in Boynton Ridge, staring at the underside of some other woman's cot, pondering the ways she'd fucked up her daughter's life.

"If you really don't want any risk," Lila said, "you can go back to working at Nestor College and getting Dad's shirts cleaned for him. I wouldn't blame you."

"The hell you wouldn't."

"But," Lila said, "I do know that isn't what you want. You tried that, and did you feel like a perfect mother?"

Jane was too furious to answer.

"If you want to feel better, stop comparing yourself to some theoretical saint and start comparing yourself to Anabel Bortnik, the Mother Who Wasn't There. And Chloe doesn't want a perfect mother. She wants a human being who will forgive her mistakes."

"You don't know what she wants. Also, I can't just applaud her when she sneaks into somebody's house, then breaks her arm fleeing the cops. I have to actually parent."

"I'm not telling you not to," Lila said. "But I remember what it was like to be thirteen. Don't you? You were doing things that wouldn't have pleased a mother, if you'd actually had one around to piss off."

"I wouldn't have done those things if she was there."

"Actually," Lila said, raising a finger, "I think you would have done them even harder. You wanted an audience for your transgressions, not some benevolent protector."

Every muscle in her body was tense; she wanted to punch her sister in the face. She wanted to, because Lila was right again. But that didn't mean Chloe should be like her! Chloe should be different! Jane had to make sure she was different.

Trout Brook had come into view. Lila parked in front of Jane's cabin. Off to the right was a large black SUV, and as the sisters got out of the car, Jane noticed that two men were standing outside it, watching them. They were trim, muscled, dressed in khaki pants and black guayabera shirts. A billow of fabric at the hem implied the presence of concealed waistband holsters.

"You've gotta be kidding me," Jane said as the realization hit. Then, to Lila, "You knew this was going to happen."

"No."

"Bullshit!"

"An inkling, maybe."

"Well, thanks for sharing, asshole."

The cabin door flew open and Chloe appeared. "Mom!" she said. Jane could see Loretta behind her, standing awkwardly in the middle of the main room. A moment later, Chloe stepped aside to make room for their visitor.

"She sure likes to dramatically appear in a doorway, doesn't she," Lila said, not without admiration.

"Hello, Mother," Jane said, and trudged up the walk to meet her.

The situation in the cabin was awkward. Anabel Bortnik hadn't changed; she still resembled the expatriate freedom fighter she fancied herself to be rather than the international drug criminal she actually was. She wore the brown work boots Jane remembered, and the green gardener's pants held up with a shoelace belt. Her tucked-in linen shirt was black, presumably to match her muscle. Her hair was pulled back, revealing a pair of round gold-and-pearl earrings that Jane recognized, from tourist shops along their Northern-Panamanian travel route, as the work of the indigenous artisans their mother doubtless believed she championed. She carried no weapon.

"Jane," she said. "Lila."

Anabel had stepped aside to admit them, and the two sisters were now frozen, arms crossed, under a row of coat hooks, next to a small pile of shoes. Chloe had backed away and stood beside Loretta, eyes wide.

The sight of her daughter instilled Jane with sudden panic. It wasn't hard to imagine the goons from outside grabbing her and tossing her into the SUV, revenge for what she and Lila had done to Anabel's home and employees. Lila had killed half a dozen people escaping the compound, likely people their mother had known for years. It couldn't have been all business for her—those were her trusted associates, friends, even. It wasn't beneath her to kidnap her own granddaughter, bring her to Panama. What could she and Lila do? The Agency couldn't help, or wouldn't, anyway; going to Panama to get Chloe would be suicide. She wished she had listened to Lila just seconds ago and kept the SIG.

She crossed the room in a few strides and cinched her daughter tightly with one arm. "Mom, ow," Chloe said, squirming, but she didn't try to escape—it was clear she found her grandmother frightening. The woman was as out of place in this quaint fishing resort as a wizard or tiger.

Anabel Bortnik laughed. "What are you afraid of? That I'm going to indoctrinate her with radical ideas? We've barely gotten the chance to know one another." She smiled at Chloe, who flinched. "I was just asking her about her arm. Do you often climb up on roofs together?"

Jane didn't answer. Chloe gripped her hand.

"If you're here to help us," Lila said, "get on with it. Otherwise, please fuck off."

Anabel feigned shock. "That's no way to talk to your mother."

"If I had one, I wouldn't."

"Touché," she said, raising an eyebrow. "I'm here to help you. I think Nutt killed Ruth."

"You've had fifteen years to decide to do something about it," Lila said. "And the second we start looking into it, there you are."

For the first time since they'd walked in, Anabel appeared piqued; Lila had hit on a source of shame. Their mother sighed, crossed her arms. "I believed she'd killed herself when Lloyd wrote me with the news. My sister was a miserable child—we both were. Our father was a depressive; our mother was a monster. We were left to our own devices."

"Sounds familiar," Lila said, throwing herself onto the sofa.

Everyone else remained standing. "Our mother didn't neglect us," Anabel said. "She violently abused us, sometimes sexually, before turning her back on the wreckage she'd created."

This last she directed at Jane with a smoldering glare that was hard to interpret. A warning? Some kind of oblique parenting advice? Chloe's face was curdled into a mixture of terror, disgust, and fascination. "Unlike me, your aunt kept the rage bottled up," Anabel went on. "She was a highly successful woman, but she harbored a bottomless well of misery. When I learned of her death, I was sad for her, but I wasn't surprised." She turned to Jane again as though trying to draw upon some suspected reservoir of sympathy—but why her? Did she perceive Jane as the weaker of the two? Or was it because Jane, like Anabel, was a mother? "I wish I'd acted then. But I was blinded by the past and by my frustrations with your aunt. Our relationship wasn't always harmonious."

A snort came from the sofa. Lila crossed one leg over the other and spat, "You're the one who hooked her up with Nutt, aren't you."

Her face hardened. "Yes."

"And you didn't think it could get her killed?"

"No," Anabel said. "I misjudged my power over him. I thought he wouldn't dare harm anyone near me. That blinded me too."

Jane wanted to join Lila in the accusations, prove she wasn't a pushover. She said, "You were doing business with Nutt, I assume. Marketing your products together. To rapists!"

"That wasn't my intention. But I learned of what he'd made and was looking for inroads into his market. In the end, he approached me. The rape angle was nonsensical. His product was dominant in the eastern US, I wanted mine there, too, and he knew it. It was a business relationship."

"But why expose your sister to risk like this?" Jane demanded.

Anabel's glare was withering. "Did you suspect your aunt of working entirely within the law? Do you think she was pure and ethical? Because she wasn't, Jane. We'd worked together for years. I made her a lot of money, and she protected many people who were useful to me. And Nutt's needs at the time were exactly in her area of expertise. She defended him when he was a disgraced academic, and she continued to work with him in the years after. My guess is that she learned something she shouldn't have, and Nutt eliminated her."

"The heifers," Lila said.

"Ah. That. No. It's true that the genetically perfect heifer is an obsession of his. And, to his credit, I suspect he's successfully created it many times over. But the rabbis keep rejecting them. They're not eager to hand over the fulfillment of their prophecy to a violent Christian kook. So they find imperfections."

"You're right about that," Lila said. "I met Rabbi Luntschitz in Oklahoma City after he stormed out of a meeting with Nutt. It sounded like the Holy Temple Center is finished with him."

"So what, then?" Jane asked. "If it's not the heifers, what did she find out?"

Anabel glanced around the room. "I'm going to sit down," she said, moving toward one of the empty chairs. The others, hesitantly, followed suit, except for Jane, who chose to stand behind the chair that Chloe had gratefully slumped into. Unconsciously, Jane stroked her head, and Chloe pushed her hand away. "I'd been planning a trip north already," Anabel went on, "before I learned what you were doing, and why. My network has been reporting business drying up in certain local markets. These locations are all in the United States, mostly in the suburbs, mostly in the Midwest and affluent South. A few months ago, people there just suddenly stopped buying my product. At first I assumed encroachment by other manufacturers and suppliers, and I braced myself for violence. But things stayed quiet. All of my sources were telling me the same thing: these customers had stopped buying entirely.

"I had my people look further into it. I wondered if there were some new government campaigns or health initiatives in these areas, but there were none. Quite the opposite, in fact—funding had dried up for these initiatives and several had ended. Law enforcement continued to look the other way, as they generally have with this category of consumer. The only explanation was that these people had gotten themselves addicted to something else. And my agents were confirming that. Except we couldn't figure out what the new product was or how it was moving through the market. I had investigators surveilling our couriers in several different corridors, and no one was moonlighting.

"The one thing I did learn," she said, "was what the new drug's effects were. Reports had it creating bursts of euphoria, energy, self-confidence. Excessive sensitivity, especially to light. A decrease in hunger and thirst—so, useful as a diet aid."

"Sounds like cocaine," Lila drawled.

"It does, doesn't it. Except, also, these effects are accompanied by others—increased relaxation and suggestibility."

"Like Yes?" Jane said.

"Not like Yes," Anabel corrected, glaring at her. "Like what Yes is *marketed* to do. Yes is just a synthetic opioid derived from Nutt's work with livestock pharmaceuticals that we combined with my product to open new markets. As I said, the rape angle was Nutt's idea. But it sold pills."

It was astounding to Jane that her mother would display this extraordinary callousness, given what she knew had happened to her own daughters. What *could* happen to her own granddaughter. She held the back of Chloe's chair, trying to suppress a wave of fury. And, as if reading her mind, Chloe reached up and laid her hand on Jane's. Jane relaxed her fingers, gripped Chloe's.

"There's one incredible detail, one thing that made me realize I had to come see this firsthand. Several people told my agents that the best thing about this new drug was that they only had to take it once."

"You're joking," Lila said.

"No. According to people who were on it, you took the drug, and its effects lasted indefinitely. It was more like an infection."

"Doesn't sound very lucrative!" Lila said, laughing.

"No."

"It's almost as though it could destroy your entire business model. And take out your competitors too."

A scowl. "Yes, Lila, almost."

"What," Jane said through gritted teeth, "is this miracle substance called?"

"Affirmation," said Anabel.

Chloe's fingers tightened around Jane's, and she gasped.

17

Lila watched her niece release Jane's hand and clap it over her mouth. All eyes turned to her.

"Chloe?" Jane asked.

Beside her on the chair, Loretta cleared her throat. "Chloe, do you want me to tell them?"

"Tell us what," Jane said. Her eyes darted from her daughter to Loretta and back.

"Chloe...found something." After a moment, Chloe nodded, and Loretta went on. "Okay. So, during her adventure with the police, Chloe found herself in possession of a small backup hard drive."

"Oh, Chloe," Jane said, slumping.

"And while you two were surveilling the compound, she decided to examine it further. She found Laurel Anne Kunstler's browsing history, which led her to an online forum that she was able to log into with Kunstler's credentials."

"Who is this woman?" Anabel asked, irritated to be left in the dark.

"Chloe's running for class president," Lila explained, "and this lady is her rival's mother. She made a deepfake video of Chloe to discredit her, and Chloe broke into their house to get evidence. And found it, I should add."

"Impressive," said Anabel.

"It's not an accomplishment!" Jane said.

"Mom," came a voice, muffled, from beneath Chloe's hands, *"stop."*

Loretta continued. "The forum is a right-wing discussion group—

there's a whole section devoted to something called Dronewave."

"Wait," Lila said, putting it together. "Do they have a logo, a bee?"

"With Xs for eyes," Chloe said.

"I saw that. On a shirt last week in Oklahoma City. People were mobbing Nutt in a cowboy bar like he was some kind of celebrity. His handler had to push them away."

"Well, that tracks," Loretta said. "Chloe and I dug around for an hour. These people think of Nutt as their leader. They're planning some mass action during the election, targeting local races and election boards that won't have much security at them. A wave of riots all over America."

"I think I've seen this before," Jane said. "The woman who was undercover at the writers' conference—she works for a congresswoman who is into this stuff. And—oh, shit." They waited a moment for her to gather herself. "My friend's brother. He had a shirt with the bee on it."

Loretta continued. "Laurel Anne Kunstler is some kind of donor hero, one of a bunch of rich people who are paying to have things sent to the rioters. When one of them gets a package, they say, 'Affirmation received.'"

"It's the product," Anabel said. "Nutt's product."

The entire situation suddenly struck Lila as hilarious. At last, somebody had figured out a way to hurt Anabel Bortnik without ever getting near her. "What does he have against you?" she said. "What did you do to him?"

"I cut ties with him. He was abusing my network, trying to influence couriers and sellers without my knowledge. Then he demanded a greater cut. He vastly overestimated his worth to me."

"Well," Lila said, "you won't be worth much yourself if this goes on much longer."

Jane said, "I don't understand. Why would anyone take this drug? You take it once and you stay high...forever? Until you die?"

Everyone was silent for a moment. Then Loretta said, "This is a golden age of medical quackery. A few years ago, people were taking horse dewormer to cure COVID. Now they're doing it because they think other people's vaccines are making them sick. If you're one of those people, and somebody wants to get you high so you can go trigger the libs, somebody who tells you doctors aren't trustworthy, institutions are against you, and politicians are liars, you'll do it, right?"

She exchanged a look with Lila. Lila understood: Loretta was thinking about her father, a farmer who'd succumbed to paranoia, believed the FBI and CIA were after him, and bankrupted the family farm building a bunker and stocking up on guns. In the end, he'd killed Loretta's mother and himself. She was seventeen. When the dust cleared, Loretta sold the farm and joined the army. She understood the mindset. If he'd survived, her father might well have been one of the people trying to treat COVID with hydroxychloroquine and bleach and popping some high-till-you-die pill a stranger sent him in the mail.

"And I noticed something else when Chloe showed me this forum," Loretta said. "There's a user on there with the screen name DiamondD1951."

Jane was startled out of her reverie. "Isn't that..."

"Yes, Lloyd Davies. I recognized it from your intel about the tobacco. It's got to be him."

"We tracked him down to Prescott," Lila said. "Chloe and Loretta were planning on looking for him tomorrow. He's likely to know something more about all this; he evidently knows Nutt."

Loretta seemed hurt, as though Lila were trying to get rid of her rather than engaging her in the same kind of work they'd been doing together for years. Lila tried to conceal her irritation. She said, "Should we reconvene here tomorrow morning?"

Everyone looked around the room. "Okay?" Jane said finally.

Lila turned to her mother. "I assume you're not staying here."

"No."

"Well, wherever you'll be, have a peaceful night."

She left the cabin, trying to appear, as much as she could, like a tired woman who needed to use the toilet. Out of the corner of her eye, she clocked Anabel's goons tracking her, their big dumb heads slowly swiveling as she crossed the gravel road to the cabin she was sharing with Loretta. Inside, she went to her pack and dug out, from the side pocket, a fresh GPS tracker. She checked the battery, applied an adhesive strip, and ripped off the paper backing. Then, palming the little device, she grabbed the car key from the bedside table and headed back out, making sure Anabel's men saw the fob dangling from her hand. "Forgot something," she said.

She opened the car door and sat behind the wheel, leaving the door open and pinging. Then she took out her phone and called Loretta. "Everyone's still talking in there?" she whispered.

"Tensely, yes," Loretta said, sotto voce.

"Come outside, be conspicuous."

"Ah. Got it."

A few seconds later, Loretta appeared in the cabin doorway. She came out into the streetlight, sniffed the air, looked around. The two guards turned. "Hey," Lila heard her say. "Are you guys hungry?"

Lila crept across the twenty feet between the two vehicles, crouched at the SUV's back bumper, and tucked the tracker up and under it. It was fiberglass and hollow and seemed to be free of dirt and debris; the adhesive grabbed and Lila withdrew her hand.

The men must have shaken their heads no. Loretta said, "You sure? We were thinking we'd pop by the lodge for a snack."

Lila stole back to the car, grabbed some papers from the glovebox as a prop. She slammed the door shut. "Hey!" she called out to Loretta. "Did you check the menu? They got chicken tenders?"

"I dunno."

"Good night, you guys," she said to the goons. To Loretta, she said, "If they have chicken tenders, get me some," and returned to her cabin.

Inside, she got out her laptop and connected to the tracker. Commercial GPS systems tended to require registration and a branded smartphone app; she had sourced ones she could root and flash with her own custom firmware, and kept a few charged and in her bag, just in case. The satellite signal here was strong, keeping her laptop securely connected to her server, and the SUV outside now appeared as a red dot on her map.

A few minutes later, she heard the slamming of car doors and the crunch of tires on gravel. She shouldered her pack and jogged outside. It took a minute to sweep her own car and discover a tracker magnetized to the chassis. She tossed it into a bush, climbed into the car, opened up the laptop on the passenger seat, and set off after her mother.

There was no hurry; it didn't matter how far away the tracker was, she could detect it anywhere on earth. She followed the car for the better part of an hour to the northwest, skirting Skeleton Flats and Nutt's compound and delving deep into the hills and scrub. Billboards advertised steak houses, bait shops, and fishing cabins. The road they were on seemed to lead to one place only, a long and spiny lake like an amoeba. A few cars passed her from the opposite direction, and she imagined that they contained doctors and lawyers from Phoenix, bringing their catches to be gutted and roasted for dinner.

A few miles from the lake, she observed that her mother's red dot had stopped, just south of the main road along the lakeshore. When Lila came to the intersection, she turned right and made her meandering way along the lake to the north until she found a disused concrete boat launch across the water from Anabel's destination. She killed the lights and pulled in, then hauled her pack from the car and took a seat on a boulder overlooking the still water. The chittering of insects and the calls of birds surrounded her.

She pulled out her binoculars but didn't need them to see the rectangles of light that marked the lakeside cabin where Anabel Bortnik and her heavies were staying. The binoculars showed the shadows of figures moving behind the curtains. She was surprised there wasn't anyone standing guard where she sat.

She put away the binoculars and pulled out a burner. This one was getting long in the tooth—a couple of days now—and would soon need to be replaced. She punched in a number and was greeted by laughter. "The same number two calls in a row?" Knight said. "You're getting sloppy, Lila."

"You asked me to rat out the great and powerful Holy Ghost of Palo Seco, and here I am."

"Wow. I didn't expect you to actually listen to me."

"A good bet," she said. "And I wouldn't have, except that I think you know exactly where she is. I think you're putting her up."

"Huh," Knight said, "is that the caw of a foraging black-crowned night heron I hear?"

"I didn't peg you as a birder," Lila said.

"You get bored sometimes, sitting on the shore of a certain Arizona lake, waiting for something to happen."

"Right. So, are you ready to tell me why you're matchmaking me with my mother?"

"I think you know the answer."

In the background, she heard the blare of a car horn, a shout. "Everything all right where you are, Knight?"

"I'm outside a bar. Watching and waiting, but there's always time to take a call from you."

"Right."

"At this point, you might know more than we do. Maybe you can give me a taste?"

"Well," she said, "do you know about Dronewave?"

"We do."

"Anabel and Nutt had a falling-out, she says. She thinks he's making something new to kill her business and is giving it away for free. It's called Affirmation. But we don't know what it is or how it works."

"So you're up to speed with us, it seems."

"Yeah, the difference is, you can do something about it. We're here to answer questions about my aunt's death. We can't stop a wave of riots."

"Well, that's the problem. Neither can we."

Across the lake, a light turned off and another turned on. Shadows crossed the windows. The wind had shifted and she smelled cigarette smoke. "Give me a break. Of course you can."

"If we had the jurisdiction, dear Lila, we could do anything. But this is more a job for our friends at the Bureau, and we are finding it difficult to get them interested. It's too decentralized and abstract. They'd rather pretend it isn't real than allocate the man-hours. I suspect they'd prefer to watch the crimes unfold before they act to remind themselves why they exist, or maybe just to feel alive."

"Don't forget the lady-hours, asshole."

"I am magnanimously conferring honorary manhood upon female officers, of course."

"Look, Knight," Lila said. "If you have something specific you need done, and something useful you can do for me in exchange, please put your cards on the table. Otherwise, I'd like to declare this annoying new chapter of our friendship closed."

"Since I've already had this conversation with Mama Moriarty—"

"Knight, ugh."

"—I'll just let her fill you in."

"We're not on the best of terms."

"Enemy of my enemy and all that, Lila. I think I see my mark, gotta run. Have a pleasant visit. Do a little bass fishing. Trip on peyote. Befriend a Gila monster." He hung up.

It was without much surprise that she detected the sound of an engine behind her, followed by the gentle squeak of brakes, the thunk of an opening door, and the racking slide of a semiautomatic pistol. "Ella quiere verte," came a deep voice.

"Yeah, yeah," Lila said. She stood up and twisted the phone in her hands, cracking the flimsy plastic into pieces, then threw them into the lake. The big man tenderly relieved her of her sidearm and backpack and guided her into the car.

The Agency's cabin was accoutered in hunting-and-fishing kitsch, including repro landscape paintings, decaying trophy heads, and antique fishing rods casually leaning in various corners as though set down there for just a minute in 1923 and never touched again. Woven creels hung from wooden pegs. An electromechanical flopping bass, motion-activated, bleated out "One Way or Another" by Blondie as Lila and her captor passed it in the hall. *I'm gonna getcha, getcha, getcha, getcha.* She was led into a sunken living room, where her mother was sitting in a canvas folding chair facing a broad, cold stone fireplace whose empty iron grate was dusted with ash. Lila took a similar chair a few feet away. After giving her a glare intended to convey, she supposed, a warning, Anabel's errand boy retreated into another room.

"Nice place," Lila said. "Airbnb?"

"Have you spoken with Knight?" her mother said, staring at the non-fire.

"Funny, I just did. He asked if we'd like to join him for a threesome."

Her mother turned and studied her for a moment. "When did you develop a sense of humor?"

"Sick burn, Anabel."

"You were not funny as a child. Your sister was funny. You were like a living ghost. Did you study sarcasm? Learn it from videos?"

"It came to me naturally via a process you weren't privy to called 'growing up.'"

Her mother nodded once, then said, "My understanding of the situation is that Knight would like us to murder Travis Nutt. At that point, he'll alert the Bureau, who will seize the compound and dismantle it. I would first like confirmation of what happened to my sister, however."

"That's my read on the Agency's ask," Lila said. "I know what you get out of it: not becoming completely obsolete overnight. But what's in it for me?"

"Freedom from Agency oversight, I suppose?"

"I was supposed to get that by burning your house down last year, and look at me now."

They stared at each other for a few seconds. A cough came from the other room, perhaps a meaningful one. The smoker, no doubt. Then the sound of someone getting up and moving around, and the shrill tones of the singing bass. *One way or another, I'm gonna find ya...*

"Why doesn't somebody turn that thing off?" Lila asked.

"There's no switch. And it's bolted to the wall. I think it is supposed to be some kind of joke."

"Could we at least get more than two lines?"

"It's the federal government," Anabel said. "Too cheap to license the whole song, no doubt."

"Jesus Christ. It reeks of Knight."

Anabel glanced around distastefully. "Everything here does."

"And what about the riots?" Lila said. "People are planning violence in Pennsylvania, Wisconsin, here in Arizona. Poll workers, election officials are in danger. Knight thinks the Bureau plans to just let it all happen."

"And you object?"

Lila recalled the callousness she'd affected with Jane, and here, elected to affect its opposite. "Yes, Mother, I object. You don't object?"

She shrugged. "There would be a poetic justice to American democracy collapsing in such a stupid way, don't you think?"

"I'm not sure that violence inflicted on innocent people is a reasonable price for satisfying your gallows humor."

Anabel appeared piqued, shifted uncomfortably in the chair. "You're a patriot now? I thought you were supposed to be a citizen of nowhere, like your mother."

"I'm hardly a patriot. I just don't want assholes to beat up old ladies in school auditoriums because they're gooned on infinite blow, or whatever the hell the stuff is."

"Hm" was the reply. And then, after a while, "So, we'll do what they wish? Eliminate Nutt? And then, if you like, you can crisscross the nation in your souped-up Volvo like some kind of avenging Santa Claus, rescuing retirees on election night."

"Fine."

"Fine." Anabel stood up. "César will see you out. I'll be in touch tomorrow."

César appeared, accompanied by the motorized fish. *I'm gonna getcha, getcha, getcha, getcha...* She followed him out to the car, which he drove with maddening slowness back around the northern tip of the lake. Soon she was alone again on her boulder, gazing out over the water. She glanced down at her hand, where slight traces of ink were still visible on her palm.

The backpack produced a new phone, which she freed from its blister pack with a slash of her folding knife. She activated it, checked the charge, then dialed the number she had memorized. "Who's this?" came a voice, and she felt it deep in her belly like hot buttered rum.

"It's Lila. Lila from the campground."

Brooke laughed. "Thanks for clarifying."

"Well, I don't know how many Lilas you fucked this week."

"There was the one on the Ferris wheel, the one in the Vatican..."

They both laughed this time. Lila said, "I'm surprised you answered."

"Ordinarily," Brooke said, "I have it set to block unknown numbers. But I thought just maybe somebody might call me from a burner."

Lila's heart lifted. She could feel her face glowing with shame. "What are you doing?"

That laugh again, like campfire smoke, like diving naked into lake water. "Actually...I can't tell you!"

"You're working."

"I'm working."

"Let me listen. Maybe I can deduce it from your environment."

"All right."

They were silent for a minute. Lila heard the groan of a big rig getting up to speed, the chatter of some children. Crickets. A car radio playing hip-hop. She said, "A highway rest stop."

"Wow, a master spy at work. Where are you? I can't hear a thing on your end thanks to this noisy highway rest stop."

"I'm sitting on the shore of a lake. Which I guess is why I called you."

"Lakes will never be the same."

"I just saw my mother."

"The way you say that," Brooke said, "it sounds like there's a story."

"Is there ever," Lila said.

"I'd like to hear it sometime."

"I'd like to tell it." She paused, then blurted out, "I miss you. Oh god. Sorry."

Brooke said, "I miss you too. Maybe when we're finished with whatever we're doing, we could get together."

"Yeah, I'd like that."

"Yeah."

Lila thought she could hear her smiling. She pictured the smile. Imagined kissing it. She groaned.

"Haha, okay," Brooke said, clearly thinking the same thing. "Gotta run, Lila."

"Okay, Brooke."

"See you someday soon."

Then the call was over. Lila felt relieved and sad and for maybe the first time in her life didn't want to do what she was doing. She threw the phone into the bag, got into the car, and began the lonesome drive back to the lodge.

18

As with everything he did that involved Peggy, discovering the identity of Alain Rampersaud came swiftly and easily, as though in a dream. They were having a working lunch together at the Cake and Kettle. He was reading another book about Cold War South America; she was jotting things in her work notebook with a monogrammed pen, as she was on duty at the public library today. Between them lay half a slice of blackberry pie that they were gradually working their way through, sharing a fork. "Do you want another fork?" the waitress asked them, and Peggy said no, thanks, but please refill the coffees. The sun was blinking on and off like a slow lighthouse as indecisive rain clouds raced across it. Harry kept looking up from his book to make sure it was all real and to steal glances at Peggy's concentration face. He said, in spite of himself, "I didn't figure you for a monogram person. Or a fountain-pen person."

"Hm?" she asked, looking up.

"A very fancy pen for a working lady." It was thick as a cigar, and the café was quiet enough to hear the scratch of it against the paper's surface.

Peggy laughed. "These did seem stuffy to me at one time. But I've got aches and pains in my fingers and toes, and a friend suggested switching to a fountain pen. You have to learn a looser grip. Plus, these old Montblancs are nice and fat and easy to grip." She held the pen up to the light. "It's funny how things old men like seem made for children. Little fast cars and big chubby pens. A special drink from a special cup. Present company excepted, Harry."

"Subaru, pencil, and a filthy old mug here," he said, raising his hand.

"I would never have bought one of these, they're preposterously expensive. Paul had a whole case of them, most of which I sold."

"Paul," repeated Harry to himself.

"My late husband?"

"Yes, yes. The monogram. PTJ?"

"Paul Theorin Jansson. Theorin is an old Swedish family name, he was actually called Theo when he was a child."

"I ask," Harry said, "because perhaps the F—perhaps Franklin wasn't referring to you in his notes. Maybe he meant Paul. Were they friends?"

Peggy put the pen down. "Huh. I wouldn't say friends, exactly. Paul found Franklin a bit ridiculous."

"Well, he was."

She laughed. "It's true!"

"You told me he worked in aerospace engineering?"

"At Lockheed, in Albany."

"Is there a chance he and Rampersaud could have met?" Harry hefted the book he was reading. "A deposed Cold War dictator, a defense contractor? It doesn't seem impossible."

"No, it doesn't. Hmm." She stared into space. "Occasionally there were job fairs, expos, that kind of thing that Paul would attend in semi-retirement. He was always escaping to whiskey-soaked lunches too. I wonder…" She froze. "Oh."

"Yes?"

"Ohhhh. Harry," she said, turning to him, "I know who he is. Alan. Alan Saunders."

"Alan Saunders?"

"I'm sure of it. It must be him. He had a British accent, but there was something else to it, the vowels were musical, the r's had a little roll to them."

"Rampersaud had a British education—there was a school in Plácidia that his grandfather founded. The British used the island as a cable station in the late nineteenth century for a while before it passed back into Plácidian hands, and some of the Brits stayed. It makes sense he would sound…intercontinental?"

"Franklin joined Paul on a few of those boozy lunches, if I remember right. Alan was…how old when he was deposed?"

"In his early twenties, I think?"

"Pfft," Peggy said. "I'm sure he's alive. He's barely older than you."

"Do you know how we can find him?"

She laughed. "I think I do. Finish that pie, Harry, and come back to the library with me."

A few minutes later he was following her through town, which in Ghorum meant across the street. The wind had picked up and rain seemed inevitable now. He had a moment of confusion, the present folding over the past, as he remembered similar weather, dashing across a parking lot with Anabel, maybe on the way to some school conference where they would be told that Jane was caught smoking.

They made it inside before the downpour began. The little library thrummed with it as Peggy led him through an employee door and into an office. Peggy greeted a coworker who was sitting at a computer, phone pinned between her ear and shoulder, and moved over to a card catalog. "We got rid of the ones on the floor, against my vocal opposition," she said. "But we kept the one where we filed the old patron information. Not everybody made it over to the new system, we just didn't have the time and money."

"Alain Rampersaud was a library patron?"

"Paul brought him here in a rare gesture of pride. I signed him up for a card, almost as a joke. We would have gotten his address so we could send it to him."

"When was this?" Harry asked as drawers slid open and closed, and her fingers nimbly moved through the cards. Muscle memory!

"A decade ago."

"I'm sure he's moved since then," Harry said, dejected.

She laughed. "Maybe, but...have you moved since then, Harry? Why should he be any different?"

Harry supposed this was true. Deposed South American dictators, they're just like you and me! After a moment, Peggy announced pay dirt with a small, satisfied sigh. He was getting to know this sigh quite well; it made him feel warm and intimate and a little turned on. She turned to him and said, "Canandaigua."

"Canandaigua! That's a day trip. Should we drop in?"

She slumped a little on her stool, frowned. "No, I don't think so, Harry. I think we need to call him."

"But if we spook him, he could slip away!"

She cocked her head. "Is that how you think of the man, Harry? A criminal we need to apprehend?"

In truth, Harry had indeed regarded Rampersaud as a quarry, though not a nefarious one—more like a rare artifact or manuscript to unearth. And of course he'd assumed the man was guilty of some kind of foul play, how could he not be? But he admired Peggy's impulse to proceed with caution and compassion. If he didn't find Rampersaud, so what? The search for him had led him to Peggy, a far greater treasure. The historian in him—and he was mostly historian—bristled at the thought of letting a lead fizzle out, but she was right. If Harry was the one being hunted, he'd want a phone call.

She held up her phone. "I've got his number. Should I?"

Harry nodded. "I can't listen."

He wandered into the stacks, the place he felt most at home since retirement took his academic office away. Not long ago, he'd gone into the old building to see who was occupying that office now and found a young bespectacled woman who had transformed it into a bright and cheerful sanctum of the intellect, garlanded with houseplants, meticulously organized books neatly packed onto brand-new dustless bookcases. She asked if she could help him, and he stammered, "S-sorry, wrong office," before scuttling off to the library where he belonged. It didn't matter to him now that he was flanked on one side by superhero comics and the other by tales of oppressive sci-fi carceral states populated by sexy vampire revolutionaries—he felt calm.

He checked his phone for texts, hoping for an update from Arizona. Had they figured out what happened to Ruth? Tracked down his missing ex-brother-in-law? But there was nothing. He texted Chloe, *How's the arm?*, and she promptly sent a selfie back from the passenger seat of a rental car, giving a thumbs-up, Jane behind the wheel looking askance at the camera.

Met my grandma, she added.

It took him a minute. Good grief! Anabel was in-country? He had just been thinking about her. Had he somehow materialized her with his gloomy reminiscence? *What!* he typed. *Why?*

She wanted to help? Or maybe get in the way. idk

What do you think of her?

Scary was the reply.

Agree! Harry responded, pleased.

Cant believe you were married to this weirdo

We were young, he typed, laughing. *She was, anyway.*

Your still young grandpa. 🌺

With immense self-consciousness, he typed, *L.O.L.* 😁

He believed that was the "rolling on the floor laughing" emoji (or perhaps a single one was called an *emojo*?) and he wasn't sure what was so funny about his text, but, as Chloe liked to say, "Take the win." He took it.

A moment later, Peggy appeared, holding up her phone as though Rampersaud were caught inside it. "I spoke to him. He'll see you?"

"Really? When!"

"Today?" she said, smiling. "Unless you have something better to do, we could drive out there, meet your ghost, and have a bite to eat. Even spend the night, if you like."

The rain had tapered off, and as they headed west out of the storm, a cold front arrived to push the clouds away, and they pulled down their sun visors against the blazing, broken-glass world. The search for Rampersaud had brought Peggy back to the latter days of her marriage, and she talked for the first time about Paul, his alcoholism, his descent into paranoia and conspiracy theories. "Honestly, Harry, we would never have split if it weren't for the politics. He wasn't mean or abusive—just a sad drunk for whom, after retirement, I simply wasn't enough. Always this air of disappointment. I used to tell him, Life is its own reward! We have money, we have time! Let's enjoy it. Of course it turned out that we didn't have money, and we also didn't have time. He didn't, anyway."

"I'm sorry," Harry said.

She patted his knee. "You say that a lot. We'll cure you of it. You're a good listener, Harry."

He told her about his text exchange with Chloe and confessed the deeper truth about his relationship with Anabel and the CIA—that she'd secretly recruited him as an Agency contractor, tasked him with eavesdropping on moneyed students connected to foreign governments, and let him believe that he was the one who'd recruited her. "Our entire marriage, I thought her trips abroad were my fault, that I'd fed her to the

Agency and let it eat her up. I thought I'd ruined her! It was only when I confronted Franklin that I learned the truth." He shook his head. "It's funny, you can feel something your whole life based on a lie, a misunderstanding, even, and not only do you never get all that emotion back, you don't even get to stop feeling it. I remember that guilt with such intensity! But also, pathetically, I still feel it, even though I know that it's groundless."

"Well," Peggy said, "you can't erase your memories, but you can stop feeling that guilt. Go to therapy, Harry! It can work wonders."

"It may be too late to change," he said.

"It sounds like you've changed more in the past year than in the previous thirty combined. You've switched careers, you've gotten closer to Chloe. Why not give it a shot?"

He was still pondering the possibility when they arrived in Canandaigua, a quaint little city at the tip of the lake it was named for—or perhaps the lake had taken the city's name. Rampersaud—or Saunders, as Harry supposed he'd prefer to be addressed—lived on a cul-de-sac on the edge of town, near a school and a business campus, and bordered on one side by woods. The house was a low ranch with several small outbuildings, including a garage and shed, shaded by maples and oaks. It had the air of a leftover from a previous neighborhood, the one the school and business park probably replaced. Harry imagined some crotchety holdout pounding his fist on a folding buffet table at some zoning meeting of the distant past, leaving this place for Saunders to eventually be forgotten in.

He was waiting for them on the porch and stood to greet them as the Subaru glided down the newly resurfaced asphalt driveway: a tall, bent branch of a man with a long, clean-shaven face and white tufts of hair over his ears. As they parked and stepped out, he climbed down his front steps to meet them, supporting himself with a gnarled wooden cane that seemed designed to complement his own knots and scars. To their surprise, he welcomed them each with a smile and a strong handshake into which Harry read a hint of defensiveness.

"Peggy," the man said. "I remember you, of course. And..." He glanced at Harry and back to her. "Paul, was it? Is he no longer living? Or..."

"He's not, I'm sad to say. This is Harry, he's a professor emeritus at Nestor College. He's the one who became interested in your story."

"Pleased to meet you," Harry said.

Saunders nodded. "Come out back with me. I've prepared some refreshments." His voice was assured, deliberate, the sounds overenunciated as Harry might expect from a man who'd been taught to get it right the first time. Not that it had mattered, in the end.

They followed him along a flagstone path, past hydrangeas and azaleas, to a patio made from concrete pavers, moss spreading from the sand in between. A deep yard extended into wooded gloom on one side, gravestones on the other. A swing set, fairly new, had been installed on a freshly poured apron of cedar chips. "For my grandchildren," he said, taking a seat on a white molded-plastic chair. A matching table anchored by an umbrella on a pole held a tray of crackers and cheese and a plastic pitcher of iced tea. It was all very informal, charmingly so, but it also seemed to Harry to convey normality, unflappability, defiance in the face of exposure. Of course, he'd only had a few hours to prepare.

"I live alone," Saunders said as they sat, as though reading Harry's mind. "My apologies for the modest offerings. My daughter-in-law comes to help out several times a week, but she'd already left when you called."

"It's fine, of course," Harry said, drawing a notebook and pencil from the pocket of his jacket. "Generous of you, in fact."

The man nodded at the pencil and paper. "I looked you up. You write books." He reached for the pitcher, poured them all glasses of tea.

"I wrote one," Harry said.

"Are you writing one about me? My father? About Plácidia?"

The question startled him. No, no, of course he wasn't. But...he'd barely cracked the Factor's notes. It occurred to him now that they could serve as a source of inspiration for a book of historical loose threads, forgotten stories set against the backdrop of the rise and fall of Western espionage. The Factor was first and foremost a gossip—who knew what else he had puzzled over in those pages, what other rumors and innuendo he'd copied into them?

"Perhaps," Harry said, carefully. "But I'm not here to...blow your cover."

Saunders shrugged. "I am not undercover, Professor. When I was brought here, I was offered a new identity, and I accepted it. I would have been happy to talk about the past, but no one asked." He nodded at Peggy. "Except for that man, your husband's friend. He asked for my story, and I told it. Part of it, anyway."

"Mr. Saunders," Peggy asked, "how did you know my husband?" Harry endured a mild wave of jealousy hearing the late Paul Jansson referred to in this way.

"Your husband was one of the American officers into whose supervision I was transferred after my extraction from my country. We bonded over a shared interest in British cars and motorcycles. When, years later, he learned that I had been settled near your home, he reached out through the appropriate channels. We were never close, but I liked him."

"Mr. Saunders," Harry said, readying a notebook page, "what happened? How did you escape? The internet has you thrown off a cliff or a ship into the sea."

"Don't forget the flagpole, Professor. Certain quarters seemed to favor the impaling theory, but imagine the effort it would take. Sharpening the flagpole, hoisting my struggling body into the air. No. Much easier," he said, holding up his hands, "not to murder me at all."

"But they murdered your father, didn't they?"

"Perhaps. But…perhaps not. You need to understand that I was a very young man, barely twenty, and sheltered. I'd been given a private education and resided in a castle on a mountaintop. My father had lived in fear for half a decade at that point, ever since the coup in Brazil that your government had supported. In addition, my mother left him the moment I was enrolled in university abroad; she eventually remarried a man in Lisbon and raised rabbits and painted with watercolors until her death. He'd become paranoid that his guards were under the sway of the junta despite evidence to the contrary. And yes, a gunshot ended my father's life, but I believe he pulled the trigger himself, on the black-sand beach of the palace grounds. No weapon was found, but…such a thing would be valuable, either as a keepsake or simply for self-defense during a very unstable time. Someone probably swiped it."

"I'm sorry, Mr. Saunders," Peggy asked, "but…why do you believe this?"

"Very simple," he replied. "If the military had executed my father, I would doubtless have been next. I was living at home at the time, hiking in the woods, photographing wildlife, reading. Wishing I could move to Portugal to be with my mother. Waiting for some manner of stability to settle over my region. News reached Plácidia slowly in those days, you see; it seemed as though we might be able to wait out the chaos. I don't think we merited more than a passing thought to Médici, or Silva before him. The drama surrounding my father's death may have been the triggering event, in fact, that sealed my own fate—news of this supposed coup reached the mainland, and before long the imagined threat became real. Why not grab the island during this interregnum?"

His mouth curled down in a frown of distaste. Harry imagined being this spoiled boy, trapped at home with his increasingly fearful father, wishing for escape to the simpler life of a wealthy, handsome expat in Europe—and then drowning in grief and in responsibility he didn't want. "I was advised to accept power immediately," Saunders went on, "and begin projecting authority and confidence, which, though it was not in my nature, I strove to do. I never met Médici but I met his foreign affairs minister—Barbosa, I believe was his name. It was clear to me that they would take over my country when they saw fit, but for a time, I could do as I pleased. So I signed over my family's land to the people as a national park. This was the apex of my very brief political career, and it infuriated my vile aunts and uncles and delighted my mother. Eventually I received word that Plácidia's independence was soon to end, and was paid a visit by an agent from British intelligence who arranged for my flight and planted the rumor that I'd been assassinated."

"Why didn't you go to live with your mother as you'd hoped?" Peggy asked.

"Ah—because by then she had died. Murdered with her husband in an apparent robbery."

"My god," Harry heard himself say.

Saunders shrugged. "Again, there was no real evidence that her death was politically motivated. Some years ago, I traveled to Portugal, against the advice of my Agency contacts, to try and unravel what happened. I visited the courts, requested the records. Most of them were gone. The only thing I learned was that the police attributed the deaths to gang violence, and once they'd arrived at that conclusion, they gave up the case. A rich foreigner killed by gangsters—you can imagine such a crime quickly falling to the bottom of the priority list."

The sun was low in the sky and cast long shadows of the three of them, the table and chairs, the swing set. A breeze shook the umbrella, and Harry's hand reached out automatically to steady his drink. "I'm so sorry, Mr. Saunders," Peggy said to him.

"So," he went on, ignoring her, "with both my parents dead and Plácidia under Brazilian control, I settled here. My experience establishing the Parque Nacional apparently qualified me for a management job in the state parks system. The Agency arranged it. I got married, had two children, divorced."

"Have you been back?" Peggy asked him. "To Plácidia?"

He shook his head. "When *abertura* got underway in the eighties, and Plácidia regained its independence, I considered going back as a tourist. There didn't seem to be much danger, though I did ponder the consequences of running into someone I knew. In the end, though, I didn't see the point. It would make me sad. My life is here now. Or was here."

"It seems to me you're still living it!" Harry said with an uneasy laugh.

"Not for long," Saunders said. "I'm ill. Terminally, I'm afraid."

Harry opened his mouth to issue some platitude, but none came out. Peggy reached over and touched his arm.

"I fear that you came here hoping for political intrigue." He threw his hands in the air. "But, sadly, that's my story. I'm sorry, Professor, that it isn't more interesting."

"It's very interesting," Harry said quietly. But he realized that he hadn't written anything down.

"You have nothing to apologize for," Peggy told him.

"Well, thank you. It's funny, I lived for years with the fear of being discovered, even though, in retrospect, there was no reason that anyone would bear ill will against me. Perhaps the businessmen who'd hoped to profit from the land I gave to the people—but it wouldn't have been very cost-effective to seek me out for revenge, would it." He looked up at the now-racing clouds. Rain was coming. "It took decades to truly accept how superfluous I was. I believe my country forgot me the moment I was gone, and the world just kept grinding on, burying the past in its wake. It's astounding to me how little is remembered." He looked up, smiled at them. "Not that it should be otherwise. The scale of human history is too large. Forgetting the past is a mercy, even if it causes us to repeat our mistakes."

"In my profession," Harry said, "we see ourselves as protecting humanity against its own worst tendencies."

"That's admirable," Saunders said, obviously not meaning it. "If you write about my story, perhaps someone will learn from it. Though the only thing I've learned, the most important thing, is how to let go. My only regrets are my failures to do that."

He stood up, indicating it was time for them to leave. They invited him to stay seated, said that they would show themselves to their car, but he hobbled along behind them, and Harry didn't know if he was doing so to be kind or to ensure they didn't make off with a souvenir. At the Subaru they turned to say goodbye, but Saunders had already climbed the porch steps and opened his door. He raised a hand in farewell without turning around, and then he was gone.

19

In the morning, Chloe woke with stiff neck and aching arm to an empty cabin. Her mother's bed was made and the sun blazed in the open window. Through it came the cry of a hawk and the chirp of insects. She popped two ibuprofen, pulled on a pair of jeans, and zombied over to the lodge, where the adults, or two of them, anyway, had already plowed halfway through their eggs and bacon and were locked in a scowly silence. Chloe helped herself to the buffet, which was housed in a giant hollowed-out log, and winked at the bighorn sheep whose head glowered down at her from above.

Loretta delivered a warning look as she sat down, against what, Chloe didn't know. She said, "No Aunt Lila? No Grandma?" and, after a few seconds of sighs and grunts, "Just kidding, jeez."

Her mother spat, "Main mission is for secret agents only, I guess. Lila vamoosed."

Loretta turned to Chloe and said, "You, me, and your mother are going to Prescott to track down Uncle Lloyd. After you went to sleep, I did some work on DiamondD1951. There's an exploit on the bulletin-board software the pipe smokers' forum uses. He bought some rare tobacco from a guy, and I got into their DMs. Lloyd had provided an address. Somebody else lives there now, but maybe they bought the place from Lloyd, or maybe a neighbor remembers him. It's somewhere to start, anyway."

"I'm allowed to come along?" Chloe asked, meeting her mother's gaze.

"Yes. But if things get hairy…"

"I know, I know," Chloe said. "I'm not going to be any good beating up villains, anyway."

"Should I bring the gun?" Loretta asked her mother.

"More trouble than it's worth" was the curt reply.

They went back to their cabins to get ready for the short trip into town. Chloe loaded her backpack with the pain pills, a book, her phone, some granola bars, and one of the bottles of water that came with the room. She lay down on the bed and, while her mother brushed her teeth, asked through the open bathroom door, "You have a gun? Here?"

"Aunt Lila brought it for me." She came out of the bathroom, arms crossed. "It's not registered to me, and I am a felon. So I gave it back to her. It's in the other cabin, I assume."

"Do you own a gun? That's, like, registered to you?"

"Yes."

"At home?"

"Yes."

"I didn't know that," Chloe said, and her voice sounded very small.

"That's by design. I have a safe for it. I hope you never have to see me use it."

The trip to Prescott was silent. Loretta drove. Chloe's arm had stopped throbbing and she had that post-breakfast, back-of-the-car grogginess that made her feel like a child; she reminded herself that she technically was one. Part of her wished she'd stayed back in the cabin, being bored.

"Why don't I try alone first," her mother said as they turned onto the street where Lloyd Davies was supposed to have lived. It was a nondescript suburban lane with a doctor's office, a small park, and a law office on one side and a row of ranch houses on the other. The few people trudging down the sidewalks looked like well-to-do retirees. Loretta pulled over in front of the park.

"Don't you think," Loretta said, "it would go better if you had a six-foot-two transgender combat veteran and a teenager with a broken arm standing behind you?"

"Haha."

They got out and squinted down the street. "That's the one," Loretta said, pointing. It was a low brown house with a gravel front yard. Colorful buckets sparsely arranged on the gravel contained what looked like plastic flowering plants. The yard was surrounded by an incongruous wooden rail fence, the kind you might see a cowboy leaning against in a movie. Two vehicles were parked in the driveway, both plugged into EV chargers, one a gigantic pickup truck, the other a tiny Fiat, both of them bright green. Chloe was fascinated by the peculiar taste of these people and wished she could get a good look at them.

She and Loretta sat on a swing set and watched as her mother approached, knocked, spoke briefly with someone through a screen door. The conversation went on for a couple of minutes. The door opened and a hand stuck out, pointing down the street. Her mother nodded, shook the hand, and returned to the park. "They barely knew him," she said. "They used to live a few streets away. Really only talked to him at the lawyer's office when the sale went through. But they said there's a guy at the end of the block he used to watch ball games with. And smoke pipes and cigars."

"Thank god for hobbies," Loretta said.

The neighbor wasn't home, but no mail or newspapers were accumulating, and a bicycle was parked in the driveway, so they figured he'd be back before long. They went out and got coffees and returned. The guy was out front, watering a tree.

This time they all got out of the car together. He was in his seventies, red-faced, with a beachy air: cutoff cargo pants, Hawaiian shirt, big straw hat. Behind him, his house was all weird angles; it seemed to be constructed out of scrap lumber and corrugated sheet metal. He turned off the hose and said, "Ah, shit. You found me."

Loretta said, "Oh, sorry to alarm you, sir, we just—"

"I didn't tell anyone the secrets." He raised the nozzle and pointed it at them like a gun. "I just needed to get away from Jeanette."

"I think you're confusing us with someone else," Chloe's mother said brightly.

"You're not from the church?"

"No, sir."

"Jesus, that's a relief." He sighed, lowering the hose again. "Who the hell are you, though?"

"We're trying to find my uncle, and your neighbor said you knew him. Lloyd Davies?"

"Never heard of him."

"Really? The guy on the corner? Sold the place to the people with the electric cars?"

"Larry."

"Maybe?"

"Larry Danson is the guy. He lived here for, I guess, eight years? I'm Mike, by the way." The man's eyes traveled to Loretta and took her in, then landed on Chloe. She tried not to squirm. "What happened to you, kid?"

"She had an acc—"

"I fell off a roof," Chloe said, cutting her mother off. "Running away from the cops."

"Huh," he said. "Anyway, maybe you people know where Larry went. Though it sounds like you don't."

"We don't. But maybe we can ask you a few things about him."

Mike dug into his voluminous shorts pockets and pulled out a little plastic box: a garage door opener. Chloe had wondered why there was no driveway; instead, a gravel footpath from the street terminated at a section of the house wall. That section now rose, and Chloe understood: he had a little golf cart that he rode around, instead of a car. It took up only a small portion of the double-wide space; the rest was occupied by a card table and a bunch of folding beach chairs. Books, papers, and figurines littered the table. "Come on in," Mike said. "Don't touch that stuff, it's my grandkids' game shit. One time I knocked over one of those little guys and my granddaughter made a sound like somebody was ripping her leg off."

They took seats around the table. Mike didn't offer them anything to eat or drink, which was fine by Chloe—for all the tidiness of the outside of the house, this garage was a mess, and she could see through a half-open door a kitchen that looked like an earthquake had hit it. She wouldn't have wanted to eat or drink anything that came from it. Among all the D&D debris was a dinner plate covered with cigar stubs and ash piles, and its odor permeated the space.

"Larry kept to himself at first," Mike said. "Decent enough fella if you caught him wandering around outside, but he didn't try to get to know anybody. Most people on this block are pretty friendly, we're all retired, just living the good life, so he kinda stuck out. Later on I found out his wife died—I guess that was your aunt."

"That's right," Chloe's mother said.

"Yeah, sorry to hear it. Anyway, one time a big tree branch got blown onto his roof, and I found him looking up at it with a big old ball pipe in his teeth, and I said, 'That smells like a rummy old burley,' and the damn thing nearly fell out of his mouth. I used to be a pipeman, now I'm more into cigars, but we talked tobacco for a while, and before long he was coming over to smoke and watch baseball. We even went out to Talking Stick to watch the D-backs train a couple of times."

"Did you notice anything unusual about his behavior? Or did he tell you anything memorable about his past?"

"Not really. He was sad. Eventually he seemed happier, got a dog, but he never had a girlfriend or anything. Then—I guess it would've been the late 2010s—he didn't come around so much anymore, he'd put me off if I wanted to get together." He seemed to remember something. "Actually," he said, "you asked me about his behavior. He did get weird before he moved. Before, he used to do everything real slow and careful, like a servant or something. Like, imagine an English butler powerwashing a house. That was Larry. But that last year, he walked around all nervous and bent over, his hands were shaky. The house kinda fell apart, it got weedy and overgrown—Linda and Ray had to rip all that out and fix things up. There was one day when I figured he already moved—it'd been weeks since I saw him—and I found him just standing in the street late at night, staring into space, with the dog pulling at the leash. I said hello and he barely seemed to notice me. So, yeah, unusual, now that you mention it."

Loretta and Chloe's mom exchanged a look. Chloe knew what it meant: Affirmation.

"Mike," Loretta asked, "do you have any idea where he moved?"

"Nah" was the reply. "Linda and Ray were bitching about it, actually, because he didn't forward his mail. It just piled up. A couple of times, they called the real estate agent that sold them the place, and she came and got it? But eventually they gave up and started throwing it out, and it finally stopped coming."

"Do you know who the real estate agent is?" Chloe's mother asked.

"Yeah. Or, no, I forget her name. But hold on." He pulled out a flip phone and pushed some buttons. After a brief conversation, he picked up a pencil from the table and wrote something down. Chloe cringed inwardly—he was writing on somebody's character sheet. They'd be annoyed. Then again, they should probably know by now not to leave their stuff lying around at Grandpa's house. Mike compounded the injury by ripping off the corner of the paper he'd scribbled on. Her mother took it from him, and a minute later the three of them were saying thanks and walking back to the car. "He's got to still be in the area. Those shots at the ball game and gastropub were fairly recent." She handed Chloe the paper. "You have your phone, right? Could you find this lady?"

Mike's handwriting surprised her—it was blocky and incredibly neat, like the text on a blueprint. Maybe he'd been an architect or something—that would explain the weird house. The name he'd written was Sunny Mansson. She looked it up and found a picture of a pretty, round-faced woman standing in front of a super-ugly development house. "Find Your Sunny Mansion in the Greater Prescott Area!" read a slogan. Not too bad, Chloe decided; better than "Join the Mansson Family." She plugged the address into the maps app and handed the phone to her mother, who propped it up in the drink holder while a voice directed their drive.

On the way, Chloe flipped over the paper the name was on. It included a fragment of a box labeled FEATURES & TRAITS, and somebody had written, *Enchanted ruby on chain around neck. Scar on face from chin to ear, won't talk about it. Some elf blood.* She snickered, then felt embarrassed and sad. Wouldn't it be fun to be one of the teenagers playing D&D in Grandpa Mike's garage? To be a mega-nerd and walk in a big loud group of other nerds to the drugstore for more Takis and Cokes? She realized that one of the reasons she'd decided to run for class president in the first place was that she didn't need friends to do it. She lived too far from the school to have many of them, and the handful who lived closest hated her, or she thought they did. Except Kay. She missed Kay, and home, and school. When would life start? Or would she just go from kid to class president to professional spy without a break? She peered longingly between the car seats at her phone—she wanted to talk to her only friend.

When they got to the real estate office, everyone was at lunch. Sunny would be back around one, a cheerful man in a bow tie told them. He recommended a place a few blocks away that had wood-fired pizzas "in case you're a little peckish yourselves," so they walked along the wide and treeless street in suddenly near-intolerable heat under a cloudless sky. Her phone restored to her, Chloe texted Kay, *I'm in Prescott AZ tracking down a missing person.*

The pizzeria was one of a row of low buildings with false fronts and was nestled between a "western heritage" gift shop and an art gallery. It smelled amazing. The second they walked in, Chloe recognized Sunny Mansson sitting alone, a giant gingham cloth napkin tucked into her shirt collar, munching on a slice of pizza and typing with her free hand on a phone. "Guys," Chloe said, when they sat down, "that's her. The house lady."

The place was high-ceilinged with a skylight and a double row of windows in the back, behind a kitchen visible from the dining room. The floor was concrete, and Chloe figured that the space used to house an auto mechanic's garage. Her mother waved a server over and said, "See that woman in the corner? Her lunch is on us."

A couple minutes later, the server brought Sunny Mansson a receipt, and, startled, she approached their table. "Thanks," she said in the soothing falsetto of a mother mouse. "I guess you folks are looking for a house?"

They invited her to sit, and once they'd ordered—"I'll have another iced tea, Sandra"—Loretta said, "What do you recommend for somebody who's just trying to get away from it all? Just vamoose, leave no forwarding address?"

She looked suspicious. "And that's you three? Just dropping out of society together?"

"Family retreat," Chloe said.

"Hm. Where do you live now?"

"Uh..."

"Warbler Drive," Loretta said confidently. "Southwest of downtown."

"I know where it is," Sunny said. The waitress brought her tea and she demurely unpapered a drinking straw and took a sip. "I don't think you guys want a house. I think you're just fishing for information." They stared at her in embarrassed silence. "You'd be surprised how many guys under restraining orders come to the office trying to figure out where their ex lives."

"That's not us," Chloe's mother said.

"No. I probably can't tell you anything, but ask away."

"It's my uncle. His name is Lloyd Davies, though it seems like he went by Larry Danson. He used to live on Warbler, then disappeared after behaving erratically."

"Your uncle," Sunny said, scowling.

"He was married to my aunt Ruth. They lived in Chicago. When she died, he came out here, and we lost touch. But now I'm worried about him." She gestured to Chloe and Loretta. "This is my daughter and my friend. They're here to help me out."

The waitress arrived with three salads in little paper baskets and the pizza, which she set down on an elevated aluminum stand so that they wouldn't have to move their drinks. Chloe awkwardly tried to separate a piece with her one good hand, failed, then accepted Sunny's help. For a while the three of them ate, stealing occasional glances at Sunny. She sipped her tea, frowned off into space. After a few minutes she asked the waitress for some Equal and added it to the tea. She drank that for a minute, then pulled out her phone.

"Fred, reschedule my one and my one thirty, please." A pause. "Thank you. Also, stop telling people where I eat lunch."

She hung up and said to them, "I sold him the land. I've been feeling bad about it for years. I'll take you there."

They took Sunny's car, which was bigger, a yellow SUV with a FIND YOUR SUNNY MANSION bumper sticker. She invited Chloe to sit in the front seat. "You can't be all cramped back there with your broken arm."

"*Thank* you," Chloe said. On the way, Kay texted back, *whos missing*.

My great uncle I never met. Grand uncle?

im at Addisons she wants to talk to you

Why

But there was no answer—Chloe was out of bars. "Is there no signal out here?" she said, and Sunny replied, with a laugh, "Honey, that's the whole point of out here."

Twenty minutes into the trip, she pulled over. "Pardon me, ladies." She hopped out and ran off into the brush, disappearing behind a boulder. A couple of minutes later she returned at a calm pace, smoothing her skirt with a pale, ring-encrusted hand. "That's my tinkle rock," she told them, climbing back into the car.

Chloe gasped when Sunny pulled onto the access road for Uncle Lloyd's plot of land; it was almost indistinguishable from the land around it, and she briefly thought they were crashing. They weaved their way along a dry creek bed and over hills until, perched on a ridge, they looked down on a trailer—not the cool nostalgic kind but a depressing-looking double-wide, its roof patched with plywood and its siding missing in places.

"He's here?" Chloe's mom said.

"Truck's there, so he's there," Sunny said. "I come out every couple of months to check on him."

She put the car in gear and descended from the ridge, then went around the trailer and pulled up behind the pickup. They all got out. A circular aluminum garden enclosure was being used as a firepit, and firewood was stored in a hut made of PVC hoops and a tarp. Two big blue drums beside it seemed to be full of cardboard and discarded mail, but the wind had swept some of it away and scattered it throughout the area. Beside a white pickup covered in dust, a couple of solar panels were wiped clean. An empty dog bowl by the front steps looked like it hadn't been filled in a long time.

"Why don't you let me go first, ladies," Sunny said. She squared her shoulders, and headed for the trailer.

They watched as the door opened and Sunny began to gesture and speak. It was possible to make out a figure in the gloom. A moment later, Sunny disappeared inside.

"What are we supposed to be doing?" Chloe asked.

"Waiting, I guess," her mother said. She looked pained.

"Was he, like, nice to you when you were younger?"

"Not particularly. My aunt was, though. Lloyd was mostly...a cloud of smoke behind a newspaper. But I was a wayward teenager and then a drug addict—*as you know*," she added, leveling a glare, "and he let me into his house without a complaint. So I owe him." She sighed. "I never imagined he could end up like this."

They heard the squeak of the door opening. Sunny leaned out, gesturing them in.

Chloe braced herself, assuming the place would stink. But it mostly smelled like the dust, with a layer of stale pipe smoke over everything. Sunny was standing next to a sofa that was covered with laundry, and it took Chloe a minute to realize that some of that laundry was her great-uncle. He was white-haired and unkempt, dressed in a wrinkled button-down striped shirt and cutoff pants. His face was lopsided—maybe he'd had a stroke at some point—and his hand was rhythmically contracting like it was petting a dog's head, but there was no dog.

Her mom's face went soft and her eyes glazed over. She said, "Uncle Lloyd? It's me, Jane. Ruth's niece. This is my daughter, Chloe, and our friend Loretta."

Lloyd nodded at the three of them and surprised Chloe by saying in a clear, papery, and peeved-sounding baritone, "I didn't think I'd ever see you again...Jane."

Relief all around that he could speak. Chloe's mother sat down beside him, and the others lowered themselves into folding chairs at a cluttered card table. Chloe noticed that these were the same cheap table and chairs that Mike had. She wondered if they'd bought them together.

"We're trying to find out what happened to Aunt Ruth. We found some evidence that she thought she was in danger before she died. The police reports say she ended her own life, but...we're not sure we believe it."

Lloyd had been nodding through all of this, and he kept nodding now. He said, pausing to draw breath, "I wish I could have talked to you... before you came. It's the truth. I was...in the house. With her. Heard... the shot. She hadn't been herself. I told her to get...help. From someone. Overwork. Stress. Difficult...cases."

He went on, haltingly, to describe her decline during a challenging intellectual property rights case in 2010 and 2011. She succumbed swiftly, descending into paranoia and, at times, rage, which was often directed at him. Ruth had a traumatic upbringing and a family history of mental illness; there had been bouts with it in the past. But it had a new intensity this time. She had bought a gun for protection, she said. "I should have...hid it. Or thrown it...in the river."

After her death, her client Travis Nutt came to him, evidently racked with guilt. He thought his case had triggered her decline. They became friends, and eventually Nutt suggested he move out to Arizona, where there was good weather and a community of retirees. Lloyd did, and he had visited the ranch, ridden horses with Nutt a few times. But after a while, they grew apart.

"I liked it...the life there...on Warbler Drive. But then..." He shrugged, waved a hand. "Got tired of all the mask nonsense."

They all just stared.

"And then everyone...got injected with poison...because the government said so. Nonsense."

"You mean the vaccine?" Chloe's mother said quietly.

"It made people sick. Once everybody had it...you couldn't avoid it. They were shedding it. They made me sick." His body had begun to shake, whether from physical discomfort or extreme emotion, Chloe couldn't tell. "And then they installed...the towers."

He glared at Sunny as he said this, as though whatever he was talking about was her fault. "Larry," she said, "I couldn't know that—"

"Whatever," he said, waving it off. "They put in the phone towers and I could...feel them. Pulling at me. Pulling at the pieces...that flaked off."

Sunny's mouth was shut so tight, it looked like it might just heal up and disappear.

"It got so I couldn't even...watch. Seeing people...get reprogrammed. I came out here...but I still felt weak all the time. My joints...hard to breathe." He coughed, squinted out the trailer window. "The bastards even did something to the sun. It's not...the same. Travis helped me out...with his medicine. I felt great...for almost a year. But it was already in me. Got sick again."

"You mean," Loretta said, "you got Affirmed."

He turned to her, nodding. "It was a miracle. Felt...young again. So much...energy."

"And it's—what," Chloe's mother said, "a pill?"

He shook his head. Another cough. Chloe sort of wanted to get out of the trailer, but she held her ground. Lloyd said, "It's a shot. Travis had it sent to me in the mail. I can't describe the feeling. I thought I would live...forever. But the shedding...caught up with me."

They sat in silence. Sunny gave the others a questioning look, then said, "Well, Larry, we'll let you get back to it. Thanks for talking with us."

"It was a miracle," he said again, as though concerned that they wouldn't understand. Chloe was startled to see that his eyes were brimming with tears. "I was never tired. My mind was so clear. The fog...was gone. I begged him for another one...tried again...but..." His chest hitched. Everyone started to get up to leave.

"Uncle Lloyd?" Chloe heard herself ask. "Do you still have them? The packages the shots came in?"

Loretta and her mother looked at her in surprise. Lloyd squinted, seemed to think. "Why do you want that?"

She shrugged. "I was just curious."

"I...don't think so. I threw them out."

Chloe's mother laid a hand on his shoulder. "I'm glad we could see each other again, Uncle Lloyd," she said, and Chloe could tell by the clipped tightness of those consonants that she was really, really mad. "I wish you luck with...all of this. And I appreciate the information. And your many insights."

"There's...a change coming," Lloyd said as they headed for the door. "It will happen...soon. I can't wait."

Chloe gulped air as they passed through the trailer's door, and she heard her mother groan with relief. The three women headed for Sunny's car. But Chloe said, "Hold on." She jogged over to the firepit where she'd seen the two fifty-five-gallon drums full of paper and used her good hand to dig through one of them. She could see now there was a label on the drum's side bearing the name of a brand of fertilizer.

Her mother materialized at her shoulder. Chloe said, "He probably starts fires with the scrap paper. We could find the packages here."

"Surely they're gone by now?" her mom said. But she moved to the other one, and they dug deep, removing layers of newspapers and junk mail. Bills, the AARP newsletter, home-decor catalogs. Would these companies still send Uncle Lloyd these catalogs if they could see his house? Probably.

It took only a few minutes for Chloe to hit pay dirt. The package resembled the box a phone or smartwatch would come in, a little white coffin somewhat beaten up by transit and life inside the trash barrel. It was postmarked IRVING, TX. Chloe pulled it out, held it up to her mother. In response, her mother held up her own box.

A movement caught Chloe's eye: Uncle Lloyd peering suspiciously out the window at the trailer's end. She offered a little wave and he withdrew.

"Let's take them to go," Mom said, and they jogged to the car, where the others were waiting.

20

As they pulled away, Jane stuck her hand between the seats and asked Chloe for her box. "Let me open them," she said.

"Why!"

"There was a deadly drug in it. If it pricked you, I'd never forgive myself."

Chloe blanched, then handed it over. This fetishy, premium packaging was not what Jane would have expected. She gave each box a shake—nothing. She noted the postmark on Chloe's, which was different from the one on the box she had found.

"Be careful," Loretta said.

Jane slowly separated Chloe's box from its lid, careful not to jostle anything that might be inside. But there was nothing. The box was empty. Its bottom was fitted with a matte plastic baseplate bearing the clear impression of a syringe. Closer examination revealed, on the underside of the lid, written and pictographic instructions for administering the drug. It recommended the thigh or buttocks as injection points. She opened the box she had found. This one contained a foam separator but was otherwise identical.

"So why is this one postmarked Ames, Iowa, and the other is from Texas?"

"Maybe the operation is larger than we imagined," Loretta said. "With warehouses all over the country."

"Jesus," Jane said. And then, "No, wait." She recalled her surveillance visit to the ranch with Lila. "We saw somebody loading a big bin of identical large Priority Mail boxes into a truck. What if Nutt is making these kits and shipping them to workers in different states? And then those people mail the individual kits. This way they never have the Skeleton Flats postmark."

Loretta nodded. "Nutt's people could even be driving to different post offices hours away, so even the workers don't know exactly where they come from."

"Wait!" Chloe piped up. "So when people on the messageboard say they've been Affirmed, they thank the other drones. And sometimes one of them says 'You're welcome' or posts a proud-face emoji. I thought it was just, like, a creepy ritual, or maybe the donors, but some of them must be the people doing the shipping."

A long, brooding silence followed as they processed what they'd just seen and heard. Jane was incensed. She scowled at the ceiling of the car, trying to think. Beside her, Loretta stroked her chin. Sunny cleared her throat as the boulder came into view, but there were no takers, and she sped by, then said, "So...sorry for eavesdropping..."

"No foul," Jane said.

"But you're saying there's a nationwide conspiracy to distribute this illegal drug that's turning people into...whatever Larry is now? Sorry—Lloyd, I mean."

"Yeah."

"Okay, but..." She glanced over her shoulder, deftly arching a plucked eyebrow at each of them. "Why don't I already know about this? Why isn't it in the news?"

"Most likely," Loretta said, "the people who make the news you consume don't know about it, and the people who make news for the people taking the drug don't think it's news."

"Uh..."

Loretta leaned forward, gripping the back of Chloe's seat. "It used to be we all had the same news," she said. "I mean, not me. Our parents, I guess. Everybody watched the same three networks on TV, everybody read the same papers. There were limited sources of truth. Not the actual truth, turns out—that's how I ended up sitting in a desert cleaning the sand out of my rifle for six years—but one everybody agreed on. Now people just pick whatever truth sounds good to them, and they find a community online that will shout it back at them. And those aren't communities you're going to just stumble across in your daily life. You have to know where to look."

"And nobody's looking?" Sunny asked.

"The kind of people who would see Affirmation as a public health catastrophe," Loretta said, "aren't ever going to learn it exists. And the people who know it exists think it's great. Everyone lives in a bubble now, and increasingly, world-altering events are unfolding in these bubbles, invisible to the millions of people whose lives they're destined to change."

After a moment's thought, Sunny said, "So it's not just this drug, you're saying. All kinds of important things are happening, and nobody knows what's going on."

"I mean," Loretta replied, slumping back into her seat, "I'd argue nobody ever knew what was going on. But now we don't even get to pretend we do."

The cell signal came back and Chloe's phone chimed. Jane watched her fingers moving, wondered who she was texting and why.

In Prescott, they thanked Sunny for the information and the ride, and she thanked them for lunch and for the eye-opening lecture on the media landscape. "If you're ever looking to relocate..." she said, and Loretta accepted the business card she offered.

"The suicide story still stinks," Jane said once they were on their way back to Trout Brook. "His brain is rotted by Affirmation and probably long COVID. His memory can't be trusted."

"I don't know," Loretta said carefully. "What he says matches the police report. They were alone in the house together. The gun was registered to her, and she had the key to the gun safe. And the increased anxiety and depression tracks with what her neighbors and coworkers said."

"Yeah, but," Chloe piped up from the back, "he was on drugs, right? Maybe she was on drugs, too. Maybe she was Affirmed like him."

"She died in 2011," Loretta said, lowering the visor against the late afternoon sun. "We didn't find evidence of Affirmation appearing before, what was it, 2023?"

Chloe said, "Yeah, but what if it was some early version of it? Like, she could have discovered what Nutt was doing, and he decided to poison her. And that's what drove her to suicide."

It sounded far-fetched, but the longer the silence lasted, the more plausible it seemed. "Do we know what else Nutt was working on around then?" Jane asked.

"I'm not sure," Loretta said. "Aside from the cocaine and the red heifers. He had only recently left academia. His research was on cattle medication, that's where the Yes came from."

Jane craned her neck, peered into the back seat. Text bubbles filled Chloe's screen, and she demurely tilted the phone up to prevent Jane from seeing them. "You have a signal? Look this up: Travis Nutt, cattle disease."

Chloe raised a single eyebrow, a Lila gesture. But she swiped the message app away and opened a browser. A minute later she said, "Uh...I'm getting some academic stuff from the 2000s that I don't have the credentials to read. But I can get the...abstracts, they're called?"

"Those are summaries of the papers. What do they say?"

"Uh..." she said, then read, "'Sedative and excitatory effects of intravenous' something or other 'on calves'...something called, um, 'anti...anti-no-ception'—"

"Antinociception," Loretta said. "It means how the body responds to pain."

"Right. Here's one on neuro...neurodegenerative prion disease—"

"Wait," her mother said. "He was working on prion disease? That wasn't in the documents Lila found. Show it to Loretta."

Chloe handed over the phone, then tensed up in sudden and obvious regret. "I'm not going to read your texts," Loretta said.

"I didn't think you were!"

"Prion disease—like mad cow, scrapie in sheep, Creutzfeldt-Jakob in people," Loretta said, reading. "Degenerative brain conditions caused by misfolded proteins."

Jane felt a little jolt of recognition and fear. "What if that's what Affirmation is? A disease. Something that breaks down inhibitions first, then everything else later. Isn't there one that comes from cannibalism?"

"Kuru," Loretta said. "Hold on." Then, after a moment: "Okay, listen to this. Kuru affects people's coordination but also causes 'mood changes.' Eventually, people who get it can't stand up or eat. It can take a year for the disease to kill them. What if Affirmation is similar, but it *starts* with the mood changes? Intensity, energy, loss of inhibition. Like cocaine. But then it moves on to the next phase, and you get shaky and lose your appetite."

"Like Lloyd," Jane said.

"And then you can't stand up," Loretta said, "and you die."

"Jesus."

Loretta was nodding. "Not a drug. An engineered degenerative prion-based brain disease."

"Nutt must have gotten the idea back then, in the 2010s," Jane said, her mind racing. "He *could* have tested it on Ruth, or maybe she just took it voluntarily. A pick-me-up that would last forever. Instead, it drove her to suicide. And when his heifer plan to start World War Three wouldn't come together and business with my mother got hairy, he decided to unleash it on the public. He found the election-truther discussion board, or maybe initiated it, and started sending people the shot. And once people began reporting results—"

"Things just snowballed. Actually," Loretta said, swiping and squinting at the little screen, "according to this study, other scientists have researched prion-based drugs. They used cattle to cultivate the prions, as miniature pharmaceutical factories. It didn't prove sustainable or reliable, though, so they gave up."

"Who were the researchers?" Jane asked.

"Uh...M. Acosta and P. Chen."

That rang a bell. "I remember now. Those were the two graduate students. The ones who were high on Yes. And one assaulted the other and was deported."

"Nutt's students."

"Nutt's research." Jane let it sink in for a moment. "So the red heifers aren't just a hobby after all. They're propagating the Affirmation."

"I guess," Loretta said, handing the phone back to Chloe, "they're helping ruin the world after all."

"Wait," Chloe said. "Are all those people on the messageboard going to die like Aunt Ruth?"

She was clutching the phone to her chest like a beloved pet that had barely escaped being run over by a car, which annoyed Jane but, a second later, filled her with sympathy and regret. She remembered being trapped in a car with her mother on the way to some mysterious rendezvous or resentfully executed household errand and feeling extraneous and unwanted. Back then, she would have killed for a way to quietly commune with friends. "I don't know," she said gently. "Maybe it's more refined than the version that made my aunt...that harmed her. Maybe it'll wear off."

The three fell silent, pondering the unlikelihood of this outcome. Chloe said, "Is it...contagious? Will everyone get it? Like COVID?"

"I don't think so," Loretta said. "With the other diseases, you have to... ingest the prions somehow. No one's going to eat the Affirmed. I hope."

They arrived at Trout Brook just after four. Chloe went to their cabin to take a pain pill and a nap. Loretta said she would do more research. Jane decided to head to the lodge, where she helped herself to a cup of lukewarm coffee from the afternoon urn and sat at a table underneath an elk head, its glass eyes looking eerily out of place, as though the taxidermist had grabbed the wrong ones from the drawer.

She drew a manila envelope from her satchel. Postmarked Chicago, it was addressed to JANE POOL, 10D3384, BOYNTON RIDGE CF, 330 BAILEY RD., BOYNTON RIDGE, NY. Inside were several pages. The top one was Uncle Lloyd's letter telling her that Ruth had died. Beneath it were two lined sheets of notebook paper, covered on both sides with blue ballpoint pen and rubber-stamped with the message THIS CORRESPONDENCE HAS BEEN REVIEWED BY BOYNTON RIDGE CORRECTIONAL FACILITY. She smoothed them out on the table.

> March 14, 2011
> Boynton Ridge
>
> *Dear Aunt Ruth,*
>
> *I'm sorry I haven't written you in a while. As you might have guessed from the address on this letter, or maybe you heard from my dad, I am in prison. So I'm not going to be able to visit this spring, either. There is a whole story about how I got here, which I will tell you sometime if you want to hear, but the short version is, I was trying to protect Lila and a man died. I wish it had happened differently but I don't have any regrets about what I did. I will not be here for long I hope and look forward to starting a new life when I am out.*

The other big piece of news is, I got married and I am going to have a baby! It's a girl and she will be born here at Boynton Ridge. One lucky thing is that there is a nursery here for incarcerated mothers and my lawyer is working very hard to get me accepted into the program, and to get my sentence reduced so I can bring her home ASAP. Her name is going to be Chloe. Everybody here has a story about a sister or cousin or friend who had a baby on the "inside," as people call it here, and most of the stories are really bad. I am hopeful I will avoid a fate like these women.

It was hard adjusting to prison life but I got used to it. As you probably know, I had problems with substance abuse and depression on the outside and was still struggling up through my trial. But I think I have benefited from the counseling here, and I'm glad that I didn't poison Chloe with the things I put into my body. She's going to be a healthy girl and I have a support system waiting for her in the form of Chance, my husband, and his parents. Dad has also promised to help, he is going to try to get me a job in his department at the college.

Aunt Ruth, there is one main thing I want to ask you about, and that's about your relationship with my mother. I know you don't like to talk about this, but maybe you would be more comfortable with the subject in a letter. I am asking because over the past few years, Lila and I have grown apart. It's difficult to love someone with addiction issues, I know that, but the more challenging things got for me, the more callous and unhelpful Lila became. And when I asked her about it directly, she said some terrible things. The last six months or so before I turned myself in, I was almost always alone, almost always high, and felt like I didn't have anyone in the world at all. So that's why the tone of this letter might be more cheerful than you'd expect. I'm in prison, but I won't be forever, and there's love in my life and I have plans for the future. But I just don't know how to make things right with Lila. I know you haven't always been on the best of terms with your sister, but maybe you can talk me through this.

I know that I'll have to make amends to Lila, even though

I feel she wronged me. I need to make them with you, too. The addiction counseling here uses the Twelve Steps. (It's mandatory for drug offenders but anyone here can do it.) So I need to apologize to you and Uncle Lloyd for taking advantage of your kindness and generosity. I did terrible things under your roof, and you didn't kick me out. I promised you I would use the money you gave me to get clean and better myself and get therapy, and instead I spent it on drugs and alcohol. I accept responsibility for what I did and I am so sorry for lying to you and causing you harm. I hope you can forgive me someday. When I have served my time I hope I can return to your home and treat you with the respect you deserve.

It will be hard, but I want to say this to Lila someday too, even though I'm angry. I haven't seen her or spoken to her in a year, though...I don't even know where she is, or if she's alive or dead. So maybe I wouldn't even get to use any advice you give me, but I want to hear it anyway.

I am out of paper! I hope you and Uncle Lloyd are well, thank you for everything, and I hope Chloe and I see you soon!

Love, Jane

She hadn't looked at this letter in nearly fifteen years and expected to feel something, but she hadn't expected this: chest hitching, tears and snot flowing down her face, sobbing like a child under the weird, watchful eyes of the moldering elk. Part of becoming an adult was realizing how many broken things couldn't be fixed, how many mistakes were irrevocable. She learned it for the first time that night in Nestor heaving George Framingham's body into the frigid waters of the lake; she learned it again turning herself in, and again when the gates of Boynton Ridge rolled shut behind her, and again when the pregnancy test came back positive, and again when she heard Chance's voice on the phone telling her he was filing for divorce. You had to learn it over and over again, because you had to forget it in order to live. Otherwise you'd end up like Dad, wasting decades of your life hiding in your office, afraid of everything.

But it hurt more than she could have imagined, being taught this particular lesson again. She'd taken and taken from her aunt Ruth and had never had the chance to give back. And just now, when she could have apologized to Uncle Lloyd, all she'd felt was resentment and disappointment.

She never made amends to Lila either. Because she'd been afraid, but also because it would have made things worse. Her apology would have been a burden to Lila, the same way her addictions had been. Anyway, she'd abandoned AA soon after her release and managed to stay sober on her own—she couldn't accept the idea of a higher power. Not that she thought she was so important. On the contrary—every human life was a ghost ship, lost at sea. No one cared, and nobody was at the tiller.

She got back to the cabin, crept upstairs, and saw that Chloe had fallen asleep, her phone unlocked on the bed beside her. Jane resisted the impulse to read what was on the screen; instead, she reached out and switched it off. Downstairs, she opened her laptop, went to her work email, and found the backup of the memoir that she'd sent herself. She opened the file and scanned the pages. She stopped halfway through and read:

> Most addicts can pinpoint the moment they hit bottom. For me, it was in the spring of 2010, during my annual visit to my aunt Ruth and her husband in Chicago. A prominent lawyer and academic, Aunt Ruth lived in a palatial home on a quiet, tree-lined street in Evanston. She had taken Lila and me in when we were runaways from home and from the police, and told me I could return for one week every year as a safe haven, no questions asked. I could always count on her giving me money, too.
>
> An addict, I took advantage of this, and then some. That year, which would be my last in Chicago and the last time I'd ever see my aunt, I asked her to give me the money right after my arrival instead of when I left. I had to pay my rent, back in California, I told her. And though this was true, it isn't what I used the money for. Cash in hand, I immediately went out, bought a bottle of scotch, and called my dealer in the area. I met him in the parking lot of the Hilton across from the public library, drinking straight from the bottle, and he sold me heroin. I walked back to Aunt Ruth's in a state of euphoria.

The house was dark and quiet; my aunt and uncle had gone to bed. I got my works out, cooked the heroin, and injected it. I knew immediately it was too much, and too powerful—it was not the stuff I was used to, and I was sloppy from the drink. As I passed out, I thought for sure that I wouldn't wake up, and the idea filled me with joy. I'd never felt more alive, just seconds from what I believed was death.

When I came to, it was four in the morning. The scotch had spilled and the bedspread must have caught fire. A big black hole was burned there, and my jeans and right calf were burned. It hurt like hell. For an hour or so I was too sick to move. I threw up in bed. Once I could get up, I gathered the burned bedclothes, balled them up, and shoved them into the trash bin outside. I found new sheets in the hall closet and made the bed, my leg screaming in pain. In the bathroom, I took a bunch of pain relievers and tried not to look directly at the burn.

By 8 a.m. I was in the hospital, Aunt Ruth at my side. Trying to hide what happened had been foolish—the smell had permeated the entire house. Understandably, Uncle Lloyd wanted me to leave immediately, and never come back. Instead, I was allowed to stay a few days and recover. When I finally left, Aunt Ruth gave me more money and said she would smooth things over with Lloyd.

"This is the last time I'll allow you to harm yourself in my home," she told me. "It's time for you to get clean. I want a different Jane to come back next year. A woman in control of her problems."

I told her sure, of course, but on the plane home, drunk, drifting in and out of sleep, I considered her a fool and a sucker and hated her for thinking she was better than me, smarter than me, and purer than me. She didn't know what it was like, going through what I went through, and never could.

I never got the chance to tell her how wrong I was.

She gently shut the laptop, trying to harden herself against what she'd read. She was angry at herself, at Lloyd, at Travis Nutt—a nice break, she supposed, from being angry at her sister.

She opened the laptop again, closed the file, and deleted the email from her Sent folder, then from the trash. She did the same in her work account. The memoir excerpt was gone.

Outside, the sun was starting to go down. Whatever Lila and their mother had been planning all day, it would soon begin.

21

A dozen hours earlier, Lila's phone rang. Not her current burner; she always kept the sound off. For a moment, still half asleep, she was transported to the past, to 2009 and the house in Mexico she'd briefly shared with a couple, sexual deviants, true lunatics. They used this very ringtone: piano arpeggios, synthesizer bass, brass hits. Both of them, same ringtone. Calls coming in all night. Laughter about whose phone was ringing. Lila hated them and ended up robbing them. They were so rich, they probably never even noticed.

She sat up in bed. Morning light coming in under the drawn shades. Watch said 5:45. Where was the phone? Not in this room. She got out of bed, opened the door. In her backpack, down in the living room, behind the sofa where Loretta, wrapped in a blanket because the night had turned cold, stirred. Lila hurried down, snatched up the pack, climbed back to the bedroom. Dug through the bag and discovered a phone she'd never seen before.

"We'll operate out of the safe house," Anabel said. "César will pick you up in five minutes."

"You couldn't call an hour ago, when he left?"

But she'd already hung up.

"The safe house I easily fucking followed you to?" Lila asked the empty room, pulling on her pants, furious that she'd allowed an unfamiliar device to be dropped into her bag, by her own mother, no less.

Three minutes later, César was waiting next to the car, placidly smoking. He didn't look directly at her as she climbed into the back seat, frantically pawing through the bag to make sure she hadn't forgotten anything in the rush.

As they drove in silence, Lila took out her laptop and idly attempted to hack into the car and control it remotely. She'd gotten a good look at the VIN passing by the windshield and had captured it with a mnemonic technique she'd developed, breaking it into pieces, creating visual place associations with the number clusters: a desert oasis, an alluvial plain where alligators crept, a featureless white room, a smelly doghouse. Combined with the email address she'd found on a flyer tucked into the pocket on the back of the passenger seat—an ad for the secure private service her mother's people had rented the car from—she reached the company's settings page through the auto manufacturer's website, using a custom Python script she'd written. In theory, via this page, she could honk the horn, flash the lights, and turn off the engine. But, to its credit, the service required an additional code to control specific vehicles from its fleet, which presumably was kept secure in their office in Sedona. A shame. Lila changed the company's username to BadAtComputer Dumb-Cars and logged out.

The air was already warm when they arrived, and Lila shed her base-layer hoodie and shoved it into her pack. She barged ahead, ignoring the other guy guarding the door, the one who wasn't César, ducked to avoid triggering the singing fish, and fell into the folding chair across from her mother in the sunken living room.

"What did you learn on your research mission with your sister?" Anabel Bortnik said.

It annoyed her that her mother knew about that. Everything about this situation annoyed her. She wanted to be alone usually anyway, but she wanted to be alone most of all when there was someone she needed to hurt. "Not many cameras, easy to hack. Four guys, two in towers, two patrolling the facility. I don't want anyone dead except for Nutt."

"That's inconvenient."

"Come on." Each refused to speak for a moment. Then Lila said, "There's also a guy, Remy, there, and his family, in a little ranch house on the west side of the compound. He's Nutt's right-hand man. I don't know how much trouble he's going to be."

"We'll keep him in mind."

"So what are we doing here? I assume we're not going to march into the facility in broad daylight. Why did you wake me? What's the plan?"

"We have a meeting."

"With whom, Mother."

The tiniest hint of a smile played at one corner of her mouth. "Travis Nutt. And his right-hand man, Jeremy Villette. We're to speak about a new collaboration based on his political ambitions and what he thinks mine are. He also would like to internationalize production and distribution of Yes."

"That's Remy's full name? Anyway, I can't go. I've already...interacted with him. In my efforts to learn what they were doing out here."

"Yes, I know. Your *interaction,* as you put it, Lila, was under my direction, a method of investigating the honesty and goodwill of the proposed collaboration."

Lila's hackles went up. In spite of herself, she said, "The hell it was!"

"For the purposes of this meeting," Anabel said, standing, "we'll pretend it was. At first I was irritated, Lila, having learned what you did. I'd falsely assumed I was long past the era when your sexual exploits could inconvenience me—"

"Excuse me, that wasn't me! That was Jane!"

"But the more I thought about it, the more it seemed like an inadvertent masterstroke. So to speak," she added. "It'll throw them off their guard."

"Or get us both killed."

"Of course it won't. Also, congratulations on eventually having sex."

"Maybe I should just kill you now instead."

"Romaldo!" Anabel called over her shoulder. A moment later, the second henchman arrived from the hall and pulled himself upright from his singing-bass-avoidance duck walk. "Get the car ready." The man nodded sternly, then fell again into a crouch as he left. Lila assumed that somewhere, Knight was watching all this via a hidden camera and laughing.

Half an hour later, the gate to the compound rolled aside to admit the car. Lila was still concerned that this was a double cross, that Nutt knew they knew about Affirmation and had brought them here to kill them. But it was too late to worry about that now; she'd deal with it when the moment arrived. They came to a dusty courtyard, where they were flagged down by a couple of uniformed lackeys and told to get out of the car. Paths led variously to the main house and horse barn, Remy's house, and the livestock and drug facilities. The lackeys frisked them for firearms and rooted through Lila's backpack but didn't notice the ceramic flip knife, designed to pass unnoticed through a metal detector, tucked into her boot. She assumed her mother had something like it too.

They were led up the long gravel drive to the main house, which was even uglier close up. Lila could see now that it was built into the hillside; the ground floor likely burrowed partway into the ground, like a rabbit warren. A log facade, intended to evoke a rustic cabin but as large as a football stadium's scoreboard, was foregrounded by a half dozen columns, each a single old-growth ponderosa, that supported an undulating canopy protecting visitors against the sun. Tall, narrow windows flanked a grand entrance featuring knotty pine double doors. As they approached, one of the doors opened and Travis Nutt appeared, pale and diminutive, wearing dark blue jeans and a yellow pearl-snap shirt. Waxen, ghostly, he tipped his Stetson and stepped aside to admit them.

They were met by the largest taxidermied bear Lila had ever seen standing in the center of a massive entrance hall and enclosed by a sweeping double staircase, like the set of *Gone with the Wind* if it had taken place in Yellowstone National Park. A pair of entryway tables made from gigantic rough-edged circular wood slabs stood on either side of the bear, and near one of them loitered Remy Villette, arms crossed, tapping a booted foot. His gaze passed over Anabel and landed on Lila, and his whole body reacted like an inflatable tube dancer.

She had to admit—silently to herself, of course—that Remy's shock was immensely satisfying. He caught himself quickly, but it was too late; she'd seen it. Travis Nutt was shaking her mother's hand, and it was clear he was attempting to employ a painfully firm grip, which Anabel Bortnik easily endured without visible reaction. "A pleasure meeting you again, Anabel," he said, and there was that party magician's voice from YouTube, nasal, fluting, somehow mesmerizing. Lila wondered if he'd taken lessons of some kind. Her mother said, "Likewise," then turned to Lila. "My associate Lila."

"This is my assistant Remy," Nutt said, triggering more handshakes. Remy would have to tell Nutt, of course, that he'd already been pumped, as it were, for information, so Lila decided to take the advantage while she still could.

"We've met," Lila said, staring into Remy's fierce and fearful eyes.

Nutt froze. "Oh?"

"In Oklahoma last week," Lila said. "For business and pleasure. Just checking you two out in advance of this collaboration." She ginned up a lascivious smile to train on Remy. "I checked this one out a little extra."

Anabel allowed Nutt to digest this information for several seconds before letting him off the hook. "Don't worry, Travis, standard procedure for our organization. The observation, I mean. What Lila does in her off-hours is none of my business."

"Of course," Nutt said dreamily.

"Real nice seeing you again," Remy growled.

"Likewise. Hope there's time for me to meet your family."

"Sadly," he said, "they're in Phoenix for a few days."

"A shame."

Nutt led them down a hallway to a boardroom illuminated by the tall windows they'd noticed from outside and dominated by a conference table made out of the largest single slab of wood Lila had ever seen. The chairs, anyway, were conventional swiveling office pieces that had doubtless replaced the tree stumps Nutt had originally chosen, then abandoned after a splinter incident.

They took seats at the table, Nutt and Remy on one side, Lila and her mother on the other. Strategically, Lila left her backpack slung over her shoulder. "So," Nutt said, his voice like the wind whistling through an asshole, "we're here to discuss the expansion of our collaboration into new—"

"Hey, sorry, excuse me?" Lila said, half rising from her seat. "I know we just started, but, where's the outhouse?"

"Lila, you couldn't have thought of this five minutes ago?" her mother scolded, but it was clear from her tone that she approved.

"Sorry, Anabel. Always have to pee when I'm nervous about business!"

"My associates are just outside," Nutt fluted. "They'll show you to a toilet. Indoors."

"Oh, wow, thank you!"

The two men were already waiting. They led her back down the hall and into another, passing several rooms, each sealed off behind a miniature barn door. They startled a blond woman with her hair in a ponytail as she emerged from an office; Lila could see computers, a server rack, some screens, through the cracked-open door before it closed. "Oh! Sorry," the woman said. "I'm—you're—"

"Headed to the ladies'?"

"It's okay, I can wait."

"Why don't you let us hold your backpack for you," one of the guards said to Lila.

She tried to blush by thinking of something embarrassing: fumbling the clip while reloading a gun. Not being able to start a motorcycle in front of a hot person. "It's got my—I'm sorry, my supplies for—I need to—" She trained a pleading look on the blond woman, who sternly glared at the guard.

"Okay, okay," the man said. "It's there."

Lila went where he pointed and locked the door behind her. She turned to find an entirely conventional washroom, with a urinal, toilet, and sink all bolted to knotty pine paneling. Incredibly, fortuitously, there was a removable panel on the wall separating this room from the office, secured by Torx bolts, but thirty seconds later she discovered that it accessed the plumbing and not the Ethernet cabling she was looking for. There must have been a drinking fountain on the other side, or a refrigerator with a faucet.

On her reconnaissance mission with Jane, she'd attempted to break into the compound's wireless network and had been pleased to discover that they were using cheap, out-of-date ISP-provided routers that had a known command-injection vulnerability. It was easy to start a new login shell and instruct the router to execute a command on any devices connected to the network, which made it possible to log in remotely through somebody's account. Unfortunately, she didn't learn until they'd returned to the motel that the things she most wanted—control of the security system and access to Nutt's personal files—weren't accessible via Wi-Fi. This was smart, smarter than she'd expected Nutt to be, and she wished that she'd had the forethought to test it before she and Jane left the area.

What she needed was access to the wired network. She'd brought along tools, concealed in a hidden compartment in the backpack, to tap into the cable directly, along with a sniffer to send the signals into the air and to her laptop.

She'd already wasted time on the wall panel. Now, swiftly, she climbed up on the toilet tank and moved aside one of the drop ceiling panels. She was lucky that the bathroom was right next to the server room; the cables ran above the wall between the two rooms, and she could reach them easily. There were two CAT7 cables running here, neatly gathered and routed with zip ties. One of them probably carried the less secure internet from a modem into the compound's routers; the other was likely the wired local network she wanted. There was no way to tell for sure without tapping them both and seeing what kind of traffic they carried, and she had no time for that. One of the wires was gray and one was green, which suggested that the installers had abided by the informal ANSI standard: gray for the routers, green for the secure network. Of course it was possible the company just used what they had, and the colors meant nothing. But she'd give it a try, and if it didn't work, she'd figure something else out.

She tugged at the green cable, creating a bit of slack, then climbed down for her tools. Cutting the cable would shut off someone's access for a few seconds, but it was a risk she had to take—hopefully no one would notice. She climbed back up, took a deep breath, and snipped the cable with her wire cutters. Then she re-crimped the ends into fresh connectors and jammed them into her sniffer.

The device came to life. An LED lit up, indicating that power was connected, and two more above each input jack began to blink rapidly, showing her that data was passing through. Into an auxiliary output she plugged a portable gigabit router, then she shoved everything back into the darkness and slid the ceiling panel home.

Sitting on the toilet, Lila opened her laptop and connected to the router. A couple of commands later, she'd injected her own code into the system. Right now, people throughout the building were seeing a box pop up with an inscrutable error message on it; as each person clicked to dismiss it, an executable of Lila's design was installed on the machine.

As she sat there, idly tapping her foot on the floor, three people across the network clicked to dismiss, which meant that three machines would shortly have her remote-access software running in the background. Unless these people all fully powered down their computers during their lunch break, which in her experience no one did, Lila would be able to tell when the machines were idle and then remotely, undetectably operate them. Also included in the executable was a keylogger; ideally, this would provide her with the passwords she needed to control any automated aspects of the security system, including the cameras, and access shared data storage. Unless Nutt jotted his secrets down only in notebooks or kept them confined to his own personal, non-networked computer, she should be able to find any records pertaining to Yes, Affirmation, and his business dealings with Aunt Ruth.

A knock came at the door. A man's voice said, "This lady out here needs to pee."

"It's fine," the woman said quietly.

"Hurry up," said the man.

"Just a sec!"

She snapped the laptop shut, tucked it in her bag, and ran the water for a few seconds. Then she smacked her cheeks, mussed up her hair a little, and exited the room like a humiliated little mouse, apologizing profusely to the blond woman and thanking the guards.

Back in the boardroom, Remy was reciting numbers from a spreadsheet. To his credit, he barely glanced up as Lila reentered, just shifted, barely perceptibly, in his chair. Lila didn't look at her mother as she took her seat and, in her peripheral vision, saw that her mother hadn't looked up at her. In spite of herself, she cheered inwardly. Teamwork.

"I'm certain," Nutt said, "that if you accept my offer, the results will benefit us both."

"Mr. Nutt," Lila's mother said, turning to her, "would like to share resources and personnel for jointly moving our product into new markets."

"Sounds exciting," Lila said. Of course Nutt's real intent was to use Anabel's people to destroy her business from the inside, with Affirmation. And, if Lila were to speak her mind, she'd say that this outcome would please her greatly, that Nutt should insist that every distributor and dealer try the product so all of them would go mad and starve themselves to death or commit suicide by cop and all of this vile and sordid business would shrivel up and disappear. But she did not, of course, speak her mind. Instead, she said, "How's the heifer project coming along?"

Ripples of wariness, eagerness, doubt, and zeal traveled across Nutt's small face. Perhaps involuntarily, he tapped the underside of his hat brim with a pinkie. "My girls are true beauties," he said.

"Have you managed to make a perfect one yet?"

Dreamily, angrily, as though to an offstage antagonist, he said, "They are all perfect."

"I'd love to see them. Remy told me so much about them."

The moments stretched out. Nutt's jaw quivered a little.

"Seconded," Anabel said. "Please show us these extraordinary animals."

Remy said, "I think that our schedule prev—"

"Of course," Nutt said, standing. He drew a breath, then made for the door, which opened before him, although not quite quickly enough for him to avoid trimming his stride. The others followed. Lila could see him consider taking the risk of getting his hat knocked off for a shot at insouciant fluidity, but he flinched at the last second and trained a hostile look at the lackey who hadn't acted quickly enough. This same man who earlier had been afraid of accidentally touching a tampon muttered something into a walkie-talkie and fell in with his twin behind them as they were led out of the building to a pair of waiting golf carts, one for Remy and Nutt, one for Lila and Anabel. The lackeys drove the carts.

Lila tamped down pride as she noted her mother's approving expression. She took careful note of the face and physique of the lackey manning the entrance gate to the ag facilities; she mentally named him Manboot and added him to the rogues' gallery that already included the Bathroom Boys. Off to the west, a woman was leading one of the horses out of the barn and onto the little training arena. Clouds were massing on the horizon and a cool wind threatened to dethrone Nutt's hat, but Nutt, confident in the adhesive integrity of his head, left it alone.

At a junction in the path, they peeled off to the right, toward the building with the fans; this indeed must be where the cattle were housed. Up close, the fans were immense, making their near silence seem like a hallucination—she had the comical impression that the facility was an airship and that they were sailing through the clouds. She and Anabel climbed out of their cart and met the men at the door.

"I don't see a yard," Lila said. "Do the cows come outside?"

"The heifers aren't exposed to the elements. Until their moment of glory, they will live their lives inside this facility."

"Don't they need light and exercise?"

Nutt swelled with pride, like an oily ball of bread dough on a windowsill. His only response was an enigmatic smile. The guard here looked a little more formidable than Manboot. Straight and square-shouldered with a bleached-blond flattop, he resembled a sixteen-ounce can of kitchen cleanser. None of the men she'd seen guarding the place appeared to have been Affirmed, though she could easily imagine them all sitting around a campfire, roasting bits of rejected red heifer on hand-sharpened skewers.

Comet Cleanser Man used a phone to trigger a motorized garage door and followed them in. Manboot remained outside.

The space was blindingly bright—somehow as bright as the outdoors—and seemed larger inside than out, perhaps because what lay before them, surrounded by white split-rail fence and verdant with natural grasses, was the missing pasture, an honest-to-god indoor pasture that looked like it had been shipped here from Tuscany. Sweet-smelling, contoured by gently rolling artificial hills, and accompanied by a soundtrack of chirping insects and warbling songbirds, this idealized plot of land had at its center a miniature lake, where cattails grew and, as Lila watched in amazement, fish jumped. Heifers, each a perfect inkblot of russet, grazed and lowed, cradled by the folds of land, or lapped at the pond, their tails idly brushing away viridescent dragonflies. A shadow passed over the landscape, and Lila looked up, convinced she would see brilliant blue shot through with gray clouds. Instead, the vaulted ceiling presented something like a giant OLED monitor, with tiny daylight-corrected lamps switching on and off to replicate the dynamism of real sky. The entire scene, an engineering marvel, had a video-game surreality that made her feel like she had died in a golf-cart crash minutes before. It was heaven, the heaven of heifers, an all-female utopia.

"This is the only reality the heifers know," Nutt told them, sweeping his arm. "All of it state of the art. It isn't necessary to give them commercial feed; my engineers have developed hyper-nutritious strains of grass. The insects deliver vital medications, as does the water, which is drawn from an underground river." He smiled beatifically at Lila, then Anabel. "That's why I bought this plot of land, which was once considered nearly worthless. My engineers discovered a heretofore unknown tributary deep in the ground that feeds the Hassayampa River and pushes up to ten thousand acre-feet a day. This," he said, pointing down, "is where it comes closest to the surface. It makes my entire operation possible and gives these beautiful girls their perfect lives. I alone have access to this extraordinary resource, and my arrangement with the state guarantees that it will stay that way."

"Wow," said Lila.

"I suppose," Anabel said, "this accounts for the purity of your product."

The man's grin lit up his face the way a flame lights up a skull-shaped candle. "You don't know the half of it. If we had time," Nutt said, "I'd bring you back beyond the pasture and show you the breeding and genetic engineering facilities. We are doing things here no cattleman has ever attempted, let alone succeeded at."

"And when," Lila asked, "will those dang rabbis finally say yes?"

His flame flickered. "They seem not to know the word."

An hour later, back in the safe house, Lila opened her laptop and began the work of digging through Nutt's nominally secure network. The security system was the easiest to manage; she simply scheduled a temporary shutdown of the cameras and perimeter alarms for the hour they planned to carry out their operation. That finished, she turned to digging for Nutt's lab records, which could clarify when he began developing Affirmation and how it was tested. These proved harder to come by. Two computers that her software had been installed on didn't seem to have access to those files; another one now harbored her exploit but its user was working through lunch—or, to judge by the wireless network Lila had previously breached, shopping through lunch. They appeared to be planning a kitchen renovation.

"Here," her mother said, handing her a fistful of objects that looked like highlight markers. Lila accepted them and took a closer look—medical auto-injectors, the kind used by people with severe allergies. They had left Nutt with a vague agreement in place; Anabel told him that her people would contact him to put the finishing touches on the deal. These injectors, Lila assumed, were not the kind of touches Nutt was anticipating.

"I assume these aren't full of epinephrine?"

"No. Don't pull the blue cap until you're ready to use it—even a small quantity could incapacitate you. Aim for the thigh, hit hard, count to three. It's unlikely any of them will manage to get their weapons out before they fall asleep, but keep an eye on the holster."

"Thanks."

She nodded at Lila's laptop. "Anything?"

"Not yet."

"I don't mind eliminating Nutt just for trying to put me out of business. But..."

"If I can't get it this way, we can get it in person."

Anabel nodded again. "Good. I want the truth about my sister." She seemed to think of something, then narrowed her eyes. "I also wouldn't mind the truth about your sister."

A little jolt shot through Lila. Was it fear? Embarrassment? Why should she care what her mother did and didn't know? She said, "I don't know what you mean."

Anabel allowed herself a condescending smile. "Of course you do."

"Tell me, Mother. I'm dying to hear your thoughts."

"I think you were the one who killed that pervert, not Jane. She was the kind of sentimental fool who would get herself into that situation. You're the kind who would overreact to it."

"There's so much wrong with what you just said," Lila said, laying the injectors down on the coffee table with a quiet clatter, "that I don't even know where to begin. It wasn't my fault that he roofied me. And murdering his sorry ass was precisely the correct reaction from Jane. Furthermore," she added, "you were cheating on Dad with the guy! You brought him into our lives in the first place!"

"That was none of your business," Anabel said with a dismissive wave. "And I didn't make your high school hire him, how long was it, five years later?"

"You made it our business, Mother, when you seduced him right in front of us at theater camp. You only let us do theater camp because you wanted to fuck him!"

"Forgive me for trying to give you the things other children had, the things you whined and begged for. Toys and playdates and...birthday parties."

"You never let us have a birthday party! Don't put that on your list of sacrifices!"

"I beg your pardon, I let you have a party at—what is that dreadful pizzeria with the animatronic rat?"

"Mother," Lila said, nearly shouting, and she didn't understand why she was perpetuating Jane's lie about the murder, or allowing herself to feel like a child again, or arguing with this woman at all, "that wasn't our party! It was Emma Kimmel's!"

"It certainly wasn't. I remember it being your birthday."

"Our birthday had been two weeks before. You were mysteriously out of town then. It was Emma Kimmel's party that you let us go to. You didn't even come inside, you just dropped us off. And you forgot to come back for us! We had to get a ride home!"

"Nonsense," she said.

"How do you even know about the rat at all!"

"Everyone knows about the rat. Anyway, I'm simply surprised, that's all. Your sister has gone soft, considering she's such a cold-blooded killer. I would have expected your partnership would be more equal."

"That's her choice," Lila said, half believing it. "She has a child. She wanted the quiet life."

"The child doesn't seem to."

"Hm."

Anabel glanced at her watch. "You should try to rest. We will leave here at nightfall."

"Yeah," Lila said, "no shit. *You* get some rest, you're the shriveled old crone in this partnership."

"You know," her mother said after giving her the stink-eye for several seconds, "if my staff had killed you in Panama as they should have, I would have mourned you, but not for long."

"Well, Mother, if you'd died in the fire I started, I also would have mourned you only briefly."

"Good."

"Good."

Instinct woke Lila minutes before her mother entered the room to do it. She got up, checked the computer. No access to Nutt's files. That was fine, she'd have them in her hands soon. She shrugged on her holster, checked her clip, chamber, and safety, and belted on the waist bag where she kept her break-in tools. She ducked under the fish and climbed into the back seat of the car with her mother, laptop in tow, so that she could set the timer for the security hack when they were ready to move.

They had Anabel's men drive them to the utility turnoff that Lila and Jane had discovered the day before. Lila set the hack to activate in half an hour and they climbed out, crossed the highway, and scaled the hill that overlooked the compound. Binoculars to her eyes, Anabel said, "Towers first? We could disable the two guards stationed there and save ourselves some trouble."

"The Bathroom Boys," Lila said.

"What?"

"That's what I named them this morning. I think they're the two guys who led me to the bathroom."

She narrowed her eyes. "Hm. You remind me of your father."

This was an insult, which Lila ignored. "Yes, is my answer," she said. She looked at her watch. "Perimeter alarm and security lighting should go off shortly. We'll want to get in before they figure out they have to reboot everything." She pulled her eight-inch bolt cutters from the belt bag and held them up. "You want to split up? I'll get the fence open behind the south tower, and you can take the cutters."

From a pocket, Anabel drew her own bolt cutters.

"Of course," Lila said. "The guard tower doors might be locked while they're in there."

"I can pick a lock," Anabel spat.

"All right, Mother, just making sure. You want to take the south one, and I'll circle around?"

"Fine."

Lila set off, preparing to circle the cattle facility while her mother headed for the near tower, but was pulled up short by a distant, strangled cry. She turned to discover her mother, crouched on one knee in the brush, her head hanging, as though she were tying her shoe.

"Mother!"

Anabel's face appeared, squinting into the darkness. "Come!"

A moment later Lila was kneeling on the ground beside her. Her cheeks were pale and drawn, her forehead glowing with perspiration. "What the hell happened?"

"I've been bitten," she said.

Lila looked down, pulled the flashlight from her belt. Anabel's pant leg was pulled up, her ankle exposed. Two little dots drooled blood.

"Oh god. Did you see it?"

"Not clearly, but it was distinctive. Dark and light rings around its body."

"That sounds like a coral snake. They're venomous. You need to get treatment immediately. Can you walk?"

"Yes." She shivered.

"Jesus."

Lila helped her mother up and bore her weight as they limped back down the hill and across the highway. Her men were standing around, smoking. They stamped out their cigarettes and led Anabel to the back of the car, where one opened the rear hatch and the other helped her sit. He gently removed her shoe, revealing an alarming amount of blood covering the bottom of her foot.

"You need to get to a hospital," Lila said. "They'll contact Poison Control."

"Absolutely not," Anabel replied, her voice wavering. "Bandage it up," she commanded. "We'll continue the mission."

"Mother. Seriously. This would be a stupid way to die. The mission will have to be postponed."

Anabel hesitated, then literally growled in frustration. "No," she said. "I will go to the hospital. But the mission must continue. Get Jane to do it."

"Mother, it can wait for you."

"She's a convicted killer, isn't she?" came the reply, accompanied by a fierce glare. "Call her now. Get her here and finish the job."

The two stared at each other. Another shudder ran through Anabel; her teeth clamped together, a blood vessel pulsed at her temple. Lila was confused and alarmed to find that she was actually worried.

"Fine," Lila said. She turned to the nearer of her mother's goons. "I'll put the security hack on hold. One of you can call Jane."

"I think," her mother said, "she'd prefer to hear from you."

22

How could it be morning already? Jane didn't feel rested; she barely felt human. Bright light shone beside her, and her body itched in the skewed and twisted clothes she'd worn to bed. She pulled the duvet over her head. Why in the hell wasn't Chance turning off the alarm? He was the one who'd set it.

No, wait. She wasn't at home. She was divorced. Chance was off somewhere doing—well, she didn't know what anymore. And that buzzing wasn't an alarm. That was her phone.

She peeked out from under the covers. The curtains, not quite closed, were bookended by black strips of night. From the distance, a voice called out, "Mom! Are you going to answer that?"

Chloe. Up in the loft. Not asleep. Actually, the lights were all on. The bedside clock said 9:47. Her laptop was still open on the bed beside her. Right.

"Yup," she groaned, and clawed the phone into the bed. To her sister, she said, "Is it over?"

"You have to come out here."

Lila sounded piqued, not panicked. Did they need help dragging a body somewhere? Did they want her to stand watch while they did their spy shit? Vacuum out their mother's car? "Why," Jane said.

"Mom got bit by a venomous snake. César and Romaldo took her to the hospital. Come to the turnoff, the one we found with the concrete shed."

Jane put her sister on speaker, sat up, pulled her hair back. "Wait," she said, "start over. Is it done? Did you get him?"

"We hadn't even started. We were just heading off to take out the guard towers when she screamed. I found her on the ground with a bite on her ankle."

"Queen of the jungle was bitten by a snake?"

"It would be a fitting end," Lila said, "after pumping poison up people's noses all these years." Now that sounded forced; a little fear was creeping into her sister's voice. About the mission, or about their mother? "Anyway, I'm just sitting in the dirt here with my laptop and supplies. I'm ready to disable the security when you get here and head in."

"All right, but...to do what? You didn't bother to share the master plan."

"It's simple," Lila replied. There, back to pique. "I'll explain it when you get here. And I'll bring your gun."

"I figured." She pulled on her boots, grabbed her jacket from the chair.

"Mom!" Chloe called down. "What's happening?"

Jane peered up. The girl's face looked pale, up there in the rafters, hovering over the railing. "Your grandmother got bitten by a snake. Gotta go help your aunt."

"Let me come!"

"No. You're hurt, and even if you weren't, it's too dangerous."

The girl stared at her fiercely for a moment before the facade fell. She blinked. "Don't die," she said for the second time in as many days.

If Jane stayed much longer, she wouldn't go. It was time to turn her back. "Never," she said, and left.

She turned the loaner's headlights off as she approached and managed to catch a glimpse of Lila, unguarded for a rare moment, sitting dejectedly in the moonlight, her back against the concrete utility shed. She looked the way she had in high school outside the stage door when Jane stood with their friends during rehearsals, laughing and flirting and smoking cigarettes. She looked like Chloe.

Then she reacted to Jane's tires on the gravel; she stood up and turned back into herself. A backpack lay on the ground next to her, and she picked it up and approached the car.

"Here's your gun," Lila said, meeting her at the door.

"You're welcome? For saving the mission?"

Lila glared, obviously irritated at having to feign politeness. "I'll thank you after we do it."

Jane accepted the gun and holster. "What else have you got for me?"

Lila handed her a pair of compact bolt cutters and a trio of medical injectors. "These are powerful tranquilizers, according to Anabel. Do you know how they work?"

Jane nodded. "Chloe used to have a friend with peanut allergies. I got lessons."

"Used to? Did she die?"

"No, she moved. Jesus Christ." She stashed the tools in her waist bag and noted Lila's expression of grudging appreciation that they seemed to have the same one. "So what are we doing?"

"I've got a hack ready to go that will power down the security system. I'm not sure how long it'll take for the staff to wake up the IT people and get it back up remotely—we should assume not long. I'll take the near tower, you take the other, we disable the two guards. Signal me when you're done, then I'll meet you in the shadows behind the ag buildings."

"Do we go for Nutt right away?"

Lila shook her head. "There are two more guys. I want them all out of commission before we head for the house. And then...Anabel wanted a confession out of Nutt, but my priority is the laptop."

"What about the right-hand man?"

"Unknown. There are two cars in front of the house, I assume he's in play."

"All right," Jane said. She squinted toward the hill on the other side of the road, pondering the towers behind it. "Are the doors going to be locked or what?"

"Beats me," Lila admitted. "Maybe they get sick of their own farts and keep 'em propped open. I've got my tools—did Loretta teach you lock-picking?"

"Nope."

"Hm. Maybe you should have brought Chloe."

"Lila. Don't. I'll put the guy out one way or another."

"Fine."

"Fine."

While Jane strapped on her holster, Lila typed something into her laptop, then stashed it in the car. They jogged across the empty highway and up the hill. The two towers were occupied, as expected; the face of the nearer guard was visible even without binoculars, illuminated by the cool light from a bank of small monitors. With her binocs, Jane could even see what the monitors displayed: an array of doors and loading bays throughout the compound. After a moment, the monitors winked out and reverted to an error message.

"That's the hack," Lila said. "Let's go."

It took six minutes to navigate the brush out behind the ag facility, and Jane was winded when she arrived. The north tower stood next to the horse barn, and the area behind it was a rocky verge that she skidded down, barely in control. It took another couple of minutes to get the fence open and wriggle through, and then she jogged to the tower's base. The structure was made of cinder block; it appeared to be a recent addition to the facility. The stairs that led to the guards' outpost and the catwalk were of modular aluminum construction and felt rickety to climb. Jane treaded lightly, but her steps still rang out through the metal. She transferred an injector from her pack to her back pocket.

Her back to the wall, she snaked out a hand and tested the latch of a steel security door. It was indeed locked. Through its wire-reinforced window she saw the rounded shoulders of a man with a walkie-talkie to his ear, saying something about the power outage. "Well, wake him up," he said, and, a moment later: "Well, somebody drive out there, then!" He signed off and dropped the handset angrily on his desk. A laptop there was displaying a baseball game; beside it stood a package of Funyuns and a can of Coke.

Jane removed her cap, freed her hair from the cinch, and messed it up with both hands. She untucked her shirt, then unbuttoned the top two buttons. It would be better if she'd been wearing makeup to muss, but you can't have it all. Hoping that Nutt brought a woman home from time to time, she thumped the door with a fist. The guy nearly jumped out of his skin. He was powerfully built, fleshy and dense, and had a stain on the chest pocket of his blue uniform shirt.

"Travis is having a heart attack! I can't get a signal on my phone!"

The guard narrowed his eyes, smelling a rat, but he opened the door anyway, because girl. Jane took two steps forward and thrust a knee into his balls. The man doubled over, giving her a moment to draw the injector from her pocket.

"You...you..." The guy gasped, then let out a little scream as the needle plunged into his leg. He shook his head like a dog, then swooned.

"Whoa, buddy," Jane said, and got behind him quickly enough to prevent his head from bashing into the desk. She lowered him gently to the floor, pulled a couple of thin leather gloves from her pack, and put them on. She wiped off the empty injector with her shirt, relieved the guard of his sidearm, leaned out the door, and flung both objects over the fence and into the weeds. Then she fixed her shirt and hair and put her hat back on.

With the binocs, she peered out over the compound to the other tower. Lila was there, leaning over the monitors. Jane waved her hands to get her attention, then gave her the thumbs-up. After giving it back, Lila pumped her fist twice. For a second Jane thought she was actually indicating approval for once in her life, but then she remembered her sister had been married to a soldier. It was just the signal for hurry up.

On the way, the horse barn, built on a concrete slab and open on both ends, served as natural cover, and Jane crept through. Its exterior was designed to appear rustic, but inside it was outfitted with new-looking equipment: tack hanging from hooks, spray bottles, shining galvanized buckets of feed—a really nice barn. Light came in from a small spotlight focused on the yard between the barn and fenced run. There were half a dozen horses in here, separated by walls that were wood up to chest height, then aluminum bars above that. The space was warm and smelled of animals and cleaning supplies. Most of the horses were standing, eyes closed, but a couple lay with their legs folded under them like giant cats. One was watching Jane move through the space. It was a beautiful, lively-looking animal, some kind of Belgian cross, she believed, with a brown coat, blond mane, tail, and fetlocks, and a long, affable face marked by a white stripe between the eyes. She stashed her gloves, stroked the horse's head, and said hello.

Chloe had gone through a horse phase a few years before—or, rather, Jane's ex-mother-in-law, Susan, had attempted to impose a horse phase upon her. It was part of the woman's ongoing project to smooth over her granddaughter's eccentricities and turn her into a proper rich asshole. So as not to seem like the terrible mother Susan was convinced she was, Jane agreed to bring Chloe to riding lessons, buy her the right clothes, and champion her progress in the sport.

Chloe gave it a good six months before bailing, but, much to her own surprise, Jane loved it—loved getting up early, loved grooming and talking to her preferred horses, loved learning their personalities and riding styles. Before she learned to ride, she'd assumed the sport to be predominantly passive, like riding in a car. In fact it was interesting, emotionally complex, and good exercise. Jane concealed her enthusiasm from Susan but pursued riding for a couple of years after Chloe gave it up. She'd gotten away from it since they'd expanded Perks, but now she realized she needed to pick it up again. She missed it.

The animal pressed its nose into her arm, nudged her with a soft lip, snorted gently into her face. A couple of other horses reacted, breathing a little louder in their stalls. A metal nameplate on the stall wall read CEDAR. Some tack hung on a hook beside the stall, including a rainbow-colored nylon halter, and there were some crayon-on-paper artworks pinned to the wall as well, a child's illustrations of herself standing next to or riding a horse that resembled this one.

Jane left the barn, pulled her gloves back on, and squeezed through the fence where she'd cut it, then walked along the fence to the east. At one point the fence passed through a declivity between the ridge and a small hillock. Lila was waiting at the back of the ag facilities, the darkest part of the fenceline. She'd already begun cutting through, and a minute later they were inside again. "There are two here. They're on high alert—the other men must have sent out a warning after the system went down."

"Where are they now? I didn't see them on my way over."

"South side of the cattle facility, scratching their heads. The approach is fairly open. We could just shoot them."

"Lila."

"Hmph. We could walk between the cattle and pharmaceutical buildings," Lila said. "The access road between them isn't well lit. If we stay close to the drug building, they might not see us, especially since they've been standing in the light."

"Let's have a look." They walked to the southeast corner and peered around it. The two men were indeed standing in a pool of light beside a loading bay, talking. One of them, tall and lanky, held a walkie-talkie. The shorter, beefier one rested his hands on his hips. Their postures were wary and confused.

"What about those?" Jane asked. She pointed to a couple of small utility vehicles. They stood in a gravel lot between spray-painted lines and were plugged into EV sockets. "We can sneak over there and drive right up."

"Right. Mom and I rode in those this morning."

"Uh-huh, been there, done that. Got it."

"Don't be a baby. So we steal the carts and drive up. Then what?"

"Chase them down, jump out, trank 'em."

"Chaotic," Lila replied, with a scowl. But Jane could tell she liked it.

They crept along the fence to the charging lot while the men's attention was trained on the entrance road and the guard towers. The carts were open to the air and had keyless ignition switches; they would start only with a four-digit code. "Maybe it's written down somewhere," Jane said, and they began digging through the glove compartments of the carts.

"Nothing," Lila whispered after a minute. "You?"

Jane didn't find a sticky note or a strip of tape; she tried *0000*, *1234*, and *4321*, then stopped herself to avoid getting security-locked out. There was a printed manual, though, which she drew from its sleeve and fanned through. The section on ignition referred to access code instructions on the inside back cover, and there she found the following:

> THIS is your FACTORY ACCESS CODE. **This code should be RESET immediately upon taking possession of your vehicle.** INSTRUCTIONS for code reset are below.

Beneath this text and above the reset instructions was a sticker, and the sticker read *3609*. Jane punched it in, and the dashboard lit up. The only sound the vehicle made was a faint whir from under the hood.

Lila found an identical manual in the other glovebox with a different number on the sticker; this code, however, seemed to have been reset. Luckily someone had written the new number in pencil underneath the factory one. She typed it in and her cart came on too. They disengaged their parking brakes and dug in their packs for fresh auto-injectors.

The two men were about fifty yards away. They'd hear the wheels on the gravel and would take a few seconds to react. The sisters looked at each other, and Lila shrugged. She raised her hand with three fingers extended, then folded them in one by one. Three, two, one, go.

The closest thing Jane had ever driven to something that looked like this cart was a lawn tractor. This vehicle was not like a lawn tractor. The torque took her by surprise; the tires spun, then caught, and the cart jerked ahead like a gazelle. A glance to her right revealed her sister, chin forward over the steering wheel, teeth clenched in a grimace of delight.

The tall guy appeared the more attentive of the two, but he wasted precious seconds squinting into the gloom, processing what his eyes were telling him. It seemed to Jane that she wouldn't waste so much time in similar circumstances, puzzling over how to react to a couple of golf carts zooming out of the darkness toward her, but she wasn't a rent-a-cop loitering outside a cow barn. The shorter man had spun around and instinctively reached for his holster, and if he'd noticed them a second sooner, he would have pulled the piece. But there was no time. The carts were too close. Jane heard the tall guy say, "Whoa, whoa!" and then the two men turned and ran, first directly away, then in opposite directions.

Tall was closest to Jane, so she went for him. She spun the wheel and the cart drifted, kicking up a spray of gravel. She felt it beginning to tip over, let up on the accelerator, straightened, and hit it.

She didn't want to kill the guy, just knock him over. She pulled up alongside him, then jerked the wheel, figuring she'd hip-check him into the dirt. Instead, an instant later, the man was in her lap, flopping like a tuna. Jane took an elbow to the face as she wobbled the cart, trying to dislodge him so she could reach into her pocket for the trank. She hazarded a glance up, and she was glad she did, because the perimeter fence was coming fast. She slammed on the brakes and skidded to a halt on the weedy verge, propelling the guard to the ground.

He rolled onto his back and his hand went for his waist. "No, buddy," Jane said, grabbing his wrist and jamming the injector into his thigh. The hand he'd curled into a fist to pummel her with wavered in the air, then fell. The guard was out. She unsnapped the holster, drew the gun, pulled the clip, and threw both over the fence. Then she turned to find out how Lila was doing.

Hard to say. All Jane could see was the underside of her cart—it lay on its side near the entrance bay of the heifer barn, flooded in light. She jogged over, wondering where the hell Lila and the other guard had gone.

There they were. The guard was half pinned underneath the cart, and

Lila was picking herself up off him. "I tried to bump him," she said, dusting off her clothes. "But I ended up rolling over. My elbow, uh, landed on his throat." She crouched, pressed two fingers to his wrist. "Okay. He's alive." Almost as an afterthought, she tranquilized him. "What did you do with this?" she asked Jane, pulling his sidearm out of the holster.

"Threw it over the fence."

"Seems like a waste," she said. "This is a good gun."

Jane shrugged. After a moment, Lila tossed it into the shadows, then emptied the clip onto the ground. "We need to get this thing out of the light." Together, they righted the cart, and Lila drove it around the corner of the barn, out of sight of the house. "Who's left?" Jane asked when she returned.

"Just Remy and Nutt."

"Remy's the guy you…"

"Right. While I was in the tower waiting for you to finish," Lila said, her voice underslung with judgment, "I surveilled the house. I saw Nutt moving behind the windows in what I assume is his office, upstairs in the east wing. He's probably been called to action at this point, so be aware."

They decided to return to the residence outside the fence, in the dark. Her sister craned her neck and scowled as they passed between the ridge and the little hill, muttering, "Security risk." They reentered the compound through the hole Jane had made.

23

Jane signaled for Lila to cut through the barn and, after a moment of irritation during which she realized it was actually a good idea, Lila followed. Several of the animals were awake and standing, peering out of their stalls in curiosity; their ears were pricked forward, their tails twitched, and their gazes followed the sisters as they passed. "Did you stop here before and make friends?" Lila asked her, confused.

"Yeah. I like horses." She reached out to stroke a brown and white one with a gloved hand. "Good boy, Cedar."

"No rush, we could just hang out for a while. Maybe you can ask Nutt for a job application while we're tackling him?"

"Already got a job as a mastermind's secretary. Why would I ever leave."

Lila opened her mouth, then closed it. There was no point. Let her have the last word. "Let's go," Lila said.

"You got it, boss."

Nutt's residence lay at the bottom of a slight incline. An illuminated track led to the front entrance; they circled to the north instead, approaching from the side, where a steel security door was set into the log wall where it met the hillside. They could hear distant voices, men arguing, through an open window. Good.

The door lock was trivial to pick, and they paused before entering, listening for any reaction to the breach. No lights, no alarm, and no change in the voices, so it seemed the security system was still offline.

Lila had guessed that anyone who knew how to reset it had gone home hours before, but it was nice to be proven right.

She found a wall switch and turned on the lights. They were in a utility room lined with industrial shelving that held cleaning supplies and nonperishable food. Nutt seemed to like French roast coffee, Pringles, and Cheerios. This room led into a home theater, where five rows of raked theater seats, each equipped with a drink holder and a footrest, faced a wall-sized screen. Popcorn was scattered beneath a couple of seats in the center, and a half-full bag of it, along with two Coke-branded cups, had been left behind. Posters around the room advertised classic westerns.

A staircase led to the upper floors of the west wing. This was the residence area. They discovered guest rooms with en suite bathrooms, a rustic-looking den made to resemble a fishing cabin, and a kitchen. A bottle of red wine, nearly empty, stood on a central hardwood island beside the wrapper from a chocolate bar. An enormous gas range appeared never to have been used, while a microwave oven above it was covered in fingerprints.

The main bedroom had its own woodstove that had actually seen some action; the ashes inside were cold, but a pile of kindling and firewood lay beside it on a fieldstone hearth. The king-sized bed was fashioned from varnished logs, and the bedclothes were mussed. A half-full wineglass stood on one bedside table, half a chocolate bar and a phone on the other. "Looks like we got him out of bed," Lila said quietly. "Should we search here? Wait and surprise him?"

Jane, eyes narrowed, was sniffing the air.

"What?" Lila asked her.

The answer came in the form of a sound: a door opening and closing in the hall, and footsteps. Wordlessly, Lila and Jane stepped to either side of the doorway, flanking it. Lila drew her gun from its holster and nodded to her sister: *You grab him.* A moment later, the door was flung open and a bathrobed figure appeared, back from the shower, holding a wineglass that tumbled to the floor as Jane grabbed the target from behind and clapped a hand over their mouth. It was a woman, surprisingly age-appropriate for Nutt, or nearly so. Her eyes widened as she saw the gun and she began to struggle.

Lila holstered it, dug in her pack for an injector.

Jane shook her head. "Stop!" she hissed. "You don't know what she put in these things."

Lila prepared an objection, then dismissed it—Jane was right. She came in close and looked into the woman's terrified eyes. "We aren't going to hurt you, do you understand? We're here for Nutt." She waved the injector between her and her sister's faces. "My associate is going to take her hand off your mouth, and if you scream, this goes in your leg. Understand?"

She seemed to relax slightly, then nodded. Jane moved her hand from the woman's mouth to her shoulders.

"Tell me your name," Lila said.

In a smoke-roughened voice, the woman said, "Wendy."

"Okay. Wendy, what's going to happen is, you're going to sit here in bed, eat your chocolate, and drink your boyfriend's wine. Is that your phone on the table there?"

She nodded. "He's not my boyfriend. It's a one-night stand."

"Sorry to interrupt it. We're going to take your phone with us. You're going to lock the door behind us when we leave and stay put until we come back and tell you it's safe to go. Did you drive your own car here?"

"Yeah, it's out at the entrance gate."

"You good to drive it?"

"What, like, am I drunk? No," she said, scowling, "I can drive."

"Okay," Lila said, "just asking."

Wendy gestured with a tip of her head. "Can she let go of me now?"

Lila's eyes met her sister's, and Jane released the woman, who adjusted and tightened her robe and gazed mournfully at the spilled wine on the floor. "Are you going to kill him?" she said, not without enthusiasm.

They just looked at each other.

"If you are, I'm going to help myself to some of his stuff," Wendy said. "And maybe just leave now? I'm not afraid."

Lila said, "He didn't hurt you, did he?"

"Nah. He just picked me up at the roadhouse on Route 10 where I work and asked if I wanted to come over and watch *Rancho Notorious*. He really meant it!" She pondered for a moment. "He's got a hog to die for but no idea what to do with it."

"Okay," Lila said. "Time to go, then."

"I never saw you," said Wendy. "And nobody but Travis saw me."

The three women looked at one another. Jane nodded. "Okay," Lila said finally. "Leave through the theater. There's a storeroom that leads to a side door."

"Can I have my phone?"

"No," Lila said.

Wendy shrugged. "Whatever. I needed a new one anyway."

They unholstered their sidearms and moved down the hall, listening for the sound of voices. During the sisters' encounter with Wendy, the men had quieted, and Lila wondered if their presence had been detected. They arrived at a double door hewn from timber that looked like it belonged on a castle keep. Jane pushed one door slightly open with her hip and listened.

"Someone's on the move," she whispered.

A door opening and closing. Footsteps. Through the slit, a figure could be seen, his back to them, hurrying down the central grand staircase they'd seen this morning: Remy. He crossed the entrance hall and passed behind the taxidermied grizzly and through the front doors. Jane said, "We should warn that woman."

"We did," Lila said. "If she puts herself in danger, that's her problem."

When Remy was gone, they pushed the door open on silent hinges and stepped onto the landing. The space was shrouded in gloom, and moonlight poured in through tall uncurtained windows. They crept along the balustrade—fucking logs again, my god, man!—and paused outside the double door to the office wing. They heard nothing.

Lila gripped the iron handle of the left door and gestured for Jane to conceal herself behind the other. She slowly pulled it open. No one there, and no sound. The women passed silently through. A hall stretched out before them, the twin of the one they'd just left on the other side of the house. The floorboards were tight, and their shoes made no noise on the woolen runner that half covered them. From somewhere came the chirping of insects, the bark of a coyote. The boardroom lay at the end of this hall, and one of its doors stood open, revealing the table Lila and their mother had sat at earlier, scattered with papers and dimly illuminated by a floor lamp in a corner.

But they never reached it. The last door on the left was standing open, revealing a study done up in dark wood and leather, glass-fronted bookcases filled with gilt-stamped volumes, a display case full of antique rifles, and, sitting open on a desk you could butcher an elk on, beside a familiar cream-colored Stetson, a laptop computer. Nutt's. A pistol lay next to it. And on the north side of the room, French doors were thrown open to a balcony overlooking the desert night. Nutt stood with his back to them, wearing jeans and a tee shirt, his hands gripping the railing, his shoulders tense. They raised their weapons.

Later, Lila would have to admit to herself that she was impressed with Nutt in this moment; she'd never in her life seen a reaction so swift and decisive. His head snapped around like an owl's; he beheld them with fierce, wide eyes, shot a rueful glance at the gun on his desk, and, without another moment's hesitation, vaulted over the balcony rail and into the darkness.

They raced to the railing and peered over. Nutt had landed on the hillside ten feet below and was running off to the west with a twitchy, chugging stride, like a miniature locomotive. The sisters paused—the laptop was right here. They could just let the guy go, grab the evidence, and learn the truth at their leisure. But to Lila's genuine surprise, Jane holstered her gun and leapt after him, deftly landing in the dirt below with a grunt. Lila followed.

It hurt to land. Her knee would swell up during the night and she'd be limping for weeks, in fact. But for now, adrenaline propelled her into a run. Jane was a dozen yards ahead of her, and Nutt was off in the distance; he was sprinting along the fence, toward what, she didn't know.

And then she did. He was going for the horse barn. Ahead of her, Jane stumbled over a rock or a bit of brush, staggered, righted herself. Lila caught up. Together, they headed for the dark opening of the barn and had nearly made it when, in a flurry of clomping and snorting, and trailing a cloud of wood shavings and dust, a black horse exploded out with Nutt clinging to its unsaddled back. Lila and Jane dived into the dirt and the horse neighed in alarm, attempting to avoid them. Its hooves skidded on the rocky ground, it caught itself, and horse and rider raced off into the night. Picking herself up, Lila saw them corner abruptly, then leap into the air.

"The rise," Jane said. "He jumped the fence! Hurry!"

Lila followed her sister into the barn and gasped to see her throwing open the stall door of the brown horse. The animals were all awake now, snorting and nickering, excited and curious. A gray-and-white-spotted one was gazing levelly at Lila, as though in challenge. Its stall bore the name SWEET POTATOES. The one empty stall had been occupied by OLD JOE.

Jane was stroking the brown horse, muttering something to it as she pulled a fabric thing over its nose and ears. Then she backed up a few steps, dashed forward, and swiftly, effortlessly cantilevered her body onto the animal. She swung a leg over and sat upright, patting the horse's neck. "Come on, what are you waiting for? No time to saddle, let's go."

Lila had ridden a horse once, as part of a tour group in a national park, where, on a job, she had followed some real estate mogul's purportedly corrupt right-hand man. It had seemed to her at the time like a good, chill way to observe the guy, who was here with another guy she was beginning to suspect was his lover—the true source of the mogul's anxiety, it turned out. In the end, she would cut a deal with the guy and let the mogul shortchange her, but at the time, all she cared about was finishing the job. The tour guide thought she looked experienced or tough or something, or maybe he just wanted to frighten her so that he could save the day and fuck her, and he gave her Cricket, a lumbering freak of a mount who nearly threw her into a canyon. Never again, she'd told herself.

Oh, well. She unlatched the stall door and threw it open. She stole a glance at Jane's horse to see how the thing went over the head, then tried to get it onto Sweet Potatoes. The horse knew what to do and wriggled its nose through. When it looked right, she took a running leap. The horse, surprised, staggered to one side, and she slid off its flank. It smelled good, warm and rank, and she stroked it, apologized.

She made it on the second try, then glanced over at Jane to see how she was sitting: scootched forward, her ankles gripping the animal in front of its rib cage. She felt the leg muscles flexing, communicating with her through the skin.

"Stay upright. Hold the reins, not her mane. Don't grip so hard with your legs."

"He's getting away!"

"They'll know where to go. Follow me! Lean into it!"

She could feel the horse growing excited beneath her, the muscles rippling. A jolt of adrenaline filled Lila with sudden confidence. When Jane dashed off, Lila leaned forward, and Sweet Potatoes burst out of the stall and out into the darkness. Jane had called it "her," which made it a... mare? *Go, girl, go.* They didn't have far to go before the jump, just about thirty yards; her sister made a wide turn without slowing, and the brown horse sailed over the fence. "You can do it, Sweet Potatoes," Lila told the horse, then didn't know where to lean—left, into the turn, or right, to tell the animal to take it wide? She chose right, and Sweet Potatoes became confused and slowed down. "No, go, go!" She tried to correct, leaning left, scrabbling awkwardly with her foot, and the mare understood and bolted for the jump.

Lila wasn't ready for the landing, and it took every muscle in her body to stay on the horse's back. She could see the blond tail of Jane's horse off in the distance, rising and falling out of view with the rolling hills north of the compound. She had another ten seconds or so of terror as Sweet Potatoes gathered speed, climbing each hill, leaping down the other side, and Lila bounced and swayed, trying not to depend too much on the straps wrapped around her fingers or on her knees, which wanted to squeeze the breath out of the animal.

But it was clear that Sweet Potatoes loved to run, and might even be showing off for her. She gained on Jane and Cedar, and soon they topped a rise, and the moon revealed the desert flats and Nutt, his white shirt a flag in the distance, moving up and down like a will-o'-the-wisp. They were getting close. They took off across the plain, rocks and brush racing by; Lila could see a faint path across the land, and the horses seemed familiar with it, deftly dodging and pivoting in response to its small changes. Up ahead, Nutt peered over his shoulder, saw them coming, tried to redouble his horse's pace.

But Old Joe wasn't up to the task. They came ever closer, gradually tacking to the east, the moon at their backs, the air filled with their breaths and the horses' breaths. Lila pulled up alongside her sister, or rather Sweet Potatoes did, and reached for her sidearm.

"No!" Jane shouted over the pounding hooves and wind. "Not near the horses!"

They must have been close enough for Nutt to hear, because he peered over his shoulder again, and Old Joe misinterpreted the movement as a command. The horse went into a wide turn, seeming to take Nutt by surprise, and he leaned, lost his grip, and tumbled into the dirt.

They were upon him in seconds, Lila hitting the ground running and snaking a hand into her boot for her knife, Jane brandishing her gun.

Nutt lay on his back panting, cradling his right arm. Coyotes yipped somewhere, but the insects around them had fallen silent. Lila knelt beside him, balancing her knife hand casually on her knee, as though she just happened to be holding it. She said, "Hi, Nutt. You ran away. Why?"

"You," he wheezed, raising his head to look at one sister, then the other. "I would have expected your mother." He groaned, let his head fall back into the dirt. "Remy told me not to trust her. What do you want."

"The truth," Lila said.

"About what? The business? It's just business," he said, trying to shrug, wincing at the attempt. "At least it is to her. The whole model is obsolete. I'm not the problem."

"No," Jane said, stepping closer. "Not the business. Our aunt."

He seemed genuinely surprised. "Ruth?"

"You killed her," Jane said.

But he shook his head, brought his hand to his throat to fondle the cross on its chain. "That's what all this is about?"

"It is," Lila said.

"I didn't kill her. I was a thousand miles away. She ended her own life."

"You poisoned her. You *Affirmed* her."

Somehow, there was enough hubris left in the man for him to roll his eyes. "It wasn't even called that then," he said. "It wasn't *finished*."

"But you gave it to her," Jane said.

"She *took* it from me."

"You administered it to her against her will."

Nutt was shaking his head. "She *asked* me for it. She was sick. Paranoid, delusional. She'd been doing patent work for me and was becoming unpredictable, unreliable. I'd found another lawyer, told her she needed help. She knew about the prion drug from my papers."

"Wait," Lila said. "Prion drug?"

"Yeah," Jane said, surprising her. "That's what Affirmation is. It was in those papers you downloaded. We figured it out this afternoon. He made mad-cow coke. That's why it lasts. At least, until it eats your brain."

"Shit," Lila said.

Jane turned back to Nutt, waved the gun. "That's what the heifers are, right? You're not trying to build the Third Temple. They're little factories for Affirmation."

"I beg your pardon," Nutt said. "I am indeed trying to trigger the restoration of the Temple. But I am also trying to make people see the light. And I am succeeding."

"Give me a break," Jane said, and startled Lila by kicking him in the face. Nutt cried out. "You forced this shit on our aunt because she knew too much."

"I *let* her take it," the man whined. "I didn't know what would happen, and I told her so. She was desperate."

"You knew it would drive her mad."

"I knew it would make her better for a while. But beyond that..." A small amount of resolve returned to his face. "I warned her! But she took it anyway. As people do." He tried to sit up. Jane kicked him back down. "How many people has your mother killed with her product?" he demanded through clenched teeth. "What if all the siblings, all the children, of everyone her product destroyed came for you?"

They stared at him in silence. He gazed at Lila, then Jane, then back at Lila. "Grow up," he went on. His nose had begun to bleed. "You're not avenging angels. You're doing the bidding of a mass murderer. You're an organized crime family. I'm trying to cleanse the world of corruption."

The insects were coming back online, chittering and chirping in the brush, accustomed to them now. The horses had wandered into a cluster and were keeping one another company, waiting for the humans to finish.

"Help me up," Nutt said. "You don't have to be tools of your mother's vile empire. We'll make an arrangement that satisfies us all."

There was a moment where everyone seemed to weigh what had just been said. Then Nutt held out a hand and, before either of them could decide what to do with it, snatched the knife from Lila and swiped it toward Jane's knee.

He missed. Jane didn't hesitate; she pointed the SIG straight down and drilled a bullet into the crown of his head. He slumped forward, then onto his side, and the dirt darkened.

The horses neighed, stamped their hooves. Jane turned to Lila with an expression devoid of emotion, her pupils dilated, her skin pale. Some of her hair had escaped the cap and stuck to her cheek. For a moment, Lila wondered if her sister was about to kill her too. Her mouth was dry as she said, "Thanks."

"You're welcome," Jane said robotically, then seemed to come to herself. "Lucky me, I already did the time."

"Har har." Lila reached out and gently plucked her knife from Nutt's hand.

"Now what?"

Lila looked over her shoulder at the faint glow of the compound, miles away. Out of her sister's gaze, she let out breath, tried to relax her features. Then, "Coyotes will arrive as soon as we're gone," she said, turning back. "Tomorrow, vultures. If they're looking for him, that might tip them off. But I doubt they will be. His bones will be picked clean and scattered."

Beside her, the body had stopped twitching. Jane said, "Let's take the horses around to the east, then ditch them on the hill. They won't wander far from home. I'm not going to jump that fence again."

"Agreed," Lila said.

Jane looked down at the gun in her hand and sighed. "I guess we should get rid of this."

"We'll find some gully on the way back to the safe house."

"All right. But I'm going to drop you off and go to the motel. I'm not interested in reporting back to her."

Lila said, "What, did he get under your skin? About us being a bunch of criminals?"

Jane shot her a look. "He's right. We are. And it's her fault. And I'm angry I ended up doing her dirty work for her."

"She didn't ask you to! She got bitten by a snake. She might even be dead now, for all we know."

This elicited, to Lila's surprise, a belly laugh. "Dude."

"What!"

"There was no snakebite. She was fucking with you. This is her idea of"—she craned her head up, as if looking for an answer in the sky—"*parenting.*"

"No! I saw the bite! Two little holes in her ankle."

"You think," Jane said, "she isn't capable of stabbing herself in the leg to prove a point?"

Lila didn't have a response to this. It couldn't be. But, she realized now, of course it could.

"Okay, then," Jane said. She holstered the gun. Then she walked to the horses, mounted Cedar, and beckoned for Lila to follow. Old Joe passed in the opposite direction as Lila made her way toward Sweet Potatoes.

Jane didn't look back, but Lila did; there Nutt lay in the moonlight, Old Joe standing at his side, looking after them in confusion. An owl cried out. The coyotes yipped. The black horse gave up and followed. They rode back to the compound, where Lila entered the quiet house, retrieved the open laptop, disabled the password protection. Then they rode the fenceline back to the empty highway.

At the safe house, César was standing outside by her mother's car and nodded to Lila as Jane pulled away. She said, "Is she all right?"

He paused a moment before saying, "Yes, ma'am, just fine."

"You got to the hospital and back pretty quick."

"I drove fast," he said after another hesitation.

"They had the antivenom on hand."

"That's right."

"Where was the hospital, again? Phoenix?"

"Yes, ma'am," he said, then seemed to regret it.

"Because Prescott is a lot closer. I'm surprised you didn't go there."

"Ma'am," he said, squirming.

"Never mind."

She thundered up the walk, head down. Romaldo, standing guard outside the door, trained a hooded, sheepish look on her, then turned away.

Inside, she heard water running. She ducked under the fish, then flopped down on the sofa in the living room and flung open the laptop. Here was everything: Nutt's plans to disrupt the election, his spreadsheet of dealers and supply lines, things he discovered on his own, things he seemed to have stolen, somehow, from Anabel. Scanned legal documents provided a history of his work with Ruth; it was clear to Lila that the relationship went sour, that Ruth became increasingly wary of his extralegal activities and no longer wanted to represent him, and that Nutt had ample reason to make her a guinea pig for his industry-disrupting new drug. She wondered who else he'd gotten sick of and dispatched in this way.

But Lila didn't plan on finding out. She was going to give the laptop to her mother and get on with her life. There were still a few days left to her planned, then abandoned, vacation. By the time she drove Louie Donough's car to Amarillo, flew back to New York, and returned everyone home in the Volvo, she'd have only a brisk sixteen-hour drive between herself and blissful solitude. And maybe a call to Brooke. Maybe a video call. Maybe a visit.

Exhaustion, and the shower's white noise, overcame her and she crossed her arms and fell asleep clutching the laptop. When she awoke half an hour later, her mother occupied the chair across from her, looking fresh as a daisy. A bit of gauze peeked out from beneath her pant leg.

"You've inherited my industriousness," Anabel said.

Lila rubbed her eyes. "I get that from Dad."

"Ha. Have you found the information I want?"

"Yeah, I found it," Lila said, hefting the laptop.

"And Nutt?"

"Dead. In a wild horse chase."

"So sad that it had to come to that."

"Jane did it."

Anabel raised an eyebrow. "Well. She is the cold-blooded one, isn't she. You see, I knew you wouldn't need me."

"Mm. How's the ankle?"

"Tiptop. They took care of me."

"Good hospital in Flagstaff, as I recall."

"Good enough. So, the laptop?"

Lila put it on the coffee table. "Everything you need to get your filthy business back on track. What are you going to do about the compound?"

"I've already called Knight," she said. "I'm sure all of this would finally be of interest to the Bureau, but something tells me the Agency would prefer to arrange for a secret domestic operation to seize the key equipment and information and destroy the rest. They're probably on their way, if not there already."

"And what'll happen to the cows?"

Anabel laughed—a startling sound, like an icicle falling off an eave. "Maybe you do take after your father. I don't know, Lila, motorcycle jackets? Dog food?"

"You don't feel anything for them? Living in their synthetic paradise, about to learn the harsh realities of life?"

"Maybe it will do them some good," her mother said.

"A bolt to the brain will make them stronger, huh."

She shrugged. "It's improved a few people I can think of."

"I think," Lila said, standing, "I'd like a ride back to Trout Brook now. I'm tired, I sprained my ankle, and my ass and thighs are killing me."

With an actual smile into which Lila dared to read a hint, just a hint, of fondness, Anabel said, "I hadn't figured you for—"

From the hallway, a faint whir. The crackle of a low-fidelity speaker.

One way—

Lila spun, reached under her arm.

Or another—

Pulled out the gun.

I'm gonna find ya—

Chambered a round.

I'm gonna—

Remy's pistol was aimed at Anabel Bortnik. In her peripheral vision, Lila could see her mother leaping to her feet, ready to dodge. But there was nowhere to go. Lila screamed his name, and as he fired, he flinched toward her.

Getcha, getcha—

She shot him twice in the chest, and he went down. Then she took three quick strides, planted her boot on the holes she'd just made, ripped the firearm out of his already-weakening hand, and spun around.

Her mother clutched her arm with trembling fingers. Her face was white and truly shocked. "Just the arm?" Lila said.

Getcha, getcha—

Anabel nodded. "My god. Romaldo. César."

Lila pocketed Remy's gun, stepped over him, and shot the singing bass in the head, silencing it forever. She thundered down the hall and into the foyer, shouldered open the door.

Romaldo, on his back, limbs splayed, and bleeding from his neck onto the concrete slab entryway. César, prone, beside the car, blood spreading through the dirt. Later, she would find the canoe Remy had crossed the lake with and, at the dock where César had collected her the day before, his car, which contained the military-issue Remington sniper rifle equipped with a suppressor that he'd used for the silent kills. It was her fault, she would understand, for forgetting he was at large, forgetting his boasts the previous week about his marksmanship.

But now she went back in, knelt over Remy, looked into his glassy, fading eyes. "You fucking dumbshit," she said. "What are your wife and kid going to do now?"

But he didn't answer. He didn't seem to recognize her. His brow furrowed as though he were thinking hard about something. And then, as death closed in, a jolt of recognition—of what, it was impossible to know. He let out a noise that seemed almost like a laugh.

Epilogue

Obsessively, Jane searched the internet for news about Nutt's disappearance and about the fate of his drug operation. For weeks, nothing. Then a report—barely a day of headlines before it was plowed under by more pressing and nationally important news—that a manufacturing facility responsible for the fentanyl-related drug additive Yes had been seized by federal authorities and was being dismantled. The owner, disgraced academic and cattleman Travis Nutt, and a trusted associate of his were missing; they were presumed to be on the run and were wanted by the FBI.

No mention of Affirmation. Nothing about Dronewave, or the right-wing messageboard, or the existence of a new engineered prion disease out in the wild.

After a while, her searches slowed to a couple of times a day, then just once, and then most days, not at all. The only additional piece of information she found was that the heifers had been sold at auction in Oklahoma City to an anonymous remote bidder. (Did the bidder know they harbored a deadly disease? Did anyone know, besides her family and Loretta?) Otherwise, silence. She had to put it out of her mind; there was too much going on. They were fully moved into the mall office now, and Chloe had taught her how to replace locks. New business was coming—surveillance, missing persons. The boring domestic stuff she'd been sick of a few months before now seemed interesting and more than risky enough. She understood that this feeling wouldn't last, but it was nice while it did. And Chloe would be back in school soon, and fourteen years old, with all the changes that would entail.

Around the end of August, she got a call from Shelly.

"I'm done," she said when Jane answered the phone. "The book. I'm done! With a draft, anyway."

"That's great!"

"I was wondering if maybe you can read it?"

"Of course, I'm dying to."

"Well, and also," Shelly said. "Maybe you can come out to the house and help me clean out some old shit. The basement's full of papers, my car's full of mail."

"Wait, your car?" Jane asked. "Why?"

"Everything that came for me when I was inside. Luke just threw it in the trunk to get it out of the house, I guess. It's mostly junk, I'm sure, but I want to go through it. Plus I need the trunk to haul all the other garbage."

"How is he? Luke?"

It had been a few weeks since Jane had asked after Shelly's brother. When the operation in Arizona was over, she'd driven out to Onteo to tell Shelly what they'd learned: that Luke was part of a conspiracy-minded right-wing internet group and that he was probably infected with a disease that might kill him. Jane believed that he'd met Congresswoman Ainsley Winter's assistant Imogen Freele on the ctznfrdm messageboard. Winter, whose upcoming campaign would be derailed if her large gambling debts were discovered (ultimately, they were and it was), had hoped to find out where her child, Katie, whom Jane and Shelly knew as Ace, had stashed the money they'd stolen from the campaign. Winter and Freele had learned about Luke, found him on the forums, and discovered via him that Shelly had been released from prison. The night of the robbery, Luke left the house unlocked for Freele and her boyfriend, who tried to make their visit seem like a normal break-and-enter, when all they wanted were the notebooks Winter was certain would contain the key to a cryptocurrency account. But when the notebooks proved to be a dead end, the congresswoman sent Freele undercover to the writers' conference to try to extract information from Shelly.

What Luke hadn't told Shelly at the time was that his IT work had long ago dried up. After a period of intense productivity, the result of his Affirmation, he could no longer concentrate and figured that the money Winter and Freele had promised him—a share of the crypto windfall—would keep the creditors at bay long enough for him to get his shit together. But that windfall never came.

Shelly was enraged by the news. Since the conference, she had been dealing with the consequences of her brother's actions while trying to find him some kind of adequate medical treatment. He was insured through the ACA marketplace, but nobody could figure out what was wrong with him or how to fix it. It was increasingly looking like nothing would. He couldn't work, and he slept most of the time. He developed weird food sensitivities and lost weight.

Now Shelly said, "Not any better. I'm afraid he's going to die, Jane."

"I'm sorry."

"Well, I'm not mad anymore," Shelly said with a sigh. "There's that."

Jane drove to Onteo on a sunny, cool Sunday morning. Shelly was out front, wearing work gloves and an N95 against the dust. She provided Jane with gloves and a mask, too, and they spent an hour hauling things up from the cellar and into the light—newspapers, broken china, old toys that Shelly didn't remember from her childhood—while Luke slept in his room. Jane filled her car with debris, and then they took a break to search through the mail in Shelly's car to make sure there was nothing of value.

There was less of it than Jane had feared, just one cardboard packing box, which had torn and spilled over onto the floor of the trunk. They sat together on the rear fender sifting through it.

"Incredible," Shelly said. "Credit card applications. I was in prison!"

"They would love for you to go into debt with them forever."

"And all this shit for my parents. Yeah, right, as if they were going to go on a cruise even before they were dead."

"Do you remember this election?" Jane said, holding up a direct mail card, a campaign flyer for a state representative race long over, featuring a man in a suit holding an assault rifle.

"Let me guess. He won."

"He actually died."

"COVID?"

"Heart attack on the stump." Jane held up a travel agency ad. "Wine tour!"

"Now, that, my folks would have liked." Shelly came to an envelope addressed by hand. The logo over the return address read TRANQUILITY SPA. "Sorry, Tranquility," Shelly said, tossing it back. "I was already chilling in the Boynton Ridge Wellness Center." But then she paused, blinked. "Wait." She fished the envelope from the trunk. "I know this handwriting."

"From where?"

"Remember?" Shelly proudly held the letter up. "The Boynton Ridge weekly newsletter. Mazes and puzzles."

"Ace?" Jane said, astonished.

Shelly ran a finger underneath the flap and carefully tore the letter open. Inside, they were perplexed to find an actual advertisement for a spa, a trifold brochure printed on glossy paper. It looked very professional. SAY YES TO TRANQUILITY! read the heading. "Huh," Shelly said. "Is this real? Did Ace actually want me to go here?"

"Where is it?" Jane asked.

"Mazuma, New Mexico."

Jane typed it into her phone. "I don't think that's a real place," she said. "The name does pop up, though. An accountant's office, a restaurant...oh my god."

"What?"

She held up her phone. "Mazuma is a cryptocurrency."

Shelly gaped, then laughed. "You have to be shitting me." She unfolded the brochure and they put their heads together, perusing it. It showed a stylized headline: THE KEY TO INFINITE RICHES IS...TRANQUILITY! And below, stock photos of hot people luxuriating in pools, or with towels on their heads, or clinking glasses of champagne. Each photo was accompanied by a paragraph of copy with a single word in bold, focusing on different aspects of the spa experience.

> Packages are available for all travelers in need of rest and rejuvenation! From the rich and **Famous** to the modest and anonymous, we have plans for you!
>
> Tranquility caters to your physical and mental **Health** with beauty regimens, massage sessions, meditation circles, and private consultations.

Explore our beautiful natural surroundings, from our desert walking paths to our world-famous cactus **Meadow**. Put your phones away and be in the world!

Don't hesitate to share your dreams. You don't know what's **Possible**...until you imagine it. Let us help you make it a reality!

"Something weird about these words," Shelly said.

"I think I know what they are." Jane did another search, this time for crypto security. "It's a seed phrase. When you start a crypto account, you generate it out of a specific list of words, like two thousand of them. That's why they're awkward-sounding." The other highlighted words were *expose, attitude, breeze, match, smooth, ugly, social,* and *offer*.

"What do we do?" Shelly said.

"We try to log in!"

Jane downloaded the Mazuma app, then clicked on the login. "So... the key to infinite riches is tranquility?" She typed *infinite riches* into the username field, then *tranquility* as a password. No luck, and *infiniteriches* didn't work either. But *infinite-riches* did. She was prompted to enter her seed phrase in a series of a dozen blank fields. Shelly read them off, in order, from the brochure, and Jane typed them in.

"Are you ready?" she asked, her thumb hovering over the ENTER button.

"Do it."

Jane did it. The screen went blank, and a little gold-coin logo appeared, spinning and gleaming. Then the coin winked out of existence, revealing two numbers, the amount of Mazuma in the account, and its present equivalent in dollars.

"Oh my god," Shelly said.

The dollar amount was $302.75.

"Scroll down, scroll down!"

Beneath the numbers they could see the value of the wallet over time, from its creation in 2018 to today, along with a graph. Ace had started the account with more than twenty-five thousand dollars that they had stolen from their mother. At its most valuable, the wallet had been worth nearly half a million. And then it crashed.

"I can't believe it," Shelly said. "The treasure was real."

"Not anymore!"

Shelly smacked her arm. "Speak for yourself, fancy-pants. Three Bennys is nothing to sneeze at. How the hell do you cash it in?"

She helped Shelly figure out the proper process, which was, unsurprisingly, convoluted, before deleting the app from her phone. A text notification popped up, a message from Chloe that consisted only of a sad-face emoji. Jane texted back a question mark and received a shrug in return. *Talk later,* Jane typed, *let's go out for dinner.* The response was a thumbs-up.

Once she and Shelly had done a couple of runs to the dump, Jane begged off. "Some unspecified drama unfolding at home," she said. "Happy to come up for a cleaning weekend anytime."

"I'll take you up on that for sure. Oh, wait." Shelly went into the house and emerged with a cardboard box. "Old-school printout. Thanks for coming to the conference with me. It really gave me confidence to have you there."

"Being there gave me a lot to think about, too." Jane took the box, gave it a friendly heft. "You want criticism or just moral support?"

"Bitch, what do you take me for?" Shelly said, grinning. "I am ready for anything." She gathered Jane into a hug.

"All right. Love you, Shel."

"Love you, Jane."

Chloe wanted to go to the brewpub and pizza joint across the road from the Nestor High School practice fields. The place made an excellent in-house root beer and you couldn't beat the vibe: picnic tables, cornhole, a DJ spinning country records, the hum of bees swarming over their heads hoping for a sip. Jane wondered if maybe it was time to talk to Chloe about alcohol. Thanks to the memoir, her addiction was out in the open now, and Chloe understood why her mother didn't drink. But at some point she was going to try it herself. Maybe she already had. The conversation had to happen.

Not tonight, though. They ate their pizza and watched girls play soccer.

"What do you think?" Jane asked her. "You want to continue at Tarbox Beals next year or switch to Nestor High?"

Chloe said, "I might stay at Beals." Not the answer Jane had expected.

"Why? Not that it's a bad idea. But I thought you were feeling alienated there."

"Well," Chloe said, "that's kind of what I wanted to talk to you about. While we were in Arizona, Kay texted that Addison wanted to talk to me. She wouldn't say why. So when we got home, I met up with her."

"Oh, boy. Drama."

"Yeah, well," Chloe said, squinting at the soccer girls. "It turns out, you know how the cops chased me and I got away?"

"Oh, yes, that."

"Yeah, that. Well…they knew it was me. The Kunstlers. They have surveillance cameras, *of course*. Her parents wanted to tell the cops and give them the footage. And Addison and them had a huge fight about it. She told her mom that she had humiliated her and she was a Nazi, and if her parents prosecuted me, she would never speak to them again."

Jane was frozen. She watched Chloe's eyes well up with tears. She imagined Chloe in prison, crying in prison.

"Mom, you know how the video made me say Addison is gay?"

"I remember, yes."

"Well, Addison *is* gay. Or she thinks probably she is. She thinks her mom, like, read her mind about it and is a homophobe and, like, outed her on the internet. She was crying and apologizing to me and everything. And I think…I kind of think…she likes me? Like, maybe that's how she realized?"

"Oh, baby." She reached out, put her hand on Chloe's, regretted it immediately, felt relief when Chloe clutched back.

"And Kay is bi, it's no big deal to her, it's just something she knows. I was wondering why she hung out with those girls, they are such annoying rich kids. But that's why—Addison pursued her because she needed, I guess, a queer friend. I'd thought Addison was the alpha in that relationship but it turns out no."

"How do you feel about all this?"

"I don't know," she said. "Kids act so casual, the girls all crush on girl celebrities, like, performatively. And there's a couple of really out trans kids in school, and like a million people are they/them. But I don't know what I'm supposed to do. Like, I can't imagine being so confident about this stuff."

"Maybe they're not all that confident. They're just trying something."

"Maybe."

Jane squeezed her hand. "So…do you like Addison?"

A sigh. "That's the thing. I don't know. I mean…if I like somebody, it's probably Kay. We were out at the golf course at night lying in the grass together, and our arms were touching and…I don't know. Am I supposed to?"

"You're not supposed to anything."

"Yeah, I know," Chloe said glumly.

"Do you like…being a girl?" Jane asked.

"I mean, I guess? I like being me in general, even though I sort of feel like an idiot sometimes. About social stuff, not homework or whatever." She thought about it for a moment. "Loretta told me about how when she joined the military, she half hoped she would die. She wasn't right with herself, she said. She actually had a fantasy of getting blown up by a bomb, not having a body anymore. When she realized she could transition, it was the most important moment of her life. It saved her. I don't feel like that. I mean, I don't cheer when I look in the mirror, but also, I don't want to get hit by a bomb."

"Well, good. And you should be happy with what the mirror tells you, by the way. You are lovely."

"My eyes are too close together."

"They are the perfect distance apart."

They both laughed. Chloe extracted her hand, took a bite of pizza. "Kay brokered a pact," she said, after a minute. "Between Addison and me. Whoever loses the election is vice president, and we work together. Maybe if all that goes okay, I'll stay at Beals. Or, if Addison and Kay go to Nestor High, maybe I'll go there."

"It's a one-minute walk from home."

"Right? No more commute. I could sleep in. But let's wait and see."

Jane was trying to conceal her profound happiness in this moment, with the summer waning and people laughing around her, and her daughter opening up to her in a context other than a fight.

Then Chloe said, "Maybe when I'm ready for dating advice, I'll talk to Aunt Lila."

Jane tried to say "You should" but it came out as a strangled squawk. Chloe burst out laughing.

"Mom, your face!"

"You were kidding?"

"Mostly. And when I need advice about liquidating my enemies, I'll call Grandma."

"That's not funny," Jane said, remembering Panama, the sound of gunfire, the burning greenhouse.

"It's kind of funny."

"It's not."

It was, though, and Chloe stared her down until she had to laugh.

Jane was getting used to the mall office and was ready to admit to herself, if not to anyone else, that she kind of liked it. Maybe even really liked it. She liked getting there before the mall woke up, greeting the custodial staff and security guard, and processing invoices while, on the other side of the glass wall, the rest of the mall slowly came to life. She liked taking breaks to watch the roller-derby team practicing in the former Sears and making the rounds of the sketchy furniture wholesalers while sipping a mango lassi from the food court. One morning she answered the phone to hear a familiar voice asking for her by name: it was Padma, her aunt's old friend, who had gotten them onto this case in the first place. "I'm so glad you answered," she said after a minute of catching up. "I wanted to thank your sister, but I can't seem to get hold of her."

"That tracks," Jane said. "I'll talk to her Sunday—anything in particular you want me to pass on?"

"I'm not sure, exactly. When we met over the summer, she asked why I wasn't a partner at my firm. It didn't seem to be in the cards for me in the near future, but...well, I was wrong. Brian Hathaway resigned suddenly, and I was offered senior partner. Which—honestly, I'm baffled. I didn't think the other partners respected me in the least. Now they seem...afraid of me? I wondered if maybe your sister had something to do with it."

"I am sure you're qualified," Jane said diplomatically. "But also, that does sound like Lila."

Padma laughed. "I'm grateful, I suppose, but...I'm not sure I like it."

"My sister's generosity often takes dubious forms."

"Hm. Well, there's a guy here now changing the sign on the door. I can't say I mind the sound of Giscombe, Koch, and Nagarajan."

They said goodbye with promises to stay in touch that they probably wouldn't keep—but then again, who knew what kind of investigative work a firm like that might need. It wasn't as though land and energy law were going to get any less demanding in the years to come.

At their next Sunday meeting, Lila confirmed that she'd pulled some strings at Padma's office. "Nothing difficult, just putting a few surprising documents in front of the right people." She had also tracked down Remy's wife and daughter and made them rich on Nutt's money, which she'd helped herself to using the information she'd found on the laptop. "I made it look like an unexpected insurance windfall." She also figured out what roadhouse Wendy worked at and determined that she'd escaped unharmed.

"Wait, who's Wendy?"

"The lady in the bedroom?"

"Oh, *Wendy*!"

When it was her turn to present, Jane provided a few mundane updates on local cases, which Lila pretended to care about. As they spoke, a figure moved across the background of Lila's screen: a woman, tall and slim, not Loretta. "Wait. Who was that?"

"A friend."

"You're talking about our private business with a friend over? *You?*"

"It's fine," Lila said with a sigh. She motioned to the woman, now off-camera, and Jane heard a door thunk shut. "She's leaving anyway."

Her voice was so wistful and lovestruck that Jane had to laugh. "You have a girlfriend. That's your girlfriend."

"Shut up," Lila said, seeming to actually mean it.

"Fine, fine. Far be it from me to question your judgment about the security of our work!"

This time it was Lila who didn't take the bait. They were learning! She filled Jane in on the cattle auction. "I don't know if you care," she said, "but the buyer was some Dronewave guy. The heifers were moved to Ohio, I don't know for what purpose. I've been monitoring the forums, though. They're still planning actions for election night. The community has lost a little steam, a few people have died, but they're not giving up."

"Died?"

"I assume Affirmation is just running its course. But nobody admits it on the forums. Lots of talk about fallen heroes."

"So what's the Bureau doing about it? What's Knight doing?"

"Nothing. It's out of Knight's jurisdiction, and the Bureau wants to wait and see. I guess they think the movement will die out with the Affirmed. Maybe they're right."

"I still haven't seen anything about Affirmation in the news," Jane said.

"I don't think you will. It's not contagious. The lab it came from has been dismantled, and the government doesn't want to start a panic. The people who are sick refuse to believe they've been deceived. They still think it's viral shedding or something. As long as nobody eats the cows..."

Later, when Jane conveyed this update to Chloe and Harry, the girl was enraged. Something about their conversation at the pizza place, or maybe about the experiences that led to it, seemed to have changed her; she was more outspoken, more confident. More adult. She planned to spend her birthday next week fishing with Kay. Fishing! If they caught anything, they would bring it back to the house and grill it over a fire in the yard. That, incredibly, was the plan.

"How can the government just ignore the problem?" Chloe shouted. "What's even the point of having a government if it doesn't *do* anything?"

"Poverty, racism, AIDS," Harry said. "Ignoring problems is a great American tradition."

"But people are *dying*!"

"That doesn't always spur our representatives to action."

A month later, Jane asked Chloe if she wanted to make a difference in a small way by visiting Shelly's brother, Luke, in the regional medical center in Rochester. He'd taken a turn for the worse, and it looked like it might be the end of the line. Chloe surprised her by agreeing to go. On the way, in a cold early-autumn rain, they talked about what to say to Shelly and whether or not there was a right way to comfort somebody when they were grieving, and Jane glanced over while they waited at a stoplight and was startled to find Chloe crying.

"Buddy," she said.

"Mom, I don't want you to die." The girl was staring steadfastly out the window, her eyes following the wiper blades as they squeaked back and forth.

"I'm not going to, honey," Jane said.

"Oh, come on. I'm not three."

"I know, I just mean—"

"I know what you mean." She sighed. The car behind them honked and Jane released the brake. "That night over the summer, when Grandma got the snakebite and you went off with your gun...I know you and Aunt Lila have been fighting about this stuff but I like the old way. Where you do...safe things."

"Oh," Jane said, "like jump off a roof and break my arm?"

"I'm serious," Chloe said. "What if you died? Grandpa's old, he could die too. And Dad just wants to hang out with his new girlfriend."

"His what?"

"I just...we're a team, Mom, I don't want you to get hurt."

This, at last, made Jane cry too. "I don't want you to get hurt either."

"It's not that I want to be in a normal family? I mean, the normal families I know are fucked up? But, Mom...we are super not a normal family."

"No."

They didn't speak for a while. Jane had planned on having a conversation like this at some point and had been waiting for the right moment, the right words to materialize, but...this would do. It didn't all need to be spoken.

Chloe said, "Just...keep trying not to die, okay?"

"Okay. You too."

"Okay."

The hospital was a sprawling structure surrounded by parking lots. Shelly had instructed them to meet her at the infectious disease center, and the signs that pointed Jane there were clearly new, as was the wing itself. The landscaping shrubs still bore their garden-center tags and the bark mulch was dark and fragrant.

Luke lay in bed in a bright, soothing, spacious room that had more of the feel of a long-term-care facility than a hospital: floral prints on the walls, a small sofa, comfortable chairs. Shelly sat beside him, writing in a notebook. She got up and hugged them, and thanked Chloe for coming. To Jane's surprise and pride, Chloe walked up to the bed, took Luke's hand, and introduced herself. Luke was beyond responding; his cheeks were sunken and his skin gray.

"I'm sorry, Shel," Jane said.

"Thanks. Not gonna lie, I'm scared." She wiped a tear off her cheek. "I don't know what I'm gonna do after. I've never been alone in my life."

"You've got us, you know."

Shelly nodded and led her over to a little grouping of chairs beside Luke's heart monitor. She asked Chloe how school was going and showed her some of her prison tattoos. After a few minutes, Jane said, "Listen, Shel, I don't want to offend you by bringing this up—"

"Oh no."

"—but this all looks expensive. Even if you guys are insured, this can't be covering it. If you need help..."

But Shelly shook her head. "Crazy thing. Somebody's footing the bill."

"Who?"

She shrugged. "Luke arranged it before things got too bad. He told me, when it's time, we come here. He wouldn't talk about it. But I think we know where it's coming from."

"Dronewave."

She nodded. "I'm trying not to get too mad about it, for my own sanity. I mean, I'm glad I won't go broke, but these fuckers are the ones who are killing him in the first place!"

At some point, once her mother and Shelly had gotten deep in the weeds about Dronewave and their days in prison, Chloe slipped out to find a vending machine. The new wing seemed determined to not look like a hospital, so it took her a good ten minutes of wandering to find the snacks, tucked behind a door marked GUEST SERVICES, a dark and floral-scented room where some kind of new age synthesizer music was playing and that also included a baby-changing table, a watercooler, and a nondenominational worship station. She bought a Twix and a Diet Coke and continued to wander. Grandpa Harry thought it was undignified to eat while walking but it was Chloe's favorite kind of meal. There was something animalistic about sitting down and tucking in! She didn't like to feel like a hyena devouring an antelope. She was a cool and casual biped!

Most of the rooms were unoccupied; so far this seemed, mercifully, like a wing without a purpose. The few that contained patients, Chloe demurely turned away from—until she recognized a familiar set of crossed legs dangling off the end of a sofa. She stopped, and a head popped up. It was Addison Kunstler's.

Thanks to Kay, there had been an uneasy peace between them since school started. But with the school election still looming, Chloe had refrained from reaching out. Now the two of them gazed at each other in shock—a lot like a hyena and an antelope, actually. Though Chloe bet they both felt like the antelope.

To her credit, Addison broke the stalemate by jumping to her feet and hustling out into the hall. She closed the room door behind her, and suddenly Chloe wondered what she was doing here. And then, just as quickly, she knew. Oh no.

Impulsively, Chloe hugged her. Addison was startled for a moment, then hugged back. Afterward, Chloe tried to figure out what to say. Did Addison know what Chloe knew about her mother? About Affirmation and Dronewave? The two girls stood there, arms crossed, each waiting for the other to speak.

"My mom's friend's brother is sick," Chloe said. "We're visiting. He's got…long COVID or something, I guess."

"Sorry about that."

Chloe shrugged. "I never met him before. Like, when he was healthy. It's still sad, though."

With a nod, Addison said, "Yeah, my mom's sick. I think she's going to die. Not, like, today, but…sort of soon."

"Oh, dude. I'm so sorry."

"Yeah. Uh…maybe don't…tell anyone at school? For now?"

"Of course not."

Addison turned away, let her hair fall over her eyes. "It's, like, a rare thing. Actually, uh, my dad donated money for, like, all this." She waved her arms around. "They're not telling me much about it. It's weird and annoying, actually, as well as fucking sad."

"Has she been sick for…a while?"

Addison gave her a look, and Chloe flinched. Could she tell she knew more than she was saying? She wanted to blurt it all out, but if Chloe's mother were here, she'd tell her not to.

"Not really. Or, I guess, kinda? Things got weird a couple of years ago, like she was super-intense and energetic and then would crash out, like she was on something? But then eventually she got tired and shaky. It was really bad on the Disney trip. Dad took her to a specialist, and…here we are."

"I'm sorry."

"Is your friend, or your mom's friend or whatever…is he going to live?"

"I don't think so."

They stood in silence for a while, Addison pivoting on her heel rhythmically, Chloe staring at the floor.

"You want some Coke?" Chloe asked, holding out the can.

Addison took it, swigged, handed it back. "So, yeah," she said, "see you in school, I guess?"

"Yeah. Uh...and thanks again. For getting me out of trouble."

She shrugged. "No worries. I was really mad at Mom for making the video, just so you know. But I barely got to enjoy being mad, because—" She nodded over her shoulder at the closed door. "Sometimes you just want to be pissed at your mom like a normal kid, you know?"

Chloe barked out a surprise laugh. "Yeah I do!"

Addison smiled at Chloe, and her heart leapt just a little. She said, "All right, see ya. May the best woman win."

"Haha, like that ever happens."

"So cynical!"

They parted with a fist bump. Then Addison turned and, shoulders low, opened the door and returned to the room where her mother lay.

A little over a month later, on Election Day, Dronewave, or what was left of it, rode their trucks into the blue enclaves of Wisconsin, Ohio, Michigan, and other swing states, many of the trucks with a red heifer chained up in the bed, lowing at the chaos, in tragic contravention of its intended life of sacred leisure. Yellow-shirted men and women circled polling places, assault rifles strapped to their chests. Local police were cowed and overwhelmed, or, in some places, joined forces with the yellow shirts. Twenty-eight people were injured and six died. Three of those were Dronewave protesters, one killed by police, the other two collapsing on the scene and perishing of unknown illness. Cattle, many of them spray-painted with the X-eyed-bee logo, were let loose in the streets. A few collided with traffic; others were shot.

The elections themselves seemed unaffected by the chaos. Ainsley Winter's last-minute replacement won, and the government prepared to limp its way into another new year.

Jane and Chloe followed the stories of the surviving heifers with interest. Many were adopted by local farms in the places where they'd been set loose, and several found a home at Farmhaven, a bucolic spread half an hour from Nestor, where animal rights activists adopted abused animals and nursed them back to health. In the winter, on an unseasonably mild, wet day, Jane and Harry brought President Addison Kunstler and Vice President Chloe Pool Kelleher, along with Kay, whom they called their Secretary of Vibe, to meet the famous beasts—exiles from paradise, survivors of insurrection. The girls petted the heifers, who really did look as flawlessly red as promised and who, even if they weren't going to usher in a new era of peace, would at least live happy lives here in the actual world. The girls cooed and squealed over them, playacting as the children they only recently were. They held baby chicks in their hands, lambs in their arms, laughed at leaping, bouncing goats and fed them milk from a bottle. Jane caught Chloe squeezing Kay's hand, caught Addison sulking, but for all that, the Tarbox Beals presidential administration had a good day, even as their federal equivalents floundered their way into another year.

On the way home, rain fell, and the rain turned to snow. Jane white-knuckled through the darkness while everyone else dozed, trusting her to get them home safe. She felt her phone buzz but didn't look at it. She tapped the brakes on the hills, watched as cars skidded off the road and into ditches, pulled over for flashing lights. It took an hour, compared to the half hour it had taken on the trip out. Every muscle in Jane's body was tense until she pulled into the driveway—then she switched off the engine, let out breath, and listened to the tick-tick of cooling metal and the gentle spatter of wet flakes striking the windshield and roof.

The text was from Lila. *Got something for us. You ready?*

Beside her, Harry stirred. "Are we home?" Chloe asked, lifting her head from Kay's shoulder.

"We're home," she told Chloe, and to Lila, she typed, *Ready.*

Acknowledgments

Thanks to my early readers, Brian Hall and Katrina Carpenter, and my editors, Josh Kendall and Liv Ryan, for making this book immeasurably better than I could have made it alone. I'm grateful to Emily Adrian for maintaining the series bible, and Catherine Nichols for naming the real estate receptionist and knowing what song the CIA's Billy Bass would play. Leela Rice offered horse advice and introduced me to the heroic beauty of Cedar. Copyeditor Tracy Roe rescued me from several errors. Stephanie and Eliza provided ongoing encouragement and jokes, as did Katrina and Olivia. Mom and Dad were supportive, as always, and my beloved chat was open in a window next to this novel the whole time I was writing it. Love you all.

Some research has been done into prion-based medication, but Affirmation isn't real. Yes is also fictional, though it's a plausible variation on common additives to cocaine. I first heard about the search for the perfect red heifer in Lawrence Wechsler's 1998 *New Yorker* article "Forcing the End," but Travis Nutt is entirely imaginary.

About the Author

J. Robert Lennon is the author of three story collections and ten previous novels, including *Familiar, Broken River, Subdivision,* and, most recently, *Hard Girls*. He lives in Ithaca, New York.